HOME IS
WHERE THE
LIES LIVE

BOOKS BY KERRY WILKINSON

THRILLER NOVELS

Two Sisters

The Girl Who Came Back

Last Night

The Death and Life of Eleanor Parker

The Wife's Secret

A Face in the Crowd

Close to You

After the Accident

The Child Across the Street

What My Husband Did

The Blame

The Child in the Photo

The Perfect Daughter

The Party at Number 12

The Boyfriend

The Night of the Sleepover

After the Sleepover

The Call

The Missing Body

ROMANCE NOVELS

Ten Birthdays

Truly, Madly, Amy

HOME IS WHERE THE LIES LIVE

KERRY WILKINSON

bookouture

Published by Bookouture in 2024

An imprint of Storyfire Ltd.
Carmelite House
50 Victoria Embankment
London EC4Y 0DZ

www.bookouture.com

Storyfire Ltd's authorised representative in the EEA is Hachette Ireland
8 Castlecourt Centre
Castleknock Road
Castleknock
Dublin 15 D15 YF6A
Ireland

ISBN: 978-1-83618-326-6
eBook ISBN: 978-1-83618-325-9

EIGHT DAYS' TIME

Emergency log. Call received: Saturday, 17:29.

Handler: Hello. Where are you calling from?

Caller: Huntington Grove. Do you know it?

Handler: Is that in High Kingsley?

Caller: Right.

Handler: Can I take your name, please?

Caller: Jennifer.

Handler: Thanks, Jennifer. What is the nature of your emergency?

Jennifer: I think I heard a gunshot.

Handler: Did that happen just now?

Jennifer: Yeah. A minute ago. Not even that.

Handler: Where are you at the moment?

Jennifer: There's a street party going on. Everyone's here.

Handler: Who's everyone?

Jennifer: Everyone. It's a party. The whole street is out. There are tables along the middle of the road. We all heard it.

[*Inaudible*]

Handler: Can you get yourself to a place of safety? I want to make sure you're safe.

[*Inaudible*]

Jennifer: Hang on.

[*Inaudible*]

Jennifer: Sorry, people are running. There are kids here. I think someone's been shot.

Handler: Why do you think that?

Jennifer: That's what people are saying. There's—

[*Sound of a bang in the background*]

Handler: Can you hear me, Jennifer?

[*Pause*]

Handler: Jennifer? Are you there?

Jennifer: Yeah, sorry. I'm moving away. Some guy came out of a house and nobody knows what to do.

Handler: Did the man have a gun?

Jennifer: No... well, I don't know. I didn't see. Sorry I'm going to move. I don't know what's going on. You need to send someone. I think—

[*Inaudible*]

[*Call ends*]

ONE

FRIDAY

HEIDI

As I wobble towards the front door with a box under each arm, I can't help but wonder whether I've made a huge mistake.

The boxes are obviously an error of judgement. They're wide and unwieldy; leaving me stumbling like some sort of tipsy crab.

It's not only the boxes. I crouch and put down both, then take another glance along the street. The long line of detached, identikit houses is relentlessly middle class. I can imagine the trampolines in the back gardens and the perils of getting the bins out on time each week. Neighbours will have kids with names like Hedge.

I never thought somewhere like Huntington Grove would be me. Who lives in a *Grove*? This sort of place is all early-morning yoga classes and skinny lattes with blueberry-banana muffins.

Standing outside our new home, I already feel like an outsider.

Freddie is late, because of course he is. His timekeeping is up there with weathermen predicting rain when it's already lashing it down.

It's my first time letting myself into the new house, which inevitably means trying every key on the ring until I find the correct one. I leave both boxes on the path and head inside, where the bright blue sky of the summer is immediately replaced by the shaded respite of the hall.

When we viewed the house, there was a moment in which I saw myself as the adult I've somehow become. I stood at the bottom of the stairs and said to Freddie: 'It's a bit dark in the hall. Do you think it's all right?'

The comment was more an observation than a panic attack – except I suddenly felt so old. My younger self would never have seen the darkness, metaphorical or actual. It would have been a new house to explore: an upstairs and down, a garden out back. So much more than the poky flat where we lived for so long.

There's probably a point in everyone's life where we start noticing things like skirting boards.

I leave the front door open, allowing some light inside, and then drift into the living room. The sofa and shelves were brought in by the moving company but there are still boxes lining the walls. Into the kitchen and there are more. Freddie's been down here for a week but there is little indication of it. Everything except the big items are still sandwiched between cardboard.

After the almost three-hour drive, unpacking is the last thing I want to do. I consider getting on with it but it's only a fleeting contemplation. Like thinking about ordering the salad off a menu. I *could* do it but life's too short. There's always tomorrow.

Back into the hall and I check the cupboard under the stairs, which is empty, then try the door near the coat pegs. When the estate agent showed us around, I remember it being a large, bare utility room. He was a typical estate agent-type with a too-tight suit and cliché every other sentence. He called us 'guys', and relentlessly referred to Freddie as 'mate', before describing the room as a 'potential office, or some sort of man-cave'.

Sticking the word 'man' in front of things seems to be an in-thing at the moment: 'man-cave', 'man-flu', 'man-scaping', 'man-splaining'. There was an article in the *Observer* last weekend (yes, I know) about 'manopause'. If women are ever going to breach things like the pay gap, we really need some sort of single-syllable description for ourselves.

I pull down the handle and push but the door sticks unmov-ingly in the frame. I try again but it's as stubborn as a pensioner doing fifty in the middle lane. It takes another attempt to realise that the door is locked. Freddie was the one who picked up the keys and I try every one he passed on – but nothing fits. I find myself heaving the handle one more time and then step back to take in the whole frame.

Why is there a locked door in our new house?

It must be Freddie.

In our old flat, there weren't enough rooms for one to be locked. We were there for ten years, doing the usual thing of trying to save for a deposit, while being lectured by six-figure columnists on how the cost of extravagances like sandwiches or avocados were the reason why we couldn't afford anything.

Hmm. I don't understand why Freddie would lock a door in our house when he knows I was driving down with the rest of our things today.

I think about texting him, or calling to ask where he is, but don't want to be that boring nag. This will be our first night in our new house and it should be a happy evening. Instead, I retrieve the boxes one at a time from outside and carry them into the hall. They're both full of my clothes and shoes; things I needed at the flat in the past week.

Neither of us were quite sure how we amassed so much

stuff. There are still four more boxes in the car – and that's on top of the ones already brought down by the movers.

Back to the car and the next box has 'kitchen' written on it in thick marker pen. It's heavier than the first pair and there's no danger of me carrying two this time. I struggle to remember precisely what's inside but fate sometimes has a funny way of answering questions. I'm two steps along the path when there's the sound of something ripping and then the box explodes as if part of a magician's trick. I'm left holding the cardboard as a wave of kitchen implements pour onto the pavement with the clanging *ding-a-ling* of a bunch of church bell-ringers hopped up on espressos. This at least explains why there are no utensils in our new kitchen: this box was left in our flat a hundred or so miles away.

There's something particularly bleak about watching a metal spatula bounce its way along a pavement towards the road. Like the final scene of the final-ever episode of *Bake-Off* sometime in the dark, apocalyptic future.

I'm not quite sure where to start. If anything is a symbol of this move being a poor decision, it's surely a ladle embedding itself in a drain cover. The pavement, road and edges of the front garden look as if a tornado has hit the homeware section of John Lewis.

A whisk is rolling around the tarmac when a voice asks if I need a hand.

There's barely concealed laughter in the question and I turn to see a young woman on the pavement, one hand on her hip with a raised, quizzical eyebrow. She's twenty at most, possibly younger. That curious fresh-faced age where no one can ever be quite sure whether a person is sixteen or mid-twenties. She reminds me of how much I miss being IDd in pubs.

'I'm moving in,' I say. 'The box split.'

I've stated the obvious and the corners of her lips twitch. It's hard not to smile back.

I put down the empty, split box and stretch out a hand. 'Heidi,' I say.

'Isabella,' she replies, nodding to the house opposite. 'I live over there.'

She crouches and picks out the ladle from the drain grate, then heads into the road to start collecting the other utensils.

The tape has given way on the box, so I concertina the cardboard flaps around one another and then start to repack. Isabella brings across the items she's retrieved and then picks up one of the other boxes from the car.

We carry them into the kitchen and add the pair to the rest of the stack.

'My husband should be home to help,' I say.

'Mum said she'd seen a guy moving in last week,' Isabella replies. 'She thought he was single.'

'I had to stay up north to finish my work notice. Freddie started his job down here last week.'

Isabella nods along, struggling to hide the lack of interest, for which I don't blame her.

We head back out for the final two boxes and put them in the living room. Isabella hovers in the doorway, ready to leave.

'Do you want a tea, or something?' I ask. 'There's a kettle around here somewhere. I definitely packed some teabags.'

She shakes her head. 'I don't really drink tea.'

Isabella's young, so of course she doesn't. Everyone under the age of twenty-five seems to be addicted to vaping and energy drinks named something like 'SMASH!' She takes a step towards the front door, so I lead her to where another woman is coming along the path. The resemblance is instant. Isabella's mother shares the same long, straight hair as her daughter. They move as if they're floating; their feet barely seeming to move.

Isabella stands outside my front door with her arms crossed, scowling: 'For God's sake, Mum. I was only helping someone move in. You don't have to check up on me all the time. I'm not a kid.'

There's a mini stand-off and then my perception of the way they each walk is obliterated as Isabella stomps past her mother, heading for the house opposite. We watch her go and then the other woman turns to me.

'Sorry about that,' she says.

'No, *I'm* sorry. I didn't realise there was a problem. She was very helpful.'

'I'm Willow,' the woman adds, stretching out her hand. Her fingers are cold and smooth as we shake. I have to bite my lip to stop the slim smile escaping. I *knew* there'd be someone around here named after foliage.

'Heidi,' I reply.

The front door slams with a booming *crash*, and Willow turns again, lingering on her house for a moment, biting her lip. 'Teenagers,' she says wistfully, although there's hesitation in her voice, leaving me to wonder if – *maybe* – there's a lot more to it than that.

TWO

WILLOW

Heidi is trying not to laugh as we shake hands, not that I blame her. Everyone has that rubbernecking jolt of excitement when spotting couples or parents with children arguing in public. We've all been there – and, goodness me, my daughter knows how to slam a door.

'I wasn't checking up on her,' I say, nodding backwards to the house. 'I saw her carrying a box into yours and it took me by surprise. I can barely get her to make her bed most days. She's almost eighteen, but...' I tail off, not quite sure how to finish.

Heidi bends and picks up a fork from the lawn, then holds it up, as if this explains everything: 'Had an accident with a box,' she says. 'Your daughter was really helpful. She seems lovely.'

It's always nice to hear – a mother can never have enough praise for her parenting skills. Except Heidi doesn't know the truth, even if Isabella's reaction to my presence gave her a glimpse.

Heidi nods towards the house: 'Do you want a tea?'

'Sure.'

I follow her inside, to where there are boxes in the hall and more in the kitchen. The house is a mirror of ours, where everything is sort of the same but not really; like going through the looking glass and coming out the other side. Here there is a box; over the road there are Isabella's shoes that she hasn't picked up. Here there is a bare dining table; over the road there is a table similarly covered with bills, letters, and all sorts of other miscellaneous paperwork that nobody can be bothered to tidy away.

Heidi explains that her husband moved down a week ago, which I sort of already knew. I nod along, not wanting to seem like a compulsive curtain twitcher.

'We were in Manchester before,' she adds. 'I finished my contract up there yesterday, then gave back our flat keys to the landlord today.'

Heidi hunts through the boxes muttering under her breath until she emerges with a stainless-steel kettle smudged with fingerprints.

'Teabags,' she says to herself, before digging into another box. 'Sorry. Freddie was supposed to unpack all this stuff.'

There's a hint of annoyance there, so I keep quiet.

After she finds the teabags, Heidi dives into another box before emerging with a pair of mugs. One reads 'I went to Brighton and all I got was this lousy mug', the other has a picture of a tree. Almost as an afterthought, Heidi checks the fridge and adds: 'At least he got milk.'

'What does he do?' I ask.

She fires back so quickly that it's like a reflex: 'Marketing manager at some PR firm.'

I almost add 'I don't really know what that means', but keep it back. It's something that I reckon most couples have – nobody really knows what the other does. In the age of 'refuse and recycling operator' instead of 'bin men' and 'front-line customer support facilitator' instead of 'checkout worker', nothing means anything.

'What about you?' I add.

'It's all a bit boring but I've been managing an office for a while. I've not sorted a job for here yet, so I guess I'm unemployed.'

Heidi smiles but doesn't do a great impression of hiding the annoyance. They moved for *his* job, then.

'What do you do?' she asks.

'Mature student. I'm doing a business management course,' I reply. 'I'm hoping to get onto something full-time in September but there is a bridging course for now.'

Heidi nods along in the way people do when they have no idea what to say. I'm closer to forty than thirty, yet still a student. Her gaze flickers momentarily towards the front of the house, then ours beyond. She'll be working out the maths of Isabella's age. I've seen this a lot.

The kettle burbles away in the corner as we stand around awkwardly. Heidi gives me a quick up-and-down glance and then presses back onto the counter and looks away. I follow her line of vision to the stack of boxes. Almost all of them have 'kitchen' scribbled on the side but there's one near the bottom on which the name 'Freddie Potter' is written in neat capital letters. It reminds me of when everyone used to have to write their name on their PE kit at school. It's when I'm thinking of those times that I suddenly realise the significance of the name.

'Is your husband Freddie Potter?' I ask, taking my turn to state the obvious.

Heidi stares at me blankly. 'Yes...'

'Did he go to Marsh Vale School?'

She pouts a lip and shakes her head slightly. 'I don't know.'

'It's near Bath.'

A nod: 'Oh, right. He did grow up around there, so maybe.'

'I think we went to school together,' I say. 'There was definitely a Freddie Potter.'

Heidi's brow creases for a moment and then she snorts.

'Small world. He should be home any moment. You can ask him.'

I think on that for a moment. It's been years since we were in the same classes.

'Have you ever been to Marsh Vale?' I ask.

'No, he doesn't have any family, so there's not been any need. I think—'

She's interrupted by the sound of a car engine rumbling.

Heidi moves into the living room, me behind, and then we head outside to where a black BMW has pulled onto the driveway front-first. A man emerges from the driver's seat, wafting his shirt to try to cool himself. He's somewhere around six feet, with sandy short hair and sweat clinging to the front of his once white shirt.

He mumbles some sort of 'Hi' at Heidi. I almost laugh because, assuming they've not seen each other in a week, it's hardly the height of romantic expression. It all feels very familiar.

What *isn't* familiar is Freddie himself. I'd love to say there's recognition but we wouldn't have seen one another in around two decades and it's not as if we were friends back then. Only the name stuck, for some reason.

'This is Willow,' Heidi says, motioning towards me. 'She lives over the road.'

Freddie crosses to her and pecks Heidi on the forehead, then turns to me, with a clear lack of interest. 'Hi,' he mumbles.

Heidi is looking to me expectantly and I feel stuck. 'Are you the Freddie Potter who went to Marsh Vale?' I ask.

There is a moment in which it feels as if Freddie is staring through me. I shiver at the way his gaze pierces. It's the chill of stepping into an air-conditioned shop on a warm day. It almost makes me apologise for asking. It's only a fleeting moment and then he slips into a curious smile. He turns between Heidi and me, before settling on me.

'How do you know that?' he asks.

'I went there, too. I was Willow Vaughan then – always the last name in the register.'

His lips crinkle and then he lets out a snorted 'huh!' 'What a strange thing,' he adds.

Heidi laughs too. 'Small world,' she repeats – although there's something unsettling about the way she turns between the pair of us.

'Are you still in touch with anyone?' I ask.

'Not really,' Freddie replies, a fraction too quickly. 'After I left, I moved up north and didn't have a reason to go back.'

It's strange the way that some recollections sit dormant until something like a word, a picture, or a smell stirs them. One moment a memory is buried deep, the next it is bright and bold, as if it happened seconds before. I suppose it's something about the way Freddie says 'reason' that has me thinking about the kid who usually seemed to have his hands in his pockets.

The Freddie I remember was gangly and awkward. Not quite one of the sporty kids but not fully one of the computer lot, either. Like most kids. I try to remember whether Freddie and I spoke that much back then. Being at school means the same faces every day – and yet people can pass one another week after week without ever sharing a word.

When it comes to Freddie, I now remember his parents dying in a car crash when we were something like thirteen or fourteen. One of the teachers said something about it in an assembly. There was a memorial service but I don't think I went.

There is something about everyone that defines a person at school. The kid whose parents have the rubbish car, or the one with holes in his blazer. Someone will get her hair cut by her mum and spend five years trying to live down the uneven fringe, long after it's grown out.

'Weren't you brought up by your grandparents?' I say, instantly regretting it.

Heidi rubs his upper arm as Freddie's eye twitches and his uneven gaze of moments before suddenly makes sense. Of course he doesn't want to be reminded of all this.

'Sorry,' I add quickly.

'It's fine,' he replies. 'You're right.'

The awkwardness is almost painful. Nobody speaks for a while until Heidi changes the subject. I think all of us are grateful.

'So...' she says. 'Is this a quiet area?'

'Really quiet,' I say, too quickly. 'I mean there was that, um...'

I can see in the way they glance to one another that I've put my foot in it again. I assumed they knew, that they'd done a bit of googling. Their joint frowns make it clear they didn't.

'What...?' Heidi asks.

'I don't want to sound all alarmist,' I reply. 'It really *is* a quiet area. There's a street party next weekend...'

'But...?'

I motion across the road towards the house next to mine. As if on cue, a man steps out of the garage that adjoins the home. His shoulder-length hair is dark and, even from this distance, I can see the fuzz sprouting from the top of his vest. His skin is tanned and he wipes his brow with his forearm.

He waves across and I wave back, then he heads into the house itself, before closing the door.

'That's Dylan,' I say, before taking a breath. I've somehow become the street's gossip. 'I suppose you'll find out sooner or later, so I should probably let you know what happened to Ciara.'

'Who's that?' I ask.

'His wife.'

THREE

DYLAN

After closing the front door, I edge into the living room and stand a fraction away from the window, watching Willow talk to the new couple across the street. With the glare, they won't be able to see me, though the rapid glances of the newcomers towards the house make it clear what they're talking about.

It's not that I blame Willow for chatting about me. Our new neighbours will find out sooner or later – but this is always how things go. I get the soft touches on my arm – 'Oh, that was *you?*' – or the thin-lipped smiles with the *poor thing*-eyes. I'm always judged for what happened.

I continue to watch them for a minute or so and then blink away darkening thoughts before heading into the kitchen. When I remove the lid of the slow cooker, steam pours out, sending the rich flavour of the lamb stew wafting airily towards the ceiling. It's warm outside, not really casserole weather – although I'm not the one who makes decisions about food around here.

'Orla!'

There is a thump from above and then the sound of scampering footsteps on the stairs until my daughter bursts into the kitchen. There's rarely a time where she doesn't explode into a room. It's a rumbling volcano and then – *bang!* – there she is. I wasn't like this at seven years old and have probably always been a bit of the recluse, even then. That must mean she gets it all from...

'Stew!' Orla says. She steps around me and inhales the slow cooker fumes.

Trailing into the kitchen a few seconds behind my daughter is her friend, Lauren.

'Hi,' she says with a nervous smile. The girls aren't quite old enough to be at the full *avoid-eye-contact-at-all-costs*-stage.

'Wash your hands first,' I say. 'Then up to the table.'

'Can we eat upstairs?' Orla asks.

'Not today.'

'But—'

'No buts – hands, then table.'

Orla's frown lasts about half-a-second and then the girls head to the sink and set the tap running. My daughter does as she was told, with Lauren following, and then I ladle some of the stew into bowls for the pair of them.

I potter around the kitchen, doing a bit of clearing up, while really listening to the girls chatter. There's something beautiful about the innocence of youth, when the world is a massive place with endless opportunity.

It's a miracle that Orla hasn't lost that.

They talk about Rey from *Star Wars* and speculate as to whether she'd be good at horse riding. I'm not quite sure how the two are connected. After that it's when *Doctor Who* might be back. They specifically talk about iPlayer and Netflix, and don't even mention 'TV'. It's a new world. Someone named Katy has a party in two weeks; Lauren's getting new shoes; the boy who lives next door to Lauren accidentally kicked his football over the hedge that separates the houses. The subjects blend into one another with a dizzying lack of cohesiveness and it's almost as if they have their own language.

They each have half a second bowl and then they're off and away to Orla's room. Even though small in stature, there is something about them that's like a herd of rhinos when it comes to heading upstairs.

I finish clearing up and then move back into the living room, glancing through the window to where the new neighbours' driveway is now clear. I wonder if they're inside now, typing my name in Google and seeing what comes up. All the reports will still be there. They will live on long after I'm gone. There's no more of yesterday's news being today's fish and chip paper – nothing is forgotten.

It's when I realise my fists are clenched that I step away from the window. I've squeezed so tightly that there are fingernail indents in my palm. Sometimes it feels as if the anger will bubble over and erupt... but then there's Orla and it goes away.

It *mostly* goes away.

I've not got far from the window when a car pulls up outside the house. A woman climbs out and then walks around to open the passenger's door to retrieve something. I open the front door and wait for her on the step.

'How was she?' Theresa asks as she hurries along the path towards the house.

'A delight, as ever,' I say.

Theresa stops and puts a hand on her hip. I've seen Lauren doing this without realising and it always makes me smile. Like mother, like daughter.

'You can tell me if they've been playing up.'

'They've not,' I say. 'I've barely heard from them all day. They had stew for tea because Orla insisted, and they were in the garden most of the afternoon. They're upstairs now.'

Theresa rubs my upper arm gently and gives the *poor thing*-eyes. Two for the price of one. 'You're a star,' she says.

I call for the girls and they scamper down the stairs once more. Lauren wants 'ten more minutes' but her mum says it's time to leave. Then they're off to the car with promises of seeing us soon. It's the final scene of a feel-good children's TV show as we wave to them and they wave to us. I feel a little silly: exposed, in the open where the neighbours can see, but there's a part of me that never wants Orla to grow out of this.

Back inside and my daughter is already on the bottom step ready to return to her room when I call after her.

'Do you want more to eat?' I ask.

'No, thank you.'

I nod her into the living room and she changes direction. 'You've got one hour of screen time,' I say. 'After that, the iPad goes away.'

I set the countdown timer on my phone and show it to her, like I always do, then press the green button to start the seconds ticking.

Orla's fingers are a blur of motion as she flits between apps and games, trying to cram as much into her time as possible.

I half-watch the news, which becomes a quiz show with me barely noticing. I'm not really paying attention because I'm watching my daughter. She might be aware of me but her eyes rarely leave the wonder of the colours in front of her.

It's barely a blink until I have to tell her she has five minutes left. She frantically swipes and pinches back to a game she was on and then there's the dreaded *beep-beep-beep* of time being up.

'One more minute,' she says, not looking up.

'One more minute today means two fewer minutes tomorrow – so it's up to you.'

That's all it takes for her to hand the device back. She could have had a full extra half an hour tonight if she wanted – but that would mean no screen time tomorrow. Choices have consequences.

'What now?' I ask.

'Lego?'

'Good thinking.'

I go to the cupboard under the stairs and pull out the large plastic tub, before emptying the contents across the floor. This enormous crate of Lego for a fiver was one of my greatest-ever car boot sale finds.

Orla and I – though mainly her – have spent the past six weeks trying to make a Tyrannosaurus rex from the random collection of different coloured blocks. Orla has an eye for what goes together. She's also a perfectionist, meaning that what I think looks a bit like a dinosaur claw can be pulled apart freely because 'that's not right, Daddy'. It's taken us this long to start work on the head, though the body itself is almost up to my knee.

There were a *lot* of blocks in the crate.

Orla tells me for something close to the two-hundredth time that a T. rex's bite is stronger than any creature alive today. 'It could bite through a car,' she says. I'm not quite sure from where she picked it up but it's one of her established facts.

This is our version of a bedtime story.

We spend half an hour building, though don't really get anywhere because my daughter is a stickler for correctness. She does build a car for the T. rex to eventually bite through, however.

I tell her it's time for bed and there's the usual rigmarole of 'Can't I stay up to...?' before Orla eventually caves and heads upstairs. I feel guilty about sending her to bed at the usual time during the school holidays but routine is good. I tell myself it's good *for her* but can rarely escape the niggle that it's more for me.

It's half-past-eight on the dot when there's a knock at the door. When I open it, Gabe is there, tapping something into his phone.

Willow's husband acknowledges me with the merest raise of the eyebrows, something which I've come to realise is one of his most excitable greetings.

'All right, pal,' he says.

I'm not quite sure when it started but Gabe has slipped into the habit of coming over two or three nights a week. I couldn't even say whether I enjoy the company.

He has a six-pack in one hand and heads past me towards the kitchen. By the time I've closed the door and followed, Gabe has already cracked open two Coronas and put the rest in the fridge. He passes me a bottle and we clink the necks together.

'Did you go running this morning?' he asks.

'Yes.'

'How far this time?'

'About twelve miles.'

Gabe lets out a low whistle. 'How long did that take?'

'Hour-twenty-five, or so.'

He puffs a long gust of breath. 'It'd take me all day. I don't know how you do it.'

He goggles, as always.

We move through to the living room and I flick the television onto the Test match highlights. Gabe takes Orla's spot on the recliner. I'm not sure I've ever sat in it. We sit in silence for a while, though it doesn't feel as if either of us are watching. I wonder if this is what masculine friendship actually is? I've never had many male mates and this is new. I don't know what to ask him.

'How's the table coming along?' Gabe asks after a while.

'I didn't get time to work on it today.'

He nods along, though it doesn't feel as if he was listening.

I spent the day with Orla, so didn't get time to head into the garage and continue working. That's where I craft the tables, units, shelves and furniture from which I make a living. I suppose *this* is what our friendship is. He asks about my runs and my work. We vaguely watch whatever sport is on the television. We're the skin of the peach, never the flesh within.

Gabe downs the rest of his beer, while I've barely had two mouthfuls. He's leaning forward on the chair, not slouching. 'I wish I could be like you,' he says.

'What d'you mean?'

'Do your own thing, set your own hours, have time to get fit – all that. I wish I didn't have to go to the factory every day. You're so lucky.'

He stops himself, his eyes slowly widening as he realises what he's said.

'I didn't mean it like that,' he adds quickly. 'I—'

'It's fine,' I reply. 'I know what you meant.'

Lucky.

Yes, I'm riddled with good fortune.

We sit and watch the television for a few minutes and, even more than before, I have no idea what to say to him. Gabe eventually asks if I want another beer and, when I say I'm fine, he disappears into the kitchen to get himself one. When he's back, there's more silence.

It's an odd sort of friendship. If he comes over to do this with me, then I wonder what things are like between him and Willow. Is *this* preferable to the relationship he has with his wife? What does it say about him – and what does it say about me?

The next hour or so passes in much the same way. We don't say much, certainly nothing of substance, while half-watching TV like an old married couple who've long since run out of subjects about which to chat. But there is something comforting about having someone around – someone who could, for all intents and purposes, be a mate.

He's not my wife but he's somebody. He's company. He keeps me out of my own head.

It's almost ten when Gabe says he's going home. We shake hands, because that's what we do, and then he's gone.

The sky is a darkening grey and I draw the curtains, before heading up the stairs to Orla's room. She's hugging her pillow, her body cocooned within the twisted bedding, as the sheets slowly rise and fall along with her breathing.

Lucky.

As if everything Orla's been through is fortuitous.

My fists are clenched once more and it's hard to blink away the hurt this time. I close Orla's door too loudly and then stumble downstairs until I'm back in the living room.

I'm on instinct now, an alcoholic on the way to the pub having promised never to drink again. I pull the bottom drawer all the way out from the cabinet and place it on the floor, then reach underneath, into the dark corners where nobody will ever look. It's only as I clasp the grip that my heart rate starts to slow, and the trembling in my fingers ebbs away.

Power lies in the pistol that's hidden here.

The truth is that I enjoy sitting in the dark, cradling the gun in my lap and dreaming of what I'd like to do with it.

I point the weapon towards the window and rest a finger on the trigger, applying the merest pressure. Nothing close to enough to actually pull it. I shut my eyes and listen to my own breathing, all the while leaving my arm extended. It is easy to picture the unknown figure in front of me; the one who wrecked my life. He's different every time I see him, sometimes with dark hair; sometimes light. He's white, Asian or black. Short or tall. Always a man.

Always.

When I open my eyes, the figure is gone again and there is only the murk of the living room. I am by myself once more, so do the only thing that feels right – press the muzzle of the pistol to my temple and say a silent prayer to a god in whom I do not believe.

FOUR

HEIDI

'I don't understand why the door needs to be locked,' I say.

Freddie hasn't got up from the sofa and doesn't look up from his phone. 'It doesn't *need* to be locked – but my work is inside. Notes and doodles, things like that for my job. I don't really want anyone to see it. Everything will look silly out of context.'

'I don't *want* to go through your things,' I reply. 'But it's my house, too. Why can't you leave it unlocked?'

Freddie finally turns away from his phone to look at me in the doorway. He gives a half-shrug and a weird blinky huff, as if he can't believe I'm being so unreasonable. 'Imagine you wrote down all your thoughts and left them on the side for me to read,' he says. 'You wouldn't, would you? I've always wanted an office. My own thinking space. If you're not going to go through my things, then what does it matter if the door's locked?'

'We never discussed this.'

When we put in the offer for the house, Freddie never said he'd use a room for an office. This was all decided while we were separated for the past week. We spoke every evening and he didn't mention it once.

He stands abruptly, riffling through his pockets. 'Do you want to go in? I can unlock it if you don't believe me.' Freddie pulls out a key and offers it.

'I *do* believe you.'

He puts away the key again: 'So what's the problem?'

I struggle to know what to say. I suddenly feel as if I'm in the wrong.

It probably shouldn't matter – there'll be nothing special in there, except for a few notes or drawings he's done for some PR campaign. Not the sort of thing worth arguing over. Not that it feels right.

Either way, before I can come up with more of a response, the door goes. I answer it to the pizza guy. His scooter is parked on the drive next to Freddie's car and he's pulling a large cardboard box out of a padded bag.

'Cash or card?' he asks.

I take the pizza and place it inside on top of a stack of still packed boxes. Over the road, Dylan's door opens and a man steps outside. He hops over the small fence between the two properties and lets himself into Willow's place. He must be her husband. There's an American-style flat-bed truck in the driveway of Dylan's place and it's hard to forget what Willow told us about him.

And his wife.

'Was that cash?'

The pizza guy bobs from foot to foot as I remember what I'm here for.

I dig around my bag to find the twenty-pound note and then watch his puppy-dog eyes fall as he waits for the 'keep the change' that I eventually offer. Before I can head back inside, my eye is caught by a flashing light two doors down. The pizza driver hums off into the distance on his scooter while I watch the lights on the house continue to flicker on and off.

Outside in only my socks, I ooh and aah across the stones of the drive onto the lawn. It might be the breeze but there are raised voices. The lights have stopped blinking but, as I edge along the street, the shouting gets louder. There's definitely a woman's voice and I realise I can only hear one person yelling. Each sentence is punctuated by quiet and then the commotion resumes. I listen for a few seconds and then, after another burst, there is silence.

Somehow, I am halfway along this stranger's path with little explanation for why I'm there.

After slowly backing away, I turn and hurry back to the house, where our front door is open, allowing the light to spill onto the drive. When I get inside, Freddie is still on his phone. It's like the shouting never happened.

'Pizza's here,' I say.

At the promise of food, Freddie finally puts down his phone. I place the pizza box on a makeshift table created from unpacked boxes, and then we sit together on the sofa. He munches his way through the first slice like a cartoon cat inhaling a fish, then moves onto second.

'I don't think I'm going to go tomorrow evening,' Freddie says.

I turn to look sideways at him as he picks up another slice of pizza. He's avoiding eye contact.

'We're going,' I insist.

'I might be late home from work.'

I say Freddie's name, waiting until he turns to look at me. 'We're going to Willow's,' I add, not letting him argue. 'She was good enough to invite us over for dinner.'

His reply is a sigh under his breath as he turns and gets to work on his second pizza slice.

'You wanted us to move here,' I say. 'I left my job for *you*. I want to make friends and fit in. I thought you'd be excited about seeing an old school friend—'

'She's not an old school friend. We didn't know each other.'

I finish my mouthful and then reply: 'She seemed to know you.'

'Yeah, well...'

That's all he has to say as he inhales his second slice. I take my time with my first as Freddie gets up and goes to the window. He opens the curtains slightly and stares out to the street.

'I'm not sure about this area,' he says.

I can't easily admit that I've been thinking the same. Our flat was small but it was close to everything. 'It's a bit late now.'

'I know... it's just...'

I wipe my fingers on the cardboard of the box and then cross to join him. The street is deserted, though there is a hint of light from each of the cloned houses. I wrap an arm around Freddie's lower back and lean my head on his shoulder. He rests his arm across my upper back and we stare towards the street as one.

'Do you think we made a mistake?' he asks.

I know my husband well enough to see the difference between a statement that's serious and something that's a joke. He means this. I could tell him about the feeling I got when I climbed out of the car earlier; that sense of being an imposter.

'Why do you say that?' I ask.

He squeezes my shoulder gently and nods across the street. 'I don't know. Maybe it's Willow? I got a funny sense from her.'

'She seemed nice enough to me.'

There's a pause and I can feel him thinking.

'Do you think he did it?' Freddie asks.

'Who?'

'Dylan.'

'Did what?'

'What Willow was talking about. Do you think he killed his wife?'

It's still warm and the sky isn't yet dark, but it feels as if the air has been sucked from the room. When I open my mouth, I expect to see my breath – but there's nothing there.

'We don't even know him. Plus, she didn't say he killed his wife, she said his wife was murdered.'

Freddie lets out a sceptical *pfft*. 'It's always someone close to the victim, though, isn't it?'

A few seconds pass and then I lever myself away from Freddie's arm. He doesn't move and instead continues to stare across the street.

'I think you're being unfair,' I say, probably believing myself.

He blows a low, disdainful raspberry: 'You can be very naïve.'

I move away from him, eye the pizza box, and then decide against it. 'I'm going to bed,' I say.

THE FUTURE

Officer: If you don't mind, can you tell me your name and job.

Samuel: Sam Longstaff, and I run a web design business but I also create apps, plus I fix computers and phones. Will you write that down? If you know anyone who needs anything fixing, I can do you a deal?

Officer: Thanks for the offer – but do you have another job?

[*Inaudible*]

Officer: Did you say you deliver pizzas?

Samuel: Well, yeah. Sort of. That's not my main job. I've been working on this app that's a cross between Uber and Tinder. You—

Officer: Is it true that you delivered a pizza to Huntington Grove on the Friday we were talking about?

Samuel: I guess.

Officer: Is that a yes?

Samuel: Yeah.

Officer: Can you remember the name of the person you delivered it to?

Samuel: It was that Heidi woman. Mum saw her photo on the news and, when I said I'd delivered her a pizza, Mum reckoned I had to call you.

Officer: We're grateful you did, Sam. Thanks for coming in. I do want to talk about the night you delivered the pizza, though.

Samuel: What about it?

Officer: Did you notice anything unusual?

Samuel: Like what?

Officer: I'm not sure. Did Heidi say anything you didn't expect? Did you see anything on the street?

Samuel: There was a bloke over the road. I saw him jumping a fence, going from one house to the one next door.

Officer: And that struck you as unusual?

Samuel: I guess.

Officer: Why do you say that?

Samuel: I suppose because of the way he jumped the fence. It felt like he was doing something he shouldn't.

[*Image shown of Dylan Wilson*]

Officer: Is this the man you saw?

Samuel: I don't think so.

[*Image shown of Gabriel Ellis*]

Officer: What about this man?

Samuel: Yeah… I reckon that's him.

Officer: Had you ever seen him before that evening?

Samuel: I don't think so.

Officer: Do you remember what time this was?

Samuel: I asked at the shop and it would've been about ten.

Officer: Thank you, Sam. Unless you have anything else to add, I think we might have all we need from you.

[*Inaudible*]

Samuel: Was it really a shooting? I know what they're saying. Mum says she heard it was a bomb.

Officer: I can't comment on what happened, Sam – but it wasn't a bomb.

Samuel: There's this video of people on the street when it happened. There are all these tables, like it's a party. They're running in different directions and there's screaming. Then there's a big bang. It sounded like a bomb.

Officer: It wasn't a bomb, Sam.

Samuel: So was it a gun?

Officer: I can't comment on that.

Samuel: Loads of people are saying it was a gun.

[*Inaudible*]

Samuel: Do you know who was shot? Mum reckons it was a girl.

Officer: I've already said—

Samuel: —Mum reckons she heard that two people are dead. She—

Officer: Sam, we need to stop there.

Interview terminated at 12:41 hours.

FIVE

SATURDAY

WILLOW

Isabella steps away from the camera and then the angle changes so that, instead of seeing her face, it is her hands that are in frame. She folds the sheet of paper once, then twice, and runs her black fingernail across the crease. All the while, she talks me through everything she's doing until, three minutes and forty-four seconds later, the camera blurs around to show the origami tiger she's created.

TikTok is the main way my daughter and I communicate nowadays, although it's an entirely one-way process. She makes her videos and I – along with, apparently, hundreds of thousands of strangers – watch. It was uploaded first thing this morning, although, from the clothes she's wearing, I think Isabella might have filmed it a week ago.

I watch the video twice, with the awful music on mute, and then scroll through the comments. It's a mix of well-wishers saying how talented she is and, in my mind at least, weirdos complimenting on her looks. I hope they are young people her own age but, in my darkest thoughts, they are predatory older men. After that, there are the trolls, of course. 'Why even bother?' one writes. 'Just kill yourself'.

I hover over the 'reply' button, desperate to defend my daughter – though we've been here before. She doesn't want protecting and she isn't after my help. 'Just ignore it,' she told me back then. 'I do.'

I wonder if she truly does. If I had strangers telling me to kill myself, I don't think I could shrug it off. And for what?

After a few minutes, I can't read any more, so close the laptop and head upstairs. I knock gently on Isabella's door, half expecting a huffed 'not now'. She instead calls back with a slightly less confrontational: 'What do you want?'

'I watched your latest video,' I say through the door.

'And?'

'Can I come in?'

I can hear her sighing and, after a moment, she mutters a 'fine'.

When I get in, it looks as if the usual clothes bomb has gone off. Tops, jeans and skirts litter the carpet, while Isabella's mirror is ringed by a blu-tacked set of art prints. A small origami tiger sits atop her dresser, which is otherwise covered with clutter. As for my daughter herself, she is on her bed, still in her pyjamas, phone in hand.

'What do you want?' she asks again.

'You know what I want.'

'You're always going on at me. It's Saturday. Can't I have a day off?'

'A day off from what? And I'm not *always* going on at you; I'm simply saying you can't do this all summer long.'

Isabella slams down her phone on the bed and scowls. We've been through this for at least six months and I was hoping she'd see things my way by now. Naïve, I know. She

wants to be a TikTok star; to spend her time making videos
about crafts, art, drawing, and all sorts of other things. I want
her to think about other things *as well*.

'I've just done my exams,' she says.

'That was over a month ago. I've given you some time to get
your head together. What about now?'

'What *about* it?'

'Are you going to apply to university for next year? Take a
gap year? Work?'

'Why do I have to decide now?'

There's such fire in her and I've often wondered whether it
comes from me. I'd like to say it was her father but he was never
this furious when we were together. I've seen things about
genes skipping generations; about kids being what their grandparents were, but I don't think it's that. Isabella is her own
person.

'Not *right* now,' I say, trying to be as conciliatory as possible.
'But I want you to start putting together a plan. The college are
running careers sessions all week and—'

'You've been spying on me?'

'Of course I haven't. It's on the college website.'

'Why would you even be looking?'

'Because I care. I want you to be a success. To—'

'Like you are?' Her eyes narrow as she glares an inferno
across her room.

I hate admitting it to myself. Hate even considering it – but
sometimes, just sometimes, she scares me. A tingle presses along
my back and I take a half-step backwards. It feels as if I've been
pushed.

'Don't be like that,' I say, trying not to falter. I don't think
I've ever been much of a crier but my eyes sting a little.

'Like *what?*' she says harshly. 'You're twenty years older
than me – and *you're* still a student. You can hardly tell me
what to do.'

'I've been trying to have this talk for months,' I say. 'You need a plan. You can't live here and make videos forever.'

Isabella pushes up from her bed and swishes her pyjamas down to cover her knees. 'So now you're kicking me out?'

'That's not what I said.'

'You're *not* kicking me out?'

'Of course not.'

'Right – so I *can* live here and make videos...?'

This is the problem with empty threats. What is my choice? Put my daughter on the streets or actually have this conversation? It feels like all or nothing.

'It's not the 1900s any more,' Isabella says. 'People make money from this.'

She smirks, largely because she knows how old it makes me feel. Things used to be thought of as modern if they were from the twentieth century; now it is ancient history.

'If you're *actually* making money from your videos, can we charge you rent?' I ask.

This, finally, has Isabella on the back foot. She is propped up on her elbows but cranes her neck away. 'You're going to take my money?'

I let the threat hang for a moment. She's made it sound like I'm about to kick a pensioner down the stairs while nicking their bag. 'It's not that, Iz,' I reply.

'Right, so can you leave me alone?'

We stare at each other and I know I'm going to cave. I probably should have thought this through better. Gabe told me not to bother picking a fight, yet here I am.

'This isn't over,' I say.

Isabella rolls her eyes.

'By the end of the week, I want to see either an application for university, or a job. You don't have to put it in but—'

'Whatever, Mum.'

I watch her for a moment more but this is getting us

nowhere. It's bluff but this is what we've come to. Isabella has recently taken her A levels and I suppose I thought she'd end up at university in September. I want more for her than what I had. She's one of the youngest in her year, which I know is hard. Some of her friends are almost a year older than her. They've thought about what's next and many had university applications in by the start of the year. The final date has already passed for this year – but Isabella could go into clearing and hope for a late spot. If not that, I suppose there are jobs out there. I don't want to judge but I *do* want her to do something.

I close her door, then return downstairs. Gabe is on the sofa, either reading the sports news on his phone, or pretending to. He doesn't say anything because he doesn't need to. I can feel his disapproval from the other side of the room. Isabella isn't his daughter and he tries to stay out of things.

Now I'm back downstairs, Gabe says he's going into the garden, so I set myself up on the dining table and crack on with my own university work. There is no summer break for us adults on the part-time course. If it's purely about the workload, I can understand why Isabella has seen what I do for my business management course and baulked at it all. Most of it is homework.

It doesn't take long before I find my mind wandering as I stare across the road towards Heidi and Freddie's place. They're coming over for dinner later and there's so much I'd like to talk about. I'd not seen Freddie in years and, suddenly, now he's in front of me, the box of memories from school has been reawakened. The fact I have a daughter who is almost eighteen makes it fairly obvious what happened to me not long after I left Marsh Vale, but I wonder what he's been doing.

That distraction is interrupted by another as Alison strides along the path. She sees me near the window, which destroys any hope of pretending I'm not in. I would happily use Isabella as a human shield if it meant someone else getting the door.

Don't worry about the uni application, love, you go over the trenches for me.

Too late.

Alison is her usual, relentlessly cheery self. I find something indefinably horrendous about people who don't see the negativity in life.

'How are you?' she beams as I open the front door. I wait on the precipice, definitely not inviting her in. She's in some bright yellow dress, her hair wound into a military-grade bun.

'Oh, y'know...' I reply, which isn't an answer, but she's not listening anyway.

'I was wondering if you could help with some of the decoration for Saturday?' She speaks with an authority I could never muster; as if there isn't an option to say 'no'.

'Saturday...?' I reply, feigning ignorance.

'The street party,' she says, with only the merest crinkling of a frown creasing her forehead. 'You've not forgotten have you? High Kingsley's 1,400th birthday. There are going to be tables all the way down the road.'

'Oh...' I say. 'I forgot that was this weekend.'

'Someone's cried off,' Alison says urgently. 'I've been going through my lists but most people have already got jobs. I was hoping you could help with the bunting.'

I don't care what anyone says, there is something intrinsically hilarious about the word 'bunting'. As in, 'This is really, buntingly annoying' or 'Sometimes Alison Hu needs a good kick up the bunt'.

I say none of this, of course.

'I've got university stuff,' I say, angling inside as if to make the point that some of us have *real* work to do. 'I'd love to help but—'

'I'll do it.'

Isabella has appeared at the bottom of the stairs as if by some sort of wizardry. I want to turn and say, 'Oh, so you *can* get up and down the stairs without stomping?' but just about hold onto it.

Alison has no hesitation, looking past me towards my daughter, almost forcing me to open the door wider, even though she doesn't ask.

'That's wonderful,' Alison says. 'Isabella, isn't it?'

'Right.'

'I think I've seen some of your videos. You're very talented. I think it's wonderful that young people can make a living from such new technology.'

She's done me there. The bitch.

I can feel Isabella smiling gleefully behind my back and then there's a stunted, accusatory snort meant only for me.

'Have you got a few minutes to come over?' Alison asks Isabella. 'I'll show you what I'm thinking of and then I can leave you to it? I know you'll be fantastic.' She turns to me and adds: 'You don't mind, do you?'

It's like being asked whether I hate puppies. There's only one answer.

'Of course I don't.'

Isabella slides around me without a word. She doesn't need to say anything. I stand and watch as she and Alison cross the road and head to the house two doors away from Heidi's.

It's not that I don't agree. Isabella *is* very talented and it *is* wonderful that young people have new ways of forging careers. Despite that, it would be nice if my daughter had an alternative plan in case her videos come to nothing.

I'm cursing myself for not being able to express that when a BMW cruises past and slots onto the drive opposite. Freddie clambers out but then ducks and reaches back into the car. By the time he's out again, I'm already down the path and off the kerb, calling his name.

Freddie turns and frowns. He takes a step towards the front door but can't pretend he hasn't seen me.

'Hi,' I say, when I reach him.

'I've only got a couple of minutes,' he replies. He's carrying a Waitrose bag and holds it up, as if to indicate there's something important inside. Those eight-quid caramelised sprouts aren't going to eat themselves.

He takes another step towards the house.

'I was wondering if you have anything from the old days?' I ask.

Freddie stops and turns back, scowling some more. 'Like what?'

'Like anything. I've got a box with photos and some odds and ends. Do you remember that we did a yearbook? We copied the idea from the US. I think everyone's in it. I used to keep it all but things got lost in various moves. I always think it would be great to see more from back then.'

'I didn't keep any of that,' he replies quickly, abruptly.

Freddie moves to the door again but there's one more thing I need to know.

'Do you remember about us?' I ask.

It's a slow turn this time. He looks me up and down, as if the moment has reawakened. He waits as I did bring it up, after all.

'We kissed,' I say, only then realising I've folded my arms. 'At that disco, house party-thing. Everyone was playing spin-the-bottle and my spin landed on you...'

He nods along slowly. 'Of course, I remember.'

'I didn't know if I should mention it in front of Heidi. It was years ago but I suppose it was one of the first things I thought of when I saw you. I think I kissed that Jan kid, too. Remember him?'

Freddie smiles but there's a distance there, leaving me wondering whether I should have brought it up. I thought he might smile, or laugh. It's not as if it means anything all these years on.

'It was a long time ago,' he says.

'I know...'

'Heidi wouldn't mind,' he adds matter-of-factly. 'You can tell her if you want. Maybe she'll find it funny?'

'Right.'

He turns back to the house, making it clear that we're done: 'I've got to go,' he says firmly. 'I'll see you at dinner.'

SIX

DYLAN

I force myself to think about what I'm doing. Don't overstretch the strides; don't waste energy by clenching my fists; keep my back straight. Perhaps it's because the spell of obliviousness has been broken but it's at this point that my stomach starts to tighten. Running is supposed to be something that can be done without considering it. As with many things in life, it gets complicated by overthinking.

The turn onto Huntington Grove is ahead and I take it before kicking on for the final sprint. My stomach twists again but there isn't far to go and then I finally reach my door. Sweat pours from my brow and my vest is so wet, I might as well have gone swimming. My water ran out two miles back and it's too hot a day to make that mistake. I take the towel from the wheel arch of the truck and wipe away the worst of the perspiration.

When I look up, Gabe is crossing the fence that separates our houses. He has a curious look on his face, as if he can't quite believe what he's seeing.

'How far did you run?' he asks.

'Just under ten.'

'Miles?'

'Right.'

He gives another low whistle and motions towards the house. 'Is Orla in?'

I don't particularly want company – but I figure Gabe probably saw my daughter leaving earlier in the morning. 'She's away for the day.'

It's the reply he wanted: 'Fancy a beer?'

'Bit early. It's not even two.'

Gabe shrugs and motions towards his own house. 'Willow and Iz are arguing again. I'm looking for somewhere to hide.'

I can hardly turn him away so wave him inside.

Gabe fetches one of the leftover Coronas from last night and I leave him in the kitchen as I head upstairs for a shower.

Lucky.

I still can't forget what Gabe said, even if it was in innocence. This house was paid off by the insurance company after what happened with Ciara. I only need enough for bills and Orla – and my woodwork more than covers that. If this is what's considered luck, I suppose I am fortunate.

By the time I've showered, changed and gone downstairs, Gabe is in the living room. I can't stop myself from glancing towards the cabinet, knowing what's hidden underneath.

'Have you heard them arguing?' he asks when I sit.

I assume he means his wife and daughter: 'Willow?'

'Right. They're always at it.'

'Not a peep.' I'm not sure why I lie but I feel the need to take Willow's side for some reason. It's impossible to miss them arguing through our adjoining wall.

'I think Willow and Iz are too alike. It's even worse when her dad gets involved. Just hope you don't have any of this to come.' He pauses and then adds: 'Where is Orla?'

'Football day camp.'

The bottle of beer stops midway towards Gabe's mouth. 'It was an all-boys' thing when I was a kid. Don't think I ever saw a girl on a football pitch.'

'Same for me,' I say. 'But we're old.'

He laughs and presses back into the recliner. There's something different about him today that I can't quite place. He seems more content and is relaxing, instead of hunching forward.

'Can I ask you something?' he says, the tipsiness talking.

'Go on.'

'Do you ever hear from the police now?'

He's staring and, even though I'm taller, I suddenly feel dwarfed. The stitch in my stomach is back.

'I know it's been three years,' he says, before adding an unnecessary: 'Since Ciara, I mean.'

'I've not heard from them in nearly a year,' I reply.

His gaze never falters as he nods slowly. 'So that's it? Someone killed your wife and that's the end?'

I don't know what to say, so remain quiet. Gabe follows up with a 'sorry' and it's only then that I realise he's drunk. Perhaps not to the stage of staggering around, or falling over – but enough that his usual guards are down.

'You're right,' I say. 'That pretty much *is* the end.'

I've never spoken about this with Gabe; nor anyone, really. Who am I going to tell? My secrets and thoughts were shared with Ciara – but she's no longer here.

'Ciara wasn't attacked,' I say, regretting it immediately. 'Not like that.' I can't bring myself to speak the R-word.

It's something I somehow feel he needs to know.

Gabe understands what I mean and, suddenly, all the awkward silences between us have been eclipsed.

'I know they reported differently – but she wasn't,' I add.

'I told Willow not to believe everything they wrote,' Gabe replies. 'I don't think she did but...'

'She was beaten. Her body was found in the bushes near the train station. They got that right.'

Gabe gulps and there's a seriousness about him that I've never seen before. Something steely and dark. He leans forward, shoulders tense.

'Did they ever have a suspect?' he asks.

'Me.'

'Oh...'

'I didn't blame them at the beginning – but, when it was clear it *wasn't* me, they still didn't move on.'

I wonder if I should tell him the rest, whether it'll sound like the rantings of a maniac. I suppose I'm most of the way there.

'There was a sighting near the train station at around the time,' I add. 'A man in a tin foil jacket. Specifically, a man.'

Gabe seems curious at this. The information was never made public. 'What do you mean?' he asks.

'Exactly that.'

He pauses for a moment, thinking: 'I've never heard of anyone wearing a foil jacket. Maybe at the end of the London Marathon when you see people in those shiny sheet things...?' He gives it a moment longer and then: 'Did the police ever ask about the, um, foil thing?'

His confusion is my confusion. It's been mine for three years.

'I don't think they believed the source,' I say.

'I don't understand...'

'It's complicated...'

I figured it would come to this if I started talking about things.

Gabe presses forward further in the seat. His beer is forgotten on the side and I sense him searching for the words.

'Are you... still... uh... looking for this person?' He speaks slowly, deliberately, choosing the words.

I wonder if I've said too much, whether I should have kept

this back in the way I have for the past three years. It might have been the moment with the gun in the dark of the living room last night but there's a part of me that wants to tell him.

There's a bigger part that can't.

'No,' I lie. My eyes wander to the cabinet. 'I suppose I'm *hoping* the police come up with something.'

Gabe is still for a moment, then relaxes. He scratches frantically at the stubble on his cheek. I watch, wondering if there's more, but he leaves it there. There's a strange few seconds in which I wonder whether we've been talking at cross-purposes? Perhaps, this wasn't about me at all.

He reaches for his beer and, suddenly, we're back to where we were last night. There's cricket on the television that neither of us are particularly watching. We're not saying much, either, and before I really know what's happening, the alarm on my phone sounds.

'I've got to pick up Orla,' I say.

Gabe pushes himself up from the chair and downs the remains of his beer. The six-pack from last night has been finished and I only had one.

We head for the front door together and Gabe mutters a 'see you soon' as I let him out. He pauses before reaching for his front door and it's hard not to wonder what's really going on between him and Willow. Is it *only* her arguments with Isabella? I could ask, of course, but it feels like our moment has passed – if it was ever there.

Gabe takes a deep breath, as if steeling himself, then he marches into the house and shuts the door.

It's a straightforward drive across town, out through the country lanes towards Orla's football camp. The sports complex is new, one of those things that locals spent years creating petitions to protest. Once it was built, it all went quiet, with people admitting that it wasn't a bad idea, after all. There is a large building, full of changing rooms, a pool and the gym; then an outdoor running track, a hockey pitch, and half-a-dozen all-weather football fields. In the winter, I'll drive here to run laps of the track because the floodlights stay on and it's safer than chancing it along the unlit streets away from Huntington Grove.

The car park is filled with expectant parents hanging around as the slow trudge of children parade away from the football pitches. Some are bouncing balls, others have their socks down to their ankles, exposing the shinpads. The kits are a rainbow of colour from the big Premier League teams and it's all very familiar. Go back thirty years, take away the advanced pitch and the multicoloured boots, and I could be among them.

Orla click-clacks her way across the tarmac with a weary sigh on her face. Her blonde hair is greasy and she has let it out of the ponytail I tied this morning.

'Good day?' I ask.

She sits on the ground and removes her boots, before pushing them into a kitbag.

'It was all right.'

'Is that, "all right" in a "brilliant"-kind of way, or "all right" in a "no"-sort of way?'

'Just all right.'

Orla seems weary, which is probably to be expected as she's been running around all day. Seven-year-olds can be ferocious bundles of energy one minute and arthritic sloths the next. She puts her kitbag on the back seat, and then climbs onto the booster seat on the passenger side, before putting on her seatbelt.

'Are we going home now?' she asks.

'I thought you might deserve some sort of treat after running around all day?'

She leans her head against the window. 'Like what?'

'McDonald's? Whatever you fancy.'

Orla says nothing for a couple of seconds as she continues to stare through the windscreen towards the pitches.

'I think I'd rather go home,' she says.

That's strange. She doesn't usually turn down the offer of fast food. 'Sure?'

'Yes.'

I start the car and set off, carefully winding my way through the traipsing children and the other vehicles. By the time I'm back on the main road, Orla still hasn't spoken.

'You OK?' I ask.

'Fine.'

'You're very quiet. Are you feeling poorly?'

'No.'

'Did something happen at football camp?'

'Like what?'

I wait for a moment. Sometimes kids can't help themselves and fill the gaps that are left. The road is clear, so I risk a glance sideways, to where Orla is still resting on the window. I should tell her to sit up straight but don't want to be a nag.

'You can tell me anything,' I say.

'I know.'

'And you're sure that everything is all right?'

She answers with a sigh: 'I'm fine, Dad. I just want to go home.'

SEVEN

HEIDI

'Alison,' the woman says, offering her hand. I shake it but she quickly pulls away. I can imagine her running home and dousing herself in hand sanitiser.

She points to the house two doors down; the one from which the lights were flickering last night, where someone was shouting.

'I live there,' Alison says. 'I wanted to welcome you to the area.'

'Oh... thank you.'

Alison moves on so abruptly that it's clear the welcome is *not* the reason why she's knocked on my door.

'You might have heard but I'm helping to organise a street party for next Saturday,' she says. 'It's High Kingsley's 1,400th birthday and there will be celebrations happening all over. We're going to have tables down the middle of the street, and everything will be closed to traffic. There will be food, party games, maybe a bit of a sing-song...'

I wonder if we've unpacked the knives yet. Is it too late to slit my own wrists?

Alison doesn't seem to breathe: 'There's an organising committee,' she continues, 'I'm not expecting you or your husband to get involved, or anything like that...'

There's a 'but' coming.

'...But this is more to let you both know.'

'Oh,' I hear myself saying, waiting for the rest. She wants me to donate a kidney to orphans, something like that.

When it's clear that *is* all she's here for, I'm left scrambling for a reply.

'Freddie's had to nip into work,' I say.

'That's your husband?'

'Right. I'd, um, invite you in, but...'

I don't want to.

'...We still have loads to unpack.'

Alison nods along sweetly and I wonder quite why I have such instant hostility to her. She's nice enough and has gone out of her way to introduce herself. I'm clearly the problem here.

I glance sideways towards her house and want to ask about the noise from last night. I also want a bit of a gossip about Dylan over the road. I saw him running earlier, and then he arrived back like a sweaty Mediterranean Adonis. I can't stop thinking about Freddie's speculation of whether he killed his wife. It *is* usually the husband or boyfriend, after all.

'So what's the area like to live in?' I ask. I should make a bit of an effort.

Alison hums slightly under her breath, either not noticing, or not minding, the shift in tone. She's prim, her hair tied in a bun so tight that it's giving a free facelift. 'Quiet enough,' she replies. 'Friendly.'

'Do you live here with your husband...?'

That's some good fishing right there.

Alison crosses her arms, which says plenty.

'I am married,' she replies, almost cryptically. 'My husband, Kenneth, is in Hong Kong. He works between the two countries.'

There's an edge there; like someone talking about how their mother-in-law has come to stay for a week.

'Any kids?' I ask, thinking about the noise from last night, though regretting it almost instantly. Only psychos ask women if they've got children.

'Not yet,' she fires back instantly, much like the way I suspect I do when asked. There's something about being mid- to late-thirties and childless that makes people view women differently.

'Me either,' I reply, in an attempt to not be such a cow. 'Why Hong Kong?' I add.

'That's where he's from.' She doesn't give a chance for a follow-up this time. 'Perhaps we could do coffee some time...?'

I can't get on board with this whole *doing* coffee-thing.

'We could *have* coffee,' I say, figuring the invitation is one of those open-ended things that will never actually happen.

Alison starts juggling her bag. 'Right, I'll give you my number,' she says, before doing precisely that. She texts, I reply, and that's that.

I'm about to make some sort of excuse to get out of the conversation when a DHL van pulls up outside Alison's house. She notices it a few seconds after I do but, before we can say any sort of goodbye, she's hurrying to her house, trying to get the delivery guy's attention. By the time he's halfway down the path, she's at a sprint to stop him getting there before her. She almost rugby tackles him, leaving the poor guy staring at her with bemusement as she catches her breath.

I can't hear what she says but she has to pull out her driving licence and then he lets her sign for the parcel on the electronic gadget.

When she realises I'm still watching, Alison turns and holds the parcel aloft, like some sort of trophy.

'Sorry about that,' she shouts.

'It's fine.'

She motions a universal finger-and-thumb phone call with her spare hand and then heads for her front door. I watch her disappear, wondering what just happened. Why the noise from the house? Why was she so keen to stop the delivery man knocking?

Back inside, and I get to work on some of the unpacking. Freddie's 'quick dash' to the office has already turned into almost ninety minutes of him not helping do the one thing he said he was going to do today. Day two of our move and I feel as alone as I was last week when I was by myself. It feels as if something has changed in those seven days. We weren't a couple of extreme work hours and locked doors before we moved but now, apparently, we are.

I start in the living room and pull out some of the knick-knacks and decorations that used to sit around our old flat. There are a few wooden animal carvings that we bought at a Tunisian market. A dreamcatcher that should've been thrown out. There are CDs that neither of us have listened to us in years, a handful of DVDs we didn't watch when we bought them, let alone now. Nothing that's really important.

I try the door to Freddie's new office, just in case, but it's still locked.

As I'm heading back into the living room, I notice Isabella crossing the road with a box in her hand. I hurry outside, catching her just as she steps onto the pavement.

'Do you need a hand?' I ask. 'Least I can do after you helped yesterday.'

She puts down the box on the pavement. 'It's only this,' she replies.

'Can I ask what's inside?'

'Bunting,' she replies, which, if I'm honest, was not what I was expecting. 'Actually, it's stuff to *make* bunting.'

We each turn to look at Alison's house together and then, bizarrely, there's a moment of connection. This girl, who is half my age, whom I've only met once, and who is someone else's daughter, suddenly has an understanding with me. She laughs first and I know I'm right, so join in.

'Alison asked you too, then?' Isabella says with a snort.

'Sort of. I think she was weighing me up as to whether I'd volunteer.'

'I *actually* volunteered. I'm going to make a video.' There must be some degree of curiousness on my face because she adds: 'That's what I do. I make TikToks of crafts, that sort of thing.'

'I'll have to look you up.'

It comes out automatically, even though anyone over the age of about twenty-five with a TikTok account needs to be on a register.

Not that Isabella agrees: 'You should! Mum wants me to get a job or go to uni. I think she's trying to get rid of me.'

'I'm sure that's not true.'

Isabella shrugs. 'She doesn't think this is a job. She acts like it's the 1900s, or something.'

I give my best closed-lip, non-committal smile, not entirely sure what to say. Either way, something must shift in my expression.

'What?' Isabella asks.

'I had the same arguments with my mum,' I reply. 'I think everyone does. I'm sure she wants the best for you.'

'She has a funny way of showing it.'

I'm not certain what comes over me but there's suddenly a part that feels the need to say something.

'Look,' I begin. 'I don't want to speak out of turn. I'm not your mum and I'm positive she means well. You shouldn't fall out and you'll only regret it later. But it's OK if you don't have your whole life figured out yet. That's normal.'

Isabella stares at me with such earnestness that I suddenly feel conscious of myself. I'm not sure where it all came from.

'OK,' she says, though it's not dismissive. It feels like she's listened, even if I'm not totally sure what or why I said it.

Isabella picks up Alison's box and takes a step towards her house. A flap of something shiny slips from the side, like a thickened sheet of foil. Isabella doesn't notice at first but then she lifts the lid a fraction and tucks it inside.

'See you around,' she says – and then she's gone.

EIGHT

WILLOW

I'm in the kitchen as Isabella strides past and unlocks the back door. 'You all right, Mum?'

I'm so shocked she's spoken to me that I almost drop the wooden spoon.

'I'm fine...' I reply. 'Trying to get everything set for later.'

Isabella puts down the box on the counter. 'I'm going to work on some of this bunting in the back garden,' she says. 'I'm going to start on a video. Is that OK?'

She has never asked for permission before and it's hard to know why she's asking now.

'It's fine,' I say, stumbling over the simple reply.

'Sorry about earlier,' she adds, not waiting for a response as she heads outside into the sunshine.

I have no idea what to say. My daughter's been replaced by some sort of android that looks and sounds like her, but actually asks before doing things.

And apologises!

Shouldn't this technology be decades away? Is this some

sort of AI thing? It feels far stranger than when we're arguing. That's the norm, this is something else. I can deal with aggression but what to do with politeness?

I watch through the window as Isabella lays out the twine and triangles of red, white, and blue. There's a large silvery sheet that feels out of place and she returns it to the box – then she pulls out her phone and starts talking into it. At least *she's* getting something from this street party.

I'm in the middle of pureeing some carrots when my phone rings. My friend Michelle's name flashes across the front. Normally, I might let the call go seeing as I'm busy – but her timing is impeccable.

'Guess who moved in opposite,' I say by way of greeting.

'Hello to you, too,' she replies.

'Do you remember Freddie Potter?'

There is a moment of silence. Michelle and I talk once on the phone once a month or so – and have done for years. Life sent us in different directions but I suppose we never completely got out of the habit of being best friends at school.

'The kid whose parents died?' she asks.

'Right. He lived with his grandparents.'

'Freddie! We went out for a couple of weeks when I was sixteen or so. I've not heard from him in years. He's moved in opposite you?'

'I've seen him with my own eyes. Spoken to him.'

'I think there was this time where we tried to kiss and almost knocked each other's teeth out. We had no idea what we were doing. Didn't you snog him once?'

'At spin the bottle one night. I was hoping for that French exchange kid but misjudged the spin.'

Michelle giggles girlishly and there's a moment in which it feels like we're teenagers once more, gossiping about boys on the way home from college.

'He couldn't get my bra off,' Michelle says. 'He trapped his finger in the catch, then accidentally snapped it into me. Kind of a mood-killer.'

I laugh this time. There's a wondrous naïvety about being young and curious.

I take a moment to open the window to let some cooler air inside, then take a seat at the table.

'I can't believe he's moved in opposite you,' Michelle adds. 'What's he like now?'

'Tallish; a bit chubby. Seems kind of normal.'

'He was always a bit scrawny when we were kids. I figured he'd be off managing an IT department somewhere.' She lets out a long, low gasp and then adds: 'I wonder if he'd like to meet...?'

'He's married.'

'Not like that! You've got such a filthy mind. Just for a catch-up. Nothing weird.'

'I'll ask. He's coming over for dinner with his wife later. I'm cooking.'

'*You're* cooking?'

'I'm not that bad.'

Michelle reminds me of the time I burned baked beans back when we were teenagers.

We spend another ten minutes reminiscing about how things used to be. It's only as the clock ticks around to four that she says she can't remember why she called, adding that she'll text if she remembers.

'Say hello to Freddie for me,' Michelle adds, before hanging up.

Isabella chooses that moment to reappear in the kitchen with her bunting box and phone.

'Everything go well?' I ask.

'The angle of the sun doesn't help but I'll make it work.'

My daughter hovers for a moment, though I'm not brave enough to ask what's on her mind.

'Heidi and Freddie from across the road are coming over for dinner,' I say.

'I'm going out with Jarvis anyway.' She stops and then a slim smirk appears on her face. 'We're planning to do heroin and have unprotected sex, assuming that's all right with you.'

I allow myself a laugh, although it's hard to wonder quite why she's being so reasonable. I was half-expecting a tantrum about how I'm kicking her out of her own house, and so on. It's happened before.

'If you need a lift or anything, make sure you get a taxi or Uber,' I say. 'I'll pay.'

'Can I have the money now?'

There's a chance this was all an act to get some cash but I take the request at face value and fish a £20 note from my purse. I'm surprised she knows what cash is.

'Here,' I say. 'Just... Nothing stupid. I'm allowed to worry.'

Without necessarily meaning to, I glance sideways towards Dylan's house. What happened to his wife is the benchmark for everything that can and will go badly. There was a time afterwards that Isabella barely left the house. What happened to Ciara scared her. Time is the only cure and my seventeen-year-old daughter is very different to my fourteen-year-old daughter.

Isabella disappears upstairs and I continue to get on with what I was doing before Michelle called. Up the matriarchy and all that.

It's almost half-past-six when I go to check on Gabe. There is one thing on which my husband and I both agree: weekends are not the times for hiking up mountains, or spending hours on the motorway in order to visit some underwhelming shopping centre. They're not for new movies at the cinema, or days at the beach. Before I went back to studying, we were both working full-time. Gabe still does. I'll never quite get my head around people who spend all week doing stuff – and then get to the weekend only to do more stuff. Weekends are for doing as little as humanly possible.

Gabe has taken this to the extreme, by sharing a beer with Dylan next door, and then retreating to the living room to play something shooty on the PlayStation. The television rumbles with the chatter of simulated gunfire as I stand behind him.

'Can you lay the table?' I ask and there's a moment in which it feels as if my husband is my grumpy teenager.

'Gimme a minute.'

I give him five – but he's still busy shooting things when I do it myself, making a special point to bang the cutlery on the table. That point is ignored as Gabe continues to grumble under his breath about the game.

Isabella comes down and says she's going out and then, after a shouted goodbye, Gabe – finally – turns off his game.

It's only another five minutes until there's a knock on the door and our new neighbours have arrived. Heidi is wearing a short, red cocktail-style dress but Freddie is still in the clothes I saw earlier. It's as if everything he owns is half-a-size too small and clings to his upper body and thighs.

We give it the usual array of enthusiastic greetings and thank yous. I hurry around, introducing them to Gabe, then ushering them towards the dining area at the back of the living room. There's a part of me desperate to impress Heidi, almost to the point that it's like being a needy teenager once more. Gabe disappears next door most nights, Isabella does her thing and I... well... it would be nice to have someone roughly my own age, who is broadly sane, and wants a chat now and then.

Not that I'd ever say as much out loud.

Heidi comments on how everything in our place is the mirror of theirs. 'Minus the boxes,' she adds, in a remark that is clearly a dig at Freddie.

For his part, it feels as if Freddie is watching me while trying to pretend he isn't. He makes small talk with Gabe about sport, work and other things I don't catch. All the while, I sense him glancing sideways, or taking me in over Gabe's shoulder. It feels as if he wants to say something.

The first course is carrot and coriander soup, to which Gabe wastes no time in adding a ludicrous amount of salt without tasting it. I flash him a quick frown but Heidi seems to be the only person who notices.

We go through the motions. Gabe manages a dairy factory; I'm back in education and have a seventeen-year-old daughter. It doesn't take much for either Freddie or Heidi to do some adding up.

Freddie's been down here for a week working as a PR marketing manager, after being headhunted. He led some youth campaign up north that I've never heard of. Heidi rolls her eyes when he says this, and it's at this moment that I know we'll probably get on.

It sounds as if Heidi has been stitched up. Her career managing an office was merrily coming along – and then they moved and she doesn't have a job. When I bring up her career, she changes the subject quickly.

I clear the table and then open the window at the front of the house. On days such as today, it feels as if the inside is broiling. These houses are the North Pole in the winter and the Sahara in the summer.

The main course is a risotto with baked halibut. There's accompanying wine but, when the bottle reaches Freddie, he waves it away.

Gabe is incredulous as he tops up his own glass. 'You don't drink wine?' he asks.

Freddie shakes his head. 'I don't drink,' he replies quietly. 'Not my thing.'

Gabe is still for a moment, unsure what to say. We got drunk together on our first date and booze has never been far from our evenings out and in.

'Have you ever tried it?' my husband asks.

'When I was a teenager. Not in years.'

Gabe passes the bottle to Heidi, who places it in the middle of the table.

'At first, I wondered what we'd ever do together,' she says. 'If you don't go to the pub, or out for a meal, what do you do?'

'What *do* you do?' Gabe asks, sounding somewhat confused.

Heidi laughs and touches her husband on the arm. 'We figure it out.'

We make small talk during the main course but I get the same sense of curiosity from Freddie throughout. It is as if he's always on the brink of saying something to me, even though he doesn't. Despite that, general chit-chat comes easily and even Gabe seems invested.

It's after we've polished off the apple and blackberry crumble that I tell Freddie I have a surprise for him. I go to the cupboard under the stairs and pull out the large box that has been following me around for a couple of decades. The one I told Freddie had dwindled over my time. My memory box once contained a pair of knee boots that I wore to death when I was fourteen or fifteen. Ever since, it's been filled with photos, letters, ticket stubs: anything I kept hold of from the time.

When I get back to the living room, I pass the top photograph from the box to Heidi – and then press a finger to the boy on the end of a long row of schoolchildren.

'Look who it is,' I say.

Heidi breaks into a grin as she takes the picture. There are almost thirty of us in two lines. I don't remember precisely when it was taken but it's definitely at the back of the school field, with the main building in the background. It's a bright day and the grass is a lush green.

'I think we were in year eleven,' I say. 'I can't quite remember. It might have been the year before.'

Heidi holds it up for Freddie to see and continues to smile. 'Look at your hair,' she says. 'What were you thinking?'

He's got a bowl cut and it's hard to believe that was ever the fashion. If everything is truly cyclical, then give it a few years and it'll be back.

Freddie takes the photo but there's no hint of a smile. 'It was a long time ago,' he says softly.

Heidi starts to dig through the box. There are swimming certificates and various commendations for everything from perfect attendance through to being a member of the young scientists' club. What a goody two-shoes.

'I kept more or less everything,' I say.

The next time Freddie appears is in the yearbook. It's been bound together with a thin hardback cover that we got for cheap from a local printer. Mine has a coffee ring on the front from where Dad mistook it for a coaster. Inside, all the students have their own small passport-sized photographs with our names and a small statement underneath.

Willow Vaughan: Don't dare to dream

I can't remember where I came up with that but it now seems so silly. It was before Isabella, before her dad, when I thought I'd end up changing the world. I suppose it is prophetic in that I didn't dare to dream of quite where I'd end up.

Freddie is on the same page.

Freddie Potter: Here, there, everywhere

He has a thin face in the photo, with wide-rimmed glasses and a peppering of acne around his neck. There's barely a resemblance to who he is now, although I don't look much like I did either.

Heidi shows Freddie his slogan and asks her husband what it means.

He takes the yearbook and shrugs. 'Thought I was a philosopher, I guess.'

'I'm so glad you sorted out your hair,' she adds.

Freddie flicks through the yearbook pages but doesn't say anything. I suppose I hoped he'd be more excited, or perhaps even name some of the people from the old days. If he remembers Michelle, then he doesn't say. She has one of the dodgiest perms I've ever seen. It is pure eighties, even though we were a decade late: wild, tight and untamed. I'll send her a photo of it later.

Heidi continues going through the box but there doesn't seem to be anything else relating to Freddie. There's plenty more of me. I'm there playing hockey for the school in a pornographically short skirt, which it's hard to believe was ever official uniform. There's an appallingly written article about badgers that I put together for the school newspaper; some order of service for a harvest festival assembly, in which I played a farmer's wife; a photo of a pineapple upside-down cake I made for home studies; a third-place certificate for the year-nine 800m race. I'd forgotten quite how much I used to do.

I ask Freddie if he wants to borrow the yearbook but he passes it back with a shake of the head, so I bundle everything into the box once more.

A new wine bottle makes a lap of the table, missing out Freddie, though it's clear that Heidi is starting to feel its effects.

'I met our neighbour, Alison, today,' she says with a snort of a giggle.

Gabe and I exchange a brief sideways glance because we know what's coming. My own youthful exuberance has just been on display – but I grew out of it. People like Alison never seem to.

'What's the 1,400 years thing?' Heidi adds.

'That's the age of the town,' I say. 'High Kingsley was founded by some blokes, I want to say the Anglo-Saxons, back in the 600 ADs. Something like that. A few people thought there should be some sort of celebration and then it all spiralled. There are going to be street parties all over, loads of roads are closed, there's some period dress contest... that sort of thing.'

Heidi nods along.

'It'll probably rain,' Gabe says, though everyone ignores him.

'Alison seemed very, um... *efficient*.'

I almost laugh at Heidi's careful choice of words. 'She's definitely that,' I reply.

'She said something about her husband being away...'

'I think he's in Hong Kong. They moved in a couple of years ago. Something about settling down and having kids but I don't know. I think Kenneth is away a lot.'

Heidi starts to say something but is cut off by Gabe's snorted: 'Wing, Ping, Ding, Dong.'

Everyone stops to look. Heidi's mouth hangs, Freddie's head is angled in confused disbelief, while I glare daggers. I wonder quite how much Gabe has drunk through the day and now this evening. Kenneth is Asian and, seemingly realising his bit of casual racism didn't go down well, my husband pushes himself up from the table. He hiccups something that might be an apology, then says he needs the toilet. Aside from his footsteps, there is silence as he stumbles his way upstairs.

'He's had problems sleeping,' I say, which is met by the muted nothingness it deserves. I'm not sure what else to go with. He doesn't deserve defending and I wonder if my husband has always been like that. If so, it's never come out before. Does the drink bring out a person's real self?

Heidi sips her wine as awkwardness descends. I turn to Freddie and find myself blurting out the first thing that comes into my head. Anything that'll move things away.

'Do you remember Michelle?' I say.

I've barely finished the second syllable of her name when Freddie fires back with a sharp: 'No'.

'She still lives in Marsh Vale,' I add. 'She's only a couple of streets from the school. She remembers you and wondered if, perhaps, you might fancy a brew, or something? The three of us.' I turn to Heidi and quickly add: 'Four of us if you wanted to come. I hope you don't mind. I'm only passing on the message.'

Freddie shakes his head. 'I don't think that's a good idea.' He pushes himself up and pats his stomach, looking towards Heidi. 'I'm not feeling too great. I'm gonna nip home.'

'Oh,' Heidi says, surprised.

'I hope it's not the food,' I add.

Another shake of the head. 'It's not.' He touches Heidi's shoulder and adds: 'Are you coming?'

'I, um...' Heidi glances to me. 'I might stay for another glass – and then I'll be over. Is that all right?'

Freddie's hesitation makes clear it's *not* all right – but he says the opposite, offers a weak smile and thanks me for the food. I let him out and then he hurries across the road, without turning back. That coincides with Gabe returning down the stairs. There is a gentle sheen to his skin, as if he's splashed water onto his face. He probably needs it.

'What's going on with you two?' he asks, nodding towards the front door and Freddie's departing shape.

'How do you mean?'

'He seemed pretty rattled when you started talking to him about school. Were you two together, or something?'

'Not like that.'

Gabe stares at me for a second and then snorts with annoyance. 'I'm going to play my game,' he says, before disappearing upstairs again.

I watch him for a moment, with no idea what to add.

After that, I head into the living room, where Heidi and I

shift to the comfy chairs. It feels as if we're both a little discon-
certed by our partners, though we don't know each other well
enough to point it out.

'How long have you been with Freddie?' I ask.

'Nine years,' Heidi says, counting on her fingers. 'What
about you and Gabe?'

'Four years. We were on and off at the beginning, then
moved in together just over three years back. We got married
fourteen months ago.'

Heidi curls her legs underneath herself and presses back
into the corner of the sofa.

'Big wedding?' she asks, airily. I think she's a tad tipsy.

I shake my head: 'We both wanted something small. Just a
register office job with a few friends. You?'

'More or less the same. Didn't want to spend all the money
on something that would be over and done with. We figured
we'd rather save for a house. I'll never get those couples who
blow thousands on rings and venues. Think of what you could
do with it all.'

She unties her hair and it cascades down around her shoulders, making her seem like a different person. I thought she was
another Alison when we first met but she's scrappier. I think I
like her.

'Did you go to uni?' I ask.

'No. I liked having money at a young age. I kind of wish I
did now. I couldn't get promoted after a while. They wanted
kids with degrees, rather than thirty-somethings with
experience.'

'You can still go. That's what I'm doing.' I sound too eager,
too desperate for someone to tell me I'm making the correct
career choices.

Heidi shakes her head a little. 'I don't think it's for me.' A
pause and then: 'No offence...'

Nobody ever says such a thing without knowing they've caused offence. I try not to let it sting: 'What about Freddie?'

There's a pause that's hard to read. It might be annoyance but maybe it's nothing.

'He took a year out and went travelling,' Heidi says. 'I think he was going to go to uni but had a bad experience while he was abroad. He ended up working in a supermarket and did a part-time marketing degree. He worked his way up from that. This job's his big break.'

She speaks earnestly, but there's definitely a twinge of something. His big break.

His.

'What happened when he was abroad?' I ask.

Heidi shrugs. 'I don't really know. He's never been keen on travelling since and it only came out when I asked why he was so against it. I figured he'd say he was scared of flying but he said he was mugged. I didn't want to push too hard. I think it's scarred him against being in other countries. I've got him to France a couple of times but never further.' She pauses and then adds: 'What about Gabe and his job?'

'He's been managing the yoghurt factory the whole time I've known him. He worked his way up from minimum wage in the packing warehouse. They've been laying people off recently, so he's stressed.'

I think of the 'ding dong' outburst from before, wishing I had an explanation. 'Stressed' isn't an excuse.

Heidi and I continue to chat for another fifteen minutes or so, until the bottle is empty. She says she should check to make sure Freddie is OK, then we say our goodbyes. It's dark when she heads across the road and I watch her, full of that instinct of wanting to know the other person is safe. When her front door opens, I close ours.

So much for finding a new friend...

The door has barely clicked into place when Gabe appears

halfway down the stairs. He must have been listening, waiting for her to go.

'Why did you say that?' I ask.

He sits on the stair and peers down. 'Say what?'

'About Kenneth.'

'I don't know what you mean.'

'"Wing, Ping, Ding, Dong". I can't believe you made me repeat it.'

There's a dismissive shrug: 'It was only a joke. It's not like he was here.'

I open my mouth to argue back but then close it again. I'm furious but we've been here before. He won't back down, nor concede he's done anything wrong. I'll shout, he'll shout louder, we won't talk for a day or two, Isabella will blame me for how awkward things are. It won't be worth it, not tonight.

'What about *you?*' he adds, accusingly.

'What about me?'

'There's obviously something going on with you and 'im over the road.'

It takes a couple of seconds for me to figure out what he's talking about. 'Freddie...?'

'He didn't want to talk about school – but you kept going on about it. So what *did* you get up to?'

I stare at him for a moment. 'What do you mean? Nothing went on.'

Gabe snorts in derision. 'I'm going out.'

He stomps down the stairs and I realise he's changed. He's now in jeans, boots and a plaid shirt.

'Where are you going at this time?' I say.

'Out.'

And he does.

I stand in the hall, speechless. Even aside from Gabe's reaction, Freddie's own to the yearbook was a bit odd. I wondered yesterday if it was because of how he didn't want to be reminded of being brought up by his grandparents. Except it didn't feel like that. It was more as if he specifically had an issue *with me*.

And now, a day on, Gabe saw the same thing but mistook it for something else. He didn't see Freddie practically run from the room when I mentioned Michelle. I should probably leave it but it's hard to forget, especially if it's now impacting my marriage. Even if that marriage is apparently to a casual racist, who seemingly now has no issues showing that in front of others.

He wasn't always like this.

Or perhaps I was somehow blind to it?

But then, Gabe is not the only problem. Because, beyond him... what *exactly* happened to Freddie at school?

THE FUTURE

Police statement: Michelle Gibson.

Michelle: I don't know if there's much I can tell you.

Officer: How about you start with how well you know Willow Ellis.

Michelle: We've known each other since school. She moved away but I suppose we've always been friends. It's easier now with phones and Facebook and everything.

Officer: And you spoke on the phone the Saturday before everything?

Michelle: We talk every other weekend or so. It's not the same through texts, is it?

Officer: But you *specifically* spoke on that Saturday?

Michelle: Right.

Officer: What did you talk about?

Michelle: Mainly how Freddie Potter had moved in across the road. We all went to school together and couldn't believe what a coincidence it was. We'd not seen each other in twenty-odd years. Willow has moved miles away, and there he is.

Officer: How did you feel about this?

Michelle: Surprised. A little excited, I guess.

Officer: Why?

Michelle: Because I used to know Freddie at school. I had a thing for him, I suppose.

Officer: Did Willow mention anything to you at that point about her husband?

Michelle: Gabe? I don't think so. How do you mean?

Officer: Was she worried about Gabe's reaction to the reappearance of Mr Potter?

Michelle: I don't think so. I mean… if she was, she didn't say. Not then. It's not like Freddie was an old flame, or anything. I don't think Willow and Freddie knew each other that well at school.

Officer: But *you* knew him?

Michelle: Sort of. We kind of knew the same people, so I knew him through that.

Officer: And you had a crush on him?

Michelle: Yeah, but I had a crush on a lot of boys.

[*Sound of laughing*]

Michelle: We went out together for a couple of weeks but it wasn't anything serious. Kids being kids. We didn't know what we were doing.

Officer: Do you know Heidi Potter?

Michelle: Not personally. I've heard her name. I think she's married to Freddie.

Officer: What about Dylan Wilson?

Michelle: I know what happened to his wife. He was living next door to Willow, so we talked about it a bit. I've never met him.

Officer: Alison Hu?

Michelle: Never heard of her.

Officer: And how well do you know Gabe Ellis?

Michelle: Willow's husband? Only through her. We've met a couple of times. I was bridesmaid at the wedding – but that was the first time I'd met him properly. It was a small thing. Isabella was the other bridesmaid but we didn't match outfits, or anything like that.

Officer: Isabella is Willow's daughter, right?

Michelle: Yes.

Officer: Do you know her well?

Michelle: I mean… I suppose not. I only see Willow once or twice a year, so I've only seen Isabella a handful of times in the past decade. I saw her more when she was a kid. I don't really know her as a teenager. I've watched some of her videos.

Officer: Did Willow ever indicate there was an issue between herself and her daughter?

Michelle: I know they argued a lot. I figured that was mother-daughter stuff, you know? Everyone's a bit like that as a teenager. I was.

Officer: But nothing more serious?

Michelle: Not that Willow told me.

Officer: Do you know if there were any issues between Isabella and her stepfather?

Michelle: Gabe?

Officer: Right.

Michelle: I don't think so. Not that Willow ever said.

Officer: OK, thank you for that. And, to clarify, you had no direct contact with Freddie Potter?

Michelle: I mean, I asked Willow if we could all go for coffee.

Officer: Why did you do that?

Michelle: I figured it'd be interesting. Like I said, Freddie and I went out for a couple of weeks when we were teenagers. After school, he dropped off the face of the earth. He wasn't on Facebook, or anything. I wondered what happened to him. I suppose that's what's different now. Years ago, people would always disappear after school. Now, with Facebook, Instagram, all that, it continues. I was curious. That's all.

Officer: Did Willow arrange for you all to go for coffee?

Michelle: No, I don't think Freddie wanted to.

Officer: Do you know why?

Michelle: You'd have to ask Willow. Or him.

[*Sound of shuffling chairs*]

Michelle: Sorry. Do you mind if we stop? I really need the toilet.

[*Sound of shuffling chairs*]

Officer: Interview terminated at 14:34 hours.

NINE

SUNDAY

DYLAN

The trio of gravestones sit in a perfect line, sprouting from the dewy grass. A thin haze of mist is lifting from the fields beyond and it feels like it's going to be a warm day. 'Ciara Wilson' is on the right, with her parents' stones adjacent. Her dad apparently put down the money for these spots when he turned fifty.

Talk about planning for the future.

Even if I wanted to be buried at her side, there's no space. I don't mind, not really. People can believe what they want about the afterlife and so on – but dead is dead. What does it matter?

I'd somehow forgotten that people go to church on Sundays. A dribble of parishioners have been passing along the path a little behind us, all muttering similar things about the mist and how pretty everything seems.

Orla is sitting on a blanket at the side of her mother's plot. We come here once a month, or so – usually when she asks. Today it was me who instigated the visit. Orla has been telling her mum about how it's been a warm summer and that she's spent a lot of time with her friend, Lauren. I'd step away if she asked, give her the privacy to talk to her mum, but she has never asked. Somehow this has become her norm.

After she finishes, Orla picks herself up and folds away the blanket into a backpack. 'Does everyone get a grave when they die?' she asks. 'Wouldn't it take up a lot of room?'

'Not everyone,' I say. 'Some people are cremated.'

She practises saying the word and then asks what it means.

There are times when I have no idea whether Orla is too young for something. She has already experienced so much that it's difficult to know whether her seven-year-old self is ready to hear some of the truths about life. I try to answer everything as honestly as I can because I figure she deserves that.

'It's complicated,' I say. 'A person's body is turned into a powder. It's called ashes. Those ashes can be spread in a place that person loved the most.'

There's a moment in which I wonder if she's going to ask the specifics of *how* a body is turned into powder. I don't think she's ready for that but, as it is, she's relentlessly positive anyway.

'Someone's ashes could be spread in a park?' she asks.

'If that was their favourite place.'

'What about a beach?'

'That would probably be OK – but the tide would come in and wash it all away.'

'Alton Towers?'

I laugh at that. 'I think you'd have to ask. Maybe.'

'I think I'd like to live at Alton Towers. You'd be on the rollercoasters every day.'

I leave her to think that and then touch a hand on her shoulder. 'Time to go,' I say.

Orla pulls her backpack higher and we make the way back to the car.

It's a straightforward drive from the graveyard through the hedge-lined roads on the way to the sports complex. Orla says very little as I drive but it's hard to know if that's because she's spent the morning at her mother's grave.

When we get to the car park next to the football pitches, I turn off the engine and open the boot to take out Orla's bag. She's still sitting in the passenger seat when I open the door and pass them to her.

Orla loosens her ponytail as if to make the point. 'I don't want to play today,' she says.

'Your mum wouldn't want you to be sad for her,' I reply. 'She'd want you to carry on and do the things you enjoy.'

Orla pushes herself out of the car with a backwards-leaning reluctance.

'I'll stay for a bit, if you want,' I add.

She nods in the way she does when she wants to make a point that she's agreeing to something against her will. It's the type of expression she makes when she finally concurs that it's time for bed.

I help Orla tie the laces of her boots and then she clicks across the car park until she breaks into a gentle jog towards one of the pitches.

I follow slowly, allowing a distance to develop between us, and then I stop on the ridge that overlooks the phalanx of fields. There are around twenty parents standing in ones or twos, looking down on the action below. The full-sized pitches have been divided into halves, with, from what I can tell, the kids divided up along age lines.

After a chat from the coach, Orla and the rest of her group do a drill of dribbling between cones, passing the ball to the coach, and then sprinting away to the end of the zone.

Orla's first run sees the ball cannon into two of the cones but her second is smooth and perfect. The coach claps as she sprints away with a grin on her face. Run three is as slick as the one before and I spot her glancing up to make sure I'm watching.

After that, the pitches are split into quarters and the coach sets everyone playing five-a-side, two-touch matches. Orla is assigned a red bib and begins in goal. I feel a prickling of annoyance until I realise the goalkeeper swaps out every time somebody scores.

It's as the games continue that the parental chatter starts to increase.

'...See what I mean?' one of the blokes says to another. 'Shouldn't be allowed. All this PC, woke nonsense. Everything's got to be equal nowadays. You're not allowed to have boys being boys and girls being girls.'

I glance sideways towards the man. He's around my age and all brawn in three-quarter tan shorts and an England shirt. The guy at his side nods along but doesn't seem to be saying much.

'How are the lads gonna get any better if they have girls slowing them down and misplacing passes?' the man continues.

I try to blank him out and watch the match. Orla is OK. I'm not one-eyed enough to believe she's a world-beater, but she's fine. At seven years old, a lot of the game is bunching around the ball anyway.

'There!' the man rages – and I realise he's watching the game on the pitch adjacent to Orla's.

One of the girls passes it to one of the boys, who miscontrols it.

'See that?' he says loudly. 'Terrible pass.'

I'm clenching my fists and, when I realise, shift a few metres but can still hear him bleating at his cohort. It would be bad enough if it was based in realism – but it isn't. One of the boys will shoot wide and there is silence – but if a girl slightly under-hits a pass, he'll be off with a barrage of 'told you' responses.

I wait until half-time, then quietly drift back to the car, knowing I can't take much more. We're far enough away that none of the children can hear what's being spouted from the sidelines, so at least Orla doesn't have to endure it. I assume the coaches would step in anyway.

I'm in the car, a few miles away, surrounded by high hedges and dense verges, when the cloud of anger begins to lift. After everything happened with Ciara, victim support offered me the chance to talk to someone. I turned them down but have never quite been able to reconcile why. There's the stiff upper lip British-thing and the 'be a man' stereotype, but I've never bought into either of those.

When I'm honest with myself, I know there's something within me that enjoys the anger. I don't think I want it to go away.

I pull onto the driveway and Willow is in the garden next door. She's trimming the bush that sits underneath her front window, although I get the sense she's waiting for something, or someone. She waves as I get out of the car and says 'Hi'.

'How's it going?' she adds.

I step across the drive until I'm standing at the short fence between our properties. 'Good. You?'

'Enjoying the sun. How's Orla?'

'At football camp.'

'*Football*? I always wanted to join in when I was a kid but was never allowed.'

I wink at her: 'Times change.'

I take a step towards my front door when Willow calls after me. 'Tell me to do one if you want,' she says, 'but I've got a friend named Beth. I used to work with her. She broke up with her boyfriend at the start of the year. She's really nice. Really normal. Not a nutter. She doesn't want to get into the whole Tinder or online minefield but wants to meet someone who's normal and sane. I was wondering if I could pass on your number...?'

It takes me a moment to process what she's asking. Willow and I don't know each other particularly well, though we've been neighbours for almost five years. We do the nod and wave thing – but that's about it. She always spoke to Ciara far more than she talked to me. It's only recently that I've started sharing beers and silences with her husband. I'm not sure if I remember how it all started with Gabe. Whether I invited him over, or he invited himself. I don't think I'd even know for certain that we're friends.

'It doesn't matter if it's not for you,' Willow adds.

'No...' I reply. 'It's not that. It's um...'

I can't think of a good reason to say 'no'.

'I can show you a picture of her if you want...?'

'It's OK. Give her my number – but it's a busy time, with the summer and Orla.'

'I think she was only wondering about coffee, that sort of thing. I said I might know someone. There wasn't anything serious implied. I think you'll like her.'

'I'll see what happens.'

Willow breaks into a grin. 'I'll text her in a bit,' she says. I'm about to step away when she adds quickly: 'Can I ask you something else?' There is the briefest of pauses before she continues: 'Does Gabe seem OK to you?'

I take a moment to think but don't know how to answer. I don't know her husband well enough, despite our evenings.

'He seems the same to me,' I reply, which is true. Gabe is quiet and likes a drink. That's the only him I know.

Willow nods, although her gaze darts back to the house, as if he might be standing there and watching. Or listening. When she looks back, she can't quite meet my eyes. 'OK. Forget I said anything.'

'Is everything all right?'

She forces a smile and replies too quickly: 'Course it is. I'll get on and message Beth. Say hello to Orla for me.'

TEN

HEIDI

I'm still hunting through job websites when Freddie wanders in, sporting the tracksuit bottoms and vest that he wears to bed.

'What's wrong?' he asks, which seems presumptive, considering I never said anything *was* wrong.

'There are no jobs around here,' I say wearily. 'I've been searching through various sites in case something new has gone live. I'll either have to drop down to general office work – or apply for jobs where I don't have the qualifications.'

I'm on the sofa with the laptop and Freddie settles behind me, wrapping his arms around my shoulders. 'It'll be all right,' he says.

'That's easy for you to say.'

'I know but I'm making enough to cover the mortgage and bills. We'll be fine.'

'That's not the point. I don't want to sit at home all day. I had a career, too.'

He releases me and stands. 'I don't know what you want me to say. You could've said "no" to coming down here.'

I turn to look at him, raising my eyebrows. We both know that's not true. 'You were coming down here for the job regardless,' I say.

I want Freddie to deny it – but he doesn't. It's not that I resent it as such – the promotion and new job would have turned anyone's head. I *want* him to be a success but I wish there was something for me, too.

'I've got a bit of work to do,' he says.

'What work?'

'Just work.'

He takes a step towards the study as it is apparently now known. The locked room.

'It's Sunday,' I say. 'Can't you have a day off?'

'I've got things to do. We have a few jobs on the go and I think clearer when I'm away from the office. They want me to take the lead on a new client and I've got to make an impact.'

Freddie remains in the doorway, awaiting permission I won't give and that he doesn't care for anyway. In the end, he turns without a word, takes the key from his pocket, and unlocks his study door. I glimpse the corners of a whiteboard and then he closes the door.

I return to the jobs websites but not for long. Before I know it, I'm browsing Facebook, which leads me off to YouTube and then I'm down the hole of losing an hour. There is an inevitability to it, like a taxi driver accelerating through a red light. I search for Isabella's name and that leads me to her TikTok 'Iz Does The Biz' channel.

She's been making videos for a little over a year and has a few hundred-thousand subscribers. Most of the videos seem to involve her creating something, or deconstructing something already made. She stitches her own clothes, or fixes a pair of boots. There are instructions of how to make things like hairbands, or bookmarks. The most-watched video is a demonstration of how to apply rainbow nail varnish. There's a bit of everything and, though the videos can be rough around the edges, she is very likeable. I wonder whether she makes any money from it and daydream about easy ways for me to have a career in this new town.

Not that it's easy to concentrate. Freddie is humming, which is something he sometimes does when he's concentrating. I stare towards the study door for a few moments but, when the noise doesn't end, I close the laptop and head upstairs to get dressed properly.

The sun blasts through the bedroom window, signalling another scorcher. Many of my clothes are still stashed away in boxes and suitcases, so I make do with shorts that are too big and a top with long sleeves.

Back on the ground floor, I knock on the door of the study and the humming finally ceases.

'Fred?'

His voice is muffled through the door: 'What?'

'I'm going for a walk. Do you fancy it?'

'I'm a bit busy in here.'

Sounds like it, I think but don't say.

'See you in a bit.'

I wait for a few seconds and then let myself out of the house.

Huntington Grove is quite the sight this morning: the lawns lush and manicured, the hush almost pristine, except for a gentle hum of distant traffic. This is modern England, I suppose. No longer the nation of cobblestones, terraces and narrow lanes. It's all red-brick semis on sprawling estates, with spaces for two cars on the driveway.

Except, there is something else: the same muffled voices I heard the other night. I amble along the street, past the house of the neighbour I've not yet met, until I'm in front of Alison's once more. I take a step onto her path, then a second. There are definitely raised voices coming from inside. She said her husband is away and she has no children... so, who?

I make the decision and stride along the path, then ring the doorbell. It's as if a switch has been flicked because the voices inside are immediately muted. Somewhere in the distance, there is the sound of children playing – probably on the backyard trampolines I pictured when moving in. That's all, though. Even the traffic has hushed.

I knock on the door but the quiet persists. Nobody is going to answer, though I can sense somebody on the other side, waiting for me to go.

'Hello?' I say. 'Alison?'

She was keen enough to tell me about the street party yesterday – but today there's nothing.

The blinds are pulled across the windows at the front, so I step backwards and keep going. Despite the heat of the day, a shiver feathers along my spine and it feels as if I'm being watched.

I'm distracted by the sound of a door opening – but not Alison's. Instead, it is *ours*. Freddie is there, fully dressed, making his way to the car. He stops when he sees me two houses down and we stare at one another across the short distance.

I head back along the street onto our drive, where Freddie is waiting by the car.

'I thought you were going for a walk?' he says.

'I thought you were working?'

Freddie shuffles on the spot, passing the car keys from one hand to another. The heat is getting to him as sweat seeps through his shirt.

'I need to pick up a few things for the study,' he says. 'I won't be long. I thought I'd be out and back before you were.'

He hovers for a moment longer, seemingly not sure how to

explain what's happening. He must've waited for me to close the front door and then dashed upstairs to change. It feels deliberate – but I can't say that.

'I'll see you in a bit,' I say, instead.

Freddie nods and gets into the car, while I let myself back into the house. It's only when I've locked the door that I remember I *was* supposed to be going for a walk.

I wait in the hallway, unsure what to do next, which is when I notice the door to Freddie's study slightly open. I nudge it with my hand, as if making sure I'm seeing what's actually there.

I tell myself I'm doing nothing wrong. This is my house as much as it is Freddie's – and it was he who arbitrarily decided to lock one of the rooms.

I'm not sure what I expect to see but it's all... *normal.* There's a deckchair in the middle of the room, which is facing a whiteboard. A small table is at the side, on which sits his laptop; there is a stack of paper pads, two felt-tips and a squash ball. At the back is a bookcase that's half-filled with various self-help titles. Even though I'm by myself, it's hard to avoid the inevitable eye-rolls at titles like, 'Think Yourself Smart', 'Why Leaders Lead', 'FADvertising' and 'Put The You In Useful'. I would prefer to Put The Books In The Bin – but that is possibly why Freddie locked the room.

'Pillow' is written on the whiteboard in large capital letters, with 'some sort of bird?' and 'balloons?' in smaller writing underneath. It's all a bit cryptic, but this is what he said it was – a place for his thoughts to manifest themselves without anyone sneering.

And it does deserve something of a sneer.

There's also another side to the situation, though. If he'd left the door permanently unlocked, I'd have little interest in being in here. I realise it's childish but the only reason I wanted to see inside is because it was bolted closed.

I turn in a circle and take in the rest of the room. There's nothing of particular note and I take a step towards the door before another thought occurs. There's little to see now – but that doesn't mean the room was in this state before. What if Freddie left the door open on purpose?

ELEVEN

WILLOW

I yawn my way down the stairs and fumble into the kitchen. The smell of coffee is drifting through the house but it was the buzz of the washing machine that woke me up. I'm not much of a getter-upper at the best of times and watching the sudsy clothes spin is hypnotically confusing.

Gabe is sitting at the table in the kitchen with a newspaper in front of him. He's relentlessly old-school, one of the few people still paying for news. I think it's a habit thing from his lunch breaks at the factory. He must have been out and back to the shop while I slept.

'I didn't hear you get in last night,' I say, hoping it won't start an argument. We need a proper conversation at some point about me and him but not yet.

He doesn't look up from the paper. 'You were out of it.'

'What time did you get in?'

'Not late. Needed to clear my head.'

I wait for a moment to see if there might be further expansion – but seemingly not.

'I heard Isabella get home,' I say.

'Really...?'

'It was almost three.'

He finally peers up from the sports pages and presses into the chair with a creak. 'She's almost eighteen. I used to stay out late when I was that age. I bet you did, too.'

'I know, but—'

'There's no point in getting into an argument over it. Pick the battles that matter.' He sounds exasperated, which isn't necessarily a surprise.

I want to reply with something wise, or smart – but nothing comes. He's right but that doesn't mean I approve of my seventeen-year-old daughter staying out until almost three.

I sit on the other side of the table and stifle a yawn as Gabe focuses back on his paper.

The washer groans and thumps its way to a stop and then finishes with the sort of beeping more usually associated with a large truck reversing. Gabe pushes himself up and hauls everything into a basket and then heads out into the back garden. It's only as he's pinning the first few items onto the line that my sleepy brain kicks into gear and I realise what's wrong.

The grass needs trimming but it's lovely and springy on my bare feet as I tread across it until I reach Gabe at the far end.

'Why did you only wash *your* clothes?' I ask. 'There's a basketful upstairs.'

'Forgot, I suppose.'

There are only half-a-dozen items – largely what he was wearing yesterday.

After Gabe has finished pegging everything to the line, he picks up the basket and waits for me to follow him back to the house.

'You don't normally put the washing on,' I say.

'I figured I'd help.'

'But you didn't wash anything from upstairs.'

'I didn't want to use the wrong settings and shrink anything. You know what Iz is like. She'd hit the roof.'

I close and lock the back door behind us but it's stifling inside, so I open the kitchen window. Gabe returns to the table and his paper. It's been an odd morning, even though I slept through much of it. I can't remember the last time Gabe put on a load of washing.

'Is there any coffee left?' I ask.

'Yes, but we're out of milk.'

That wouldn't be a problem for Gabe or Isabella. He prefers black and she's all about the calories. I'm more of a milk and three sugars-kinda person – especially in the morning.

'Do you want anything from the shop?' I ask. 'I'll get some milk.'

I could point out that he's been to buy a paper and could have bought milk himself – but it's another argument that doesn't feel worth having.

Gabe looks up and shakes his head. 'Don't think so.'

He scratches the stubble on his cheeks, showing a smear of purply-red on the underside of his wrist. It looks like a birth-mark, except I know he doesn't have one.

'Are you bleeding?' I ask.

He turns his hand over to see and then rubs the mark with his other hand. 'I was moving some of the paint cans last night. The fence needs treating and you know what that stuff's like. It gets everywhere.' He holds up his wrist once more: 'Has it gone?'

'Yes.'

'Damn stuff.'

I watch him for a moment, wondering if there's something to add, but he turns back to his paper and flips the page.

'About last night,' I begin.

'What about it?'

'With Freddie... I don't know how to explain it.'

'Explain what?'

We do this sometimes – both of us. Pick a fight and then pretend we haven't. Last night, Gabe seemed annoyed about Freddie but now he's seemingly fine. Maybe it was the same thing with his remark about Kenneth? See how I respond. Perhaps we each want the arguments?

Because of that, I don't reply. There won't be a winner and I don't have the energy for it. As if to prove as much, a yawn rattles through me before I can say anything else. The smell of the coffee has me anticipating like a Pavlovian dog.

I change quickly and then grab my bag before heading onto the sweltering street. There's no car on Dylan's drive and it's a pleasant walk along Huntington Grove, out onto the wider estate. It took me months to figure out where all the cut-throughs lead. That knowledge turns what would be a twenty-five-minute walk into something that barely takes ten.

The corner shop serves much of the local area and is one of those that are rapidly going out of fashion. It sells everything from eggs to magazines to car batteries to smoke alarms. Essentially, it is a supermarket that is somehow crammed into the equivalent of a cupboard, via some sort of physics-defying trickery.

I pick up a bottle of milk from the chiller and head to the counter, where a bored-looking middle-aged woman with the name tag 'Pam' is flicking through the *Sunday Mirror*.

'You always have less milk than you think,' she says.

'I think there's something philosophical in there,' I reply.

She laughs and asks if it's warm outside.

'Scorching,' I say. 'What time are you here 'til?'

Pam rolls her eyes: 'Three. Manager's given himself the day off. All right for some, ain't it?' She pauses and then adds: 'Did you hear the sirens earlier?'

'What sirens?'

'Someone said one of the homeless guys in the centre ODd.

I don't know the details. Was wondering if you'd heard anything?'

'I've only just got up.'

She winks: 'Lucky you.'

We do the usual hand-wringing thing of saying how awful it all is. The homelessness is terrible, someone should do something, all that. I know none of it will actually lead to me doing anything. That done, Pam asks for the money and I get out my purse. It's only as I'm going through it that I realise the forty quid I had yesterday has gone. I flick through the side pockets in case I've somehow moved it, but the two twenty-pound notes aren't there.

'Everything all right?' Pam asks.

'Yeah, sorry...'

I end up tapping my card to pay. Pam seems keen for more of a chat but I tell her I've got to head back and then hurry my way back through the alleys towards home.

When I get in, Gabe is still at the table, having apparently not moved since I left. Despite the open window, the kitchen remains baking hot.

He grunts as I open the fridge and put the milk inside.

'Did you borrow some money?' I ask.

He looks up and blinks. 'What?'

'I took some money from the cashpoint on Friday. There was sixty pounds. I gave twenty to Iz yesterday – but the other forty has gone. Did you take some? It's all right if you did...?'

He shakes his head and stares blankly. 'It'll turn up,' he says.

I have no idea why people say things like this – as if something will appear from thin air. The only reason the money is missing is because it was taken. Aside from Gabe and Isabella, the only people who've been in the house are Heidi and Freddie – and it's a stretch to think it was either of them.

As I'm trying to think it through, there is a thump from upstairs and then a shambling, zombie-like slow clattering on the stairs. Isabella eventually appears, eyes half-closed, hair jutting at matted angles.

'Don't suppose there's any toast?' she asks.

'I can do it,' I reply.

'Cheers.'

She turns to head back towards the living room when I say her name. 'Did you borrow some money from my purse?' I ask. 'It's all right if you did, but—'

It is as if I've flipped a switch. Isabella pushes her hair from her face and her eyes open wider. 'Are you asking if I stole money?'

'No, but—'

'You're not even brave enough to ask outright, are you? Go on, accuse me of stealing to my face.'

'I'm not accusing you of anything. I—'

Isabella throws both hands into the hair: 'I didn't steal *anything!*' A momentary pause, and then: 'I'm going to Dad's.'

She slams the kitchen door and then thunders upstairs with a series of booming stomps. That's followed by another slammed door, which I can tell from the tone is the one to the bathroom. It's come to something when I can distinguish between the sound of slamming doors.

I glance to Gabe but he's making a special effort not to make eye contact. I can practically hear his: 'Told you.'

The thing is, I believe Isabella when she says she didn't take the money – but, if she didn't, then who did?

TWELVE

DYLAN

I'm in the workshop-garage when my phone buzzes. My first instinct is that something's happened to my daughter. It's always there in the back of my mind: Orla is injured, she's missing, she needs me. For a while after what happened to Ciara, I would barely let Orla out of my sight. I'm not as bad now but, whenever we are apart and my phone goes, there's that flickering sense of panic.

It's a text from an unknown 07 number:

Hey! This is Beth. I got your no from Willow. All mysterious, innit? No pics, no details. Kinda exciting. I'm off work 2moro AM. Fancy a coffee?

I read the message through five times, looking for any sort of hidden meaning. It appears straightforward enough. Willow said Beth wants to meet someone who's 'normal and sane' and I have to wonder whether that's me. I don't think there's much about my life from the past three years that hit either of those points.

My first three attempts at a reply are started and deleted, then I put the phone down and consider not responding. I need to think about Orla, not myself. Then I wonder what's the worst that can happen. It's a question I ask a lot – but rarely in a positive way. Orla's at football camp without me and the worst that can happen is that someone snatches her and everything starts over again. Everything in our lives is a calculation of what I consider to be the worst that can happen.

I can do tomorrow. Is 10am OK? Where do you want to meet?

I send the message and a reply fires back less than a minute later:

Awesome. Do u know Wake Me Up Before You Dough Dough on the High St? They do good croissants. 10 is good for me

I have never heard of the place but a quick Google search shows that it is a bakery-café nearby. It's rated a respectable 4.7 and I have a nose through the reviews. It's almost universally good but there are, of course, the one-star nitpickers with far too much time on their hands.

A quick message later and we're set.

All I have to go on is a phone number and the name 'Beth'. I don't know her age but she's right in that there's something exciting about that.

At least there should be a decent croissant out of the experience.

I try to get back to work but it's a strange, somewhat distant, feeling of having something to look forward to. I barely have five minutes to bask in the glow of not embarrassing myself through a series of texts when my phone rings.

'Is that Mr Wilson?'

I'm expecting some sort of spammy call from a charity but it's not that.

'Who is this?' I ask.

'It's Zac from football camp. I'm looking for Orla's dad?'

It feels as if the bottom has fallen out of my stomach. Everything I feared has happened. She's missing, she's been taken, she's hurt. I shouldn't have let her go.

'That's me,' I manage.

'She's got a bit of a stomach ache. Is there any chance you could pick her up? She's asking for you.'

It takes me a moment to process it. 'She's OK?'

'I think so. It might be a bit of a stitch, something like that. I don't know for sure.'

'I'll be right there.'

Orla is sitting on a bench at the side of the car park when I arrive. The coach, Zac, has seemingly been waiting with her and shakes my hand. He's young and fit with spiky hair and tattoos on his arms. I'd guess he's possibly a lower-level pro or semi-pro, who's earning a bit of money on the side.

I crouch so that I'm at eye level with Orla. She turns away, apparently unable to meet my gaze. Her arms are folded, her boot bag on the floor. The true sign that she's done is that her hair is untied and scraggy around her shoulders.

'How are you?' I ask.

'My tummy hurts.'

'Is it a sharp pain, or more of an ache?'

She shrugs. 'I don't know.'

I press a palm to her forehead, the parent's version of a four-year medical degree. It's cool and, as far as I can tell, normal. That's me out of ideas. 'OK, we'll get you home.'

I give her the keys, send her off towards the car, and then turn to Zac.

'Thanks for waiting,' I say.

'No problem.'

'How has she been?'

'Fine.' He stops and then adds: 'Actually, she's been better than that. She had a good morning session in the five-a-sides and then we had a reshuffle after lunch to split the teams up more by ability. She was in one of the better teams for the seven-a-sides – but she wasn't joining in. That's when she said her stomach was hurting and she wanted you.'

I peer towards the verge, to where the man was cursing earlier. There's no one there now, which is hardly a surprise given the length of the day.

'I hope Orla's back tomorrow,' Zac says.

'I'm sure she will be. She wanted to come. She had a few options for summer activities and chose football. It's not like I pushed her into it.'

By the time I've said it, I realise this is what it would sound like if I *had* pushed her into it.

Zac smiles, as if to say he doesn't want to get involved. He shakes my hand again, before jogging back to the pitches.

In the car, Orla has already taken off her football socks and strapped herself into the booster seat.

'Are you sure you're all right?' I ask.

'Just belly ache.'

I look across to her but she's refusing to catch my eye. It's clearly more than her stomach – if it's that at all – but there are only so many times I can ask the same thing. I probably shouldn't have taken her to her mother's grave earlier. We go semi-regularly but usually on a Sunday, when she can have a quiet time the rest of the day. She's still only seven.

As I pull away, Orla rests her head on the passenger-side window and sighs. She'd usually be chattering about whatever she'd been up to – but not today. She's also not touching her stomach.

I wait until we're away from the complex, into the solitude of the country lanes. The emerald carpet that rings High Kingsley stretches far into the distance, banking up and over a hill until it drops down to the town on the other side.

'Are you sure everything's good?' I ask.

'Yes.'

'You can say if it's not. We tell each other everything, don't we?'

There's a short silence but enough for me to realise the lies I tell. Orla doesn't know what's under the cabinet in the living room, nor how I spend some of my days when she isn't there. The things I do.

The pause is almost her acknowledgement of that. *Do we tell each other everything, Daddy? Do we?*

'It's fine,' she says. 'Can I put the radio on?'

THIRTEEN

WILLOW

I'm sitting in the living room when I spot the familiar Vauxhall parking at the front and blocking our drive. I hurry to reach the front door before Craig can ring the bell. My ex – Isabella's father – and I exchange the most cursory of nods. He will have driven for an hour and a half to pick up his daughter. I'm not exactly on bad terms with him, but it's not as if we're mates. I don't think we ever were. That was the problem.

When we met as teenagers, Craig was in a band. I keep reminding myself of that whenever I wonder why we got together – largely because it's all I have. He wasn't the lead singer, he wasn't even the lead guitarist. He played bass in some dreadful knock-off Oasis-style indie band that had all the attitude but none of the talent. Their best-known song, which wasn't known outside of my social circle, had a chorus that rhymed 'twiglet' with 'piglet'. I suppose Lennon and McCartney never managed that.

When I was a certain age, that was enough.

Two decades on and Craig couldn't be more different. The

long hair and rake-thin physique have been swapped for a receding hairline and, to be kind, 'middle-aged spread'. He's a middle-manager at an out-of-town Asda, which is, admittedly, more than I've ever achieved.

'Is she ready?' Craig asks.

'I don't know. Isabella didn't say you were coming right now.'

I peer around Craig to notice his wife, Sarah, in the passenger seat of the car. She is, of course, stunning. I have no idea how he managed to punch so far above his weight – metaphorically and literally – but Sarah is the type of woman I always hoped to somehow grow into when I was a gawky teenager. There's blonde and boobs, while, perhaps worst of all, she's smart and runs her own estate agency. I could handle looks and I could accept brains – but don't go putting it all together.

What a bitch.

Craig married her five years ago in some sort of whirlwind romance that must have been based on her low self-esteem, or the depression I imagine she must have gone through. I figured it would last a year but here we are.

'Did you have some sort of argument?' Craig asks.

He knows me too well.

That's the other annoyance with my ex and his happiness – his is real.

I fell for Gabe, although it's often hard to remember why. He listened a lot back then, said nice things. The bare minimum, I suppose – although I didn't realise it then. It seemed like more. That first bite of a pudding when it's the greatest thing ever. Then, the more you eat, when it starts to become sickly and claggy, when your stomach feels full, you wonder why you wanted it in the first place.

Is it me?

I think that a lot. I make bad decisions, especially when it comes to husbands.

Lost in the thought, I don't get a chance to reply before Craig continues: 'You and Iz? She sounded a bit upset when—'

Isabella has once again materialised out of thin air. She breezes past me in a pair of tiny denim shorts, a loose vest and a duffel bag slung over her back.

'—She accused me of stealing,' Isabella says. She doesn't wait for me to add anything as she Doctor Martens it across the path and gets into Craig's car, closing the door *carefully* behind her.

'I didn't *accuse* her of anything,' I say, trying to sound calm.

I watch over Craig's shoulder as Sarah turns around and immediately strikes up a conversation with my daughter. Craig follows my line of vision and then turns back.

'It's just... Maybe lay off her for a bit,' he suggests, quietly and calmly.

'You're not here,' I retort, too quickly. 'It's not like I *want* to argue with her. I want her to have what I didn't.'

Craig puts his hands in his pockets and half-turns so that he's standing sideways between me and the car. 'She's only just finished her exams,' he says.

'That's the point, though. What now? If she takes too long, all the other kids will get ahead of her. She'll get left behind and she's already one of the youngest in her year.'

Craig nods along but it's difficult not to get the sense that he's patronising. 'I know...' he coos. 'Her videos are going well, though. Have you watched them?'

'Of course. It's not like it's a career, though, is it?'

'Maybe – but it's like telling someone they can't be a footballer, or a movie star, isn't it? Some people *are* footballers. They *are* movie stars.'

I sigh at the thought of that. It's hard to argue with the idea that a person *might* win the lottery. I mean, yeah, they might. Someone has to.

'I'm not saying she can't keep doing this,' I reply, quieter now. 'All I'm trying to do is get her to start thinking about alternative options, *as well*. She can do two things. She's almost eighteen, not fourteen.'

Craig sighs and runs a hand through his hair. His *thinning* hair.

'Are you encouraging her just to spite me?' I add.

Isabella's father remains annoyingly calm about it all, not taking the bait. 'Not everything is about you, Willow.'

He lets it sit, probably waiting for some sort of volcanic reaction. The problem is that, deep down, I know he's right. Sort of right.

'This is why we broke up,' he says and, for a moment, I'm that twenty-one-year-old kid with a child of my own again. There's a lump in my throat and the memory feels so close that I know I'm going to cry if I don't do something.

'Sometimes, you can be so negative,' he says. 'I don't think you realise how it comes across.'

I pinch the loose skin around my knuckle and squeeze for all I'm worth.

'I'm not negative,' I say – which is, of course, a negative way of phrasing it.

'You're the one who told me the band was going nowhere. Maybe it was, maybe it wasn't – but it would have been nice to give it a go.'

We're back to the place we always end up: 'That was twenty years ago!' I say, trying not to shout. 'And you *did* give it a go.'

'Not really.'

He stops and nods towards the car, where Isabella has said something that's made Sarah explode with laughter. I can hear her from here, which only makes me closer to tears. I pinch my skin harder.

'I'm *realistic*,' I say.

'Our daughter is creative,' Craig says. 'She wants to be arty and expressive.'

'I want that for her, too! But I also want something for her to fall back on.'

Craig sighs again and nods at the car. 'How's that working out?'

I pinch the skin near my knuckle so hard that I almost yelp. It's hard to keep it back but then the fire erupts through clenched teeth. 'She chose to live with me, remember. She chose *me*.'

Craig turns to look at me and opens his mouth to reply. I'm expecting an argument, a long-overdue slanging match, but I can't even get that right.

He nods shortly, says, 'I know', and then saunters off towards the car.

Moments later, he, his stunning wife, and my daughter are out of sight.

I watch them go, knowing I shouldn't have said it. He went high, so I went low, knowing how to hurt him.

Well done, me.

There's a part that wants to text him and apologise but I know I can't handle a messaging chain today. I turn to head inside when an even more familiar car rumbles up outside the house. It's a Mini that's only done a few thousand miles – except all of them will have been perilous due the state of the driving.

The car stops, starts again, bunny hops forward, and then stops for a final time. After that, my mother clambers out. She slams the driver's door and, without turning towards the house, heads to the boot and starts wrestling a suitcase.

'Mum,' I call.

She ignores me until the case has been successfully bashed into the hood, the back bumper and her own leg.

'What's going on?' I ask, as I take the luggage from her.

She bats me away with an errant flap of the hand. 'It's your father,' she says. 'He's done it now.'

'What are you on about, Mum?'

Not today.

She grabs the case back from me and sets off along the path towards the house.

'Mum!'

My mother stops and turns. People have always said I look like her but I've never seen it. I certainly don't now. For a reason I can't entirely fathom, she's had a blue rinse. Senility must be on the way.

'He's having an affair,' she snaps.

'Who is? Dad?'

'With that barmaid from the football club.' She clicks her fingers irritably. 'Whatshername?'

'I don't know, Mum. Are you sure?'

She bustles along the path and then drops the case outside the front door. 'Are you going to invite me in?'

FOURTEEN

HEIDI

Freddie comes to bed a little after eleven. I'm already on my side by then, taking long, slow breaths and letting the air out gradually. Freddie says my name and, when I don't respond, there's the clatter of his wallet, phone and keys all being dispatched onto the nightstand. He's done this almost every night since we met. It only takes a few seconds until he has his clothes off and then there's a flutter of covers as he slots himself into bed.

'You awake?' he mutters.

I say nothing and lie with my eyes closed, listening as he tinkers with his phone and then, eventually, turns the light off. It's only five minutes more until he's wheezing gently. Freddie isn't actually a big snorer, it's more heavy breathing than it is full-on trumpeting, but he does chunter at the same level night after night. He always has.

After he got back earlier, we did very little for the rest of the day. It's been the laziest of lazy Sundays. We couldn't even be bothered to unpack more of the boxes, instead rattling through half-a-dozen episodes of some *Bake-Off* rip-off that's not as entertaining as *Bake-Off* but was easy enough to watch while barely looking up from a phone.

Throughout it all, I couldn't escape the thought that Freddie had left his study open because he wanted me to see how normal it was inside. After he got home, I never mentioned that I'd been inside and he never asked. I suspect he knew. In a backwards way, it makes me believe even more strongly that there's something in there he doesn't want me to see. He left the door unlocked to stop me bothering him in future – but whatever was in there was either well hidden, or he took it with him.

This is, obviously, nutty conspiracy theory stuff... except it feels as if something has changed in the week we were apart. Or, perhaps, it was something more than that? Something to do with Willow over the road? I don't feel as if I can ask outright and, even if I did, what would he say? It seemed like an odd disconnect between them at dinner, something to do with being at school together – though it's hard to know what.

But is it her? Or him? Or me?

We either have complete trust in one another, or we don't.

I wish I could say differently – but we don't.

It's funny how things can change so quickly. How such small actions can have such large ramifications. Locking the study felt like a trigger for feelings that run much deeper.

I slip out of bed and creep around to Freddie's side, watching as his chest rises and falls in slow, rhythmical grunts. His eyelids are fluttering as his lips mouth a silent conversation. I edge slowly towards his dresser and, when I'm near enough, stretch for his phone. We've never been one of those couples who check one another's devices, nor one who hide our phones away. I've never really had the urge to go through his messages, and doubt he has for me.

But maybe that's changed?

I tread carefully out of the room, heading to the toilet and closing the door, where I press the button to light up Freddie's phone screen. He gets a new one every year, saying he needs it for work, although I think he really just likes new gadgets.

The Face ID blinks and says I'm too far away, then that I need to enter the passcode. I figured this would likely happen, although I'm surprised to see it wants six digits, as opposed to the four that unlock mine. We've never spoken about this sort of thing but I always assumed his code would be the same one we use for the debit card of our joint account. That's what works on mine... except that's four digits.

I try the six digits of his birthday – day, month year – then the six for mine. Neither work, so I try month, day, year – but that's not it, either.

I can't remember whether a person gets locked out with too many incorrect codes, so turn off the screen, while sitting on the toilet and staring at the back of the door.

Do I trust my husband? *Should* I trust him?

The fact I've just tried accessing his phone probably answers that – but I'm not sure if that says more about him, or more about me.

Either way, it doesn't say much that's good.

THE FUTURE

Police statement: Pamela Johnson.

Pam: I've got to be at work in an hour. Do you think it'll be longer than that? I don't want to be late.

Officer: We'll try to get you away as quickly as possible, Miss Johnson. I wanted to ask you about your interaction with Willow Ellis on the Sunday before everything that happened.

Pam: She came into the shop and bought milk. That's all.

Officer: Did you talk to each other?

Pam: We probably did. I try to chat with most of the customers, y'know?

Officer: What did you talk about?

Pam: Probably the weather. It was a warm day and I was annoyed at being stuck in work. My manager gave himself the day off and called me in to do the early shift. Found out the day after that he'd gone off to Weymouth. Didn't even pay overtime.

Officer: And is that the type of thing you spoke about with Miss Ellis?

Pam: I don't know. Maybe.

Officer: Did you know Ms Ellis?

Pam: Sort of. I knew her face. She'd come into the shop sometimes and buy odds and ends. Lots of people do.

Officer: Were you friends?

Pam: No. I only found out her name when it was all on the news. That's why I called you.

Officer: And we're glad you did, Miss Johnson. If I may, is there anything else you particularly remember about Ms Ellis when you saw her that morning?

Pam: Like what?

Officer: I'm not sure. Did she say anything surprising? Did she seem angry, or particularly upset? Happy, perhaps? That sort of thing?

Pam: Um...

Officer: You can take your time.

Pam: She might've been a bit upset, I suppose. I don't know. Confused, maybe?

Officer: Why do you say that?

Pam: I think she was missing money, something like that. She went to pay and looked in her purse. Then she kinda leapt back a bit, like 'Huh?' You know? It felt like something unexpected had happened. She went hunting through the pocket, then paid on a card.

Officer: Did she say anything about missing money?

Pam: No – it was more her reaction. Like, if I was missing something, that's probably how I would have reacted.

Officer: For the benefit of the recording, Miss Johnson has made a motion with her hands as if to indicate she's surprised. Is that fair, Miss Johnson?

Pam: Yes. She was surprised.

Officer: So, she acted surprised and then paid on her card?

Pam: Right.

Officer: Then what happened?

Pam: She hurried away really quickly. Almost ran.

Officer: Did she say where she was going?

Pam: No. I assumed she was going home. She'd bought milk.

Officer: And she didn't say anything else about missing money, or being upset?

Pam: I don't think so.

Officer: Did you see her in the week afterwards?

Pam: I don't think so. If I did, I don't remember.

Officer: Is there anything else you might have to say?

Pam: I don't think so.

Officer: OK, thanks for that. And thank you for coming forward.

Pam: Do you think it'll make any difference?

Officer: I'm afraid I can't say. Interview terminated at 10:39 hours.

FIFTEEN

MONDAY

DYLAN

I don't need to check Orla's temperature to know my daughter is fine. The truth is in the way she tries to talk me out of taking it. She squirms as I put the pistol-shaped thermometer in her ear and then press the magic button to wait for the digital readout. It wasn't like this when I was a kid – it was a cold, glass traditional instrument under the tongue and a struggle not to gag on it.

I perch on the edge of her bed and wait, though it's not long before the device beeps to show a round 37°C.

'It's normal,' I tell her.

'I don't feel normal.'

'What hurts?'

'My belly.'

'OK, I'll take you to the doctor.'

Orla shakes her head rapidly. She's still in her nightclothes, bundled up in bed next to her giant soft sheep, who is named, imaginatively, Sheepy. There was a time when it was as big as

she was but not so much now. It's a constant fluffy reminder
that nothing stays the same for long.

'Why don't you want to go to the doctor?' I ask.

'I don't want to.'

'I *know*. I'm asking *why*?'

We've switched parental roles. I'm the one with all the 'whys'.

Orla shakes her head and mumbles something I don't catch.
It's not worth pushing because we both know there's nothing
particularly wrong with her.

'At least come downstairs and have something to drink,' I
say. 'I'll put some toast on and we'll see how you go. Perhaps it'll
settle your stomach?'

Orla agrees and I leave her to get dressed as I head downstairs and plop two slices of bread into the toaster. I pour her
some juice and then wait at the table until she appears.

She's not wearing her football kit, so I suppose her mind is
made up.

There is a moment halfway through her first slice when
Orla forgets she's ill. The first few bites are accompanied by the
expected grumbles of how it hurts but then she demolishes the
rest in no time. It's only when she's most of the way through the
second that she remembers it's supposed to be painful.

'How are you doing?' I ask.

'It hurts.'

'What do you want to do today?'

'Don't know.'

She sips her juice and I clear the plate into the sink.

'Are you going to dry up?' I ask. 'You're at eight stars…'

Orla glances across to the chart on the fridge, where she's
decorated her name onto a large sheet of paper using glitter and
felt-tips. Every time she helps around the house, or does something good at school, she gets a star. Ten stars means she gets ten
pounds. Inflation and all that. It was 50p in my day.

Belly ache, or no belly ache, the lure of being one step closer to spending money is too much. Orla leaps up and grabs the tea towel from the drawer. There's a melancholic twitch as I realise she no longer needs to push onto tiptoes to reach.

I wash up her plate and glass, plus my own mug and a few other things. Orla dries everything and puts them away – and then we go through the somewhat sacred ritual of extracting a star sticker from the pad on top of the fridge. She chooses a green one and then presses it onto her chart, before counting the nine.

'One more,' she says with a smile.

'You can have number ten if you get through football camp today.'

Orla shakes her head: 'I don't want to go. I don't feel well.'

'Did something happen yesterday?'

'No.'

'You can say if it did.'

'It didn't. I just don't feel well.'

We're at an impasse because there's no point in me accusing her of lying, even though she is.

'Is there something else you want to do?' I ask. 'I could see if Lauren's free today?'

There's a slow realisation on Orla's face that she has to make a choice. Either spend the day indoors, pretending she's ill – or get to do something she wants with her friend.

'O-K...' She speaks slowly and cautiously, almost as if the two letters are two words.

'The only thing is, if you're sick, I don't think Lauren will want to catch it.'

I can almost see the cogs turning. My daughter shakes her head very slowly, narrowing her eyes. 'I don't think she'll catch it.'

'How do you know?'

closer. Her eyelids seem heavy and she can't fight away the yawn.

'Sorry,' she adds. 'Mum's walked out on my dad, so she's staying over. It's been a crazy day or three.'

I wonder how Gabe is feeling about having his mother-in-law stay. Or how Willow feels about him. It's hard to know what she sees in him. Or, maybe, what she *saw*. His comment about Kenneth had that 1970s-vibe. There will sometimes be a clip of an old TV show, with a casual bit of racism that nobody blinks at.

'You look like you need some sleep.'

Perhaps it's the word 'sleep' – but it sends Willow into another yawn, which quickly becomes a laugh. 'What gave it away?' she says.

She angles between the house and me – and I get the sense she'd rather escape for the day. Real life wins, however, as she moves onto her path.

'I better get back,' she says, before quickly adding: 'You didn't mind me asking Freddie about school, did you?'

'Why would I?'

'I don't know. I realised how weird it sounded when I said my friend wanted to meet for coffee. I didn't want you to think it was as a date, or anything weird. It was only an old schoolfriend thing.'

'It's fine. I understand. We're not a clingy couple. We do our own things and have our own friends.' I stop myself from the correction – *had* our own friends. 'I don't think Freddie's that keen on his old school life anyway.'

'No...' Willow says. 'I figured...'

She says goodbye and then heads into the house. I watch her, though it's all a bit odd. There's definitely an atmosphere between Willow and my husband, though I'm not sure what – or if it matters.

I cross back over the road and lock myself inside before plopping on the sofa once more with the laptop. I recheck the job sites I looked at an hour ago, then make a call to a job agency whose adverts keep appearing. The call rings off without being answered, which at least indicates they need someone to answer the phone.

I poke my head into Freddie's study, where the door is unlocked and everything is more or less as it was when I last looked. The whiteboard now has 'Penguin?' written on it, with no apparent progress for whatever that campaign is. I flick through a small stack of papers, that largely seem to be invoices. It's all a bit dull and I can't remember why I was so annoyed with him over it.

It's when I'm unpacking more of the boxes from the kitchen that there's a knock at the door. It's a slight surprise to see Alison there. My neighbour, who's organising the street party, looks a little less manic today. She has on a pair of glasses and is wearing yoga pants, with shorts over the top. There is a worrying moment in which I wonder if she's going to invite me along to some godforsaken class, where I'll have to pray to the air, or learn how to breathe from my fingers.

Instead, she nods over her shoulder. 'Do you fancy that coffee?' she asks. 'There's a good café in town if you do.'

When she offered before, I figured 'coffee' was code for 'Let's never speak of this again'. My instinct is to make up a reason why I can't – but then I decide I'm not making any friends by sitting at home unpacking boxes. My job hunting is also going nowhere.

I tell Alison I need a few minutes to get dressed and then meet her back at the front of the house. She's doing short jogs on the spot, while typing out a text at the same time.

'You look wonderful!' she exclaims, which is, at best, an overstatement.

I'm in my only pair of yoga pants, which I haven't worn since January. That was a failed attempt at a new year's resolution for the usual things. Get fit, lose weight, run a marathon, maybe a half, possibly a ten K, perhaps a five at worst. All that. I abandoned the plan by early February when I came to the logical conclusion that cold + exercise = no chance, while warmth + a morning muffin = happiness.

'So do you!' I reply, which instantly riddles me with self-loathing. I'm one step away from having a conversation about matcha and hummus.

'I know this great little place,' Alison says. 'It's walkable – and I'm friends with the owner. Shall we go?'

I want to ask whether 'walkable' means a few minutes', or an hour at a brisk hustle. Both are technically 'walkable', although one is preferable to the other.

There's no opportunity for any of that, however. Alison is off like an Olympic race-walker, bounding along the pavement as I have to quick-step to catch up.

'Do you walk much?' she asks.

I manage a disingenuous 'sometimes', although can barely get my breath.

'There are lots of places around here to get out and enjoy the countryside. Some fabulous walks out and over the moors. You can lose yourself out there.'

I think she means it in a good way but I can't imagine getting lost on the moors would be a great slogan for the tourist board.

I try to remember the route as we charge through a series of alleys until we reach a towpath, where, mercifully, Alison stops to say hello to a bloke who's walking a pair of French bulldogs. One's called Pickle, the other is Dill – and the pups seem less enthused about walking than I am. Pickle is the smaller of the two. She has laid flat on the path and is refusing to move, which seems appealing.

By the time I've given them a quick pet, Alison is off again. She reminds me of a teacher I used to have as a kid. School trips were organised with military levels of precision. Lateness was up there with being a mass murderer.

Thankfully, her pace is closer to mine this time.

'How long have you lived here?' I ask.

'Kenneth and I moved back to the UK about two years ago,' she says.

'You were in Hong Kong before that?'

'Right...' She tails off somewhat wistfully, a pleasant thought, then adds: 'I went there on a business trip. I was staying in this massive hotel in the centre. Two gyms, restaurant, all that. I was sitting at the bar and there was this guy I couldn't stop looking at.'

Alison giggles to herself and it's hard not to see her in a different way. The ruthless organisation is the front but there's a woman in love behind it all. I wonder if I still feel the same for Freddie.

'One thing led to another,' she continues. 'Next thing you know, I'm living over there with him.'

'Why'd you come back?'

'We wanted kids but I suppose we're not there yet...'

'It must be hard with him working overseas.'

'Right...'

Alison leads us through a gate, away from the canal and back towards a row of houses.

'Do you live on your own?' I ask, remembering the voices and banging.

There's a pause and then Alison points off towards a clutch of swans on the side of the bank. 'Careful around them. They can be vicious if you catch them on an off day.'

I follow her past the first few houses, away from the swans, and then she says: 'What are you going to do about work down here?'

The change of subject was expertly done and I let it go for now.

'I'm looking into it. There doesn't seem to be too many jobs for office managers, or even much that's similar. I'm sure something will come together.' I wait and then add: 'What do you do now?'

'Not much...' she stops for a moment, apparently thinking: 'I was in marketing before I went to Hong Kong. I did a bit out there but then we were trying for a baby.'

There's an implication that the 'trying' hasn't gone well but we don't know one another enough for me to pry.

'Freddie's in marketing,' I say instead. 'That's why we're here. He's managing a division now.'

'Really?'

I'm not sure why I say it, though I suspect it's to show off. To make myself seem more influential and important than I am. The words are out before I can take them back, however: 'If you're still in the market, why not come over later?' I say. 'We can see if Freddie knows someone that's looking for a person like you. He does have a lot of contacts.'

'Oh...' Alison slows her pace a little further and then adds: 'That's really kind. I might just do that.'

SEVENTEEN

DYLAN

It is exactly 10 a.m. when I walk into Wake Me Up Before You Dough-Dough. A large counter is off to the side, filled with sandwiches, cakes, and the promised croissants. The main area is bustling with parents and sugar-crazed children.

The problem is immediately apparent. A blind date is fine – except I have no idea who I'm looking for. I don't want to be the creepy weirdo, checking out every woman, so hang around the cabinet, vaguely reading the menu, while briefly taking in the scene around me. There are lots of people, though many appear to be parents. I'm starting to worry that Beth might be the pensioner in the corner, with a walking frame, when a woman appears at my side.

'Are you Dylan?' she asks.

'Beth?'

'Yes! Thank God. A bloke came in ten minutes back wearing Crocs. I thought he might be you and I was like, "Er, no, mate. You're a grown man and it's 10 a.m.".'

There's a hint of a northern accent, plus an infectious laugh that seems permanently close. Beth's in denim shorts and a Fozzy Bear T-shirt.

'How did you know it was me?' I ask.

'The guy walking cluelessly around in circles kinda gave it away.'

She laughs and it's easy to join in, then I turn to the counter and the menu beyond. 'What would you like?'

'How are we gonna do this?' she replies.

'Do what?'

'The whole feminism thing. I can't have a man buying me everything. It only reinforces the patriarchy, don't you think?'

'Um...'

She catches my eye and laughs once more. It takes me a moment to realise Beth is joking. She's so forward that I'm not sure how to react. So different to Ciara, except the moment I have that thought, I have to shoo it away.

'You can buy and I'll get the next round in,' Beth says. 'I'll have a black coffee. Simple and easy. None of this almond milk, double mocha, syrupy stuff. Oh, but I will have a chocolate croissant if there's one going. I'll get us a seat outside.'

Beth waits in the doorway for a moment, straightens her top, grins, and then heads into the sunshine. The entire conversation was a blustery, blistering few seconds and I wonder if she's as nervous as I feel. Whether this is the real her, or a front for a first meeting. Maybe it doesn't matter because her energy feels infectious.

When I join her, Beth has found a table at the end of the row on the pavement. The sun is behind us, with a parasol providing some respite from the heat. Beth is on her phone but slips it away as I try not to drop the tray of drinks and cakes.

When we're settled she points to the two croissants. 'So... this is awkward. Who gets the big one. Paper, scissors, stone?'

'I thought we might arm wrestle,' I reply.

'Ooh, yes. I'm up for that.' She rests an elbow on the table and eyes me up.

'Actually, you can have it,' I reply, pointing to her bicep. 'I can't compete with those muscles.'

She laughs, then grabs the larger of the two croissants and begins picking flakes from the side. 'So, Willow, eh. All this blind date stuff...?'

'It was a bit out of the blue.'

'I'm just glad to see you've not got two heads, or something. That would've been a deal-breaker for me.' She sips her coffee but doesn't break eye-contact. There's a momentary twitch, the real her, and then a quieter: 'I talk a lot when I'm nervous.'

'I think I'm the opposite.'

She thinks on that for a moment as she returns to picking apart the croissant. 'They reckon opposites attract, so we've got that. If we're ever arrested together, let me do the talking.'

'What would we be arrested for?'

'Something white-collar. Nobody ever goes to prison for that stuff. Embezzlement could be fun?'

I laugh at that, then get to work on my own croissant. Beth continues picking for a while, then digs into her bag and pulls out a couple of sheets of paper.

'Right,' she says. 'I didn't want this to be awkward, so I went online and printed out a list of questions that are apparently good to ask on first dates.'

'And you think *this* isn't awkward?'

She glances up to the sky, then back down. 'Um... let's ignore that. Question one: What type of things make you laugh? For me, it has to be kids falling over.'

I bite my lip, unsure if she's being serious. 'I have a young daughter,' I say.

'Oh, I knew that. That's more or less all Willow told me about you. She didn't want it to be, quote, "a massive bombshell".' She makes bunny ears with her fingers and then adds: 'And, yes, I am one of those people that does air quotes.'

There's a comfort about the way Beth talks that makes it easy to go along with whatever she's saying. A large part of me enjoys it but I think, maybe, I liked that moment of vulnerability as well: when she said she spoke too much when nervous.

Beth presses forward and lowers her voice. She speaks with hushed resonance. A priest giving a blessing: 'I'm not being mean. I know you've got a young daughter, but you have to admit, it is *really* funny when kids *who aren't yours* fall over.'

I laugh, partly because she spoke with such seriousness, but also because it's one of those things that clearly *is* hilarious, except that no one is brave enough to admit it.

'It's not funny,' I tell her.

'Come off it. There's this Instagram account—'

'Fine! When other people's kids fall over, I laugh hysterically.'

She slaps the table gently. 'The prosecution rests, your honour.'

Beth has another bite of croissant and then: 'What's your daughter's name?'

'Orla. She's seven.'

It gets a nod of approval: 'That is a cracking name. You never know what you're gonna get 'round here. There was a kid at the park the other day named Pond! Pond?! It's child abuse.'

'Orla's mother chose the name.'

Beth nods along without taking the bait of asking about Ciara. There's a part of me that wants her to, another that doesn't want to spoil whatever this is.

'She's into football,' I say. 'And Star Wars. And climbing things. She's talking about going up Everest when she's older. She was annoyed that other women have already done it. She wanted to be first.'

'Good for her. Not the climbing, more the life goals.' Beth

shuffles her paper and then adds: 'OK, question two. What do you do and how long have you been doing it? I'm a teaching assistant and I've been doing it for two years.'

I begin to answer and then stop myself: 'Hang on, you work in a school but you laugh at kids falling over?'

'I laugh *inwardly*,' she says. 'You're the one who said you got hysterical. I help them up first and *then* laugh when their backs are turned. There's a difference.'

I grin and then tell the truth: 'I'm a woodworker.'

She narrows her eyes as if wondering if I've made that up: 'Is that a euphemism?'

'Ha! It should be but it's also true. I sell pieces around the country.'

'I did not expect that.'

'What did you expect?'

'Hmmm...' Beth plays with her hair and stretches her legs into the sun. 'I don't know. If you'd been a banker or a Tory, or something, I'd have had to call it a day. Woodwork is good.' She looks down at her page and then adds: 'Number three: This is a big one. Are you ready for this?'

'I'm primed.'

'This goes beyond politics, or religion. I want to make sure you are suitably braced.'

I shuffle in my chair, have a sip of coffee and swallow a mouthful of croissant. 'I'm braced,' I say.

'Good. What combination of toppings makes the perfect pizza?'

It's not what I expected but I laugh as she adds: 'There is a right and wrong answer.'

I shrug: 'I'm a pineapple guy.'

She bangs the table: 'Yes! The right answer. I was worried for a moment. This is the hill I'll die on. You're either on the side of pineapple, or you're not.'

We continue to chat and, before I know it, it's gone eleven

and Beth heads into the café to get her 'round' in. She returns with more coffee and more croissants – 'you only live once, right?' – and then we're off again.

We get to question twenty-one: 'Are you now, or have you ever been, a wearer of cord?' – to which we both answer 'no', and then Beth announces that she has to go. She's helping run an art class during the school holidays and 'those little monsters aren't going to cover themselves in paint without me'.

The pair of us get up, ready to leave and we have an awkward handshake before she opens her arms to invite a hug.

'C'mon, mate,' she says, 'we're pineapple buddies.'

We hug briefly and sweatily before she pulls away.

'I don't want to impinge on your time with Orla,' she says, 'but do you fancy doing something one evening this week?'

It surprises even me that the reply comes instantly: 'That sounds great.'

'You can come to mine...? It's expensive going out nowadays. We can get a pizza? Some wine?' There's a pause and a wide smile to let me know the joke's coming: 'A massive bag of ket...?'

'I'm up for that,' I say, then add: 'Not the ket.'

That gets a laugh. 'I'll text you the address.'

We hover inelegantly, post-hug, post-handshake, wondering if there should be anything more. Then Beth bobs on her heels and turns all in one go. 'See ya soon,' she says – and I know that we will.

EIGHTEEN

WILLOW

Is your mum staying over again tonight?

The text from my husband arrived ten minutes back but I can't think of how best to reply. The truth of 'probably' is not going to go down well with Gabe. It's bizarre that my house seemingly has a one-in, one-out policy. Isabella stomped away, in bumbled my mother.

I always hate leaving Mum by herself at the house because I know I'll return to find things deftly moved with ultimate levels of passive-aggression. None of it is overly important but it's still disconcerting to find my coats have been rearranged on the rack because 'it looks better like this, don't you think?' Or she'll have switched the mugs in the cupboard because 'I couldn't find the one I liked'.

Sometimes it is unavoidable to leave her alone, however.

It's hard not to feel the passing of time as I let myself into my parents' home. It's the same front door, the same key, as when I was a teenager. I always have that tug of being a girl again. The deep fat fryer would be bubbling away as I got in from school and it's as if that smell permeates from the walls. There's the spot where I once tripped down the bottom three stairs and cut my lip on the skirting board. The shred of tinsel that hung in the corner of the hall for almost five years because Dad didn't want to go up the ladder to get it down.

This will always be home, regardless of anything that happens in the rest of my life.

'Dad...?'

The call goes unanswered as I edge through the shifting plates of time and continue into the living room, where Dad is sitting in front of the TV. The sound is overpoweringly loud. Both of my parents insist neither of them are going deaf but they will have conversations about what to put on the shopping list at a volume more usually associated with jets taking off.

My father didn't hear me come in and jumps as he spots me. He's in his usual comfy chair and makes a soft yelp and then straightens himself, pretending it never happened. He grabs the TV remote and changes channel, before swearing under his breath and scrambling to change it back. That done, he accidentally turns the volume up, starts to alter the contrast and then, finally, finds the button to mute it. I assume that's what he was trying to do in the first place.

'What did she tell you?' Dad says, without prompting.

I take a seat on the sofa. 'Something about a barmaid at the football club.'

He wafts a dismissive hand. 'Oh, that's nothing. What about her and Derek at the Legion? I bet she didn't tell you about that, did she?'

I massage my temples with my fingers, trying to find the right words and hold back the wrong ones. I can't believe they've not grown out of this yet.

'You're both in your seventies, Dad. Do you honestly think

there's something going on with Mum and some bloke at the Legion?'

'He paid for her entry into the meat draw.'

I should've come prepared for this with a bottle of Jack. There's a big part of me that doesn't want to know: '*Meat draw?*'

'Did she tell you about that? She'd forgotten her purse, so he paid for her to go into the meat draw.'

I assume the 'meat draw' is some sort of raffle to win meat, as opposed to a meat *drawer*, but my parents are seemingly so barmy that anything could be true. This is a new low, even for them.

'Is there anything going on with this barmaid?' I ask.

'Course not!'

'Can you tell Mum and then we can all go back to normal...?'

'No – she's gone now. She made her choice.' He sounds defiant.

'Dad, you've been married more than forty years. Can we all have a bit of dignity here?'

He turns away to watch some more of the racing. '*If* she apologises, I'll think about it.'

'Apologises for what?'

'For going on about that barmaid. I didn't do anything.'

'*If* he apologises, I'll think about it.'

I ease off the accelerator as I approach the roundabout, fighting the urge to swear. Mum is shouting into the phone because that's what she does. I'm not sure she's ever quite got her head around how phones work.

'Are you there?' Mum says.

'I'm here, Mum. I'm going round a roundabout.'

'You shouldn't be on your phone while driving.'

'I'm on Bluetooth. It's fine.'

'Who's Blue Ruth?'

I indicate, exit the roundabout, and settle into a queue of traffic.

'Why do you want Dad to apologise?' I ask. 'He says there's nothing going on with the barmaid. It's all a misunderstanding.'

'That's what he *would* say.'

'He mentioned something about Derek at the Legion...'

That gets a huffed sigh: 'He's not still going on about the meat draw, is he?'

'He did mention it.'

'I don't know what his problem is. I forgot my purse and Derek was being a gentleman. Your father could learn a thing or two.'

'If *you* don't want to say sorry first – and *he* doesn't want to say sorry first – could you both say sorry at the same time?'

There's a ruffling and then Mum's voice is distant. Even through the phone, I can hear she has the television at a level more usually heard on a building site.

'*Loose Women*'s coming on,' she says. 'We can talk later.'

I start to reply but she's already gone.

This time, it's me who sighs. I don't know how my mother and father manage to fall out so often. All they do is watch TV and then go – separately – to either football or 'the Legion'. Isabella was born more mature than either of them.

I consider calling Mum back but know it won't be worth it. I'll end up getting a running commentary of what some menopausal Z-lister is saying about the current political situation in Iran.

The fact she's staying another night means there is definitely going to be a price to pay with both Isabella and Gabe – when Isabella returns from her dad's – but I do my best to forget that as I pull into the university.

Even in the summer months, there is never anywhere to

park. I end up leaving the car on a side street around half a mile away and then walk towards the main buildings.

Education is, clearly, a good thing but there is something unquestionably humiliating about being in classes with those half a person's age. It's even worse that many of the people with whom I share a class are a similar age to my daughter.

As I get closer to the lecture theatre, I spot Mohammad leaning on a post close to the café. He's on his phone but the very fact he's here is something of a relief. Mo is ten years younger than me, closer in age to the late-teen and early twenty-year-old students – but there is a definite disconnect between students of that age and anyone older.

Mo waves as I approach. I'd like to think that my presence is as much a relief for him as his is for me. Much of the work is completed online but there are two days a month for which we have to show up.

He slots his phone into his pocket and gives me the briefest of hugs. 'I didn't think you were coming,' he says.

'It took me ages to park,' I reply. 'Plus, Mum and Dad have fallen out, so I've been Switzerland all day.'

Mo looks puzzled for a moment, which makes me feel even older than I am: 'Aren't you a bit, um... *advanced* to be having parent problems?'

That's one way to put it. Isabella would say *she* was having parent problems – but she's a teenager and that feels more normal.

'There is nobody more aware of that than me,' I say.

I buy a coffee as we chat about our respective weekends, although it appears that our lives are full of not much going on.

We head into the lecture hall together and the following two hours are a blur of coffee, drifting thoughts, gobbledygook and general inattention. When it comes to formal education, my attention span shrinks to that of a three-year-old. It doesn't help that our lecturer has the charisma of a retired accountant with a fondness for analysing soil at the weekends.

The end of his lecture is more of an act of mercy than anything else. A kidnapper finally letting the victims go. Nobody seems to be speaking as we zombie-walk our way towards the exit and it's only when we reach the warm air that reality kicks in.

'I feel like I've been punched in the face,' Mo says blankly. 'Did you get all that?'

'I was paying attention for the first five minutes and then it was all a blur.'

'Isn't there a human rights act for things like this?'

'Not since Brexit.'

We continue towards the car park together and, through some miracle, Mo has found a parking spot adjacent to the disabled ones. He could only be closer if he'd ploughed into the bollards and barrelled through the glass doors of the lecture theatre.

He holds his hands wide and grins: 'I know!' He waits a beat, then adds: 'What do you think of the customer data analysis project?'

'It's on a par with gonorrhoea.'

He smiles, then replies: 'Do you fancy working on it together?' A momentary pause and then: 'The project, not the gonorrhoea. I don't fancy asking any of the kids.'

'I was hoping you'd ask.'

'Are you free now?'

'I could be.'

Mo plips his car fob and the orange lights flash as the doors click open. 'Can I come to yours?' he asks. 'My roommate is home today. If not that, we could go to the library...?'

It's not much of a choice. I always feel like a bored, widowed spinster at the university library, surrounded by half-asleep youngsters.

'Let's go to mine,' I say.

Mo says he'll follow and it's only when I'm halfway across the car park that I remember I'm going to have to introduce him to my mother.

Mum is watching some auction show when we get in. She's set herself up on the sofa with a bag of Thai Sweet Chilli Walkers Sensations and doesn't look to see who has let themselves in. I doubt she's left the living room since this morning.

'Had a good day?' I ask.

She doesn't turn from the TV, where someone is holding a vase in the air. 'They're never going to make fifty quid for that.'

'Mum...?'

She finally spins and notices Mo at my side. He's striking in the sense that he's tall, has a beard – and she's never met him before.

'Oh...' she says, with something close to an audible blink.

'This is Mo,' I say.

'No...?'

'*Mo* – as in *Mo*hammad.'

She nods but I'm not convinced she's heard me over the TV.

'We're going to do some uni work in the kitchen.'

More nodding and then: 'A tea would be nice.'

She turns back to the television and starts muttering to herself about vases. I leave her to it and lead Mo into the kitchen. The kettle is safely switched on as he takes a seat at the table, suppressing a smile.

'Your mum seems, um... nice,' he says.

'This is nothing,' I tell him. 'She gets up every hour in the night because she needs the toilet. When she's not doing that, she's snoring like an asthmatic elephant.'

I throw my hands up as he laughs: 'Your husband must be delighted with it all.'

'That's one way of putting it.'

I make three teas and then get to work with Mo. It's hard to achieve much, however, because Mum calls through every fifteen minutes or so, primarily to relay whatever it is she's just watched. Judge Judy has laid into some guy without a job, so she fills me in on the details 'because I thought you'd find it funny'. Then some woman gets something wrong on a quiz show and she wants to test the question on me because 'even you'll know the answer to that'.

In her mind, there is no difference between *being* at home and *working* from home. By the time she tells me that 'You don't see Bob Monkhouse on TV any more, do you?' I'm close to breaking.

'He died almost twenty years ago,' I tell her.

She frowns and shrugs, as if this is all new information. 'What's the name of the other one?' she asks.

'What other one?'

'You know – the one who does all the presenting. Like Bob Monkhouse but still alive.'

I try to explain that I have work to do and she waves her hands around, before adding: 'It'll come to me. I'll let you know.'

'You don't have to.'

Mo is starting to realise that this wasn't a great idea. The sheets of data we are supposed to be analysing are sprawled across the table, with our notes just filling the margins.

There are twenty minutes of blissful non-interruption until the front door goes, as Gabe arrives home. The living-room door opens – but my husband quickly gets himself out of there before moving into the kitchen. He looks at me, looks at Mo, and then rolls his eyes.

'I'm going to get some dinner,' he says.

I start to call him back, saying we're finishing up, but he is already in the hall. A moment later and the front door sounds again.

'Sorry...' Mo says.

'It's not you,' I reply.

'I think I should probably go.'

He closes the textbook symbolically and I almost ask him to stay. It's not for work purposes – we're getting nowhere fast – more for moral support. A bigger part of me wants to follow him to the door. I seem to have fallen out with everyone.

Mo packs the rest of his things into his bag. 'We'll catch up soon,' he says.

'Thanks for coming over.'

There's a moment in which I think he might hug me. There is pity in his eyes and he gives a closed-mouth smile instead. He doesn't even know the half of it, with Freddie's weirdness over our schooldays, Gabe's general hostility and absence, plus Isabella's ambivalence.

There's one other person as well, of course.

As soon as Mo's gone, Mum calls from the living room. I ignore her and head for the stairs, planning to lock myself in the bathroom and enjoy a few minutes of peaceful solitude.

Sooner or later, something has to give.

NINETEEN

DYLAN

As I stand on the bank and watch the kids playing football, there is no sign of the loudmouth from the day before. The overwhelming noise is fun and enjoyment as the babbling of children's laugher ebbs up from the pitches.

It's after I've been there for ten minutes or so that I spot one of the coaches making his way up the bank towards me. For a moment, I think it'll be trouble. I'm a solo man watching kids – and the connotations are hard to miss. Then I realise it is Zac and that he's smiling.

He shakes my hand and stands at my side.

'We've been missing Orla today,' he says.

'She's still got a bad tummy,' I reply. 'She's gone to her friend's to rest up.'

'Hopefully we'll see her tomorrow…?'

He sounds optimistic and interested. I try to think of a more diplomatic way to phrase things but nothing comes to mind, other than bluntness.

'I was wondering if there have been any problems with her?'
I ask.

I look for Zac's reaction and he blinks with surprise. 'Not at
all. She was very engaged on Saturday and a bit less so yesterday. I assumed her bad stomach was the reason why. Do you
have any concerns...?'

'I'm not sure.'

I go back to watching the match and it's only a few seconds
until the ball skims out of bounds. The players argue over who
touched it last, so Zac heads down to mediate. He ends up
making them play paper-scissors-stone to decide and it's a
matter of seconds until everyone has calmed down and got on
with it.

It's as play resumes that my phone goes. Theresa's name
flashes and there is that usual uneasy panic. My daughter is at
Theresa's house and something terrible has happened. Orla is
badly hurt, or she's missing. I try to control the wave of rising
alarm in my voice – but it must be there because the first thing
Theresa says is: 'Everything's fine, Dylan.'

I wonder if this is how other parents, perhaps other people
in general, view me. I'm nervous and jittery, constantly on the
brink of a breakdown.

'Do you know someone named Alfie?' Theresa asks.

I take a moment to think: 'I don't think so.'

'Neither do I. Orla was saying the name to Lauren. It could
be nothing but they went quiet when they realised I could hear.'

'Alfie...' I repeat the name but it doesn't stir anything.

'It could be someone off YouTube,' Theresa adds. 'Some sort
of personality. You said to keep an eye on her, so I thought you
should know.'

I thank her for the call and she tells me she can hang onto
Orla for as long as needed.

'The girls are talking about doing some baking,' she adds –
which brings forth memories of flour across the kitchen and

smeared butter on all the cupboard handles. With a laugh, I wish Theresa luck and then she's gone.

It's hard to know what I'm looking for, so I sit on the bank and watch. Perhaps more importantly, I listen. The shouts from the various matches overlap with one another but it's not long before I find myself focusing on the pitch adjacent to the one being coached by Zac.

A lad with a shaved head, who is bigger than anyone else, is bounding around as the smaller children call 'Alf' after him. I watch for almost ten minutes as Alf dominates the game – or tries to. He is stronger than many of the other players, but possesses no particular skill. His passes go astray and he consistently mis-controls the ball.

The coach's whistle sounds after a while and I watch as 'Alf' strolls off the pitch, up the bank. He passes me and continues towards the car park. In a blink, I realise I'm following. It feels as if I'm watching myself as I call after him.

He was the tallest player on the pitch but still significantly shorter than me. It's hard to judge his age – I'd guess seven or eight because that's the group with which he was playing – but he's rugged, with a snarl to his top lip. He's not remotely intimidated by me as he glares up.

'Are you Alfie?' I ask.

'What's it to you?'

We're almost at the tarmac of the car park but there's a gap between the pitches behind and the cars in front.

'I think you know my daughter,' I say. 'Orla.'

The smirk tells me everything. I can see the bully within him; the glimpse of the way he uses his size to get his own way.

Alfie turns to walk away, so I call his name once more.

'You're gonna leave her alone,' I say firmly.

He turns and leers once more. 'Where is she?' he says.

'She'll be back.'

'Will she? She's not as good as she thinks she is.'

'Leave her alone.'

'Or what?'

He stands squarer and taller, then snorts with derision. It's terrifying to not be in control – but there's something about his arrogance that burns within me. Orla has been through so much – and this was her summer treat.

It's as if the gap between Alfie and myself has evaporated. I'm looming over him before I know I've moved and then I've grabbed him by the shirt. The cockiness seeps from the boy as the defiance in his eyes turns to uncertainty. He's no longer the biggest and strongest. No longer the one with power. I twist the material in my fist, squeezing the shirt tighter into him. I could lift him off his feet and he knows it.

'Don't walk away from me,' I growl – and, in that moment, I feel such power. Such fury.

Alfie starts to say something but then, from a few steps over, a woman's voice breaks me from the trance.

'Oi!'

I instantly release Alfie and he drops onto his studs with a clack. The woman is standing by a battered brown Astra. She drops a cigarette and stamps it out with her foot as she starts to walk towards us.

Alfie steps away from me and straightens himself. 'It's all right, Mum,' he calls. 'This *paedo* was trying to feel me up.'

He trots across the tarmac to the car and takes a spot next to his mother. His confidence is back as he grins from behind her.

The woman narrows her eyes and folds her arms.

'Get out of it,' she shouts.

The scene has attracted onlookers as other children make their way from the pitches towards the car park. There are parents watching: nobody quite sure what to make of it all.

There's nothing to say, so I do the only thing I can – get my head down and stride quickly towards my car.

This is why Orla doesn't want to come to camp any longer.

She's getting bullied. After all that's happened to my daughter, this boy, this absolute scumbag thinks he has the right to intimidate her.

My heart is thundering, fists clenched, jaw tight.

I have to stop myself from turning around.

From running back and grabbing him.

Throwing him to the ground.

Reeling back and slamming my fist hard.

Right into his stupid face.

Let him smirk then.

Let him grin and sneer and laugh and bully as I give him what he deserves.

If he even glances in Orla's direction—

I'm at my car and my hand is shaking. It's hard to catch my breath as I fumble with the key, then throw myself into the driver's seat and slink down. There is a lump in my throat. I picture the pistol, hidden under the unit in the living room, and can feel it in my hand. It's heavy but my finger is on the trigger, not quite pulling it all the way, but knowing I could.

There are tears now, as there always are when this image is in my mind. I can see the gun, feel its weight, I just don't know whether the barrel is pointing at my own head, or someone else's.

TWENTY

HEIDI

After listening to Alison's enthusiasm about the street party, we say goodbye, and I spend what's left of the morning unpacking boxes. Despite that, the pile never seems to get smaller, so I head into the garage to see how much room there is. It's as I'm hovering there with the main door open that a car pulls up over the road and Isabella gets out. Willow's daughter slings a bag over her back and says goodbye to whoever's driving, before sighing her way onto the pavement. Even from the other side of the road, it's obvious she isn't happy.

It's possibly to avoid going into the house, but when she spots me, Isabella crosses the road.

'Did you hear?' she asks.

'Hear what?'

'Gran's moved in. I was only away a day!'

She sounds furious. 'I saw your mum earlier and she didn't seem too pleased about it either,' I reply.

'It's not the first time,' Isabella says, shaking her head. 'Last time, she was here for almost a month. I was trying to revise for exams and she kept trying to "help", while telling me exams are so easy nowadays.'

She huffs a long breath and glances back towards the house, as if waiting for a better offer.

'I used to argue with my mum all the time,' I say.

There are a couple of seconds in which I think I've misread the situation. Isabella doesn't reply and instead stares at her feet.

'What about?' she asks eventually.

'Everything... nothing.'

'When did it stop?'

'The arguing? When she died.'

Isabella peers up and catches my eye before quickly looking away again. She gulps. 'Oh.'

'She was in a car accident,' I say. 'Suddenly all the little things didn't seem that important.'

Isabella nods along.

'I didn't mean to get all morbid,' I add. 'It feels like a long time ago but it also feels close. Sometimes, it's like it was yesterday.'

'I get it,' Isabella says quietly. She gulps again and then turns back to her house and sighs. 'I should probably go in. I was at my dad's last night.'

She steps off the kerb onto the empty road and then I say her name. 'I'm around any time,' I add. I'm not even sure why, other than I see a little of myself in her. I remember those furious looks towards my mother and how I felt about them when it was too late.

'Thanks,' Isabella replies. She waits a second and hurries across the road, into her house.

It's strange the effect that something seemingly small can have on a person. It's only that short interaction and I find myself upstairs, unpacking the boxes I've spent the weekend ignoring.

When the front door goes, I realise it's close to half-six and I've spent hours at the task. Freddie calls my name and I head downstairs to meet him. We go through the motions of comparing days, though there isn't a lot on my end. He thanks me for clearing so many of the boxes, while I keep quiet about the lack of job opportunities.

He has barely been home for two minutes when we are interrupted by a knock at the door. Freddie opens it, and Alison is there, clutching a cardboard folder, dressed far more smartly than her yoga gear of earlier. She's in a tightly fitted pencil skirt, shirt and jacket. The visual is so striking that Freddie takes a step backwards.

He looks to me: 'It's for you, Heid...?'

Alison straightens herself as I remember I told her to come over to discuss careers with Freddie. I should've messaged him but it's a bit late now.

'I was here for you, actually,' Alison says, talking to my husband. She looks between the pair of us, seemingly realising she's interrupted something. 'Sorry, is it a bad time?'

She doesn't wait for much of an answer and it's like she's a different person from who I was talking to on the towpath hours ago. There was vulnerability but now there's breathless efficiency.

'I'm Alison from a couple of doors down,' she says. 'I was telling Heidi earlier that I used to work in marketing. She thought I could ask you for a bit of advice about getting back into it...?'

'Right...' Freddie turns between the two us, caught in the middle. His brow creases momentarily. 'I suppose that's fine.'

'I don't want to impose,' Alison says.

That is, of course, what everybody says when they know

they're imposing. I did invite Alison over but she must have been watching and waiting for Freddie to get home. He was barely in the door before she was here, too.

'It's not an imposition,' Freddie says.

Alison takes that as an invitation to step inside.

I figure he'll take her into the living room but, instead, he nods the other way.

'I've set myself up with a study,' he says as he opens the door to her side.

'Ooh, very fancy,' she replies.

'Do you want to wait in there? Don't mind the mess. I'll run upstairs and get changed, then we can have a chat.'

The strangeness of before, when Freddie's study was locked and out of bounds feels like a distant annoyance now. The room is open for anyone.

I wait in the kitchen, making myself cheese and onion on toast, listening to Alison laugh from along the hall. Freddie joins in and, after half an hour, they're still in there.

I've finished my food and clear up, before doing laps of the living room, not quite sure what to do with myself.

It's almost forty-five minutes until the study door finally reopens and Alison giggles her way into the hallway. I quickly fall onto the sofa, as if I've been there all along. Nothing to see here. I'm not a nutter. Freddie emerges behind her and she touches him on the upper arm, before moving towards the door.

'Thanks so much,' she says.

'My pleasure.'

She turns, spots me on the sofa and flashes a toothy smile. 'Thanks to you, too, Heidi. What a day!'

Freddie sees her to the door and lets her out with a cheery: 'See you tomorrow'. After that, he comes into the living room.

'I didn't think you'd be that long,' I say.

'Me either. She's got a great CV. Better than mine in some

ways. She's coming in for an interview tomorrow. I think we might have something for her.' He stops himself and then crosses to the sofa. 'That's all right, isn't it?'

'Of course,' I reply, probably too quickly, not quite sure why I'm annoyed, or at whom. 'Why wouldn't it be?'

TWENTY-ONE

WILLOW

'Do you think he hates me for some reason?'

It's hard to tell solely from the tone of Michelle's voice on the phone but my friend seems personally affronted by the idea that Freddie has no interest in her. There's almost something comical about it all, like being gossipy teenagers again, fretting over which boys like which girls and, perhaps more importantly, why.

'I don't know,' I reply. 'He *is* married. It is a bit weird to meet up with a random girlfriend twenty years later.'

'I know but we weren't really going out. I was only interested in finding out what he's been up to since school.'

'Did something happen between you?' I ask.

'Not really.'

I think on that for a moment. 'It's not just you. It feels like he's avoiding me. He came out of the house to get into his car this morning and pretended he didn't see me, even though I was waving from the other side of the road.'

Michelle makes a humming sound and then says: 'We had a

kiss and a fumble – but that's all. Like you do as teenagers. What about you?'

'One kiss at spin the bottle.'

'Perhaps it's something to do with his parents dying while he was at school...?'

'Maybe...'

There is still a sense of being that spurned teenager. It's not that either of us particularly mind that Freddie has no interest in going over old times; more that, because he's *so* against it, there's a desire to know why. Is it something about us in particular? Or the school? Something that happened around that time of which we're unaware?

'Do you know if he's on Facebook?' Michelle asks.

'I've not asked.'

'If he is, tell him to join the Marsh Vale leavers group. A few of his old crowd are on there. There's bound to be someone he wants to say "hi" to.'

'I'll ask – but he runs away every time we see each other.'

I'm not sure what else to say – but the sound of the front door interrupts the conversation. I tell my friend I'll catch up to her soon and then Gabe walks into the kitchen. My husband looks around, as if making sure Mo and our coursework has disappeared, then he slumps into one of the chairs. He sighs and takes out his phone.

'Did you have something to eat?' I ask, somewhat tentatively. That's what he said he was going to do when he stormed out.

He looks up and there's something fierce in his expression. 'All I want to do is come home after work and rest,' he says, which is nothing to do with what I asked. This has clearly been on his mind. 'Watch some TV or play some games. That's it. It's not like I want to have dinner on the table, or anything like that. I don't think it's a lot to ask.'

There's some truth there – Gabe has never been an old-fashioned working man who wants food ready and the house spotless – but that's not the entire picture. He doesn't help much around the house, either. Except for, obviously, when he did his own washing and nobody else's. There is a time and place for pointing out facts such as this, however, and his glare makes it clear now is neither.

'I know…' I reply.

'What is going on with her?' he says, annoyed.

I presume he means Mum.

'She's in bed,' I reply.

'I mean, in general.'

'I'm trying to sort it between her and Dad. Another day or two. I'm sorry – but I can't just kick her out. Dad won't have her back until *she* apologises and she won't go back until *he* apologises.'

Gabe rubs his crinkled brow and I know how he feels. A long, wide yawn erupts, showing off his tonsils as he doesn't attempt to cover his mouth. His eyes water and he smears the tears of tiredness into his skin. I think about him disappearing late at night on Saturday and it feels like something is broken between us that's deeper than my mother being here.

Does everyone eventually feel like this in a relationship? You sort of get sick of one another? Or are other couples *actually* happy? It's hard to know how Gabe and I ended up here. We once went for a really long drive in the country, where we talked for hours about our lives. I'm sure we liked each other then, at the beginning.

There was never a specific moment that made me question this life, simply a series of small *chip-chip-chips* that slowly etched everything away.

'Is Isabella back?' he asks.

'Yes and no. She was home – but then she went over to her boyfriend's.'

Gabe widens his eyes and I know he's assuming Isabella and

I argued again. We didn't, not this time, but I know why he'd think it. This is Isabella's life: a night with her dad to get away from me. Out with her friends when she comes home. In-out, in-out. I don't know if I have a problem with that. Probably not.

'What about your man?' he asks.

'My what?'

He motions the table, making it obvious he means Mo.

'We're working together on some coursework,' I say.

Gabe nods along and, for a moment, I figure that's the end of it. Then he turns away and mutters 'that's convenient...'

'What do you mean?'

'You know...'

I watch him, looking for more, but I'm not sure I *do* know. 'All I want is a job I can enjoy,' I say. 'I didn't get a chance to study when I was younger, so I'm trying to change things now.'

'And who's paying for all this?'

It's relationship bingo: I've fallen out with my daughter, my mother and now my husband. *Ding-ding-ding*. Full house.

'You said it was OK,' I reply.

Gabe shakes his head, dismissively. 'What about him over the road?'

It takes me a second to realise that Gabe is talking about Freddie. Again. 'What about him?' I say. 'I've barely spoken to him.' We've been over this.

'But there's something going on, isn't there? I saw the way he looked at you the other night.'

'What way?'

Gabe slaps a hand on the table: 'You know what I'm talking about.'

'I don't.'

He pushes himself up and shakes his head. 'I'm going to bed.'

I have no idea what to say as Gabe stands and stomps through the house before attacking the stairs with the gusto of the world's strongest man wearing steel-capped boots. He slams the bathroom door and then there is merciful quiet.

The problem is that I *do* know what Gabe is talking about, even if it's not what he might think. I knew the first time he brought it up. There was unquestionably something between Freddie and myself. A sense that Freddie knows something I don't. That something important happened at school that nobody else seems to remember. It felt like he did not want to be in the same room as me.

I want to tell Gabe all this, but how can he see things my way if I don't understand it myself?

When it comes to Freddie, me, and our past, there is something quite seriously up. I just wish I knew what it was.

THE FUTURE

Signed statement from Valentina Grujic:

I was sitting outside the Wake Me Up Before You Dough-Dough café when I saw Dylan Wilson with a woman whose name I do not know. I also didn't know his name at the time but I did recognise something about Mr Wilson. I thought he might have been on TV once, something like that? Maybe Big Brother *or* The Traitors*? I sort of knew him without knowing him. It was only after everything happened, and his face was on the internet, that I realised he was the same person whose wife had been killed a few years ago. I remember feeling sorry for him back then.*

They were sitting a couple of tables away from me and I assumed they knew each other, or were boyfriend-girlfriend. They were laughing a lot and seemed to be enjoying themselves. I can't remember what they ordered but they were definitely drinking and eating something. One time, the woman went into the café to order more – and Mr Wilson got his phone out. I think he was texting someone but I don't know for sure. When he noticed me looking at him, he smiled – and I smiled back.

They looked happy, which is why I noticed them. I would say they were in a good frame of mind. They were by themselves, with no children or pets. I did not see a weapon of any sort, including a gun.

I hope Mr Wilson and the woman are both all right. They seemed like a nice couple. I don't know what else to write.

TWENTY-TWO

TUESDAY

WILLOW

I finally decide to get out of bed after Mum goes to the toilet for the fourth time. She flushes it each time, which is one thing, I suppose, except the sound of gushing water wakes me every time. Gabe is sleeping, or at least pretending to, though the ruffled covers on his side tell the story of a restless night. I don't blame him for being annoyed. It's a few minutes to five and he has to be up for work in ninety minutes. Home isn't much of a sanctuary at the moment.

Downstairs feels cooler than usual and I pull my dressing gown tighter as I head into the kitchen. Through my blurry, hazy morning eyes, it takes a few moments to notice that the window is wide open. It's been so warm during the day that we've been leaving windows open throughout the house – but I was sure I closed them before I went to bed. If not that, then I pulled them *almost* closed, and left this one on the latch. I try to scratch out the memory but my mind is scrambled and slow. It comes with age, I suppose – but the clarity isn't there. Perhaps I did leave the window open?

I poke my head into the living room but the obvious things are there – the television, the speaker system, my purse on the side. In the kitchen, our keys are hanging on the rack and the tub filled with change is unmoved. If anybody has broken in during the night, then there are no signs.

After setting the coffee machine murmuring, I yawn my way through trying to make some breakfast. The box of Corn Flakes is empty apart from crumbs – which is an Isabella trade-mark. If she had *completely* emptied the box, she'd have had to squash the cardboard down for recycling – and she'll do anything to avoid the egregious task of having to clear up. I settle for coffee and peanut butter on toast, then move into the living room. There, I watch the endless loop of TV news, while wasting an hour on my phone.

It's only as the thumps begin from upstairs that I realise the time. Gabe appears at the bottom of the stairs in his work suit and stands in the doorway, yawning.

'Does your mother ever stop pissing?' he asks. For once, it's a fair question.

'I don't think she does.'

As if on cue, there is a thunderous bang from upstairs, the sound of the spare-room door being wrenched open, footsteps, and then the toilet door opening.

Gabe and I catch each other's eye and start giggling like giddy children who've been told not to laugh. It's infectious as our snorts quickly become full-on guffaws. Something has shifted overnight, though I'm not sure what.

He crosses the room and I stand as he welcomes me into his arms. This is how we used to be.

'I'm sorry for being grumpy,' Gabe says. 'I'm just tired.'

He releases me and I step away to look up at him. He's freshly shaven, ready for work. Light and dark. We argue, we make up. I wonder if it's me. Whether it runs in the family? Mum and Dad are always falling out, and so am I.

'I'll get it sorted,' I say. 'I'll go full United Nations to get Mum and Dad talking again.'

Gabe nods upwards. 'Imagine our water bill if she stays long term.'

'I know!'

'What about you and Iz?'

'We're getting on. Sort of.'

'And the uni work?'

'It's coming along. I feel so old.'

I'd like him to deny things – 'You're still young' – but he doesn't. 'I'm going to head off,' he says instead.

I'm about to ask if he wants coffee or breakfast but it's obvious he wants to be out of the house before Mum bounds down the stairs. The flush of the toilet upstairs is his signal to leave.

'See you later,' he says, pecking me on the forehead.

I press myself into him once more, then watch him go. He's being nice today but it's been a long week. I wonder if I bring these mood swings out of him. Words like 'bipolar' and 'schizophrenic' get thrown around so much nowadays – but it does often feel like I'm living with two husbands. There's this side of Gabe, with whom I can giggle about toilet habits. Then there's the suspicious husband who's endlessly on edge. The one who has some degree of obsession about Freddie and myself.

The front door closes and Gabe's car starts just as the footsteps begin from upstairs. When Mum appears, she is wrapped in a dressing gown with outrageously large pink slippers on her feet.

'Was that Gabe?' she asks, nodding at the door.

'He had to go to work early.'

Mum nods along, though her nose twitches in anticipation of possible tea.

'What happened with him last night?' she asks airily.

'What do you mean?'

She finally gets off the bottom step and limps towards the living room. It's hard to know if she actually has a problem as the limp comes and goes, depending on how much she wants doing for her.

'I heard him going out last night,' she adds.

'When?'

'About half-twelve, I guess. Dunno what he was up to. My hip was playing up.'

I watch her, looking for some sort of malice, or confusion, though she moves on almost instantly. I was asleep by half-past midnight and assumed Gabe was still at my side.

'Is there any tea?' Mum asks, apparently not realising the impact of what she's said. 'I could murder a cuppa.'

TWENTY-THREE

DYLAN

Theresa welcomes Orla into her house for the second day running with a grin and a gentle pat on the arm for me.

'Thanks for having her again,' I say.

'It's my pleasure – they keep each other occupied. If it wasn't for Orla, Lauren would be climbing the walls.'

I watch my daughter disappear inside with her friend and ready myself to leave when Lauren's mum asks the obvious question: 'Did anything come of the Alfie thing?'

I try to fight away the shuddering memory of me, essentially, threatening a child, then my near breakdown in the car park. The idea of slamming that bully of a boy into the tarmac has barely left my thoughts since it occurred the first time.

What was I thinking?

What *am* I thinking?

If it hadn't been for the adults around, I don't know what I would have done to him.

With a shake of my head, I bat away the question. 'I don't think so. Alfie might be a TV character, something like that.

Orla seemed a lot happier last night, so I think she's feeling better.'

Theresa nods along, taken in by the lie. The truth is being well and truly skirted. 'I can feed her again later if you want? Let me know.'

I thank her once more and then head back to the car. It's Tuesday and so, summer holidays or not, I have a routine.

I drive through the streets of High Kingsley, enjoying the warmth through the window as I navigate the endlessly bewildering one-way system. There are parents and children wandering up and down the High Street, and I pass the café where I sat with Beth barely twenty-four hours before. Things felt different then – hopeful, perhaps – but then the darkness descended once more.

I'm so engulfed by thoughts of Alfie and what I might have done had his mother not shown up that I miss my turn and have to filter the entire way around the system once more. Eventually, I pull into the car park at the back of the crown court and pay the six pounds it costs for an all-day pass.

I am on my way up the steps heading into the court when the usher waves me across.

'You must be sweltering in all that,' I tell him.

He's wearing a suit underneath the usher's gown and tugs at the sleeves. 'Supposed to be the hottest day of the year today,' he says.

'Rather you than me.'

I wait as he helps out a woman who is looking for a certain case and then he turns back to me.

'What's on today?' I ask.

'Court one is the same as last week but number two looks interesting.'

'What is it?'

'Assault.'

I thank him for the tip and then follow the steps up and into

the main building. The court itself is some sort of 1970s archi-
tectural throwback: all faded wood and dull, tiled, echoing
floors. The overwhelming colour is beige-brown, as if everything
is being viewed through a sepia photo.

I follow the passages up into the public gallery of court two
and have barely taken a seat when everyone is rising for the
judge.

The defendant in the dock is a stereotypical thug. He has a
shaven head, with a suit that's far too tight and possibly hasn't
been worn since his previous court appearance. Letters are
tattooed on his knuckles and he winks at his pregnant partner,
who is sitting next to his solicitor.

It's not long until the prosecution is laying out the case that
the defendant – Dan Somebody – used a pint glass to seriously
wound the victim. The victim himself is a far smaller man, who
is sitting behind his own solicitor and barely looking up. Even
from the distance I'm at, I can see Dan trying to make eye
contact with the person he apparently glassed.

The victim is the first person to give evidence and the story
sounds straightforward enough. He was in the pub with his
friend, sitting next to the quiz machine, while a football match
was on. He noticed two men at the machine, one of whom –
Dan – seemed agitated.

When asked what that means, he says the defendant was
banging the side of the machine whenever he got a question
wrong. Dan shakes his head vigorously at this, staring holes
through the victim.

'They were swearing and kept putting in more money,' the
victim adds. 'They would read the question to each other and
then punch the button to give the answer.'

'What happened?' the solicitor asks.

'There was a question about how many sides a nonagon has.
One of them read it out and then they both said, "None", saying
that they weren't going to be caught out by a trick question.'

There's a snigger from someone on the jury, which is met by a stony-faced look from the judge.

'Then what?' the lawyer asks.

'I laughed.' He takes a breath and then adds: 'I didn't mean to. It was an involuntary thing. Before I knew it, I was on the ground and there was blood in my eye.'

He holds his face, indicating the pain, as the prosecution solicitor lays out the evidence, which includes – from what I can tell – some rather graphic images of the violence.

Dan is still shaking his head but it's not hard to see from the looks on the jurors' faces that he's toast. Nobody will believe whatever defence he might have, including me.

After the first set of evidence, the judge calls for a break and the jurors filter out. I leave court, too, navigating the passages and then heading around the side. There's a small garden, hidden by a series of hedges and it's behind there that I find the usher having a quiet puff on his e-cigarette. The sun has disappeared over the top of the court and the high bushes are providing a comforting shade.

'How's it going in there?' he asks.

'Grimly.'

'I'm not surprised.' He draws deeply on the cigarette, holds it, and then breathes out a waft of fruity smoke. After a series of sideways glances, he finally comes out with it. 'Can I ask you something?'

'Sure.'

'Why are you here? Not today... in general. Every week.'

It's such a raw question, with such up-front honesty, that I am temporarily lost for words.

'I'm not sure I know...'

The usher has another gasp and then dispatches the device back into one of his many pockets. 'I get the sense you're looking for something...?' he says.

'Maybe...'

We stand uneasily, neither sure what to say next. Some-times passing acquaintances are meant to be only that. Nods, waves, and the briefest of enquiries as to the other person's well-being is all there's supposed to be.

'Time to head back,' he says, nodding towards the court.

'See you in there.'

He strides past with a swish of his gown, leaving me alone in the shadows of the court. It suddenly feels cold, like waking up in the middle of the night to find the quilt on the floor.

It wasn't as if I could tell him the truth. Someone murdered my wife and I don't believe whoever it was could kill one person and then stop. The police don't have answers but whoever it was is out there somewhere. Maybe they're in here?

I move back towards the front of the court but then change my mind about going in. Whoever did this to Orla, to me, to my wife, isn't some bloke with a pint glass in a pub. It's someone far more cunning than that. Someone who wouldn't be caught up in something so trivial.

I will get those answers – and then my wife, then Ciara, will have her vengeance – but it won't be today, and it won't be here.

TWENTY-FOUR

WILLOW

'I'm not going in.'

Mum folds her arms across her chest and pulls the seatbelt tighter, even though the handbrake is on and the car's not moving.

I look past her towards my parents' house and fight the urge to ram-raid the damned place. If nothing else, it would get her inside. This is why I wouldn't let her come in her own car – she'd have waited for me to indicate in one direction and then floored hers to go in the other.

'I'm going to talk to Dad,' I say. 'Don't go anywhere.'

She harrumphs, as if to say she'll do whatever she pleases, so I use the central locking to trap her inside, knowing there's no way she'll figure out how to escape.

Dad is in the same spot as I saw him yesterday, wearing the same clothes, and I can't be certain he's moved. He once again jumps as I enter the living room and scrambles for the TV remote, changing the channel five times and then turning it off, on, off and on, before finding the mute button. It is perhaps no surprise that he's watching an auction show. A couple are holding onto a vase and there's every chance it's either the same as yesterday, or that it may as well be.

'She back, then?' he says.

'Mum's in the car outside.'

He harrumphs and turns back to watching the screen with the sound down.

'She says she's sorry. She's going to come back in, OK?'

Another snort and then: 'If that's what she wants.'

That done, I flick on the kettle because tea is their Good Friday Agreement, then head back out to the car. Mum is busy trying to find the lock button on the door, not realising it's actually under the dashboard. When she notices I'm on my way, she sits up straight and acts as if she's not moved since I left.

I let myself back into the car and slot into the driver's seat.

'Dad says he's sorry,' I say.

'Oh, is he indeed...?'

'Come and see. He put the kettle on.'

Mum fiddles with the seatbelt, somehow getting her finger trapped in the release mechanism before finally extricating herself. She clambers out the car and saunters across the road with her chin high. While she's doing that, I grab her luggage from the boot and drag it towards the house, before dumping it in the hallway. By the time I get into the living room, my parents are both watching the auction show, with the volume at an ear-splitting new high.

'They're never going to make fifty quid for that,' Dad shouts, presumably in an effort to be heard over the TV.

'What?' Mum yells back.

'I said they're never going to make fifty quid for that.'

'I heard you the first time.'

I make them each a tea and place both cups on the table, although each of my parents shuffle in their seats to watch the screen around me. They're back to whatever normal is for them.

'I've got to get home,' I say.

'What?' Mum shouts.

'I'll bring your car back tomorrow.'

I wave instead, hoping it will get the message across but neither of them seems too worried. By the time I'm back in the sunshine, it feels as if at least one of the weights on my shoulders has been lifted.

After Isabella, I told myself I wouldn't be ready for any more children. It wasn't her, it was me. Now I wonder if it was because babysitting two parents is enough by itself. I don't think they used to be like this – and I know that, one day, I'll miss this sort of thing. It's hard to see how I'll specifically miss *this*, however. This whole charade was likely to enable them to have a mini holiday from one another.

Without Mum at my side, it is a stress-free drive back to the house. There's no 'look out for that car', when another vehicle is half a mile away; or 'what's the speed limit here?' every time she senses I might be a mile or two-per-hour over. If only the passive-aggression didn't run in the family, we might all get on.

By the time I get home, Craig's Vauxhall is parked outside the house and I have to manoeuvre around it to get onto the driveway. I've not seen Isabella's father since I goaded him two days ago.

I take extra care to pull off the perfect reverse job and, by the time I'm out of the car, Craig's partner, Sarah, is bounding along the pavement towards me.

There's no sign of him but she's wagging her finger, that wavy blonde hair cascading behind her as if she's in a shampoo advert: 'Who do you think you are?' she storms.

'Sorry...?'

'Using Isabella against her father. Saying that she chose you over him. You ought to be ashamed of yourself.'

'Oh, right...'

It's hard to know what to say. I'd forgotten my pettiness – but Craig's wife doesn't give me any time to respond anyway.

'You *know* that he stepped away so that she didn't have to choose. He didn't *want* to make her pick sides. We'd have her living with us in a heartbeat if that's what she wanted.'

'I know, I—'

Sarah moves closer, moving her finger nearer to my face. 'You don't know how much he misses her, how much he loves it when she calls and he gets to see her. He's missed out on most of that growing up – and then you throw it in his face!'

The onslaught has left Sarah out of breath, finally giving me a moment to get a word in.

'I'm sorry,' I say, meaning it. 'I regretted it the moment I said it.'

She pushes herself up high onto the tips of her toes, making herself taller than me and then, when Sarah realises what I've said, she sinks down once more. 'Oh... well, so you should be.'

Sarah steps away, seemingly not expecting anything conciliatory.

'You need to say sorry to him,' she says.

'I know. I will.'

Sarah moves closer to the car, rage apparently satiated, before she turns back. 'And don't you *ever* talk like that to him again.'

She finishes with some sort of pirouetted flourish and then flounces off to the car before I can reply. I don't particularly blame her, although it's a relief to see there is nobody else on the street who witnessed the humiliation.

I wait for Sarah's car to be out of sight and then go through my bag in an attempt to find my house keys. When there's no sign, I knock in case Isabella's home. If she is, she doesn't answer.

I reopen the car and check the various cup-holders and storage spaces. I look in the boot and then tip my bag out onto the driver's seat, all without a result as I'm left contemplating the drive back to Mum and Dad's in case I dropped my keys there.

It's a last resort as I hunch down and peep underneath the driver's seat and then the passenger's, which is where I spy the glimmer of stainless steel. I would bet that, as Mum was hastily pretending she *wasn't* looking for a way out of the car, she somehow sent the contents of my bag sprawling.

The keys are a fingertip too far away and I start to look around for a hook, or something similar. There is, of course, no reason for something like that to be in either the car, or the garden.

As I'm picking myself up from the ground, there's a rumble of an engine and then Freddie's BMW pulls onto the driveway opposite. I'm low and out of sight as he and Alison clamber out of the car and then meet on the driveway. They stand together for a minute or so, with her laughing at something he says and then angling forward to brush his shoulder for a reason I can't fathom. Is she flirting? Is he? I'm so used to seeing Alison as the neighbourhood organiser, that it's a shock to view her in any other way.

I wonder whether Heidi's at home, although there's no sign of anyone in the windows. Alison says something else, giggles, and then turns to head towards her own house. As far as I know, she's living by herself, her husband overseas, so it's all a bit curious. I take that moment to stand, revealing my position and then calling to Freddie across the road. He looks directly at me and there's no way he can pretend to have missed me this time.

'Can you help?' I ask. 'I can't reach my keys.'

Freddie takes off his jacket, revealing huge patches of sweat on his shirt. He checks behind, possibly looking for Heidi, and then crosses the road slowly.

'What do you need?' he asks, not catching my eye.

'My door keys are stuck under the passenger seat. I can't reach them. Could you have a go?'

Freddie replies with neither a yes or a no. He simply crouches, stretches and retrieves my keys, before handing them to me.

'That it?' he asks, already turning to go.

'Thank you,' I reply – and I almost let him leave... except I feel a tug of wanting to talk to him. Being with people who have shared experiences can make a person feel both young and old at the same time.

'Did you hear anything last night?' I ask.

Freddie twists back to me, standing sideways, not committing to listening but not leaving either. 'What do you mean?'

'There was a window wide open at our place. We didn't know if someone broke in. It doesn't *look* like anything's missing but I was wondering if you heard or saw something...?'

He shakes his head: 'I was asleep early.'

'Can you ask Heidi?'

'Fine.'

Freddie takes a step away but I continue speaking: 'Are you on Facebook? It's just there's a Marsh Vale leavers group with people from our year.'

His face is a hesitant mix of confusion and curiosity. His gaze is so piercing that I temporarily stop speaking until I remember where I was up to.

'There's a few people on there who would probably want to say hi,' I add.

The silence is brutal. Icebergs break apart; royals marry, divorce, and marry again. It's as if the passage of time has shattered.

When he speaks, it is slow and deliberate: 'Have you been telling people about me?'

'No, but—'

He steps forward, standing tall, and there's a moment in

which I suddenly feel vulnerable. It doesn't matter that we're in public, or that we're neighbours.

'*Don't*,' he says, almost in a whisper. 'I'm *not* on Facebook and I *don't* want to say "hi" to anyone.'

I barely have time to explain myself because he steps away, turning and storming across the road back to his house.

It takes a few seconds to get my bearings and run through what's just happened. In the instants afterwards, it's hard to figure out quite why he felt so imposing. The entire incident lasted barely a blink, yet I'm trembling as I watch him go.

For a moment, just a moment, I thought he was going to hurt me. There was such simmering, desperate anger.

Inside the house and I call for Isabella. There's a stutter in my voice, a nervousness that wasn't present before.

There is, unsurprisingly, no response. I would usually let it go, except for a sense I can't entirely explain that I'm not alone.

I head upstairs and knock on my daughter's door, which is when the 'don't come in' echoes out.

I think about asking why she didn't answer the front door when I knocked – but then remember what Gabe said about picking the battles that matter. This is not one.

'I'm just checking you're home,' I say.

'I am.'

'Your nan has gone home.'

'OK...'

I wait on the landing, plucking up the courage to ask if she might want to do something, even if it's have a sandwich together. After those seconds with Freddie outside, I'm craving company.

There are no sounds coming from beyond her door and I wonder if Isabella's father was right. I *am* too negative. Isabella wants to be arty and expressive – and I'm constantly trying to mould her into the adult I wasn't.

I press my head to her door. 'Iz...'

There is a hesitation and then her voice seeps through from the other side. She's so close, yet so far. 'What?'

'Do you want to do something?'

'Like what?'

'Have something to eat? Sit in the garden...?'

I know she's going to say 'no' moments before she actually does. Her exact reply is a diplomatic 'maybe later', though the rejection is clear.

I wait a few seconds more and then head downstairs.

I am restless on the sofa, considering getting back to my university work, knowing I won't. I want to call Michelle and tell my friend about the weirdness with Freddie – except the very thought still gives me chills.

Why is he so keen to avoid talk of school? I know his parents died, that he was raised by his grandparents, but it can't only be that? What happened that makes him so desperate to avoid me?

I can't come up with anything, so I begin scanning Isabella's TikTok channel when a text arrives from Beth:

Met yer mate from next door. Don't tell him i told you – but i think i like him

It takes a moment to remember that one of my other friends had a coffee date with Dylan from next door. With the whirl-wind of chaos surrounding my mum, plus my husband's mood swings, it had slipped my mind.

I tap out a reply:

I'm telling him right now

Dont u dare

I reassure Beth that I'm not really going to tell Dylan, and realise that I'm smiling. It would be so great if they got together. They have both been so lonely.

I wait to see if she's going to reply, and, when she doesn't, remember that I owe my ex an apology.

With that, I tap out a message to Craig:

Sorry about the other day. I didn't mean it. Thanks for looking after Iz & the advice. I should've listened

I check it through, then press send. I should have sent it in the minutes after I argued with him on Sunday. It now feels like I was pressured into it by his other half, which, in a way, I was. Better late than never and all that.

There is no immediate reply but it's then that Gabe gets home anyway. My husband pops his head around the living-room door and puts his satchel on the floor. His suit jacket is over his shoulder as he stands listening.

'It's quiet in here,' he says.

'I told Dad that Mum had apologised, then told her that Dad said sorry.'

He nods: 'Iz upstairs?'

'Yes.'

'No arguments?'

I'm not sure if I should be offended that this is his first thought. 'Not today.'

'Good.'

He picks up his bag and is on the bottom step when I call after him and trail into the hallway.

'Did you leave the house last night?' I ask.

Gabe starts to cross his arms but can't quite manage it because he's holding his satchel in one hand and suit jacket in the other. 'Course not.' A pause and then: 'Why?'

'I thought I woke up and you weren't there...'

He pouts a lip and shrugs: 'Could it have been a dream?'

His eye is twitching and there's something about the way he's standing that means I don't believe him. Why would Mum lie about him going out? Why would he wash his own clothes but nobody else's the other night? Why would our kitchen window be open when I was certain I closed it?

So many questions.

'I suppose it might have been a dream,' I tell him, not mentioning it was Mum who heard him leave.

He eyes me curiously and I sense him wondering if there's going to be a follow-up. Is this why I'm always arguing with the people in my life? I can't let things go, I can't just trust them. We've been reduced to this sort of bland, perfunctory conversation about whether I've had a fight with someone that day.

When I say nothing more, he spins and takes the next step. 'I'm going to have a shower,' he says.

TWENTY-FIVE

DYLAN

I force myself to lean back slightly, telling myself not to hunch or clench my fists when I'm running. It's a waste of energy.

Breathe...

It's funny how the advice of almost every sporting coach, regardless of the discipline, is to breathe. All those hours of expertise and education – and the best guidance they come up with is to do the one thing every human does without thinking.

My watch beeps to signify thirteen kilometres, which means three more to go to get up to the ten miles. I run around the flagpole in the park and then loop back to the gates, before jogging on the spot while waiting to cross the road.

It's Alfie who is stuck in my mind. I have barely stopped thinking about him since I grabbed him in the car park.

A bully is a bully – but is that him, or me?

It's obvious now what I should have done. I should've spoken to Zac or one of the other coaches, asking if Alfie and Orla might have had an issue. What I definitely should not have done is the one thing I did.

I don't think I regret threatening him, though – only the fact I was spotted doing it.

I'm still considering that as I near the corner of Huntington Grove. My watch beeps for sixteen kilometres and I realise I've somehow blanked out the past three. If it wasn't for the evidence on the screen, I'm not sure I'd be able to say I'd moved at all.

I try to put on a final sprint back to the house but there's nothing left in my legs and I end up slowing as I reach my drive. I stop my watch at 16.3km and then grab the towel from the wheel arch of my truck and start to dab away the damp from my brow.

'Good run?'

Willow is standing at the barrier between our houses. My neighbour is holding a pair of secateurs but her hands are clean and I get the sense she has been waiting for me. Somehow, I missed her as I got in. It feels like we've done this before.

It's always a strange question, of course, albeit a typical one. Runs are *never* good – that's the whole point of them. Exercise is hell and anyone who says otherwise is a liar.

'Not bad,' I say, trying to catch my breath.

She nods along, weighing up whether to ask something, before deciding to go for it. 'How were things with Beth?'

Ah, of course that's why she's waiting. She knows her friend and I had coffee. Beth has probably given her version of it all and now Willow is after mine.

'Did Beth say something?' I ask.

A glimmer of a smile creeps across Willow's face, which is answer enough. 'Only that you had a good time.'

'That sounds true.'

I try not to smile. That's two of us who thinks we had a good time. Willow waits, probably after more, but then takes a small step back towards her house. 'Can you make sure my husband gets back at a reasonable hour later?'

'I'll see what I can do.'

Willow says thanks and then retreats inside, while I wipe away the sweat from my arms and face. If I'd been swimming, I'd probably be drier than now.

When I get inside, Gabe is in my living room, beer in hand, watching more cricket highlights. He looks me up and down, then laughs: 'How far this time?'

'Ten miles.'

He puffs his lips, then holds the beer can aloft: 'I've been working hard, too.'

I nod upstairs: 'Anything?'

'Not a peep.'

I tell him I'll be down shortly and then head upstairs. I ease Orla's door open as quietly as I can and then squint through the darkness to where she's curled up, asleep under her covers. It's always a pull to drag myself away from watching her. The sheets rise slowly with each of her breaths and there's an urge to wake her, so we can have a few more minutes together. I could have had that earlier, of course, except I left her with Theresa in order to chase more fantasies at the court.

I'm stuck in that Tuesday routine at the court, knowing I get nothing from it, yet unable to stop.

After showering and changing, I head downstairs and get my own beer from the fridge, another for Gabe, then join him in front of the television. He takes the can and frowns at the other thing I've brought through.

'What are you eating?' he asks.

'Hummus and flatbread.'

'There's no way that's food.' He holds up his family-sized bag of kettle chips to emphasise the point.

'Thanks for keeping an eye on Orla,' I say, even though she was in bed when he got here.

Gabe says it's no bother and then nods towards the window. 'You spoken much to them over the road?'

'Who?'

'The new lot.'

I shake my head. 'I've waved a couple of times but that's about it. I don't think I know their names.'

'Heidi and Freddie,' Gabe says, though it's through clenched teeth. He sounds furious for some reason. 'What do you reckon?' he adds.

'Of what?'

Gabe doesn't reply at first. His jaw is moving, though I don't think he's actually eating. His gaze is fixed on the window and what's beyond.

'Have you seen him talking to Willow?'

'Freddie? I don't think so.' I wait and then add: 'Should I have?'

There's an ominous pause before we're interrupted by the doorbell. I check the window but can't see anyone on the driveway. I don't want whoever it is to ring a second time, and risk waking up Orla, so I hurry into the hall and open the front door.

I'm half expecting it to be kids messing around – if that's even a thing nowadays – and am surprised to see a man standing on the step. There's a vague recognition, though I can't quite place him.

'You Dylan?' he asks.

'Who's asking?'

'You think you can go around touching up kids, do you?'

As he steps forward, I realise it is the man from the bank overlooking the football pitches who was going on about how bad the girls were. He's still in three-quarter tan shorts, though the England top has been replaced by a red polo shirt.

'What are you on about?' I say.

He doesn't answer, instead trying to push his way past me into the hallway. I have to decide whether to shove him back, or allow him in. It happens so quickly that I'm already shuffling backwards as he continues towards me, a sausage finger jabbing towards my face.

'My missus saw you grabbing our Alfie.'

At the sound of the boy's name, I finally clock what's going on and stand my ground. The man stops moving, leaving us at a stand-off near the bottom of the stairs.

'Maybe you should talk to your son about bullying other kids,' I say.

'Maybe girls shouldn't be playing football.'

By the time my reply is out, it's too late. I point to his over-hanging gut: 'Sorry, mate. I forgot it takes a real man to be an athlete.'

I can see the comment ticking over in his brain. There is a second or two in which he doesn't quite realise what I've said and then, when he does, he launches himself forward, right fist swinging.

I'm seeing things in slow motion as I move to the side, feeling the swish of the air as the man's knuckles skim the front of my jaw, not making contact. He is slightly off balance but I have no time to process what to do next before Gabe launches himself from the living room, connecting with a thunderous punch of his own. There is a deafening crunch as the man's head jack-knifes sideways. A blink later and my attacker is on the floor, groaning to himself.

Nobody moves.

Gabe is in the living-room doorway, I'm at the bottom of the stairs and, between us, Alfie's dad is on all fours. He starts to push himself up – but Gabe is a tectonic plate of fury. The first kick connects squarely with the man's head, sending him spin-ning closer to the stairs. The second is even more brutal. The skull of Alfie's father bounces from Gabe's foot into the newel post and then the other man slumps to the ground with a splat.

It's the splash of blood onto the bottom step that wakes me from the stunned inaction. Gabe is lining up for a third kick and

I scramble to get my arms around my neighbour, pushing him into the living room.

'No!' I shout.

Gabe is fighting against me and, as I turn, I half expect to see Alfie's father motionless on the ground. I've never heard anything like the smack before. There's a relief as he moans – but it's only momentary. He turns towards us and I know what's going to happen before it does.

Perhaps I let it?

Things always sound worse in retrospect than they feel at the time. A split-second thought becomes a drawn-out investigation. A momentary action, or inaction, is examined with forensic detail.

Before Alfie's dad can get to his feet, I have allowed Gabe to slide around me.

Allowed him.

My neighbour is spitting with righteous fury and rocks back, before kicking the other man in the stomach like a rugby player punting for touch. Gabe howls like a mistreated wolf and drops to his knees, rattling a punch into his opponent's jaw. There is a crack and the man's head shoots sideways once more, pinging back in time to receive another splintering blow to the temple.

This time, it is Gabe who stops himself. Alfie's father slides sideways, his ear colliding with the already-bloodied bottom step once more. He flops onto his back, eyes closed; body limp, lifeless.

He's dead. Surely, he's dead?

TWENTY-SIX

HEIDI

I slot onto the sofa close to Freddie, who angles his phone away from me. Since getting home, he spent half an hour in his study, fifteen minutes outside on his phone, and then heated himself up some soup.

The less said about my day, the better.

'How was Alison's interview?' I ask.

He looks up: 'Huh?'

'I thought Alison was being interviewed at your place today?'

He blinks at me, as if this is all news to him. 'Oh, right. Yeah, it was good...'

I glance across the house, in the vague direction of our neighbour's house. 'Did you hire her?'

He ums for a second, as if confused about the question. 'She only wants part-time hours but her portfolio is excellent. I talked it over with one of the other managers and she's going to do a couple of days a week to see how it goes.'

'That's great!'

Freddie nods and then turns his phone towards me. There's a photo of a house on the screen. 'I've been looking at places a bit closer to the office,' he says.

The picture is of a house uncannily similar to the one in which we're sitting: two storeys, semi-detached, a garage at the side and a glimmer of green at the front.

'Why?' I ask.

His eyes flick to the window and then back to me. 'Can't you feel it here?'

'What?'

He shrugs: 'I don't know... something doesn't feel right.'

The thing is, as mad as it sounds, I almost know what he's talking about. I felt something a bit *off* when I stepped out of the car four days ago. That twinge of being out of place and, perhaps, out of our depth. I couldn't quite describe it then but figured it was a class thing. We're renters of a small flat, not owners of a big house. It doesn't make sense.

'We've literally just moved in,' I say. 'We've not even unpacked.'

There's a glimpse of a frown on his face, as if pointing out that I've been home the entire day, not finishing the unpacking. Or that's what I tell myself. I spent part of the morning re-checking my emails, searching for jobs, sending new emails, going down wormholes on LinkedIn, that only made me feel worse. I'm getting nowhere with my job hunting and it's hard not to wonder if the problem is me.

Not that Freddie says any of that – he's too focused on wanting to move. 'If we've not unpacked, that's why it's good to be thinking about this sort of thing.'

I look to him, wondering if it's a joke. The firm stare makes it clear it isn't.

'Is there something else going on?' I ask.

'Like what?'

'I don't know...'

I glance across the road towards Willow's house. We both know there's something odd there. Freddie is *so* determined to avoid any talk of their time at school that I'm not sure what to make of it. I think Willow feels it too. I wonder if they had a fling when they were teenagers. It's not that I'd care – we've all been young – but I don't know why he'd be so reluctant to mention it. It wouldn't be a problem.

'I don't want to move again,' I say, firmly now. 'It was enough planning and effort to get here.'

'That's because it was a distance. We'd only be going across town.'

'Precisely – so why bother?'

Freddie opens his mouth, then closes it again. What can he say? He's accidentally made the point for not doing what he suggests. He slumps back in the sofa, chastened and annoyed at himself.

I think about what to say next, or whether to say anything at all. There was the initial weirdness over him locking his office, then those moments with Willow and his reaction to the talk about their lives at school. It's like I missed something.

'Is there something I should know?' I ask.

'Like what?'

'I don't know... things haven't seemed right since I got here.'

Freddie sighs and runs a hand through his hair. 'I'm just busy. There's so much on, plus new people. I don't want to mess up this job.'

I wait for a moment, wondering if there's more. Everything he's said is true. It's been a big change for both of us. I'm stressed from a lack of a job – but he's stressed because of a brand-new one.

I rest a hand on his knee and squeeze gently.

'Some of them are useless,' Freddie adds. 'They couldn't come up with a campaign to market walnuts to squirrels.'

I was going to ask him about Willow but it's hard not to laugh and the moment is lost.

'I'll figure it out,' he says, resting his head on my shoulder. 'I don't mean to be grumpy... just bear with me.' He pauses and then adds: 'And perhaps think about the other house – or *any* other house.'

I don't reply but it feels like this is an issue that won't be dropped any time soon.

'Was Alison pleased?' I ask.

Freddie lifts his head and shuffles back to the other side of the sofa. 'She seemed to be.'

'I think I'll go and congratulate her.'

I wonder if he's going to ask for more details of my own job hunting. I'd messaged him earlier but only to say I was trying. Freddie is already back on his phone, possibly searching for houses.

I put on my sandals and head out into the evening warmth. The sun is on its way down, cascading a glorious orangey-red across the horizon. I've not lived here for long – but a few days are enough to get a sense of the cars that are usually parked on the street. Because of this, I notice the battered brown vehicle parked haphazardly across the front of Dylan's drive, blocking him in. I wonder to whom it belongs and then catch myself. It's easy to see how people can become busybody neighbourhood-watch types in a place like this. These communities are one step away from the gossipy cliques of being back at school.

Ignoring the car and whatever's going on at Dylan's, I head along the street until I reach Alison's. I knock and there is, perhaps predictably, no answer. The bell gets a similar result, even though I can hear a definite scrabbling from inside. I think about letting it go but then head to the side window. I cup my hands to shield the glare, though there's little to see as the curtains are pulled. I try knocking on the glass anyway, before waiting at the front door, which isn't answered.

I should leave but there are already too many unanswered questions in my life and I know I won't. Instead, I edge around to the side of the house. Alison's place is the same as ours in terms of shape and layout. There is a wooden gate and fence but it only takes a little effort to hoist myself up and over. Depending on one's perspective, I either land on the other side as gracefully as a nimble kitten, or more of a drunken hippo.

There is a window on the side of the house next to the back door. Both lead into the kitchen and I creep along before peeking through the glass. I have to stop myself from yelping when I realise Alison is hiding in the far corner.

She's pressed against the wall, peeping around the doorframe towards the front of the house, presumably waiting to make sure I've gone. She's in comfy jogging bottoms and a vest, as if she's recently got home from a yoga class. I watch her for a few seconds until she turns slowly and notices me. Even through the closed window, I can hear her yelp of alarm. Alison pats her chest and there's a second in which I think she might keel over. As she takes a breath and composes herself, I give a friendly wave. She checks over her shoulder and then crosses to open the back door.

'The gate was open,' I say, nodding behind me, even though it's a lie.

Alison glances past and frowns a fraction. She's so different from the composed organiser who was so keen to tell me about the street party. Now, she's jumpy and nervous.

'Nobody was answering,' I add. 'But it sounded like someone was in and I was worried you might have been hurt and couldn't come to the door...'

It's not the best of reasoning – but also plausible.

There's a box on the table, which I think is the one Isabella was carrying the other day. The one that had the bunting supplies inside.

Alison straightens her clothes and again checks over her shoulder: 'I didn't hear the door,' she says.

It's an obvious lie but not worth pointing out. 'I wanted to say congratulations. Freddie said you were going to be doing a couple of days a week.'

'Right...'

She looks behind for a third time – and that's when a short, hunched East Asian woman appears. She does a double-take when she notices the back door is open and then shuffles into the kitchen.

'Who is it?' she says, looking at Alison, who sighs.

'This is Heidi,' Alison replies. 'She lives a few doors down.' After that, Alison steps to the side. 'This is my mother-in-law, Chen. She's staying with me for a *bit*.'

There's a definite emphasis on *bit*, as if this indeterminate length of time is certainly not Alison's choice.

Chen hobbles across the kitchen until she's only a step behind Alison. She eyes me up and down. 'Who are you?' she asks brusquely.

'Heidi.' I poke a thumb over my shoulder. 'I moved in a couple of doors down.'

Chen leans in and squints: 'You're like my chubby Alison. She could lose a bit of weight, too.'

I'm so stunned that I can't speak.

Without another word, Chen turns and totters away back through the door.

When I turn back to her, Alison is open-mouthed, eyes wide. I have no idea what to say but Alison is more alarmed than I am.

'I am *so* sorry,' she says. 'She's, um, from a different culture and, er...' Alison stops herself. 'Sorry, it's not that at all. It's not cultural and it's nothing to do with where she's from. I know loads of nice people from China and Hong Kong.' Alison checks her shoulder and then lowers her voice. 'She's just a cow.'

'Alison! Alison!'

Chen's sharp, snappy voice chimes from the room beyond and Alison's shoulders droop. She waves me into the kitchen and closes the back door. 'I'll be right back.'

I'm left leaning awkwardly on the worktop as Chen loudly scolds Alison in the other room. After a minute, Alison returns, offering a forced smile as she fills the kettle.

'Sorry about everything. Things aren't normally like this.' She indicates the kettle and then adds: 'Do you want something?'

'I only dropped round to say congratulations about the part-time job with Freddie.'

'Thank you.'

Alison is so different to the other times I've seen her. No longer is her chin high and back straight. She's somehow cowed and shorter. It's no wonder she doesn't answer the door. If I was living with such a monster, I wouldn't either. I feel bad for cheating my way inside, for dispelling the myth with which she's surrounded herself. To everyone else, Alison is strong and confident: here, alone with her mother-in-law, she's shy and embarrassed.

I take a step to the door but Alison snaps a pleading: 'Stay for a minute.'

When I turn, she's angled her head towards the living room, making sure we're not being eavesdropped upon.

'How long has she been here?' I ask softly.

Alison answers without turning back: 'About six weeks. She almost never goes out. Says she doesn't like the air here – what-ever that means.'

The kettle is bubbling away in the corner. I have no idea what to say but don't feel as if I can leave.

It takes me a while to come up with: 'How long is she here for?'

Alison shakes her head: 'Too long.'

'Is your husband due back any time soon?'

There's something close to a sigh. 'That depends on how long a piece of string might be...'

'Sorry...'

As the kettle clicks off, Alison turns and shakes her head. 'Don't be. It's not your fault. I'm the one who should be sorry.'

She fills a teapot with hot water, a strainer and a small scoop of leaves, and then stacks a tray with the pot, a saucer and a cup. I'm left alone in the kitchen as she carries it into the living room. It's only been a few seconds when there's a bang and a yelp. Alison scampers back into the kitchen, grabs a cloth from the sink and disappears once more. When she finally returns, she leans on the fridge and closes her eyes. She seems shattered.

'She refuses to eat anything she considers British,' Alison says. 'I know it's hard for her...'

'Looks like it's hard for you, too.'

A slight nod. 'Yes...'

'It'll be good for you to get back to work.'

Alison's eyes snap open. 'True. Thank you for that. You don't know how much it means.'

She's halfway through another word when Chen snaps her name from the other room.

'Thanks for coming over,' Alison says. 'We'll have to do coffee again some time.' She smiles weakly as Chen's calls continue. 'I've got to go.'

TWENTY-SEVEN

DYLAN

I nudge open Orla's door and it feels as if the world has stopped. There's a second, two... three... and her chest does not rise. I push further into her room, not worrying about the creaking door. I'm almost at my daughter's side when, finally, the sheets rise. I stand and watch her for a minute, maybe longer, counting the breaths in and out, watching as her grip tightens around Sheepy. She's taken the toy to bed most nights since we got it and I dread the day she stops.

If my daughter was disturbed by anything that happened downstairs, she's not showing it. It seems like she hasn't stirred.

Back downstairs and Gabe is leaning against the hallway mirror, bouncing on his heels as if on the start line for the 100 metres. He's panting short, sharp breaths, staring at the blood on the bottom step.

'What was that?' I say.

Gabe's eyes flicker towards me and then back to the blood. 'What?'

'You nearly beat the guy to death.'

There is a nonchalant shake of the head: 'Nah...'

'He stopped moving! I can't believe he managed to get up, walk out, and drive off.'

For me, there's relief. For Gabe, there's only a shrug. 'He'll be fine.'

I watch my neighbour, my... *friend?* but he's a stranger. I wonder if this side to him has always been there. Perhaps it has and I've somehow missed it, or maybe he's perfected how to hide it? As Gabe continues to huff breathlessly, there's a manic frenzy about him. A dangerous fury.

'You can't just... do that,' I say, stumbling over the words.

Gabe doesn't look up from the floor, though his shoulders tense. 'He came into your *home.*'

'I know.'

'Your *daughter* is upstairs.' I shiver as Gabe peers up and fixes me on the spot with his stare. 'He swung the first punch.'

'I know, but you—'

'You need to get yourself together, mate. What would've happened if I wasn't here?'

'I'm not saying—'

Gabe's eyes narrow as he cuts me off once more: 'Think of your missus. If I'd been there, maybe it wouldn't have happened.'

I'm open-mouthed as Gabe spins and marches along the hall, then out of the house without another word. He leaves the door open, allowing the warm breeze to drift up the stairs. I sit and stare at the blood and then turn sideways, towards the living room and the cabinet beyond, knowing what lies underneath. I can almost feel the grip of the pistol in my hand, my finger resting on the trigger. The only thing that stops me is knowing that Orla is upstairs, in bed, clutching Sheepy in her arms.

Think of your missus, Gabe said.

And I do. I think of Ciara and I think of our daughter. I have to do something to fix this. Except... what if it's already too late?

THE FUTURE

Police statement: Zachary Mendleton.

Officer: Thank you for coming in and confirming your details, Mr Mendleton. Could you tell me what you were doing during the week in question?

Zac: I was working at the football camp.

Officer: Could you explain a bit more about this camp?

Zac: It was for children from five years old up to fourteen. We ran it six days a week, with all the coaches taking different age groups. The idea was to run a tournament at the end of the six days – then we'd start again with a new group the following week.

Officer: Which age group were you in charge of?

Zac: The seven- to eight-year-olds.

Officer: Is it correct to say that boys and girls are allowed to play together at that age?

Zac: Right. It's fully mixed. We only divide by ability for certain things, so that the kids don't get disheartened. That's nothing to do with gender, though.

Officer: Could you tell us how you became familiar with Dylan Wilson?

Zac: His daughter was in my age group.

Officer: Can you remember her name?

Zac: Orla.

Officer: I believe the first day of the camp was Saturday. Is that correct?

Zac: Yes. The football week ran from Saturday to Thursday. Everyone was off Friday – and then back the next day.

Officer: Sounds like a lot of work.

Zac: I guess… but it's football, so…

[*Sound of laughing*]

Officer: Do you remember whether Orla Wilson came to the first day of camp on the Saturday?

Zac: She definitely did. They have to wear stickers with their names for that first day and hers is unusual. I learned it straight away.

Officer: Did you notice anything else unusual about her?

Zac: I don't think so. She fitted in OK. Not the best, not the worst. Like most of them.

Officer: When did you first come into contact with her father?

Zac: The Sunday. Orla had stopped running and, when I asked how she was doing, she said she had a stomach ache. I asked what she wanted to do and she said to call her dad.

Officer: Is that what you did?

Zac: Yes.

Officer: Then what happened?

Zac: He came and picked her up.

Officer: Did you actually meet him then?

Zac: Yes. I was waiting with her while one of the other coaches covered my pitch. Dylan – her dad – came and got her.

Officer: Did you talk?

Zac: Not much. He asked what happened, so I told him that Orla said she had a stomach ache. He said something about how she'd chosen to do football camp above other options.

Officer: Was there anything else?

Zac: I don't think so.

Officer: Was there any talk about a gun?

Zac: With who? Orla's dad? No. Why would there be?

Officer: When did you next see Dylan?

Zac: He came back on the Monday.

Officer: Isn't that normal?

Zac: I suppose – except Orla wasn't there. He came on his own.

Officer: He was at the football camp without his daughter?

Zac: Right.

Officer: Did he say why?

Zac: It was to tell me that Orla was still ill.

Officer: Did that strike you as odd?

Zac: Maybe. I didn't think about it too much.

Officer: Couldn't he have called to tell you or one of the other coaches?

Zac: I suppose – but I thought he probably lived in the area.

Officer: Did he stay long?

Zac: I did notice him on the bank next to the pitches watching the session for bit.

Officer: What did you think of that?

Zac: Not much, I suppose. I don't think he was there for long.

Officer: Did he say anything else about why she was missing camp?

Zac: Not really. I got the sense she was unhappy about something.

Officer: What gave you that impression?

Zac: The way Dylan asked if there had been problems. He didn't seem clear about what.

Officer: What happened after you spoke to him on the bank?

Zac: Break time was only a few minutes after that. By the time I looked back up to the bank, he'd left. I assumed he had gone home.

Officer: Did you hear or see him after that?

Zac: No.

Officer: But something else happened during that break time, didn't it...?

[*Inaudible*]

Zac: I didn't see anything. I was supervising the kids who'd brought food.

Officer: But you must've known something happened...?

Zac: Only in the sense that some of the kids were talking afterwards.

Officer: What were they saying?

Zac: Something about an argument between parents in the car park. I asked the head coach but he'd not seen anything.

Officer: Was there any follow-up from the apparent argument?

Zac: Not that I know of. I got on with the second session.

Officer: Do you know who was in the argument?

Zac: I heard something about one of the kids, Alfie, arguing with an adult – but that was all.

Officer: Did any of the children mention whether they'd seen Orla's dad on the Tuesday?

Zac: Not that I heard.

Officer: And did anyone, at any point, say anything about a gun?

Zac: I don't think so. I mean, no. It wasn't like that.

Officer: How did Mr Wilson seem when you spoke to him on the bank?

Zac: Normal, I guess. I don't know what to say.

Officer: Did he seem particularly happy? Or angry? Upset?

Zac: Just normal.

Officer: Did many other adults come and watch the training sessions when their children weren't involved?

Zac: I don't know. There were always adults on the bank I didn't recognise – but there were loads of age groups and I was only in charge of one. I can't say.

Officer: Did you see Mr Wilson there on the Wednesday?

Zac: Not that I remember.

Officer: Could he have been away from the pitches, perhaps in the car park?

Zac: If he was, I didn't see him.

[*Inaudible*]

Officer: I think that's probably it but is there anything else you'd like to say?

Zac: No... well... it's just... I didn't know who Dylan was until after all this. I remember the story about him and what happened to his wife. It's got to mess you up, hasn't it?

Officer: Did Dylan Wilson seem messed up to you?

Zac: No, that's not what I mean. I'm just saying. You know? It's got to mess a person up. I'm not putting it very well. If anything, the opposite is true. He seemed really normal but, if it was me, I think *I'd* be messed up.

[*Inaudible*]

Officer: Thank you for coming in, Mr Mendleton.

TWENTY-EIGHT
WEDNESDAY

HEIDI

The digital clock reads 05:03 when Freddie hauls himself out of bed with a grunt. He heads off to the bathroom and then, just as I'm on the brink of dozing off again, he flushes the toilet. If that's not enough, there's a short pause and then he does it a second time.

I don't want to know.

He heads downstairs and there's the sound of the door as he enters his study.

I've been sleeping on this new mattress for five nights now and it doesn't feel right. It was as if our old bed in the flat had contorted itself to fit around me – but this is too stiff, too new. I turn over and shuffle deeper into the covers, then try a second pillow. I roll one way, then the other, then try on my front. Nothing makes any difference, so I get out my phone and realise Freddie has sent me half a dozen links to various houses around the area. I don't click any of them.

By the time the clock has moved to 06:41, Freddie is back out of his study and the smell of coffee is wafting through the house. There's no way I'm going to get back to sleep, so I slip into my dressing gown and head down, into the kitchen. Freddie is at the table, thumbing his phone while he drinks from a mug.

'Didn't wake you, did I?'

He gets his answer in the form of The Look.

'Sorry,' he adds quickly, suitably chastened. 'Did you get the links I sent?'

'I've not looked at them yet – but I don't understand why you're so desperate to move again. We've not been here a week yet.'

'It'd be nice to be a bit closer to the office.'

'But *I* might end up getting a job that's closer to here...'

My husband chews the inside of his mouth and nods shortly. 'We can talk again later.'

It's probably the dismissive way he's said it, as if there's no debate to be had, but it leaves me spoiling for an argument: 'Is it something to do with Willow?'

His brows crease: 'Why would it be?'

He replies so quickly that it ends up being an answer of its own.

'Because, ever since we ate with Willow and Gabe, things have felt different.'

'How?'

I watch him, not sure of the precise words. I can't think of a specific instance: it's more a sense.

'It's nothing to do with her,' he adds. 'I'd just like to be closer to the office.'

'Did something happen when you were both at school?'

Freddie doesn't move from the table but fixes me with a gaze of such intensity that it is as if I can feel myself shrinking. 'Like what?' he asks.

I can't look away but my mind is suddenly blank. 'How would I know? I'm asking you.'

'Ask *her*,' he says, voice rising. 'Go on – go over there now, knock on the door, and ask.'

'I believe you.'

'It doesn't sound like it.'

I don't know what to say next. Freddie lost his parents when he was young and was raised by his grandparents. It wasn't long before they were gone, too. I can see why his hometown holds little except bad memories, and that's probably why we never particularly got into his upbringing. When he told me about his parents and grandparents, I figured he'd say more if he wanted. It's not as if it mattered. Some people are open books; reciting every minor incident they've ever experienced. Others are quieter and more private. Freddie is the latter and that's fine. I'd rather that, compared to everything we ever do being plastered across Facebook.

Freddie's phone beeps and, after checking it, he crosses to the sink and tips away the remains of his coffee. 'I'm going in early,' he says.

I force away a sigh and manage an optimistic: 'See you later.'

We've barely seen each other since moving in.

I follow him out to the front of the house, only to see Alison waiting patiently at the end of the drive. She's a different person from the evening before, as if she has switched with a twin. She's dressed smartly in a tight skirt, top, and jacket. Her hair is back in that bun that comes with a free facelift. When she spots me, she waves with a waggle of all four fingers and a thumb, and then Freddie unlocks the car for her to get into the passenger side.

Freddie says 'see you later' and then gets behind the steering wheel. He mutters something inaudible and Alison throws her head back and laughs. Moments later, they're off the drive and down the road.

So much for 'part-time' if she's in at seven the day after an interview.

I should probably leave it there – but there's a twitch of a curtain from Alison's house. I wait and watch, and then, not long after, the front door opens. Alison's mother-in-law is there, dressed in what I first think is a spotted pink shower curtain. Chen is balancing on a walking stick with one hand, waving the other towards me, mumbling something I don't catch. It's only as she gets nearer that I realise she's wearing a faded red, ankle-length dressing gown. It's a horror show – somehow offensive to all five senses, even though I can only see it.

I'm not sure if I'm supposed to approach but Chen can hobble pretty quickly when she wants. It's like watching a startled crab as she scuttles along the pavement and continues onto our drive.

'You do this?' she says, aggressively.

'Do what?'

Alison's mother-in-law wafts the walking stick in the vague direction of the road: 'You do this?'

'I don't know what you mean.'

'You! You!'

Chen starts talking quickly in another language as I stare at her blankly. I hold my hands out, palms up, as if to say I don't know what she wants. At that she spits an audible 'bah!' and then turns and disappears back the way she came.

TWENTY-NINE

DYLAN

It's only when I notice the depth of the shavings on the garage floor that I realise I've planed far too much from the strip of wood. I've been on autopilot since last night and it was only the sleeping tablet that gave me any rest.

Orla chooses that moment to enter the garage from the side door that links to the house. My daughter already has a backpack together and her shoes on.

'What are you making?' she asks.

'It's supposed to be a table.'

'It doesn't *look* like a table.'

I hold up what should have been a leg, although it is now far too thin. I'm going to have to start again. 'What does every oak tree begin with?' I ask.

'An acorn.'

I waft the table leg around. 'And every table starts with a leg that's far too slim.' I put it down again. 'You don't have to stay at Lauren's overnight if you don't want...'

She hoists her backpack higher. I read somewhere that it's

good to start allowing children their independence at a young age. Let them make their own choices, although – sometimes – they might need to be guided towards a decision.

'It'll be fun at Lauren's,' she says. Neither of us brings up the idea of her returning to football camp.

'I'll go and wash my hands then.'

I leave her in the hall as I move through to the kitchen and squeeze some washing-up liquid onto my palms. Or try to. It's only as I grip the bottle that I realise I am shaking. It was twelve hours ago that Alfie's dad picked himself up from my hallway floor and ran back to his car. It simultaneously feels like an age and a blink away. I've been expecting a knock on the door ever since: the police, or... I don't know.

Something. *Someone.*

The water splashes up my arms, onto the front of my trousers as I curse under my breath, trying to get control of myself. I need to be better than this. I need to be better *for my daughter*.

I use the tea towel to dry my hands and clothes as best I can, then grab the car keys. Orla is on the bottom step, obliviously and innocently sitting atop the exact spot on which there was blood pooling last night.

She grins with mischief and intrigue: 'Are you ready for your *date*?'

I frown as we head outside and I lock the door.

'It's not a date,' I tell her as we slot into the truck. 'I'm meeting a friend. More to the point, where did you hear about "dates"?'

Orla smirks to herself. I know it will have come from something she watched. It's a staple of school dramas on TV, or in the movies. If she didn't see it herself, Lauren or one of her friends will have. There was talk of a primary school prom this year. It never happened but I suppose it's inevitable in the future. I remember myself at that age: all I wanted to do at any such formal occasion was go skidding on my knees.

'You don't have to be such a drama queen, Dad.'

'Where did you learn about drama queens?!'

She laughs to herself.

We had the talk about how, just because I was seeing a woman later, it doesn't mean she's a replacement for Orla's mother. I thought it was adult and honest. Turns out, my daughter finds the whole thing hilarious.

I don't get an answer because, as I'm about to start the engine, I spy Gabe in the rear-view mirror. He's standing at the bottom of the drive, about to head towards the house. I've only ever known him cross the fence between our properties, so this is new. He's wearing a suit and gives a small nod when he realises I've seen him.

I tell Orla to wait, then get out of the truck and close the door, meeting him at the back of the vehicle.

He holds his arms wide – no harm done and all that. 'Sorry about last night,' he says, not making eye contact. 'I got a bit carried away.'

I glare at him, replying through clenched teeth. 'My daughter was upstairs. You nearly kicked a bloke to death.'

Gabe checks both ways, making sure nobody can overhear. He doesn't have to worry about that – the pavement is clear.

'I know,' he says with a breathy sigh. 'I overreacted. I was worried about what he was going to do but that's not an excuse.'

I wait and he glances up.

'Have you heard from the police...?' he asks.

I let him stew for a second, knowing this is the reason he's here. 'Not yet,' I reply. 'But, if I do, I don't know what you expect me to tell them. That bloke didn't kick himself in the head.'

'No... I just thought, maybe he fell...?'

I stare at him again, not quite sure what to say. A part of me, maybe the biggest part, doesn't regret any of what happened. I know I let Gabe step around me when I could have stopped him. I saw that man on the ground and pictured his son bullying my daughter. It hadn't been that long before that I'd been riddled with such fury that I might have done something similar to that man's child.

But I'm trying to be the adult here. To be the reasonable one. There is a difference between us in that Gabe *did* kick that man while he was down. I merely *threatened* his son.

'I *am* sorry,' Gabe says, though it's hard to tell if he means it. 'It was a moment of madness. Can we agree that he slipped, though? He was inside your house without permission and you've got those varnished floors. He slipped and hit his head. We both saw it...'

It's hard not to sigh. I turn back to make sure Orla is still safely in the vehicle, which she is. 'What if there's a shoeprint on his neck?' I ask.

Gabe shrugs. There's no answer to that.

'I don't think you should come over again,' I say.

He nods acceptingly. 'Will you think about how he slipped?'

'He didn't slip.'

'Maybe he did?'

I don't reply and, eventually, Gabe takes the hint. He turns and slopes back to his own driveway, where he gets into his car. I assume he's going to be late for work and has been waiting for me.

The truth is, I don't know how to feel. If Gabe hadn't been there, I don't know what Alfie's father might have done. It's not the violence in itself that shocked me; it was the extent of it – and the way Gabe wouldn't stop. If it had been just them, not me, Gabe could have killed Alfie's father. Maybe he would have?

If I'm honest, I was frightened. I've never seen anything like that. I've had those revenge fantasies of what I might do if I was alone with Ciara's killer. It's only after seeing Gabe like he was that I realise I might not have it in me.

Back in the truck and my fingers are trembling on the steering wheel. I don't think Orla notices. She seems content to tell me about the plans she and Lauren have made for their overnight 'party'. From what I can tell, it largely involves Disney movies, dress-up and cookies. I tell myself to enjoy this while it lasts. It's not long that young people can be entertained with cartoons and sugar.

I drive her to Lauren's house and thank Theresa for taking Orla overnight. We go through the usual small talk – yes, everything's all right; yes, it's warm; no, I don't have any particular plans for the weekend – and then I'm off again.

I know I should head home but it's almost as if the truck is driving itself. Before I know it, I'm on my way up the drive towards the large car park at the back of the sports complex, next to the football camp. Orla should be here – but it's clear she doesn't want to come.

It's drop-off time, easier to be anonymous, so I pull into a space in the back corner of the car park and wait.

Alfie and his parents are easy to spot as they hang around the front of their brown Astra. Even from a distance, the bruises are clear on the face of Alfie's father. There's a cut angling away from one eye, which is surrounded by a thick panda rim. The other is covered by a bandage.

I wait until Alfie has set off towards the pitches and then hurry across towards them. I copy Gabe's pose from earlier, holding my arms wide, trying to show I'm no threat. It's only as I'm getting closer that I realise I don't know either of their names.

Alfie's mother spots me first. She points and says something I don't catch and then Alfie's dad spins.

'I want to say sorry,' I call.

A part of me wonders why I'm apologising. We're only here because their son was bullying my daughter – and then his father started swinging his fists. They should be saying sorry to me. To Orla.

I'm trying to be the adult.

Except they're not listening anyway. In a flash, they are back in the car. The engine starts and, by the time I get to where they were standing, they have already pulled away with a squeal of tyres. I hold my hand up, wanting them to stop – but the only thing I can see is my fingers shaking as I wonder whether I've just made things worse.

THIRTY

WILLOW

I'm finally feeling like I'm getting somewhere with my uni work when the doorbell rings. I'm not sure why considering he has a key but, for a second, I think it's Gabe. He inexplicably left late for work this morning. He claimed something about 'trying to give the other staff some responsibility', which would make sense except for the fact that he's *always* on time.

I stayed awake until almost two this morning, wondering if he was going to get out of bed and disappear. He didn't – and all that happened was that I've been trying to stop myself falling asleep all morning.

As I head into the hall to get the door, Isabella bounds down the stairs and launches herself forward to get there before me. If I'd known she was that fast, I'd have suggested athletics as a possible career.

The reason for her speed is quickly apparent as her boyfriend, Jarvis, slouches his way into the hall. I'm not one of those parents who automatically disapproves of their child's boy- or girlfriends but it *is* hard to take to Jarvis. He's a yawn in human form. The fact he's vertical always surprises me.

He grunts something akin to a 'hello' but he could be clearing his nose for all I know. I don't imagine him to be one of life's great conversationalists.

It's only when Isabella turns to have him follow her that I notice her eyes are ringed red, her cheeks puffy.

'Is something wrong?' I ask.

'I'm fine. Why are you always interfering?'

I'm about to protest her abruptness but it's nothing compared to the venom Isabella has for Jarvis. She turns and hisses a furious, 'come on' to him, before heading up the stairs. He nods blankly in my direction and then trails after her like a scolded puppy.

I stand at the bottom of the stairs, listening, and then edge up until I'm on the landing. I'm half expecting shouting but the reality is far more familiar than that. Isabella and I do the shouting – but her father and I, probably Gabe and I, too – do the hushed, hissed arguments.

I creep along the landing until I'm outside her door, trying to tune into their muted disagreement. The closed door obviously doesn't help.

When Isabella was young, her father and I would do this. Craig and I could begin and end an argument over the course of an hour while barely speaking a word out loud. There were two things we were good at together – the biggest one of which was fighting. Perhaps that was why Gabe felt so compelling at first? We would talk about our feelings and our days. But then, over time, we stopped. Does that mean it's me? I've seemingly done this twice.

I'm not quite sure how it happens. There might be the subtlest of realignments of the tectonic plates, or perhaps I simply can't stand still. Either way, the floorboard underneath me creaks and then the only sound from beyond Isabella's door is a stony silence. I have to think quickly, so begin humming to myself and then dash to the bathroom. I doubt Isabella's taken in but there's no way I'm going to be caught outside her door. The upshot of that is spending a couple of minutes sitting on the toilet, then running the tap and washing my hands far more loudly than any human would ever need to do.

By the time I'm back on the landing, the silence from Isabella's room is exemplary. The charade has been broken, so I head back downstairs, making a special point of hitting all the creaky parts just to let my daughter know I'm *definitely* not eavesdropping on her.

I wonder if she and Jarvis are breaking up. I have no idea what she sees in him anyway – plus it's not as if they spend every waking moment together. Perhaps she's decided to apply to university after all, and this is what they're arguing about? I can only hope.

At some point between later today and the beginning of the next ice age, I'll likely find out.

With whatever's going on upstairs, it's hard to concentrate on my work and, perhaps inevitably, I end up staring across the road once more, wondering about the enigma that is Freddie Potter. I wish I could understand why I'm so intrigued by him. Perhaps the only condolence is that it's not only me.

I phone Michelle, half-expecting her to be at work, which is why I'm slightly speechless when my friend actually answers.

'What's going on?' she asks. There's a clatter in the background.

'The usual: a stroppy teenager who's probably broken up with her boyfriend. I'll probably find out on TikTok if she has. You've got all this to come.'

'Don't even joke,' Michelle replies. 'He turns thirteen next month.'

'Good luck with that.'

There's a beat and then she adds: 'I take it you're calling about our mutual friend...?'

'In a not calling about him kind of way. We're weird, aren't we?'

Michelle laughs. 'At least it isn't just me. I keep wondering why I care.'

'Why *do* you care?'

'Probably the same reason you do.'

I would imagine she's right – except I'm not completely sure what it is.

'I've been trying to remember whether there was any big thing at school,' Michelle says.

'With Freddie?'

'In general with our year. Do you remember that girl who got pregnant? Nicole Somethingoranother...?'

'Didn't she end up in prison?'

'She nicked a load of money when she was working at the Post Office. I can't think of anything else that happened, though.'

'Some lad got suspended for bringing a can of Heineken into school but I don't remember much other than that.'

There's a mutual silence. There isn't anything I can think of that would make Freddie so hostile to the idea of acknowledging the school we went to. Can it really be about his parents' death?

'I'll ask around,' Michelle says.

'We should probably leave it,' I say, not meaning it. 'Don't make a big deal.'

I don't mean that either.

'I'm sly when I want to be,' Michelle replies. 'I'll ask without asking.' She waits to see if I'm going to stop her, then adds: 'Don't you want to find out why he's so against talking about school? Maybe he got secretly expelled? He could be one of those lads you read about who got seduced by a teacher – and then they run off together.'

'I doubt it.'

'You never know, though. He could be a secret arsonist? Or a drug dealer? There has to be some reason why he wants to forget.'

'Maybe we should let him...?'

Michelle is quiet for a moment and then says: 'I'm the new Poirot. I'm Miss Marple. I'll get to the bottom of this.'

Before I can reply, there's a bang from above and then an ever-approaching rumble until a Jarvis-shaped blur flashes past the living-room door frame. The front door clatters open and closed.

'Sorry, I've got to go,' I say. 'Teenager problems.'

I hang up and then make my way upstairs carefully. When I get to the landing, Isabella's door is partially open and she's hunting through her wardrobe.

'Everything OK?' I ask.

She turns to me and rolls her still-puffy eyes. 'Can you leave me alone?'

I hover in the doorway. 'I only want to help, Iz...'

My daughter turns away. 'I know, Mum. Just not now.'

THIRTY-ONE

DYLAN

The front door is grubbier than I remember. Flecks of dust and dirt have caught in the grouting around the rippled glass and the 'No doorstop sellers' sign is largely redundant given the state of the place. Even the Jehovah's Witnesses would take one look and think, 'No chance, pal.'

I knock and it's only a few seconds until the door is opened.

Tom seems so much older than he was when I last saw him. He's unshaven and greyer than I remember. I get the merest hint of peppermint but it's mainly whiskey as he holds the door open.

'Is it a year already?' Tom asks. He looks me up and down and then turns away. 'You wanna come in?'

'I don't have to.'

He pulls the door wider, until the handle is touching the wall inside. 'What kind of guy would I be if I sent you away?' he says.

I head into his hallway, trying to ignore the smell of stale marijuana and booze. I don't need to ask how he's been doing because it's largely self-evident. Instead, I follow the hall until I end up in a small, cramped kitchen. The stacked boxes of crisps and crates of pop make it look like he's just done a cash-and-carry run, while the sink is full of dishes. There are six toasters in a pile near the back door and five kettles on the counter. I take a seat at the table, though it feels cramped because of the drum of cooking oil that's there for no apparent reason.

'Wanna brew?' Tom asks.

'OK.'

The sound of the television seeps through from the living room but, in all the times I've visited, I've never ventured that far into the house.

Tom stands with his back to me as he sets the smallest of the kettles boiling. None of this clutter was here last time and, despite the smell of weed and booze, it's hard to know quite what's going on.

Tom rests with his palms on the countertop, head bowed, still facing away. 'I don't know what you want me to tell you that I haven't before,' he says.

'I think I need to hear it every now and then.'

Tom slumps a little further. 'What about me?' he says. 'What do you think I need?'

'I know. I'm sorry.'

We hang around each other in silence as the kettle boils. Tom puts milk and sugar into a pair of grubby-looking mugs and then pours in the water, before adding the teabag last. He places both mugs on the table, one either side of the oil drum, and then sits with his head in his hands.

'It was dusky,' he says. 'Sort of dark but not quite. It's like that in summer, isn't it? I'd been at the pub and there was football on. The Euros, I think. I was walking home, down past the junction where Franklin meets Edgley Street, near the station.'

He reaches onto the table and removes the teabag from his mug with his fingers, dropping it on the table.

'Is that it?' he asks.

'What then?' I reply.

He shakes his head and somehow manages to sink even lower in the chair. His head is almost between his knees. I think about telling him to stop, that I've heard enough, but I know I haven't. I need the rest.

'I heard some sort of noise,' Tom says. 'When I looked over, there was a bloke in a tin foil jacket.'

'Where?'

'In the shadows near the park entrance. He was by the gates. He must've seen me because he turned and ran off in the other direction.'

Tom peers up, neck craning as he waits for reassurance.

'That's it,' he adds. 'That's literally all I saw.'

'What about his face?'

'No.'

'Hair colour?'

'I don't remember. It was dark.'

'But you saw the jacket?'

'Yes.'

'I don't understand what you mean by "tin foil". Nobody wears tin foil.'

'He was. Honestly. I wouldn't say it if it wasn't true.'

Tom squeezes the bridge of his nose and returns to staring at the floor.

The park he speaks of is where Ciara was found. Nobody, least of all me, seems to know why she was there in the first place. Her train arrived and the park was in the opposite direction to our house. I would have met her but she said she'd get a taxi. The CCTV shows her walking past the cab rank until she disappears. Perhaps she was dragged into the park? Perhaps she went for a walk? I've resigned myself to never knowing the answer.

'I can't go back,' Tom says. 'I wish I hadn't been drinking but I had.'

'Have you been drinking today?'

A pause and then: 'Aye...'

I've not touched my tea and the bag has probably been in for too long now anyway. The water is a mucky brown – but that's not as filthy as the mug itself. There are green stains smeared along the outside where it says 'Welcome to Glasgow'.

'I can't make the police believe me,' Tom adds. 'All I can say is what I saw.'

We both know that's true. Why would they believe an alcoholic? Tom slept on the streets that night. His word is hardly confirmation and yet this is what I've been clinging to for three years. An alcoholic drug addict saw a man in a tin foil jacket and I've decided it's fact, even though the police insist it's not.

Tom finally lifts his head, pushing back into the chair and staring across to me. 'How long are you going to keep visiting?'

'I don't know.'

'I could call the police. Witness harassment, something like that.'

I eye the tea, thinking about trying it. 'I know,' I reply. 'It's not like I plan all this. Not like I *want* to keep coming back.'

We sit silently for a minute. *Minutes.* I don't know what to say and Tom would never ask me to leave. I could end up moving in and he'd not say a word.

'I know what I saw,' Tom says.

'I know you did.'

'I was pissed but I'm not blind.'

I push myself up from the table, ready to leave. I've heard enough – or enough for now. I might need to hear it again tomorrow, or the next day. Maybe the day after that, or next week? I once went six whole weeks without needing to visit Tom, to hear his side.

'I know,' I tell him. 'I believe you.'

THIRTY-TWO

HEIDI

There is something in Freddie's office that he didn't want me to see. I know that, even though there's no evidence. It's why the door was locked when I first got here – except he realised that couldn't continue long term.

It's only now, as I stand in the doorway of his study, that I wonder whether he had something to hide at our old flat.

If he did, there's no sign of it in here. A squash ball sits on the side, while the whiteboard still has the word 'Penguin?' written on it. There are some files and, as best I can tell, the same books as before. His laptop is on the chair, lid down and charging. I have checked this room every day since he left it unlocked, not sure what I'm looking for.

I wish I could explain why it matters but it's hard to dive deep into a feeling. Some call it gut instinct and maybe it's that. I've known Freddie a long time – and I know, *really* know, that something about Willow and this house has him rattled.

I'm so certain the answer might be in this room.

It's as I'm staring at the whiteboard that my phone pings.

It's unexpected enough to make me jump as, for some reason, I think it might mean that Freddie is home.

It's not. There is a text from an unknown number:

Hi. It's Iz from over the road. Can I come over?

It takes me a short while to realise that 'Iz' means Willow's daughter, 'Isabella'. I can only assume she got my number from her mother's phone because I didn't give it to her.

Of course. I'm in now. I'll be out back.

I'm not actually sure why I tell her to go around the back but I get the sense that, whatever's going on, it is a conversation of which she doesn't want her mother to be aware.

I head through the side door, out to the garden and then wait in the centre of the lawn. Everything is overgrown, with weeds from the flowerbeds growing into the grass. When we were in the process of moving, Freddie said he would sort it – but I can't see it happening now, not with work as busy as he says. I could do it myself – but the lawnmower never made it down with us.

There is a creak from the gate and then Isabella appears. Despite the heat, she is largely covered up in a kaftan-type dress. It would look ridiculous on me but, somehow, it's perfect for her. I was never as confident or self-knowing when I was her age. I was self-*aware*, of course – but had little concept of what made me happy, or what I wanted.

There is a flush around Isabella's eyes and cheeks from where she's been crying.

'What's wrong?' I ask.

She bites her lip, not wanting to say, so I figure we can start with something else.

'How did the bunting go?' I ask instead.

The teenager blinks with surprise at the question. She smiles gently. 'Good, I think. I gave Alison back her box. She seemed happy with everything.'

'Did you make a video?'

A nod.

'And did it come out as you hoped?'

'I think so. I've not posted it yet. I was going to wait 'til after Saturday, so I can show how it looks on the day.'

Isabella bites her lip again, then checks both ways, making sure there's nobody near either of the fences that border the house.

'If I tell you something, does that mean you'll tell my mum?' Her voice is croaky and soft.

It's not what I expected and I stumble over my words until I eventually manage: 'Well, no... I mean, it depends what it is.'

'Something personal.'

'I wouldn't necessarily say something but if you'd...' I lower my voice, 'killed someone, or something...' From the way Isabella reels away, it is immediately obvious that this is not what she meant. 'Sorry,' I add.

'I'm pregnant.'

I stare at her and there is a sudden, rushing sensation of having no idea what to say or do. Not only have I never been pregnant myself, but I've never had to give anyone advice about it.

'I *think* I am,' Isabella adds. 'I've done three tests. The first said pregnant; the second said no; the third didn't change colour at all – but I don't think I had enough wee by then.'

'Oh...'

'I'm a few days late.'

Isabella angles forward and, before I know it, I'm patting her on the back as she sobs onto my shoulder. It's a strange thing to realise but it's only now I notice that she's taller than me. Probably taller than her mum, too.

'I won't tell anyone you don't want me to,' I say, wondering if I'll regret it. It's a big ask to keep things from her mum.

Isabella continues to press herself into me for a few seconds more until she pulls away and wipes her eyes.

'Sorry,' she says.

'You don't need to say that to me.'

She nods solemnly and stares at her feet.

'If you are pregnant,' I say, 'you'll start to show sooner or later. You're going to have to tell your mum at some point.'

'I know...' She tails off and pats her eyes again. 'Can you come with me to the hospital? I don't really have any friends who are girls. I never have.'

I glance towards the gate, half hoping Willow will be there to take over. I am as out of my depth as the token politician on the first week of *Strictly*.

'I'll come if you want me to,' I find myself saying. 'But you probably *should* tell your mum. You don't *have* to...'

'I've got an appointment on Friday,' Isabella replies, which is when I realise she's already way ahead of me. 'It's at half-nine. Is that OK?'

I blink. What can I say? Like when a new mother shows a photo of her potato-faced newborn and says, 'Isn't he cute?' Only a complete psycho would say 'no'. She must be desperate if her over-the-road neighbour is the only person she can turn to.

'Of course I'll come,' I reply.

Isabella breathes out with relief. 'Thank you.'

'Do you know who the father is?' Probably the wrong question but it's a bit late now.

She quickly glances away and starts to scratch her shoulder.

'Sorry,' I add. 'That came out blunter than I meant.'

'It's my boyfriend's,' Isabella says, though she isn't asking him to go with her: she's asking me.

'Have you told him?'

'I went to do it earlier but it came out wrong. One minute I was talking about feeling tired, the next I said I wanted to break up. I don't know how it happened.'

'Do you want to break up with him?'

'No! It's all a bit of a mess.'

I end up stroking Isabella's arm as if she's some sort of rock from which I'm trying to get a crayon rubbing. I have no idea what I'm doing. It is these sorts of conversations that are literally the reason why having children isn't on my horizon.

'I wanted to tell him I might be pregnant,' Isabella adds, 'but, if I'm not, it might spoil everything.'

'I'll come with you on Friday,' I repeat. 'I won't tell your mum unless you want me to – but, really, have a think about telling her or your boyfriend. You don't have to – and I'll come with you regardless – but just think about it.'

Isabella nods along before a low 'I will' comes out as a breath.

I already know that she won't tell anyone except me and there's no point in pushing things further. I'm trying to figure out why it's me she's asked when she gives me the answer unprompted.

'I liked your advice,' she says. 'When you told me that I don't have to have my whole life figured out yet. I think I needed someone to say that.'

It did sound like good advice at the time but, when Isabella puts it into her own words, it sounds like I might have potentially wrecked her life. Sure, a seventeen-year-old doesn't have to have all the answers – but if she took my words to mean she can drift through the next ten years, then that's a definite mistake on my part.

'Mum doesn't get it,' Isabella adds, on a roll. 'She wants me to have this whole life plan. It's because she had me when she was nineteen. She thinks that if I go off to uni, or whatever, then I won't end up like her.' There's a momentary pause and then Isabella pats her abdomen. 'And look what I've done.'

'Not much. You?'

Beth grins: 'Not much.'

We laugh and then, without me noticing, she has shuffled a little closer.

'How do you know Willow?' I ask.

'We were volunteering at this sports day fundraiser for leukaemia research last summer. We ended up having to run the same event and got on well enough that we stayed in contact. We have the odd coffee and I hear about the trials and tribulations of raising a teenager.'

I think on that for a moment. I only know Willow from living next door to her. We nod and say hello but not much more.

'What did she tell you about me before we met?'

'Not much. You were her neighbour, a good dad, you're kinda normal.'

'Only kinda?'

'I'll take "kinda". What percentage of people do you think are non-psycho, non-creepy, non-weird, non-thick, non-Tory?'

'Fifty per cent?'

Beth snorts loudly: 'Ten per cent tops.'

'It's got to be higher than that.'

She shakes her head. 'No way. Have you ever *been* on Tinder?'

I haven't – and say as much.

Beth taps my knee momentarily, then motions towards the kitchen. 'Do you want something stronger to drink?'

It's early evening and, with my daughter staying at her friend's, I have no plans.

Beth and I agree on a bottle of white and then, when she's back, Beth is staring through the window, avoiding eye contact. 'I need to tell you something,' she says.

It sounds ominous and I find myself flashing back to the dark of the living room the other night, holding the gun to my

own head. About the visits to court and others to Tom, who says
he saw a man in a tin foil jacket. About how I grabbed that
bully, Alfie, and only stopped myself from hurting him because
there were adults. How I let Gabe slide around me and almost
kick a man to death.

There are things I should tell her, too. I don't know if I'm a
good person. I don't know whether I deserve to be happy.

Except I blink it all away.

'I googled you,' she says quickly. 'After we met and I knew
your full name, I looked you up.'

I don't reply at first. A big part of me expected as much.

'That tends to happen when I meet new people,' I say.

'Is that a problem?'

I give myself another second, considering the question.
'When Orla gets a bit older, this is the world she'll inherit.
Nothing's forgotten and everything lives on.'

This is something I've thought about a lot. I can live with
my name always being synonymous with my murdered wife.
Orla has got this to come. If she goes off to college, or university,
someone will type her name into a search engine – and there it
will be. Friends, boyfriends, work colleagues. Anyone who will
ever end up in her life will know what happened to her.

'Is it a problem *for you*?' I ask, almost hoping she says it is. I
don't know if I am worthy of a normal life.

'No,' she says firmly. 'It's not a problem. I did think about it.'

Beth stares off towards the window, lips pressed into one
another. At some point the record finished playing but I didn't
notice. Beth is at the other end of the sofa, hugging a pillow, and
the fizz of a few minutes before, when we were closer, seems
gone.

'You can ask whatever you want,' I tell her, sensing that's
what she wants.

The reply comes so quickly that it's clear this was on her
mind: 'How long were you with her?'

The image of Ciara floats into the front of my mind. There could be so many – the way my wife looked on our wedding day, her hair high; or when we first met and she was going through a phase of wearing black every day. Except the picture I get is as we left the hospital after Orla had been born. The nurses said we could go and we looked to one another cluelessly, wordlessly, as if to say, 'Is this all right? What do we do now?' There was no one to guide us then, no manual for what it all meant.

'We were together for almost ten years,' I say.

Beth takes a breath: 'That's a long time.'

'I know.'

'And since...?'

'Nobody... but it's not like I can just forget her.' I glance away. 'I wouldn't want to...'

I worry that we're done. That the few hours we've spent with one another is a mirage of a life that I'll never have again.

I wait for Beth to speak but she doesn't – not until I turn to face her, when she nods.

'I won't pretend to do the whole, "I know how you feel"-thing, because I obviously don't,' she says. 'But I get that you'll never forget her. It would be far weirder if you did – and you know there's only ten per cent in the non-weird category.' She smiles humourlessly.

'Orla is only seven,' I say. 'There are a lot of years where she has to come first.'

It gets a nod: 'I know. That's how it should be.'

Beth shuffles closer, crossing the ocean of the sofa until our knees are touching. She is so near that I can see the gentle peppering of freckles across the tops of her cheeks. It's the first time I've noticed them.

'Perhaps we can see how it goes,' she says quietly. 'We don't have to go all-in and swap rings tomorrow, do we?'

'No...'

I sometimes wonder about the person I am now compared to the one I once was. Couples can fall out, with accusations of how one or both of them have changed – but that is surely what is supposed to happen? I'm so different to the person I was before. The old me would have never watched my neighbour almost kick a man to death. He'd have never grabbed a schoolkid and threatened him. I think something in me is broken and wonder if it will ever heal.

But then, from nowhere, Beth angles forward and kisses me very gently on the lips. There's barely any pressure and she instantly slides away and smiles slightly.

'Is that OK?' she asks.

I surprise myself: 'Yes.'

And it is.

Beth moves nearer, pressing harder this time. I push into her and then she's sitting on my lap. Her fingers skim through my hair until she touches my ear.

Except...

I'm on instinct, jolting from an electric fence. I find myself shuffling away and Beth can't disguise her look of confusion.

'Are you OK?' she asks.

I don't know what to tell her. Ciara used to touch me in the same way – and, in that moment, I am frozen by it. It's too soon.

'I'm sorry,' I say.

Beth shuffles from my lap back onto the sofa. 'It's OK...' she says, though I know it isn't. I sound mad and perhaps I am.

'I thought I was ready,' I say.

'You don't have to—'

'I think I'm going to go.'

THIRTY-FOUR

WILLOW

It's four minutes past midnight and Gabe has been out for more than an hour. He said work has been stressful and that he was going for a walk to clear his head. It was late – ridiculously so – but I didn't see the point in arguing. I could hardly demand he come to bed with me. We've never been a couple to check up on one another's every move.

It feels like he was caught out by Mum being here. If she'd not told me, I wouldn't have known about his apparent early-morning trip, or *trips*, out of the house. I wonder whether he's been creeping out for long, or if it's a recent thing? If it had been long term, wouldn't Isabella have noticed at some point? Or perhaps he only chooses the nights when she sleeps at Jarvis', or her father's?

So many questions.

Those are the simple questions.

The bigger ones are where he is and what he's doing. The walk to clear his head is plausible, except Gabe has never been one for exercise. If I asked to go with him, I have little doubt he'd say it was fine. I'd then end up trawling around a park, or some back streets, at midnight.

Perhaps he's telling the truth? Perhaps not.

It feels like he told me he was going out this time in case I had the urge to stay awake in an effort to catch him out.

He's unquestionably still annoyed at whatever he thinks I'm hiding from him about Freddie. He saw the unease between us and has read far too much into it. Bringing it up will probably mean another argument.

The door sounds at 12:09 and Gabe trots up the stairs, heading into the bathroom. There is the sound of running water and sink splashes that last for a good five minutes until there's silence. A couple of minutes later and the water is gushing once more.

Gabe has never been one for extended washes or soaks in the tub. He'll shower, plus brush his teeth and wash his hands – but it's a few minutes in and out. It's never fifteen minutes of solid time at the sink... until now.

It's hard to forget how he washed his own clothes unexpectedly the other day.

As I'm considering going to knock on the bathroom door to check on him, the water stops, the light clicks, and then Gabe creaks across the landing until he edges through the bedroom door.

He speaks in a hissed whisper: 'You awake?'

I'm on my side, eyes closed. I almost reply to say that I am but, for a reason of which I'm not entirely sure, I take a long, deep breath through my nose. I can sense my husband watching me from the end of the bed, so I hold it before slowly letting the air back out through my mouth.

'Willow?'

I take another breath, wondering how long we'll continue this charade. Was Gabe ever the right person for me? The right person to be a stepfather to Isabella? She's never called him

'Dad', not that either of us asked. He's been more of a mediator than a father but I don't think he wants that either.

Then there's the racism from the other night that I haven't forgotten. I didn't realise he was capable of saying something like he did. I've not brought it up since and don't feel able. I challenged him once and he laughed it off. Where do we go from there?

There are two truths and I'm worried that I know them both. The first is that Gabe and I are very different people, each incompatible with the other.

The second is that, back when we first split up, I saw Isabella's father, my ex, with his new girlfriend. She was gorgeous and smart – and I was embarrassed for not keeping up. I had to be with someone – *anyone* – because the alternative was to be alone. That led me to Gabe.

And, if that's the case, it means it's not him. It's me.

Which is more or less what Craig said the other day: my problem is that it's always about me.

THIRTY-FIVE

HEIDI

It's a little after midnight when the movement from across the road catches my eye. Willow's husband lets himself into their house and closes the door. I wonder why Gabe is getting in so late, especially as there is something about him I didn't warm to. I don't think I understand why he and Willow are together. During the dinner at theirs, they barely spoke or interacted with one another. Then he said that thing about Kenneth that embarrassed everyone but himself.

It doesn't seem like they have a lot in common. I know opposites are supposed to attract but is that really true? Freddie and I can have our moments of angst but...

I don't know where that thought finishes because, as I blink away from Gabe, something feels broken in my relationship, too.

Perhaps it *is* this house?

The bloke over the road had his wife murdered. The woman a couple of doors down is seemingly two different people, depending on whether her overbearing mother-in-law is around. Freddie could be right, after all: we should get out while we can.

After he got home from work, Freddie spent two hours by himself in his study. He said he had been distracted from his main project at the office and was now behind. When he went up to bed, he apologised with a yawn, and mumbled something about making it up to me at some point. I told him I was going to stay downstairs and read. An hour later and now I'm in Freddie's study, eyeing the whiteboard with 'Penguin?' still written on it. 'Hoody?' has been added underneath.

I suppose it doesn't seem as if there's anything out of the ordinary. There's every chance this is his creative process that I'm seeing for the first time proper. There was no home office in our flat to compare it with.

Which is probably why I'm not sure I understand my obsession with his space.

But I *am* obsessed. I think it was something about it being locked on the day I moved in.

I open Freddie's laptop lid but it asks for a password – and I wouldn't know where to start. I picture my husband, upstairs in bed, and wonder whether he'd be annoyed at me snooping through his things. How would I explain it?

Maybe I'm losing it? That's what scares me. The pressure of having no job, of not knowing how to spend my days, of moving away from our friends to this new place... it's taking a toll. I've had almost no contact with people we used to live near. Workmates were always that – colleagues, not friends. Covid broke something when it came to those relationships and I don't think I ever recovered. Moving has only made it worse.

And now I'm alone in a new place with a husband who would rather lock himself away than spend time with me.

I am about to leave Freddie's office when a final creeping idea takes hold. What if I'm not seeing something *because* I only

look in here when it's bright? I switch off the light and stand
momentarily in the dark.

It takes a short while to notice – but things *are* different.
The flashlight on my phone suddenly makes the big things – the
bookcase, the table – peripheral. It's the smaller, inconsequential items that catch the light. I realise Freddie has left his watch
on the bookcase when the strap reflects the beam. There's a
random CD case of an early Oasis album jammed onto the
shelf, between a stack of books. I don't think we own a CD
player any longer but it probably got caught up with everything
else in the move.

The two things are nothing by themselves but I'd missed
both when the room was fully lit.

I scan my phone from side to side, letting the light lick
across the surfaces, telling myself I've lost it but unable to stop.

But then, from nowhere, I notice the small slit in the middle
of the skirting board between Freddie's bookcase and table. It
would be normal if it was in a corner, where the boards join, but
this should be an unbroken strip of wood. I scan the light across
the opposite wall to check but there is no gap there.

I stare for a moment, wondering why it matters, why I care,
but then find myself cross-legged on the floor, phone propped
against the chair leg to angle the light. As soon as I run a finger
across the top of the board, it's clear that it's loose.

It only takes a gentle tug and it pops away from the wall,
revealing a series of Blu-tack blobs that were holding it on. It
reveals a gap of around thirty centimetres – and there can't be
much question that the wood has been sawn away deliberately
from the rest of the board. There are minuscule grains of
sawdust in the corner that haven't been fully vacuumed, so it
was recent.

There should be solid plaster, or brick, behind the space but
there's not. Someone has very deliberately carved a hole into the

partition. Tufts of insulation hang from where a lower portion has been sliced away.

It can't be an accident. This must have been something Freddie did last week. He'd not quite finished when I arrived, which is why the door was locked.

I'm not crazy.

At first, I can see nothing but a dark space, but, when I crouch even lower, ear pressed to the ground, the phone light catches a small, rectangular box that has been pushed deep into the crevice. It's the sort of metal lockbox often used by market traders or car boot sellers to store cash. Considering it's made of metal, it is light for what it is. There's a slight rattle from something inside – but it can't be coins or anything hard.

The box is locked and, when I shine the light into the recesses of the hidden space, there is no sign of a key.

I hold the lockbox for a while longer, weighing it in my hands, wondering what's inside and why it's hidden. Trying to think of where, or if, Freddie used to keep it in our old flat. Is it new?

After a minute or so, I return the box to the space and re-tack the board in place. It's late and it's dark. The search for the key can happen another time, especially as he's at work all day.

I let myself out of the study and creep upstairs. As I enter the bedroom, the light from the hall slips across the bed. Freddie is on his side, asleep. It's a little after one in the morning and I watch him for a few seconds. He breathes in deeply, holds it, and then gently huffs it out.

I moved here for him. Upended my life because he asked.

And yet, behind that study door, in a secret alcove, inside a locked box, my husband has his secrets. As I watch him sleep, it's impossible not to wonder how much of our relationship rests on whatever's inside.

THE FUTURE

Police statement: Jarvis Williams.

Officer: I know you're nervous, Jarvis, but I want to assure you there's nothing to worry about. This is perfectly normal. The duty solicitor is here for your benefit. I'm sure she's already told you that but nobody is trying to catch you out.

Jarvis: OK.

Officer: I'd like to ask you about your relationship with Isabella… um, what's her last name?

[*Inaudible*]

Jarvis: North. Her mum is Ellis but Iz is North, like her dad.

Officer: Right… yes, sorry about that. Isabella North. How do you know her?

Jarvis: I suppose we're going out.

Officer: You suppose?

Jarvis: She said she wanted to break up.

Officer: When was this?

Jarvis: The Wednesday, I think.

Officer: So, are you broken up…?

Jarvis: I don't know. She didn't invite me to the street party but I probably wouldn't have gone anyway.

Officer: Any particular reason?

Jarvis: It's not my thing. She knows that.

Officer: Did you hear anything from her between the time she said she wanted to break up on the Wednesday, and what happened on the Saturday?

[*Inaudible shuffling*]

Jarvis: —a few texts. She said we needed to talk but we didn't get further than that. I had stuff to do and so did she.

Officer: Do you know what she might have wanted to talk about?

Jarvis: I suppose about the break-up.

Officer: What about the break-up?

Jarvis: I don't know. You'd have to ask her.

Officer: She must have given some clue...?

[*Inaudible*]

Solicitor: I don't think you can expect Mr Williams to read the mind of his girlfriend. He told you what he knows – and indicated to me that he'd be perfectly happy to show you the messages he exchanged with Ms North. I've seen those messages and there's nothing he hasn't already told you.

[*Inaudible*]

Officer: Did Isabella seem particularly upset when you last saw her?

Jarvis: What do you think?

Officer: I'm asking you.

Jarvis: Well, she broke up with me.

Officer: And she was upset about it?

[*Inaudible*]

Solicitor: I think you can take that as a given, considering what Mr Williams has already told you.

Officer: What reason did Isabella give for the break-up?

Jarvis: I'm not sure.

Officer: She must have given some idea...?

Jarvis: Not really. She said it wasn't working and she needed time to think.

Officer: Think about what?

Jarvis: I don't know.

Officer: You must have some clue?

[*Inaudible*]

Solicitor: Can we move away from questions that are trying to second-guess the reasoning, or mindset, of Ms North? You can't expect Mr Williams to make blind guesses about a different person's thought processes. As you should be able to see, he is incredibly upset by what happened on Saturday. He is here of his own volition as a witness, not a suspect.

[*Inaudible*]

Officer: How long were you and Isabella North boyfriend and girlfriend?

Jarvis: Since Christmas, so, er…

Officer: About eight months…?

Jarvis: Yeah.

Officer: Did you have a good relationship in those eight months?

Jarvis: Think so.

Officer: What was Isabella like in that time?

Jarvis: How'd you mean?

Officer: Did you get on well? Did you argue much?

Jarvis: She argued with her mum all the time.

Officer: But not with you?

Jarvis: Not really. Little things.

Officer: Like what?

Jarvis: She makes TikToks. I was telling her to keep at it because she's good but she was thinking about listening to her mum and applying to uni.

Officer: You didn't want her to do that…?

Jarvis: No.

Officer: Why not?

Jarvis: Didn't want her to go away, I suppose.

Officer: You wanted her to stay with you, as opposed to apply to university…?

[*Inaudible. Sound of crying*]

Jarvis: Is she going to be OK?

Officer: I don't know.

Jarvis: Is everything they're saying true? About what happened? With the shooting and—

Officer: I don't know what you've heard, Jarvis – but I can't comment on what occurred. I'm sorry about that.

Jarvis: No, right... It's just...

Officer: What?

Jarvis: I don't think it can be true.

Officer: What can't be true?

Jarvis: She's just—

[*Inaudible. Sound of crying*]

Officer: Jarvis?

[*Inaudible. Sound of crying*]

Solicitor: I think we might have to leave it there. Do you want to come with me, Jarvis? There's a room down the hall we can go to.

[*Inaudible. Sound of crying*]

Officer: Interview terminated at 10:22 hours.

THIRTY-SIX
THURSDAY

HEIDI

Freddie is out the front door before Alison manages to knock or ring the bell. For someone who's 'part-time', she's now been at his office three days in a row. He holds the passenger door open for her and she does a strange curtsey before climbing in. When he gets into the driver's side, he says something that makes her laugh – and then he drives off and away again.

I should probably be jealous but this sort of flirting has never particularly bothered me. Some couples get together and somehow expect one another to stop being attracted to anyone ever again. The important thing isn't having those feelings, it is what we do with them.

With that, I see why my husband might have a crush on Alison. There's a degree of unavailability and mystery about her. I sense it, too. Is she the cowed woman living in fear of a domineering mother-in-law, or is she the powerhouse at the forefront of organising town-wide celebrations? Is she the career-less woman who can't get pregnant, or is she a semi-single woman whose husband is often away?

Alison *is* the barometer of this street, though. On the surface, there is a middle-class idealism but, below that, there are secrets.

Big ones.

Gabe is across the road at the same time, getting into his own car. He can't have slept much given the time he got in – a fact I know because I also did not sleep much. He notices me in the window and waves in a way that's part-dismissive yet part-friendly. So much of the interaction we have day-to-day is this type of barely concealed scorn. *Hey. I've noticed you – and I will offer the simplest gesture I can – but let's not actually talk to one another, yeah?*

I wave back and then Gabe drives off and away down the street, too.

With Freddie gone, I lock and bolt the front door, meaning he cannot get in, even with a key. I head into his study and remove the skirting board, before pulling out the lockbox once more. Among the fleeting glimpses of sleep last night, I dreamt about the box. It wasn't locked then, except, whenever I opened it, the vision would end and I'd not see what was inside.

The size of the hole means the key will be small. I'd have noticed if Freddie kept it with his others, so know he doesn't. I doubt he'd keep it separately on himself, as there'd be a chance of losing it. He wouldn't risk leaving it around the main part of the house to be discovered – especially when we *still* haven't fully unpacked.

All that means it is probably in this office somewhere.

I spend forty-five minutes wasting my time by searching through the pages of books and running my hands under shelves in case there's something taped there. There are needles in haystacks and there are small keys in slightly cluttered studies. That's if it's here at all.

I could smash open the box to see what's inside but there's no going back from that. If I were to buy a replacement box,

Freddie would realise as soon as his key doesn't work. I could simply take the box, re-fix the skirting board, lock the door and pretend I was never here. Freddie wouldn't know for certain I'd been in... although there would be no other rational explanation. We'd be left in a world of me pretending I don't know what was hidden in his study, while he's almost certain I do.

I would take that risk *if* I had some clue as to what's inside the box. It could be keepsakes from his parents or grandparents. Perhaps an old passport of theirs, something like that. How could I justify my actions then?

My other option, of course, is to simply ask Freddie what's going on.

I'm at a crossroads – but then I am at something of an advantage. That's the thing with not having a job: I can spend the entire day searching for a key.

And so the hunt continues.

THIRTY-SEVEN

DYLAN

It's a theft case at court today. Days like this are what make me feel as if I'm here only out of habit. There has to be something wrong in that I crave the serious stuff. Someone up on an assault charge is probably going to be violent... and perhaps the type to harm lone women who are out after dark. That's what I tell myself. I sit, watching a defendant's reactions and listening to their history. I find out where they live and wait to hear whether any of their habits involve late-night escapades close to the train station. I'm searching for specifics in a world of generalisations – but what else is there to do?

None of those things feel as true for someone who nicked a bit of money from the cash register at a late-night garage where they worked.

I've heard many things like that in the past couple of years. There's been good and bad cases, but my definition is different to others'. For me, domestic violence cases are the best. It's not because I revel in the details, it's because I see the darkness of those on trial. I watch these hawkishly, returning as often as I

can to stare at the heart of the people accused of beating and
battering those supposed to be closest to them. I wonder if
Ciara's killer is among them.

It takes a lot to beat a person to death. I suppose I never
realised that until after what happened to my wife.

After domestic violence, it is other cases with violence that I
look for. I know the difference between Grievous Bodily Harm,
Actual Bodily Harm, Section 39 Assaults – and the others. I
used to think the most serious violent cases would be the best –
but the opposite is true. The lunatics who end up on GBH
charges wouldn't have been able to beat Ciara to death and keep
quiet about it. It's the quiet ones who are up for stupid acts of
aggression who interest me. Someone throwing a pint glass in a
nightclub: yes, please. A bloke slapping a bus driver for missing
a stop: that's the one. Some fella punching a cyclist for existing:
he's my guy.

This is who I am and what I've become.

This is the person I couldn't reveal myself to be around
Beth. The person my daughter will never see. The me that
knows what is hidden under the cabinet in the living room.

My phone is on silent but I feel the gentle buzz from my
pocket and get that tingle. Orla is still with her friend. Something's happened to her and Lauren's mum is on the phone,
telling me I need to get there quickly.

I slip the phone from my pocket, holding it low so the judge
cannot see. I'd be booted out of the public gallery if she did.

It is not a call from Theresa, of course. Orla's fine. It's Beth:

Are you OK?

I read it quickly, then slide my phone back into my pocket.
Even if it was the time or place to reply, what could I say?

Beth and I had two dates – and the fact I'm here in my spare time is why I don't deserve somebody like her. How could I possibly explain this obsession?

Back in the courtroom, there's a sense that someone on the prosecution side might have shot me a look, so I focus back on what's going on below. The defendant is a bingo caller accused of stealing a weekend's takings from his employer. It's semi-familiar in the sense that the hall is close to the train station. I've spent so much time stalking that area in recent years that it would be impossible to miss.

I've seen football fans kicking off when results haven't gone their way; climate protestors blocking roads; stag and hen parties descending into chaos. I've been in pubs when fights break out or glasses are thrown. All of that is little compared to the rowdy hordes of old people who spew from the bingo hall at closing time. They're off their faces on cheap bitter and Werther's Originals. Mix that with an evening of narrowly missing out on winning something like a shower curtain, or an almost out-of-date six-pack of Quavers, and it's a toxic blend. They'd have Millwall fans running in the opposite direction.

The defendant is James Bernard Gallagher, who is 'more commonly known as Jimmy'. He shuffles from side to side in the dock and I figure the poor sod must've seen some sights. If he *did* steal the money, he's probably earned it. Given the number of rampaging pensioners over the years, he'll have post-traumatic stress.

Jimmy is short and seems permanently itchy. He tugs at his poorly fitting suit and reaches around to scratch his backside.

The basics of the case seem to be that he let himself into the hall one night in the early hours, raided the safe, and made off with the money. The CCTV had been disabled and the two sides are arguing over who had enough access to turn off the cameras.

It's not the sort of case from which I'll get much – but I

always feel uncomfortable about standing up midway through and walking out. I'm here too often to be that guy.

I'm biding my time when the prosecution lawyer says that the bingo hall's CCTV system was disabled at some point around the closing time of 11p.m. The final image is a still shot of Jimmy in the hallways, close to the control room.

I am so keen to leave, so oblivious, that I almost miss it.

The prosecution lawyer points to an enlarged screengrab and asks Jimmy: 'Is this you?' I nearly don't look.

Nearly.

But, when I do, the image is extraordinary. Jimmy is only visible from the side. He's pacing, not looking at the camera, though it isn't that which leaves me open-mouthed.

It's what Jimmy is wearing.

His bingo-caller's jacket is sparkling and extravagant. It's as shiny and silver as it is ridiculous. It glimmers, reflecting the lights from out of shot.

And on first glance, without knowing it's a jacket he wears to put on a show, I could have sworn it was made of foil.

THIRTY-EIGHT

HEIDI

I've been through every item of clothing in Freddie's wardrobe and there's no sign of the lockbox key. I've checked inner pockets, outer pockets, coat pockets, even those weird tiny pockets that jeans have on the front that are too small to fit anything. I've tried his drawers, in both senses of the word, then his socks. I peeped under the carpets and in our cupboards.

Nothing.

Spying on my husband has essentially become my full-time job – and I'm very bad at it.

It is into the afternoon when I find myself checking through the DVD cases, wondering why we kept so many appalling films – or bought them in the first place. I can't even remember the last time I watched any of them. I'm busy opening and closing the case for Adam Sandler's *Jack And Jill*, which I have mercifully never watched, and whose container definitely doesn't contain a lockbox key, when the doorbell goes.

It's almost a relief, a temporary release from this self-inflicted madness.

I get to the door just as the bell rings a second time. When I open it, there is an East Asian-looking man there. He's wearing rimless glasses and is in a smart suit. He seems out of place in the heat of the summer and it crosses my mind that he's definitely at the wrong house.

'Is Alison here?' he asks.

It's definitely my own prejudice – but his perfect English accent throws me.

'You must be Kenneth...?' I say, assuming he is Alison's husband, who has been abroad.

He stares back, not confirming or denying. Alison said she met her husband in Hong Kong and her mother-in-law is East Asian. If it *is* Kenneth, it's been a day since his mother came across, bafflingly claiming, 'You do this', while pointing a walking stick at me.

'Who are you?' I try again.

'Alison.'

For a second, I think he's telling me that Alison is his name. Then, I realise he's demanding to know where she is.

'I can't tell you anything unless I know who you are,' I say, trying to be as firm as I can.

The man stares back at me, blinks, then turns on his heels to head along the driveway. I call after him but he doesn't respond. Instead, he strides purposefully along the pavement, turns onto the path that leads to Alison's, and lets himself into the house. I stand watching, wondering if anyone else might emerge, though the street is otherwise quiet.

If it *was* Kenneth, then why didn't he say? Alison didn't seem to know when he might be back, saying something about the length of a piece of string.

Back inside and I return to my own insanity. There is no sign of a key in any of the DVD cases, nor the kitchen cabinets or drawers. Another hour passes.

In an effort to do something else, *anything*, I head out for a walk, following the towpath like I did with Alison. If anything, it's warmer today. A couple are busy mooring a canal boat, the wife bellowing at her husband for apparently not doing it right. It has to be a long holiday in such a confined space when people aren't getting on.

I trail towards the centre of town, past the row of cafés, bars and betting shops, then loop around, back towards Huntington Grove. The town is busy with weary parents traipsing along as their children race around. We're only a couple of weeks into the school holidays but the adults already look as if they're trapped in the trenches, waiting for the order to go over the top.

As I complete my route and arrive back outside the house, a taxi pulls up outside Alison's place. It mounts the kerb and then bumps back down because it goes without saying that the worst drivers are the ones who do it for a living. There is a slight delay, then the rear door bangs open and Alison appears. She's in the same office uniform as she was wearing earlier but there is a straight-backed urgency to her now.

She hurries towards her house as I call after her. There's a moment, barely a glimmer, in which she misses a step. She motions as if to turn but then continues moving. With a bang of the door, and without a glimpse over her shoulder, she's gone.

THIRTY-NINE

WILLOW

I sometimes wonder when 'coffee' started to become a thing. I don't think it was an activity people did when I was younger. My parents never went out for a caffeine hit. They never spoke to their friends about 'doing coffee', or visiting cafés. They went to the pub occasionally, but that was about it.

I'm looking for a mop of curls, when I spot Michelle sitting at a table outside Starbucks. My friend is scrolling on her phone and doesn't notice me until I'm almost over her. She jumps up and wraps her arms around me for a clammy, warm hug – and then sits back down. It's way too hot for all that.

'You found me then,' she says.

I take a seat opposite her on a scratchy metal chair that must have been designed for pain enthusiasts, or people who hate sitting down.

'It wasn't hard,' I say. 'Although I'm not sure how a motorway services can have *two* Starbucks.'

'They multiply,' she says. 'I was in London the other month

and they're everywhere. Take your eye off a Starbucks for a short while and two more will spring up on the same road.'

I laugh, let it sit, and then: 'How was your journey?'

'Lorry drivers trying to overtake other lorry drivers while doing the exact same speed and taking up all three lanes. Pretty much normal. You?'

'The same.'

We're at a service station that is roughly in the middle of High Kingsley and Marsh Vale. It is as grim as every other similar place I've ever visited. A mix of barely awake truckers on a break and kids who are desperate for a wee.

Michelle and I go through the routine that people do when they haven't seen one another in a while. She tells me I look 'fab', so I respond by letting her know that she's 'terrific' herself. I ask about her top, so she says she likes my sandals. If it wasn't for this type of stuff, I have no idea what human beings would ever go on about. Michelle is probably my oldest friend. We've known each other since we were kids – and we're still saying the same things.

'Do you want another drink?' I eventually ask.

'It's so expensive here,' Michelle replies. 'I was going to get a sandwich but I'd have to auction a kidney.'

'I've got a credit card.'

Michelle doesn't need a better invitation. I head to the counter and order some fruity slushy thing for Michelle, an iced latte for me – plus two scones. It costs somewhere in the region of the average UK worker's annual salary but I'll deal with that at another time.

Back at the table, I put down the tray and sit again.

Michelle wastes no time. My new neighbour has been on both of our minds for days: 'So... the mysterious Freddie...'

'I've been trying to think of why I'm so interested in him.'

'Me, too.'

'I think it's because it's so weird. A hundred miles away

from Marsh Vale – and Freddie ends up moving in opposite. It's such a coincidence.'

Michelle is nodding along. She tried to get me into true-crime podcasts six months ago. This is her thing. 'I have been asking around,' she says. I start to reply but she talks over me: 'Don't worry, I was stealthy. Like a talkative ninja.'

It's hard not to picture Freddie's anger – *'Have you been telling people about me?'* – but my curiosity wins out. I wouldn't have agreed to meet otherwise.

'What did you find out?' I ask.

'I went for a beer with one of the lads Freddie used to knock around with at school,' she says. 'All casual, like. Told him I was thinking about arranging a reunion and then we got to reminiscing.' She pauses and then adds: 'He remembers you.'

'What's his name?'

'Alistair Dale.'

I consider the name for a moment. 'I have no idea who that is.'

'He had an afro and used to eat Dairylea triangles every day.'

'Ohhhh... Cheese Boy. I didn't know his actual name.'

The image is clear now – the bewildering sight of a teenage lad nibbling one cheese triangle after another, day after day, for years.

'You should see him now,' Michelle says. 'Like a rake with legs. He's some sort of county athlete.'

'Cheese Boy?'

'I don't think he's into cheese any longer. Anyway, do you remember that school assembly where we found out Freddie's mum and dad had died in a crash?'

'I think it's the first time I properly knew who he was. What were we? Thirteen? Fourteen?'

'Something like that. What I didn't realise is that his

*grand*parents also died while we were in our final year of sixth form.'

It takes me a moment to take that in. After his mum and dad died, everyone knew Freddie was being raised by his grandparents. But then, before he was even a full adult, they had gone as well. It must have been terrible.

A twinge of guilt hits. It's obvious why he never wants to talk about the past.

'I don't remember that,' I say. 'I guess we *weren't* friends.'

Michelle raises an eyebrow ever so slightly, as if to say *I know*. 'Alistair said they were only a week or two from taking their A levels when Freddie's grandparents died within a week of each other. He reckons it was a mix of old age and exhaustion. That sort of thing.'

I think of Isabella, who has just got through her own exams and is at a similar time in her life. 'What happened then?'

'Alistair says Freddie took his exams, then went travelling.' She clicks her fingers. 'Like that. The day after the final test, he got on a plane. I couldn't find anyone who's heard from him since.'

It takes a moment for that to sink in: 'Nobody?'

'Not a soul. Definitely none of his old friends. After he left, he never got back in contact.'

I suppose it's not a total surprise. Marsh Vale must have held bad memories for Freddie, given everyone he knew died there. He probably did want to get away.

Michelle is still talking: 'Alistair said he tried to look him up on Friends Reunited, MySpace, Bebo, Twitter, Facebook. All of them. He couldn't find him, so left it at that.'

'You didn't tell him that—?'

Michelle shakes her head. 'I figured Freddie was our little secret.'

She cuts into her scone and then goes cream and jam, like a psychopath. I slice my own and add the jam *first*.

'Nobody has a bad word to say about him,' Michelle adds. 'Everyone was like, "Oh, yeah, I remember Freddie. Whatever happened to him?" I was trying to figure out if he'd done something bad at school, or around Marsh Vale. If he did, nobody seems to know about it.'

We sit quietly for a moment, partly because we're scoffing scones but also because, in these times of mobile phones and social media, it is genuinely unusual for someone to go off grid to such a degree.

But then, not everyone has to live their lives online and reveal each part of themselves. I constantly wish Isabella wasn't so open with everything and wonder if people from her generation will regret it all one day.

'Gabe is convinced there's something between Freddie and me,' I say.

Michelle more or less gulps down a mouthful of scone. We've known each other long enough that she replies with her mouth open: 'Why?'

'I guess because it was so awkward between us. Gabe figures it can only be that weird if we're hiding something. I can't convince him otherwise.'

I consider telling her about my husband's late-night disappearances but it's a lot to admit if there's nothing to it. I'm sure people *do* go for late walks to relax. There are far stranger habits.

Michelle thinks for a moment and then: 'What's he talking about? How can you prove that something *didn't* happen?'

I shake my head: 'I have no idea.'

FORTY

DYLAN

James 'Jimmy' Bernard Gallagher's defence seems to be that he either lost his key to the bingo hall's control room, or had it stolen. Whoever found it is the person that disabled the camera system, and subsequently stole the money. He claims he had no idea of how to turn off the CCTV, even if he had his key.

What I didn't realise is that he's on trial alongside a woman who worked in the office of the complex which contains the bingo hall.

I haven't moved from my seat in the public gallery since seeing the enlarged photo of Jimmy in his sparkly jacket. I've always been so focused on Tom's claim that he saw a man in a 'tin foil jacket' near where my wife was killed that I've not thought around it. Entertainers: Singers, magicians and, I suppose, bingo callers obviously wear outlandish clothes. By his own admission, Tom was drunk – so that sort of clothing could appear to be foil.

The cross-examination is not going well for Jimmy. It

doesn't help that he *looks* guilty. He never stops moving and is constantly tugging at his clothes and hair.

The debonair prosecution lawyer has the grace of a man who could do this sort of public speaking in his sleep. He wafts a hand towards Jimmy and says: 'You have an eye for the women, don't you, Mr Gallagher...?'

It's hard to suppress the shiver as I think of my wife, of Ciara, and what happened to her.

There's an objection from Jimmy's defence but the question is allowed. Jimmy's childish smirk makes it clear he wants to answer.

'Guilty as charged, your honour,' he replies impishly. From someone more charismatic, it *might* be charming. From a fidgety man in his fifties, it's creepy.

His response does not go down well, especially with his own defence. One of the women working for him puts a hand on her head, while the bloke at her side tries to get Jimmy's attention with a waved gesture that must mean, 'Stop talking!'

The judge adjourns for lunch shortly after that. Everyone files out and I hurry to catch the usher before he disappears. He gives me one of the court lists, which is where I find Jimmy's address. It only takes a few seconds on Google Maps to discover his house is five minutes' walk from where Ciara's body was found. It's another five minutes past that to the bingo hall.

My hand is trembling as I struggle to type Jimmy's name into the browser search bar. It turns out that James Bernard Gallagher – Jimmy – isn't simply a lowly bingo caller. He ran for the local council almost a decade ago with the bewildering slogan of 'GO BIG WITH JBG'.

There was a series of publicity stunts; one of which involved him abseiling from the roof of the local shopping centre without permission; another where he tried to long jump over the canal. He ended up getting rescued by an off-duty life-guard who happened to be passing. These would be odd occurrences in any case but, for a man who would have been comfortably into his forties at the time, it is bizarre.

The circumstances around the election itself are also something of a curiosity. By the time polling day arrived, Jimmy was not on the ballot. He withdrew due to what he described as 'unfortunate personal issues'. It's only as I dive deeper into the article that the truth becomes clearer.

The hairs stand up on my arms as I read the quote from the political party Jimmy was supposed to be representing: 'Mr Gallagher is the subject of an indecent assault allegation and, until the investigation is complete, we do not feel it appropriate for him to stand in this election.'

My thumbs are again refusing to cooperate as I search clumsily for more information. All I can discover is a short update saying that the allegation would not be continuing to court due to 'lack of witness cooperation'. That could indicate many things – but it doesn't mean the accusations were false.

I think of Jimmy's smirk from the dock and try to remember if it came with the wink I now think it did. Does he have an eye for the ladies?

Guilty as charged, your honour.

I've been visiting court week after week, hoping Ciara's killer would reveal themselves. A violent person isn't violent only once. But maybe it isn't the violence that's key – perhaps it's the attitude to women...

And Jimmy, with that smirk, lived so close to what happened to my wife.

I am the first person back in court after lunch, waiting in the public gallery for the parade of ushers, solicitors, judge, jurors and everyone else.

When Jimmy, JBG, or whatever he wants to be known as, finally reappears, I can barely take my eyes from him. The more I watch, the more I dislike. He has no attention span and is constantly smiling, as if this case is no big deal.

This is day two of the trial and it is almost at its end. If I had been here yesterday, I could have seen more.

The prosecution's summing up is straightforward. Only Jimmy had access and opportunity to enter the room where the cameras were disabled. He lived near enough to return in the early hours and let himself in, undetected. Even I can tell it's circumstantial.

The defence says Jimmy's keys were lost or stolen. He did not realise until after the burglary had occurred. How is he supposed to be able to prove what happened to his keys? He claims he didn't know the safe code and, though he was aware of the alarm code, didn't know how to disable the cameras.

Jimmy's biggest hindrance has been himself. If he's found guilty, it will be the smiles and fidgeting that does it. The defence lawyer seems to acknowledge this, although not explicitly.

'A person's conduct and demeanour should have no effect on a verdict,' he says, punctuating his words and leaving scattered pauses. 'In a court of law, facts and *only* facts are what matters. If Mr Gallagher stole the money, then where is it? He hasn't been on a spending spree, he hasn't paid off his house, he hasn't been on long foreign holidays. He's lived the same modest life he always has. If Mr Gallagher broke into the safe, then how? He didn't know the code. He's not some James Bond figure.'

There's a snigger from one of the jurors, which, I suspect was the desired result. Jimmy is in the dock and I'm not sure he realises this was a dig about his appearance.

'Mr Gallagher might not be perfect,' the lawyer continues. 'He might have personal foibles, like us all, but none of that means he is a thief. Proof is key and there is zero proof that he had anything to do with this burglary. *Zero.* A person is innocent until proven guilty *beyond all reasonable doubt*. In this case, there is far more than *reasonable* doubt – and, for that reason, I urge you to acquit.'

He takes his seat and nods momentarily to Jimmy as if to say, *That's the best I could do, pal.*

The jury is sent out and then Jimmy disappears outside with his defence team. I follow them and sit in the hallway, a bench length away, trying – and failing – to listen into their conversation. Jimmy can barely stop talking. I take a few photos of him on my phone, while pretending I'm reading an article. As he continues babbling, I eye the pictures, wondering if he truly is the person for which I've been searching. I always hoped I'd discover who killed my wife. Perhaps that hope has finally become belief? Perhaps the man in the foil jacket is real.

It's Jimmy the bingo caller?

Barely an hour has passed when everyone is called back into court. It is probably no surprise when the foreman announces the verdict is not guilty. Before any other words are uttered, Jimmy punches the air and bellows 'get in' as if his football team have scored. He is told to quieten down but the beam on his face is fixed. The prosecution seem comfortable with the defeat, as if they knew it was coming.

Afterwards, Jimmy hustles into the hallways once more with his solicitors. He shakes everyone's hands, though is repelled when he tries to hug the woman who is a part of the team. She pats him on the arm and shakes his hand instead. Her disdain is barely concealed.

There is no entourage outside. No family members with whom Jimmy can celebrate, no media to show any interest. He gallops down the stairs and turns towards the car park. I'm a few steps behind, seemingly drawn to his trail, unable to let it go. It's only as we pass through the gates into the car park itself that Jimmy notices me. He stops and turns, eyes narrowing as he realises I'm there and recognises me from the courtroom.

'You all right, mate?' he asks, curiously.

I picture the pistol underneath the cabinet in my living room and dream of pulling the trigger. No, not a dream. It's more than that: it's reality now.

'I'm fine,' I tell him flatly. 'Congratulations.'

Jimmy smiles, perhaps wondering if he knows me, then nods, before turning and heading off to his car.

'See you soon,' I whisper.

FORTY-ONE

HEIDI

Freddie calls a chirpy 'Hello' as he gets back into the house after work. I watch from the living room as my husband drops a duffel bag next to his study door and heads in to see me: 'Good day?' he asks.

I could tell him about the hours I spent looking through everything we own for a lockbox key I couldn't find, but don't.

'Not bad,' I tell him. 'I saw Alison getting out of a taxi earlier, though...'

This doesn't seem like news to him: 'I had quite the day,' he says. 'She quit.'

'Alison?'

'Right. No reason – completely out of the blue. She came into the office and said she couldn't be there any longer. I thought she meant she wasn't feeling well, something like that, but then she said she shouldn't have taken the job in the first place. Next thing, she's out the door, down the stairs and getting into a taxi. That was in the middle of the afternoon. I tried calling but she didn't answer.' He pauses and then adds: 'I was going to go over and ask if she's OK.'

'I wouldn't. Her husband's back – or, I think he is. A man knocked earlier asking after her. He refused to say who he was, so I didn't tell him. After that, he went back to Alison's house and let himself in.'

Freddie seems confused – so then I tell him about Chen, Alison's mother-in-law, wagging fingers and seeming annoyed. It's all a bit baffling.

'Do you think she called her son and told him to fly home?' Freddie asks.

'Maybe.'

'What do you think Alison's mother-in-law was annoyed about?'

'Possibly because Alison took the job. I don't know.'

Freddie bobs towards the front door and back again. 'I'll probably leave it,' he says. 'If her husband is home and kicking off, the last thing she wants is either of us getting involved.' He stops for a second and his gaze shoots momentarily towards the window and the street beyond before he adds: 'There's enough of that going on around here.'

We stand for a moment and I don't know what to add to that before he says: 'Did you get a chance to look at that house out by the school...?'

I don't bother to hide my sigh. 'I don't want to move so soon again, Freddie. Maybe in a year, or so? We've not even tried to fit in properly yet.'

He stares at me piercingly.

'*You* chose this house,' I remind him. 'I was happy with it but this is something you can't change your mind about on a whim.'

'It's not a whim.'

'So, what is it? Everything was fine until we met Willow.'

Freddie's shoulders tense and I know this is the truth. 'It's nothing to do with her,' he says, gaze flitting away from me, inadvertently admitting it *is* because of Willow. I wish I knew what had happened between them. It has to be something.

'I'm not moving,' I say. 'Not again.'

He stares for a moment longer but seemingly realises he won't change my mind.

'I've got work to do,' he says, with a huff.

He turns and picks up the duffel bag, then opens his study door.

'Where's the bag from?' I ask. It's only now I realise that he left the house without it this morning. 'I've not seen it before,' I add.

Freddie turns and blinks, surprised I've noticed, or said something: 'Freebies from a client,' he replies.

He stands tall, silently challenging me to push the issue. When I say nothing, he heads into the study and slams the door, leaving me alone in the house I insist I won't leave.

FORTY-TWO

DYLAN

My daughter is restless as I try to put her to bed. Theresa says the girls were allowed to stay up late the night before, which means Orla's routine has been broken. I can hardly blame Theresa, seeing as she looked after Orla for so long.

I try tucking her in but Orla has decided tonight that, after years of *wanting* to be wedged in by her sheets, she now wants the covers loose enough that she can wriggle her legs free.

I crouch at the side of the bed. It's too late to continue work on the Lego dinosaur tonight: 'Do you want a story?'

'What about the story of your date?' Orla says.

'It wasn't a *date*,' I say. 'And you're too young to know about dates.'

'Date-date-date-date-date-date-date.'

She arranges the repeated word into some sort of ditty that she either invented or I don't recognise.

'It was fine,' I say. 'But you don't need to worry because you're my number one and you always will be. Now... do you want a story?'

Orla wriggles against the covers again, until she's on her back. She closes her eyes and the shadows cast by the dim night light dance across her face.

'Two chapters,' she says.

'Are you sure you'll manage that much?'

'Two...'

I open the copy of *Prisoner of Azkaban*, which I've read to her twice already over the years. I'm no Stephen Fry, but give the voices a bash and watch as her lips twitch when she finds something funny. She is, as ever, asleep before the end of the first chapter. I allow myself to tail off and then sit to watch her. I want to tell her everything that happened today, except I know I won't. Of course I won't. She knows nothing of the foil jacket or the pure violence that took her mother. I just want her to know that she's safe.

I remain at my daughter's bedside for a couple more minutes, assuring myself she's asleep, and then head downstairs. I've spent much of my time this afternoon and evening reading and re-reading everything I can find about Jimmy from the bingo hall. Many of the articles are recycled from one another. I keep focusing in on the line: 'subject of an indecent assault allegation', looking for hidden meanings that aren't there.

Lack of witness cooperation...

I wish I could find out what that means. Victims of sexual assault are, obviously, granted anonymity. But that means I have no way of knowing who might have accused Jimmy – and what he supposedly did. It never reached court.

There is a gentle knock at the door and I assume it's Gabe. He had got into the habit of visiting at this time – except that I specifically told him not to.

When I answer it, I'm almost right.

'Hey,' Willow says. 'I don't suppose you've seen my husband, have you?'

She smiles hopefully. It looks like she has a lot on her mind.

'I don't think I've seen him all day,' I reply.

'Oh…' She glances past me, as if expecting her husband to be at the end of the hallway. I realise Gabe probably used me as an excuse when he's really disappeared elsewhere.

'Is there a problem?' I ask.

'Nope.'

She replies so quickly that she might as well have said 'Yes'.

Willow twitches nervously, then lowers her voice. 'Did something happen when he was here the other night?'

I'm not sure why her question takes me by surprise but I'm left blinking at her, lost for words. What should I say? *Your husband nearly beat a bloke to death while my daughter slept upstairs.*

'Not that I know of,' I reply, though there is a definite stumble. 'Why?'

Willow thinks on it, likely noticing my hesitation. 'He's been a bit distant since then,' she replies. 'It's probably work. I know he's busy.'

My neighbour hovers on the doorstep, apparently not sure what to do with herself. 'How did things go with Beth?' she asks.

I stare at her for a moment, needing the time to remember she set me up with her friend. Since today in court, I've been so focused on Jimmy the bingo caller that more or less everything else has escaped me. When Willow last asked about me and Beth, there was enthusiasm. This feels more like going through the motions. She seems distracted.

'Beth's great,' I say, which doesn't answer the question.

'She is,' Willow agrees, before taking a step backwards. 'If you see Gabe, can you ask him to call? Or just tell him to come home.'

'I can call him if you want…?'

'I've done that.'

'Maybe he'll answer if it's me…?'

Willow twists back, as if it never occurred to her. 'Maybe.'

She waits on the drive as I phone Gabe. There's a long pause and then nothing. 'It didn't even ring,' I say.

'Same for me.'

Willow edges back to the gap in the fence. She says thanks and then heads into her house. I'm about to turn to go inside myself when a woman's voice calls my name. When I twist back, Alison is hurrying along the path onto my drive.

'Only me from over the road,' she says cheerily. There's something different about her. Her smile feels forced – or more forced than usual.

I wait, wondering what she wants, and it's only as she gets closer that I notice the discolouration on her face. It's not quite a black eye but there's definitely something darker.

'Can I ask a favour?' she says.

I want to say 'no', to get back to researching Jimmy, but there is a certain etiquette to living in Huntington Grove. It's easier to go along with things.

'What do you need?' I ask.

'You know it's the street party on Saturday...?'

'Of course. Orla can't wait. She's invited one of her friends.'

'Excellent! It's just there's still quite a lot of things to pick up. Everyone's kind of been chipping in and you have a really big car...'

She tails off but the sideways glance to my truck says enough.

'I was wondering if you might collect a few things tomorrow?' Alison adds. 'It's mainly decorations – tablecloths, place mats – that sort of thing. There's lots and it's all too big for my car.'

I don't resent helping but, even if I did, Alison has a way of asking that's more of a telling. She likely figured this out weeks ago and it's only now I'm being let in on it.

'It should be fine,' I reply.

'Everything's at a party shop out near Poplar Place.' She hands me a business card. 'The details are on there.'

I check the card, which reads: 'Poplar Place Parties'. There's an address and a phone number.

'Any time after ten tomorrow,' Alison adds. 'I'll tell them you're coming. We don't need them until Saturday morning but, obviously, it's peace of mind if they're here...'

The bulldozer-like hint is impossible to miss. She wants them tomorrow.

'I'll sort it,' I say.

'Wonderful.'

She turns to leave but I call after her. 'What's up with your eye?'

Alison touches it self-consciously, then her eyelid starts to twitch.

'Hayfever,' she replies. 'I get it all the time. I've been rubbing my eye and now it's swollen.' She pauses, perhaps wondering if I'm going to question the obvious lie. When I don't, she turns and heads back across the road to her house.

It's only then I realise that her husband, Kenneth, is in the front window, watching. I give him a small wave that is unreturned, because he's already spun away. I hadn't realised he was back from Hong Kong, not that I was paying attention. It's not as if we're friends. I don't know if we've ever had a one-to-one conversation.

Back inside, and I sit in the living room searching for what turns out to be the same repeated information about Jimmy. Time and again I come back to the line about indecent assault. It's nothing but it's everything. Then there's Tom and his insistence over three years that he saw a man in a foil jacket.

A bingo caller's jacket...?

I'm distracted by a flicker of movement through the window. A blur of brown that was there, then not by the time I reached the glass.

Except I know what it was – or think I do.

A brown Astra...

I head upstairs to the top bedroom and look from one end of Huntington Grove to the other. There's no sign of any moving car, let alone the one that belongs to Alfie's parents. After the beating his father took in the hallway below, and the fact they wouldn't accept an apology, I've been half-expecting a return. Nothing good will occur if that brown Astra turns up outside the house again.

I stand a pace away from the upstairs window, out of sight from anyone below, but with a view of the street. The sun is on its way down as five minutes pass... ten... until I convince myself I was seeing things. It's been a long day and it's almost over.

Back downstairs, I close the curtains, then turn off the lights at the front of the house. All that's left is the orangey glow from the dim lamp at the back of the living room.

I've been craving this all day, removing the bottom drawer of the cabinet and reaching underneath, removing the gun. It feels heavier than the last time I held it – but then it always does. As if the mass grows the longer it is inactive.

I place the pistol on the table underneath the lamp and watch. There's a pull to lift it again, to hold it, to use it...

The gun remains on the table as I rush upstairs and change into jeans and a light hoody. I check Orla, watching for a few seconds as she breathes in and out softly, deep in the throes of sleep. It's very rare that she awakens before morning.

It's instinct now as I hurry downstairs, double-check the front door is locked, and then grab the pistol from the table. I bury it in the large pocket at the front of my top, then leave the house via the back door. I lock up and hoist myself over the fence into the alley at the back. There are too many nosy people watching the world through their front windows – but nobody will see me leaving this way.

I don't need to check where I'm going because the route is

burned into my mind. I've made it so many times that I wouldn't be surprised if I sleepwalked it one night.

It's dusky and the streetlights are starting to turn themselves on as I follow the back alley to the main road. From there, I trace the pavement towards the centre of High Kingsley, before darting into the lane at the back of the old Grey Goose pub. That becomes a flattened track which skirts the rear of the bus station and then I'm outside the park gates near the train station.

There is no memorial for Ciara here. It didn't feel right that she should be remembered by the place she died. She wouldn't have wanted it – and I know I didn't. In the weeks after her body was found in the flowerbeds, after the police had left, people avalanched the area with bouquets. I've still got the cards of condolence. Some wrote letters, many left small cards with 'so sorry' or 'RIP' and a signature. I didn't read them all.

I couldn't.

I only let Orla visit once. She wanted to come, even though I'm not sure she understood it all. I told her the flowers were from people who loved her mum and she took it at that. She didn't even cry.

I glance towards the flowerbeds and there's a blooming rose bush there now. If I were to close my eyes, I'd still see the mound of flowers but there's no time for that.

It's a few minutes more and I'm outside Jimmy's house. The nearest streetlight is a house width away, leaving a gloomy patch of darkness directly outside his. Even in that light, I can see the stencilled JBG on the front door. I have no idea why he figures his initials are such a brand. At least I know I've got the right place.

Jimmy is there. His curtains are open and he's in the living room across from a television. It feels so brazen to watch him, so voyeuristic, and yet he's not bothered. Along the rest of the street, there are drawn blinds and curtains. I can't see a soul except for James Bernard Gallagher.

He swigs from a bottle and scratches his head, oblivious to the fact I'm at the end of his garden, swallowed by the shadows, watching him.

He laughs at something, throwing his head back like a cartoon figure. In many ways, he is.

I creep away from the garden onto the path, then towards his front door. The gun feels heavier in my pocket than before.

I take it out to check it, as if expecting it to have grown an extra barrel or something in that time. It hasn't, of course, yet my arm strains from the weight. I tell myself this is it. Now is the time and this is what I've waited for. All those days stalking the court have led to this. All those evenings alone in a darkened house with this gun.

This is what I wanted.

This is what Ciara would have wanted.

I ring the doorbell.

FORTY-THREE

HEIDI

Freddie and I have barely spoken since I made it clear I did not want to move again. He spent almost two hours in his study, then warmed himself up some soup. After that, we sat on our phones, at either end of the sofa, like opposing magnets. Then he said he was going to bed.

I wonder how long the silent treatment can continue. Will it be until I cave and agree to start looking at other houses? In many ways, all it's done is to confirm there is something not right about Freddie's relationship to Willow. I wondered at first if it was because she reminded him of his parents' death. But, if it's that, it might be a reason to avoid her, not a reason to move entirely.

Freddie uses the bathroom, then he's moving around the bedroom. I wait almost an hour for things to go silent before disappearing into his study. I close the door quietly and turn to see the mystery duffel bag he said came from a client. He's had freebies in the past and there would be no reason to disbelieve him, if not for the way he's been behaving – plus that hidden compartment I'm certain he cleared for himself, with the lockbox inside.

I wasted a whole day looking for the key.

Inside the bag is a pile of tat. There are keyrings, cheap wristbands, a flask, embossed paper bags and headed notepaper, all with the branding from some movie that must be coming out soon.

It's a relief in a way, because at least he's telling the truth about this. It has been a strange few days, an odd week. We didn't have these problems when we lived on top of one another in our flat.

A better job for him, more money, more space, this house... I wonder if we were trying to fix something that wasn't broken. Answer a question we hadn't asked.

But I wish I knew what there was between Willow and my husband. What is in his lockbox he has tried so hard to hide.

I shove the junk back into branded duffel bag and move it back to where it was. I'd been waiting for Freddie to go to bed so I could check up on him – and it was all for no reason.

I should follow him up, I know that, but there's the draw of that lockbox and what might be inside. Before I know it, I'm on my hands and knees, levering away the piece of skirting board, then hunching to reach for the box.

Except it isn't there.

No... it *is* – but something is in front of it. Something bigger.

I know what it is the moment I see the coffee ring on the front.

It's Willow's yearbook. Not just a copy of the yearbook, the actual one Freddie and I both handled the other night.

I remove it from the hidden space almost disbelievingly, wondering if she gave it to my husband. Except... I was there when she *offered* it and he turned it down. Did he change his mind? Why wouldn't either of them have said?

The other class photos Willow showed us are pressed inside

the book but it's been done hastily and one of them now has a large crease across the corner.

That's not the only odd thing. Willow's things are also in the secret alcove – her swimming certificates; a handwriting commendation; exam results.

She might have lent Freddie the yearbook and photos – but not the other items. There is no reason for him to have them.

I flick through the yearbook and look for Freddie's photo.

Freddie Potter: Here, there, everywhere

It doesn't sound like him, which I suppose is a testament of how much we've changed. The photo was taken more than half a lifetime ago.

I continue looking through the pages but am bemused by its presence in our house until I remember Willow asking something about an open window in her house. She didn't think anything had been burgled but was obviously concerned enough to ask. Freddie was supposed to have asked me about it but didn't.

When we went there for food, the windows were open because it was so hot. Our house is on the other side of the road and, though it's still warm, the sun sets in such a way that her side of the street gets the evening warmth. Perhaps a window was left open and Freddie... what? Broke in?

I wouldn't have believed him capable and yet...

When I peer up from the pages, there's a small key sitting on the ground, in the space, next to where the yearbook was sitting. It definitely wasn't there earlier and I almost turned the house upside down looking for it. It's as if it appeared from thin air, that I willed it into existence.

I already know it will fit and the key slots perfectly into the lockbox. I turn it and flip the lid.

There's only one thing inside: A small rectangle of card.

The words 'birth certificate' are written across the top and it's hard not to be disappointed when I see the name 'Andrew Westley'. I check the back but there's nothing else written there. That's all there is. I've never heard of Andrew Westley and the name means nothing. Whoever he is, he's around 18 months older than me.

It suddenly occurs to me that the box could have been in the house all along. Someone named Andrew Westley lived here and his birth certificate was left behind. It doesn't explain the key – but Freddie could have found it lying around the study. Maybe he found the hidden compartment and figured he would use it as well for the yearbook. This great conspiracy I've created is nothing of the sort?

I go to re-lock the box but stop myself long enough to take a photo on my phone of the birth certificate. The flash goes off, which is only a surprise because I didn't expect it. In the moment it takes me to gasp, there is a creak from the stairs and I drop everything. There is a louder scrape and then silence. I hunch frozen, trying to think of an answer for when Freddie comes through the door to ask what I'm doing. I'll point to Willow's yearbook and ask what *he's* doing. It'll be the row to end them all.

...Except he doesn't come in. There is quiet from the hall and the stairs. I wait for a minute, maybe two, until I convince myself Freddie is not there. I stuff the lockbox and yearbook back into their hidden spot, then stick the skirting board in place.

Upstairs, Freddie is in bed, rolled on his side, an arm draped out of the covers. I whisper his name but there is no response. If he had answered, maybe I'd have asked about it all. Why is he so strange around Willow? Why does he have her yearbook? Does he know Andrew Westley? Did he break into Willow's house?

Except he's asleep, so I don't. And because I've missed the moment, I wonder if I ever will.

FORTY-FOUR

WILLOW

It's almost two in the morning when Gabe slides out of bed. My husband got home about ten minutes after I spoke to Dylan, telling me he'd been walking off some stress after a hard day at work. His phone battery was dead but he didn't realise until when he was back.

Dylan said that nothing had happened between them – but the fact Gabe hasn't been next door in two days is testament that it did. I'm surrounded by people who are lying. There's Gabe and whatever he's doing when he leaves the house; Dylan, who won't say why he and Gabe have fallen out; and Freddie over the road – who has any number of issues.

I keep my eyes closed as Gabe moves quietly around the room before creeping down the stairs. I strain to listen, wondering what he's doing, until there's a click and clunk of the front door.

In a flash, I'm out of bed and on my feet. I hurry downstairs, grab a big coat to go over my pyjamas, slide on some shoes, and head outside.

It feels like this is it. Perhaps I'm finally admitting to myself that Gabe and I are done and should probably have never been together in the first place. *This* – the late-night walks – is part of that. He doesn't trust me with Freddie.

And I definitely don't trust him.

It's dark but the night isn't particularly cold. I turn both ways, looking to see where Gabe has gone. There are no lights from within any of the houses on Huntington Grove and, at first, I think I've been too slow. It's only a flicker of movement from the end of the street that lets me know where he is.

I have to run to catch up, traipsing across people's lawns in an effort to stop myself making much noise. By the time I reach the corner, I'm sweating. The coat is thick, more suitable for cold winter days than calm summer nights.

It's hard to run at all, let alone silently – but, when I spot Gabe further up the street, I know I'm closer to him. I hurry once more, keeping my eyes up as he skirts another corner. By the time I get there, he's further on again.

We continue going through this routine until I dash around one more corner and almost collide with him. Gabe is standing outside the park, close to the war memorial. If he was paying any degree of attention, he would have seen me a few metres from him. Instead, he is staring at the memorial. It is a large dome-shaped structure, with pillars around the sides and a stone circle base.

I dip back behind the high hedge and peep around the side as Gabe crosses to the collection of homeless people in sleeping bags. A few seem to be sleeping but a couple of the men acknowledge Gabe by looking up to him. They exchange some words I can't hear and then, as abruptly as he approached them, Gabe strides away in the opposite direction.

I'm not sure what to do. I stand still for a moment, trying to figure out where my husband is headed. It's certainly not in the direction of our house. I continue to wait. My husband *could* simply be going for a walk. Apart from a brief word with a homeless man, that's all I've seen him do.

I consider heading home when a homeless man stands, shakes off his sleeping bag, and sets off in the same direction as Gabe. I follow as he walks away from the memorial, traces the line of a large warehouse, then cuts into an alley.

I hurry some more, crossing the road and following the building until I'm in the shadows of the alley. My first thought is to wonder whether Gabe is gay? He's never shown any inclination but wouldn't be the first. I almost don't want to peer around the corner, knowing what I might see – except, before I get there, there is a loud, echoing *thwack*.

When I reach the mouth of the alley, I am frozen. The homeless man is on his knees, a hand clutching his head, Gabe looming over him. My husband reels back with a closed fist and then throws a wild, booming punch. There is a resounding *crunch* as the homeless man falls to the side.

I want to shout, to stop this, but there are no words.

Gabe hunches over his victim and swings two more quick blows into the man's ribs. *Whump, whump!* It's only then that I finally find my voice.

'Stop!'

Gabe is on the brink of throwing another punch but stops and turns to look at me. His face is half hidden by the shadow but, even in the one eye I can see, there's something I've never witnessed before.

Rage.

Fury.

He stands taller and edges towards me. There's a metre or so between us. His fists are balled and there is a moment in which I wonder what he might do. Past him, the homeless man is crawling on the floor towards us. A series of £20 notes are on the ground near his feet.

'What's going on?' I ask.

Gabe is panting, eyeballs shooting from side to side: 'He tried to mug me.'

'Who?'

'Him.'

He points to the homeless man and I wonder if I've misread everything. I saw Gabe talking to the man at the memorial and then, a minute or two later, the homeless guy got up to follow. Perhaps he *did* try to mug Gabe? It makes sense... doesn't it?

The homeless guy is wearing a 'Frankie Say Relax' T-shirt and there are now browny-red stains across the front. Blood seeps from his nose.

'I'll call an ambulance,' I say.

'No,' Gabe replies.

'What do you mean "no"?'

The homeless man pushes himself onto his heels and rocks woozily from side to side. 'No,' he says.

There is a glance I don't quite understand between the two of them. Something like recognition, although I don't get how they can know one another.

'Are you all right?' I ask.

The homeless man nods and grunts something that might be 'Yeah'. He pushes back into a sitting position as his nose continues to stream blood.

'I'm going home,' Gabe says.

He steps past me, heading towards the end of the alley and rubbing his knuckles. 'Is this what you've been doing at night?' I ask.

'What?'

'Beating up homeless people...?'

He scowls. 'Why are you here?'

'I heard you leave the house. I was worried...' It's not the case – but it could be.

'You followed me.'

It's not a question – but I can hardly deny it's true.

'I was worried,' I repeat, faltering. I'm not sure how I'm the bad guy here.

'I'm sleeping on the sofa,' Gabe says. He's somehow made me feel as if it's my fault again but, this time, I know it isn't. Perhaps this is what it's always been like, although, until now, I didn't see it.

This time, it's not about me, it's about him.

Maybe he knows it as well because, without another word, my husband turns and heads for home.

THE FUTURE

Police statement: Aiden Styles.

Officer: Thank you for coming in, Mr Styles. Could you confirm for the recording your name and job?

Aiden: I'm Aiden Styles and I work as a court usher.

Officer: How long have you been an usher?

Aiden: Almost eleven years.

Officer: Thanks for that. Can I ask if you know this man?

[*Image shown of Dylan Wilson*]

Aiden: I do.

Officer: Who is it?

Aiden: That's Dylan. I think his last name is Wilson.

Officer: How do you know him?

Aiden: He visits the court.

Officer: What do you mean by 'visits'?

Aiden: He sits in the public gallery once or twice a week to watch the cases.

Officer: How long has he been doing this?

Aiden: A couple of years, I think? I couldn't say for sure.

Officer: Is there any timeframe of which you *can* be certain?

Aiden: It's definitely been two years. That would be the minimum. It might be closer to three.

Officer: Do you have any sort of relationship with Mr Wilson?

Aiden: How do you mean?

Officer: Are you friends? Do you spend any time together?

Aiden: Nothing like that. I only know him from court.

Officer: How did you find out his name?

[*Inaudible*]

Officer: I'm sorry. I didn't catch that. Can you repeat what you said?

Aiden: Is everything I say here confidential?

Officer: It depends what you say.

Aiden: It's just… well, I got his name from the sign-in log. I'm not sure if that's a big deal. My job is, um—

[*Inaudible*]

Aiden: —I don't want to lose it.

Officer: I can't make any promises, Mr Styles – but I don't think there are any issues with what you've told us. When you found out Dylan Wilson's name from the visitor log, what did you do with that?

Aiden: Googled him.

Officer: What did you see?

Aiden: I found out that his wife had been killed.

Officer: And what did you do with that information?

Aiden: What do you mean? I didn't do anything with it. I just found it interesting that his wife had been killed and then he was coming to court every week.

Officer: Why do you think he was doing that?

Aiden: I have no idea.

Officer: Did you ask him?

Aiden: I did. Recently, actually.

Officer: What did he say?

Aiden: He said he didn't know.

Officer: He didn't know why he was coming to court...?

Aiden: I can only tell you what he told me.

Officer: What do you think he meant by that?

Aiden: You'd have to ask him. I don't know. Going to court used to be entertainment, though. Before radio and TV – and even when I was a kid – people would go to court. I don't think it's *that* surprising. I'm surprised more people don't go. It's free and it's in the centre of town. If I didn't work there, and had free time, I'd go.

Officer: Fair enough. Tell me about the last time you saw Dylan Wilson.

Aiden: It was a week ago, give or take a day. He was watching a theft trial.

Officer: How do you know that?

Aiden: I pay attention to most people who come through the doors – but he was there so often that it would have been stranger if I didn't pick up on him.

Officer: What was happening in the theft trial?

Aiden: I think it was a guy who worked in a bingo hall who'd been accused of taking some money. I don't know for sure but could probably find out.

Officer: Did Dylan often focus on theft cases?

Aiden: It was mainly whatever the big trial of the day was. I don't think there was any particular pattern. It got to the point where I'd tell him what we had on.

Officer: Do you have this level of relationship with many other people?

Aiden: Not really – but then, aside from the legal staff, there weren't many faces I saw regularly. Perhaps a few defendants…

Officer: Would you say there was anything particularly noticeable about Dylan when you last saw him?

Aiden: I don't think so. It was like any other week.

Officer: Did he seem particularly distressed? Or upset? Happy?

Aiden: Not that I noticed.

Officer: Are you sure?

Aiden: I think so. He was there a couple of days that week. He seemed fine.

Officer: OK. I think I've got it. Is there anything else you want to add?

Aiden: Not really, well… maybe. I don't know if the rumours are true. I suppose it's just… how unlucky does one guy have to be? He loses his wife – and now this happens. Some people just can't get a break, can they?

FORTY-FIVE
FRIDAY

WILLOW

It's not long after five when I traipse down the stairs and stop in the doorway to see Gabe asleep on the sofa. I've never been able to sleep well on anything other than a proper bed – but he's in his underwear, dozing with no blanket or cover. There is an open can of lager on the floor next to his dangling hand. He is one of those who can sleep anywhere. One of life's great superpowers.

I head into the kitchen and put on the kettle, then return to the doorway and continue to watch my husband sleep. We've been together for four years, been living with one another for almost three. Our marriage is only fourteen months old and we should probably still be in the throes of our honeymoon period. Aside from our *actual* honeymoon – a week in Scotland – I'm not sure we've ever had that. Isabella is at such an important time in her life and I wanted to be there for her. Perhaps it's that, or maybe Gabe and I are not the people we thought we were.

The kettle bubbles, so I head back to the kitchen and fill a

French press with hot water and granules. By the time I get back to the living room, Gabe has rolled over. The whites of his eyes glimmer through the gloom and his voice is husky and lethargic: 'How long have you been watching?'

'Not long. Do you want a coffee?'

He pushes his way up into a sitting position and stretches tall. 'That'd be good.'

I pour two mugs, add milk to both, sugar to his, then join him in the living room. I take the chair he would usually have, while he has the sofa to himself.

'What happened last night?' I ask.

He doesn't answer at first, instead sipping the coffee and rubbing his eyes.

'I should be asking you,' he says, not looking at me. 'I went for a walk, almost got mugged, and then you were there.'

'It was after two in the morning.'

'Exactly.'

The sun is creeping around the curtains, chopping the living room into squares of darkness and light. We stare at each other through the glittering particles of dust that catch the brightness. We're both lying – and we both know it.

'Why did you get up and go out?' I ask.

'Couldn't sleep. Needed to clear my head. Why did you follow?'

It's a strange feeling when the world flips and you're left wondering whether you're in the wrong. Is this how soldiers feel sometimes? The stories of war are always told by the winners, so those victors automatically become the good guys. But, within that, there must be times those fighters wonder whether the other side has a point.

Darkness and light.

'You've been going out late a lot,' I say. 'There was blood on your hand the other day. A homeless guy was taken to hospital last weekend...'

Pam at the corner shop told me that, when I was there for milk. She asked if I'd heard the sirens and I hadn't thought much of it until last night.

Gabe stares: 'You think that was me?'

I turn away from my husband, not sure what to believe, not ready to say it out loud. Do couples come back from this sort of thing? I think Craig, Isabella's father, was right when he said I was a negative person. I make things about me and put down everyone on my radar.

'What about you?' Gabe says, eerily echoing my thoughts.

'What *about* me?'

'What's with you and Whatshisname over the road?'

I huff. We're back to this. 'I keep telling you – there's nothing with me and Freddie.'

'Come on – we all saw how he reacted when he was here. I'm not blind – there's something going on there. His missus saw it, too.'

I think of Heidi and wonder whether she saw the strangeness of her husband's reaction. Perhaps everyone did? I'm lying to myself, even if I don't know what's going on with him.

'There's nothing between us,' I say.

Gabe bats a dismissive hand in my direction: 'Why were you following me?'

It feels like a big moment in our relationship, perhaps the biggest. A watershed where our lives will change depending on what I say next. It also feels as if I'm ready for this, as if I want it.

I pick my words with clarity, knowing their impact. 'Because I don't trust you,' I say.

Gabe stares at me, but I am defiant in response. He might have already guessed I didn't trust him – but me saying it is another thing entirely.

'Perhaps you should look at yourself,' he says, a little

quieter. 'All the arguments with Iz. With Craig. Who's the constant in that?'

'This isn't about me.'

His lips curl into a sneer: 'People can't hide who they are,' he says.

It's a short sentence; poetic, perhaps. The sort of thing that gets pasted onto the photo of a cloud and then passed endlessly around Facebook. There's something about the way he says it that is like a physical blow.

When I don't reply, Gabe puts down the mug and strides past me towards the stairs. 'I guess that's that,' he says.

I sit in the chair staring into nothingness, wondering if this is how all my relationships will end. There was Craig and now Gabe. It's not as if my daughter and I have ever particularly been on great terms, either. Somehow, I alienate everyone in my life.

At least this one was deliberate, I suppose. I *don't* trust Gabe. I *don't* trust my husband.

The bathroom door bangs, then the shower starts. I finish my coffee, then down what's left in Gabe's mug before heading into the kitchen to make more. A few minutes pass and the shower stops. There's some shuffling, then Gabe clumps downstairs. I brace myself for him to come into the kitchen and say something devastating – but the silence is worse. The door sounds and, by the time I get to the front window, my husband is reversing the car off the drive.

It's as I'm watching the road that I notice Freddie appear from his own house opposite. He's also in a suit, clutching some sort of duffel bag. He checks his pockets and unlocks the car.

It feels like the night before, when I was on autopilot, acting without thinking. Perhaps that's my problem in all this – but, before I know what I'm doing, I'm across the road, standing in front of his car.

Freddie goggles through the windscreen but has little option other than to either run me over, or talk to me.

His window hums down and he calls: 'What are you doing?'

'I need a word.'

'I've got to get to work.'

'It'll only take a minute.'

He sighs and unclips his seatbelt. When he gets out of the car, he rebuttons his suit jacket and bears over me.

'What's your problem?' he asks, spitting the final word.

It's probably not right to blame my issues on Freddie. It's not as if the mutual mistrust between my husband and I has suddenly appeared because new people moved in.

But things have undoubtedly been worse since the meal last weekend. Everyone knows Freddie reacted oddly to me and there are only so many times I can say there's nothing between us. If I'm not that problem, it *has* to be him.

'I remembered something last night,' I say.

'What?'

'That time Alistair Dale climbed to the top of the science block roof.'

Freddie shrugs: 'You stopped me to say that?'

'Don't you remember? He refused to come down. He was protesting against that dinner lady who'd told him off for fighting. He reckoned the other kid hit him first. It went on for the whole afternoon and we all got sent home because they wouldn't let anyone in the science block.'

'So what? That was years ago.'

I pause, lips pressed together, but only for a moment: 'I just thought it was funny. Imagine if someone at work did that. An office worker goes up onto the roof, so everyone gets sent home...'

Freddie stares at me like I'm mad. Maybe I am?

'I need to go to work,' he says.

'Sorry to have kept you.'

I move out of the way and Freddie gets back into his car. He barely checks anything he's doing as he continues to stare at me while putting on his seatbelt. Moments later and he's pulling away. It's probably my imagination but, as he's driving off, I even think I see his eyes watching in the rear-view mirror.

I turn to his house, wondering if Heidi might be watching and what she might be thinking. There are things I should probably tell her – and I'd bet there are things she could tell me.

There's no one at the window and I take that as a sign that we should do this another day.

Back at my house, there is the sound of movement from upstairs. Isabella rarely moves before ten, so it's a surprise to hear the shower going again.

I stand in the hallway, alone, not knowing what to do with myself after the conversation with Freddie. There's university work, of course – there always is – but I have no chance of being able to concentrate. It's only as I get into the kitchen, craving more coffee, that I notice my purse and remember another curious thing about this week.

Someone took money from it.

It wasn't one of those middle-aged, absent-minded moments that are creeping into my life with alarming regularity. I know the cash was in there and, by the time I went to get some milk, it was gone. I blamed Isabella because that's what I do. Speak first, think last. But if I *had* been thinking, I'd have realised that she had no reason to steal. I'd *given* her money before that. If she wanted more, she would have asked.

I'm such a terrible mother.

I make more coffee and sit in the kitchen, partly feeling sorry for myself and partly wondering what to do when I next see Heidi from over the road.

When my daughter appears, she smiles thinly but Isabella is ashen-faced, eyelids heavy.

'Rough night?' I ask.

'Something like that.'

She pours herself some coffee, then sits at the opposite side of the table. It feels like she wants to say something, although I'm not sure how good I am at reading the signs any longer. Perhaps I never was and that's the problem.

'There were doors banging,' she says quietly.

'Gabe and I... had a disagreement.'

Isabella nods. It's nothing new, I guess – although it's usually me and her.

'Is there anything I can do for you?' I ask.

She squeezes her eyes closed and rubs them, then suppresses a yawn. 'No,' she replies. 'But thank you for asking.'

'Is everything all right with you and Jarvis...?'

I almost don't ask because I know this could be seen as prying, or sticking my nose in.

Not today, though. Isabella simply shakes her head. 'Not really,' she says. 'I've got to go out in a bit.'

'Do you need a lift somewhere?'

Another shake of the head: 'Not today.'

FORTY-SIX

HEIDI

Waiting rooms at doctor's offices have to be the most depressing places on earth. I realise there's a bit of first-world angst about that – there are plenty of countries in which it's hard to find a surgery – but, on the plus side, at least they're spared *this*.

I have no idea who designs the posters but it's basically a collage of everything that could go wrong with a person's body. One screams: 'Thyroid Problem?', which could be a name for a band. Another goes for the catchier: 'Do you have trouble urinating?' In case anyone is unsure what that is, there are yellow droplets along the length of the page. There is a giant picture of a condom with 'Contraception' written through the centre. The 'N' even narrows down to fit in the little tip at the end. I can only imagine the instructions given to the design company. *You know the tip at the end of a rubber johnny? Do you reckon you could fit the letter 'N' in there?*

Away from the posters, there's a general sense of malaise. Some bloke is coughing up a kidney in a corner; one woman keeps keeling over and groaning at the floor; there's a kid running up and down with tissue stuck to his shoe. The magazines on the rack are so old that one of them has a rumour about Michael Jackson getting married on the cover.

I'm trying to ignore it all by skimming around my phone, which is when I settle on the photo of Andrew Westley's birth certificate. I google the name and year of birth but everything is somewhat common. There's a guy with a law office in San Francisco; some singer-songwriter, which is probably shorthand for 'unemployed' – not that I can talk; a second lawyer; an author, and a teacher. It's only as I get into the deeper realms of the search that I stumble across a news story. Someone named Andrew Westley died on his gap year in Guatemala eighteen years ago. There are two hits for 'Andrew Westley Guatemala' – both of which come from newspaper websites linked to the Nottingham area. Details seem scant, although Andrew's age at his time of death would be close to the birth certificate.

There's a quote from someone named 'Zoe Swanson-Young', who is described as a 'backpacker' and says: 'It was such a shock. I only spoke to him the night before.'

That's more or less it.

Zoe is somewhat easier to find than Andrew and I would imagine having such an uncommon name can be a blessing and a curse. She works as a party planner and was recently highlighted in a *Sunday Telegraph* magazine feature. Her company name is listed and searching for that gives me a possible phone number.

Before I can do anything else, Isabella emerges from the corridor. I'm only just on my feet when she collapses into me, her chin cradling into the crook of my neck.

She can barely speak as she sobs silently. It takes a few seconds until she's composed enough to say, 'I'm not pregnant.'

I don't know what to say – I'm not sure if this is a good or bad thing – so I simply hold her until she's ready to pull away. Her tears have trickled onto my neck and underneath my top.

When she does step away, Isabella blows her nose long and loud into a tissue.

'Thank God,' she adds, which I guess answers the question about whether this is a good thing.

'Is there anything I can do?' I ask.

She shakes her head: 'Sorry for all this. I didn't mean to dump on you.'

I say that it's fine. I can understand the stranger thing. It's easier to thrust secrets on a person who isn't close.

We stand for a moment and, for the first time since we spoke on the street, there's a strand of awkwardness.

'Can you give me a lift home?' Isabella asks.

'Of course.'

'Maybe drop me around the corner from the house...?'

'If that's what you want.'

The journey back is completed in near silence. Isabella rests her head on the window and, when I glance sideways, I can see the slim smile on her face. We're nearly home when she says: 'Thank you for this.'

'It's not an issue – but you should think about telling your mum.'

She's quiet for a moment but then says: 'She has problems of her own.'

It's impossible not to be nosy. 'Like what?'

'I'm not sure. It's been weird all week.'

We reach the corner of Huntington Grove, out of sight from Willow's place, so I pull in. Isabella unclips her seatbelt and rests a hand on the door.

'Are you ever going to have kids?' she asks, out of the blue.

Sometimes blunt is the best way. We grow out of direct questions and instead go around in circles, never getting the answers we want. There's no malice in what she's asked, more interest.

'I don't know,' I say. 'We've never said "no". Sometimes it's

We're probably the same age but Zoe has some sort of ageless quality about her. She's in a suit but has perfect skin and long, braided hair. There's little more annoying than when someone is effortlessly alluring.

'Sorry I'm late,' Zoe says, motioning towards the bedlam behind us. 'One of the caterers pulled out this morning and I've been ringing around to get a replacement. Then there are only eight doves and there are supposed to be twelve. The breeder was trying to force pigeons on us.' She waves a hand. 'I don't know why I'm boring you with all this.'

'It looks like it's in hand,' I say.

'If you could tell that to the bride, it'd be much appreciated.'

I'm not sure if she's joking. But then Zoe steps towards the hotel entrance and tells me to follow. There are nerves as I trail half a pace behind. She's a busy woman, doing a busy job, at her busiest time – and yet she's stopped to talk to me. A person wouldn't do that for something small and inconsequential. This is what happens when someone's been brooding for years, for decades. When a niggling, dangerous thought has never quite left them.

Zoe leads me out the front and around the side. There are acres of plush grass, manicured flowerbeds and, with the blue sky and sun overhead, it's easy to see why people get married here.

We end up on a swinging loveseat in a shaded area next to a small pond. Zoe checks something on her phone but then swipes it away.

'There are koi in there,' she says, nodding at the pond.

'Fish?'

'I arranged a wedding last summer and one of the groomsmen got drunk and tried to grab them out of the water. Somehow, he ended up falling over and nearly drowned. The happy couple tried to sue the hotel. This is the first time I've been back.'

Zoe stares into the distance like a disappointed parent with a hyperactive child who's just been banned from the McDonald's PlayPlace.

'Anyway, I've not got long,' she says. 'So you're married to Freddie Potter. There's a name I've not heard in a long time.'

'How do you know him?' I ask.

'We were gap-year kids. You know the type. Travelling across countries, drinking whatever we could afford, trying the local drugs.' She stops and turns to me: 'This isn't news, is it?'

'I know he had a gap year.'

'I'm not saying we were addicts or anything but we dabbled, you know...?' Zoe adds.

'It's fine. It's not like I was an angel at that age.'

Zoe takes me in for a second and I wonder if the 'drugs' remark was some sort of test to see the type of person I am. She nods and then continues: 'We'd sleep on people's couches and stay up all night listening to Led Zep, talking about the meaning of life. We thought we knew everything. We were little dickheads, to be honest.' She sighs wistfully and breaks into a smile.

'I knew Freddie was on a gap year but not the specifics,' I say. 'He doesn't even drink now. He hasn't the whole time I've known him.'

Zoe nods along and I wonder if she's going to question why I'm here. I'm not sure what I'd say – but there's something about the way she chews on her bottom lip that makes it feel like she *knows* why I'm here. As if she sensed this moment would always come in the end.

'Freddie's never said much about Andrew,' I add, which is a bit of a gamble, considering I don't know anything about a connection between them, other than Freddie having his birth certificate.

Zoe doesn't flinch: 'I suppose he wouldn't, given what happened.'

She stops and fixes me with a stare.

'Do you *really* want to know?' she asks. Her eyes are deep and brown and say so much more than her words. She's been living with whatever this is for half a lifetime.

'I think I do.'

She waits a moment, giving me a chance to change my mind, and then continues: 'Andy and Freddie were really similar and yet also two very different characters. Sometimes, you'd think they were brothers; other times they were like two people who'd never met. Freddie was a computer geek but growing out of it. Andy was really quiet. The two of them had met up somewhere in Honduras, I think. I met them in El Salvador. I'd been travelling with a friend who had to fly home because her mum had been diagnosed with cancer. I was going to go with her back to Britain but then met Freddie and Andy in a bar the night before I was due to fly.'

Zoe glances off towards the pond and the hotel beyond. She tugs at her jacket and rubs her eye.

'I've not spoken about this out loud in so long,' she says.

'Sounds like you remember it well...?'

There's a wistful, thoughtful pause, and then: 'Not saying it doesn't mean I don't *think* about it.' Zoe turns away from the water and is suddenly in the moment once more: 'It was this grotty bar,' she says. 'I remember the smoke pooling around the ceiling and rows of spirit bottles on the back wall. If you slipped the bartender a US dollar, he'd hand out free drinks. I was in there with Freddie and Andy, thinking about going home, and then I realised that I didn't want to. What was I going to do in England? Get a job?'

She laughs to herself, at the absurdity of how things have changed since then. She now runs her own company.

'I asked if I could tag along with them,' she continues. 'I wanted to keep pushing against reality. I knew we'd have to go home one day and go to uni, or get a job, but I wasn't ready. The only thing was that they were so tight with one another. I didn't know if their duo would be as comfortable as a trio. Both of them had lost parents, so I think they found solace in each other. I had both my parents back at home. I'd sneak off to make calls and would end up writing postcards after it was dark because I didn't want to upset them.'

I can picture the scene of a young woman hastily scribbling a card by candlelight as her orphaned companions sleep. Freddie's lack of parents has always been a background to our relationship. I knew early on that there would be no trips home to meet his folks. It was one of those things. He didn't want to talk about it and I figured there was no point in me bringing it up over and over. What would it achieve? I can see how he would have been drawn to another young friend who'd lost his parents.

Zoe's story is cut off as a man in a shirt with rolled-up sleeves trots over. 'It's the fondue man,' he says.

'What about him?'

'He's got bronchitis.'

'Are you sure?'

'He's in hospital, apparently.'

'He better be.' Zoe smirks slightly and adds: 'I obviously don't mean that. You haven't told the bride, have you?'

The man shrinks away: 'I'm not going anywhere near her. She threatened to strangle the hairstylist earlier.'

Zoe sighs. 'I'll do it in a bit. I'll need to build up to it.'

'What about the fondue?'

'That is the most middle-class sentence I've ever heard. Either way, I'll deal with that, too.'

The man cannot hide his relief as he thanks Zoe, then disappears back to the front of the hotel.

Zoe checks her phone, taps out a quick message, and then turns back to me: 'This is a long way from those days in Central America,' she says. 'The me of then would definitely hate the me of now.'

'It looks like you're doing all right to me...'

Zoe blinks away the compliment. 'Everything was day to day back then. Hour to hour sometimes. We'd be chatting to someone in a bar or a hostel. Before we knew it, we'd be in the back of a car on the way to Belize, or wherever. I think there's a part of me that misses that.'

'The lack of structure?'

'Right. It's all work and bills and houses nowadays. It's nice, obviously. It's secure – but there was something fun about never having a plan.'

Zoe's phone buzzes and she glances at it before swiping away the message.

'I fancied Freddie a bit,' she says, turning to me. 'Nothing serious, just that sort of young person infatuation because we spent so much time together. He'd pay for everything. I think he inherited some money...'

She waits for confirmation.

'Something like that,' I reply.

'Andy let Freddie pay for everything, too, and I wondered how long it had been going on.'

'You did say they were different...?'

'Right but it wasn't only the money. Andy was a really bad drunk. Freddie would get happier and jokier but Andy would get loud and violent. Then he'd get through to the other side and end up crying, saying how sorry he was. He'd say he wasn't going to drink again and then he'd be back on it the next day. It was only Freddie who was able to control him.'

'What did Andy get up to?'

'There were a couple of times where, if it wasn't for Freddie, Andy would've probably been arrested or beaten up. Freddie had that calming thing going for him. He could sweet-talk bar owners, or locals – plus Andy as well, of course.'

I think of the birth certificate in the lockbox belonging to the drunken friend whom my husband constantly had to calm.

'How long did you travel with them?' I ask.

'Maybe a month? Five weeks? Six? It felt like a long time but I don't think it was. Everything was really intense. We'd spend day after day together. You know how sometimes a week can fly by but, other times, it's like a year in itself.'

'Did you come back to England together?'

Zoe turns away, back towards the pond. 'No...' She takes a breath and checks her phone again. 'There was a fire...'

There's quiet for a moment; only the sound of birds chirping on the other side of the water.

'At the hostel,' she adds. 'Well, sort of. It wasn't an official hostel. It was more of a back room in someone's house. This was before Airbnb, Tripadvisor, all that. It was illegal but we knew that. We stayed there because it was cheap. We were in Guatemala by this point and had been at the market. We got chatting to one of the stallholders and must've mentioned that we didn't know where we were sleeping. He showed us this room. I didn't want to sleep there but the boys did. We stayed up drinking and smoking, then I went off to the *actual* hostel. It was more money but I had bad vibes about that place.'

It's probably my imagination but it feels as if the temperature has dropped by a degree or two. The birds have stopped bleating.

'I went to see them the next morning,' Zoe says. 'Only the building wasn't there. The air smelled like it does after a bonfire, when that smoke catches in your lungs. One of the walls was scorched black and I remember this huge hole where the windows used to be. I was looking for Freddie and Andy but the stallholder from the day before was telling me to go. He kept saying how he'd never rented the space to the boys; trying to pretend it hadn't happened. I spent the day going around the streets looking for them both. I thought they'd be in the market, or there was this little café we used to go to smoke. They weren't anywhere and my Spanish wasn't good enough to ask around. We'd made some local friends that week but, all of a sudden, it was like they couldn't speak English anymore.'

Zoe stops and takes a bottle of water from her bag, from which she swigs.

'What happened?' I ask.

'Looking back, I think it was some sort of cover-up. There were a lot of these illegal hostels and hotels. When it started to get dark later in the day, I still didn't know what had happened to them. It was the next morning when a girl in the hostel said she'd heard that someone named Andrew had died in the fire.'

Zoe's phone starts to ring but she presses the button to cancel the call without glancing down.

'Andrew's dead...?' I say, even though I already know.

'I tried to find Freddie but people were saying he'd already left. I found the taxi driver, who said he'd taken Freddie to the airport the day before.'

I don't want the answer to the next question but ask it anyway: 'Why did Freddie leave?'

Zoe bites her lip again and takes a breath. She glances to the heavens. 'I'm not saying this as fact. I've not seen Freddie since that night we were all drinking and smoking. I wasn't there when the fire broke out.'

'But...?'

'Freddie used to do this thing with a lighter. He'd flick it and light it, flick it and light it. He would do it over and over, like the way people play with their hair, or whatever. I always wondered if maybe...'

'You think he accidentally set fire to where they were staying?'

Zoe looks to her phone and checks the identity of the missed call. 'All I know is that, if I'd done that in a foreign country, maybe I'd have run, too...' She stands and taps the phone screen again. There's urgency to her once more. 'I have to go. I don't want to cause trouble. This was a long time ago but I guess it's been at the back of my mind ever since. I've probably been waiting to tell someone for ages – then you called, and, well...' She takes a step away and looks back. 'I was going to ask if Freddie wanted to meet again but I don't think I want that. I doubt he would, either. Different times, you know...?'

'I know.'

Zoe starts to walk away, her phone at her ear. I watch her leave and it's hard not to think of how much a person changes. One moment, we're young with a life ahead, the next it's houses, bills, endless responsibility.

There is no reason for Zoe to lie. If this is true, it explains why Freddie rarely wants to travel and why he doesn't drink any longer.

Except it's hard to get past one enormous question.

Did my husband accidentally kill his friend – and then do a runner?

FORTY-NINE

DYLAN

Jimmy stumbles backwards and collides with the fridge as I barge into his kitchen. He slips to the floor as I shunt the door closed and bear down upon him.

'Whuh?' he grunts.

I dump my bag on the floor and, as Jimmy tries to wriggle away, I straddle him, pinning his arms to the ground. I'm younger, taller and stronger than him – and he knows it.

'You were in court,' he says.

'How many women have you killed?'

I'm surprised at how calm my voice is. There is a stillness I could never have expected.

Jimmy's eyes flare. 'What?'

'It's a simple question.'

'None.'

Of course he's not going to admit it. I stretch to the side and unzip my bag, then pull out a photo of Ciara. I hold it, so he can see. 'You know her, don't you?'

Jimmy shakes his head frantically, so I push down harder with my knees, making him wince and groan.

'I don't,' he says.

'You killed her, didn't you? You wore your silver jacket when you did it.'

'I didn't. I don't know what you're on about.'

I'm not sure if I can explain what happens next. It's as if I'm suddenly self-aware. I can see myself pinning a man to the ground in his own kitchen – but for what reason? Because a drunk told me he saw someone in a foil jacket?

And then it's over and I'm done.

I press backwards, allowing Jimmy to haul himself away. The next thing I know, I am sitting with my back against the door, bag at my side, my wife's photo in my lap. I don't remember crossing the room.

Jimmy gets to his feet and turns in a circle. He eyes the knife block, then reaches for his phone on the counter.

It's in his hand when I manage to croak: 'Please don't.'

He stares down over me and knows the same as me – he has the power now. A man like Jimmy craves that. 'JBG' is the type of person who waits a lifetime to end up with authority.

'Who are you?' he asks.

This all seemed so easy in my head but I'm not sure how I let it happen. How it got so far. I was so certain but it was all built upon nonsense.

I turn the photo around for him to see. 'She was my wife,' I say.

I'm slumped, defeated.

Jimmy looks to the phone again, then places it on the counter. He stands on the furthest side of the kitchen, arms folded. 'You were in the news,' he says.

'Right.'

'I was in Lanzarote. When I got back, she was everywhere.'

'You were on holiday when she was killed...?'

Jimmy looks blankly at me: 'I go every year. The only reason I'm not there now is because of that stupid court case.' He waits and then adds: 'Why are you here?'

'Because I made a big mistake.'

Jimmy frowns, nose wrinkling: 'You think I killed your wife?'

I can't look at him. Of course he didn't do it. I can't quite figure out why I thought he did. I saw his jacket and was so certain. I couldn't think of anything else.

'I was wrong,' I say.

'You can say that again.'

There is a moment in which neither of us knows what to do next. I push myself up to my feet as Jimmy motions to grab the phone. I hold my hands up in surrender and he stops.

'I should go,' I say. 'I'm really sorry. This was the biggest mistake I've ever made.'

I pick up my bag and open the back door, hoping I can somehow get away with this.

'Hey,' Jimmy calls.

I turn and he hasn't moved. He's next to the phone and my fate continues to rest in his hands. There's a long pause in which I have no idea what will happen next.

When Jimmy next speaks, his tone is quieter.

'You should talk to someone,' he says. 'You can't go doing things like this – even if you have lost your wife.'

'I know.'

I think about asking whether he's going to call the police after I've gone. He probably should. It'll be easy enough to find out my name. I've invaded his home, threatened him.

'I've got a daughter,' I say, knowing what I'm doing.

Jimmy stares back. 'OK.'

'I need to be a dad to her.'

'Not much of a dad now, are you?'

It's hard to argue.

I wait, although he doesn't have anything else to say, so I exit the house. I'm calm at first, although the composure leaves me as soon as I reach the corner.

I run.

I'm not sure where I'm going at first and it's a minute or so until I remember I am parked at the railway station. I'm expecting police cars to be there, blocking me in, a line of officers waiting to bring me in.

There's nobody except a woman with a trolley.

I loosen the tarp at the back of the truck, remove the photo of Ciara from my bag, then re-zip it and toss the bag in with the linens. After that, I refasten everything and practically throw myself into the driver's seat. It takes a few minutes until I'm able to start the engine.

'This wasn't you,' I tell myself out loud... but there's a part of me that wonders if it is. Beth was so kind to me on those dates. I told her that my daughter, that Orla, had to come first, though that's definitely not what I did here. If things had gone badly – and they still could – where would that leave Orla?

I'm shaking as I turn the key.

The drive home is slow and careful as I try to think past the crippling shame. Jimmy is right: I need to talk to someone. I should have done it three years ago, yet I was so consumed with thinking it would make me weaker.

I notice her as I pull onto Huntington Grove. Beth is sitting on my doorstep, playing with her phone. She wipes her forehead with her hand before standing when she sees me pulling onto the drive.

When I get out of the cabin, she is so close that I can see the sweat on her brow. Her hair has stuck to her forehead and there's a damp patch in the centre of her top.

'I don't *need* to be in a relationship,' she says. 'You know that, don't you?'

'I—'

'I'm happy to be single, I really am, but I thought we had a good connection.'

'We did.' I'm stumbling, not expecting this.

'I'm going to give you one pass because of everything. That's it, though – and you've used it now. If you want me to nick off, I can do that. If you want to invite me in for a drink because it's like an oven out here, we can do that, too. It's up to you.'

My mouth is dry and there's a part of me that wants to collapse and confess my disgrace. But then I wonder if this is my second chance? I don't deserve this.

And maybe it's the kindness I don't deserve but the next thing I know, I am sobbing into my hands. The cries come from deep in my stomach. Three years' worth pouring through the surface.

'Well,' Beth says, 'I didn't expect that.'

FIFTY

A group of four homeless people are sitting on the war memorial. Their sleeping bags have been packed into a shopping trolley, which is next to a trio of battered suitcases. They notice me coming and I try to remember if any of them were there the night before.

As I get closer, I give a nervous 'hi', although none of them pay me much attention.

'I'm looking for someone,' I say. 'A man in a Frankie Says Relax shirt.'

Three of them turn away but a man grunts 'What?'

I show him the image of the Frankie T-shirt on my phone. It was easy enough to find and I didn't realise it was so popular. It's only as I do this that I realise the lack of tact in shoving an expensive smartphone into the face of someone who has nowhere to live.

He doesn't seem to mind.

'Do you know the guy who wears a shirt like this?' I say.

'What d'you want 'im for?'

'For a chat. Nothing serious.'

'Pete,' he says.

'Do you know where Pete might be?'

'Kitchen.'

I start to ask which kitchen but then figure I can work it out myself. I give the man a ten-pound note for his trouble, although there's something awkward and embarrassing about it all. It's my fault, of course. It's like I've bribed him. There's a moment in which it feels like he's going to hand it back but he doesn't.

It only takes a quick internet search to discover there's a homeless kitchen a few streets away. When I get there, I realise it's at the rear of a church. A few more homeless people have congregated near the back doors and I spy Pete immediately. There's a bandage across his eye and he's still wearing the Frankie T-shirt.

I cross towards the group and hate myself for feeling vulnerable. They're homeless, not criminals, yet I cannot shake off the angst of being out of my depth.

I head for Pete but, when he spots me, he turns away.

'Pete?' I call. He half spins back – but everyone else turns to stare. There are men and women across the entire spectrum of ages.

'Can we talk?' I ask him. 'Do you remember me?'

It is perhaps because of the pressure of everyone looking that Pete slowly turns. He's tall, though his back is hunched. There is a speckle of grey in his otherwise gingery beard but he seems younger than I thought last night. He is thirty at most, not even as old as me. It's hard not to wonder how it came to this. An unlucky moment here, perhaps a bad choice there? Nobody deserves this.

He nods towards a tree that overhangs a fenced-off electricity substation, covered with signs, promising death to anyone who looks at it the wrong way.

I walk in the direction Pete indicated, stopping near the fence when I feel the metal boxes humming.

'Did you try to rob my husband?' I ask, trying to sound blunt and confident, just in case he is a mugger.

Pete blinks away sleepiness and shuffles on the spot. 'What do you think?' he asks.

'I don't know what to think.'

'I reckon you do.'

He speaks so clearly and eloquently. I'm not sure what I expected. I try to be that respectable thirty-something who bridles against racism, sexism, and all the other isms – but I'm as guilty as anyone.

'I saw my husband beating you up,' I say.

Pete shrugs.

'Why?' I ask.

It's only one word – and Pete doesn't answer. He doesn't need to because it's as if I've had a cartoon moment with a light bulb going off over my head. *Ding!*

The missing money from my purse, the blood on Gabe's hand, the way he washed his clothes for no reason. Why did it take me so long to figure out?

'He pays you...?' I say.

Pete shrugs a second time.

'Does he do this regularly?' I ask.

I stare at Pete properly, noticing the purply-black marks around his eyes, the scabbed scratch near his ear.

'Is it other people as well?'

Pete looks past me towards his group once more. 'I think you need to talk to your husband,' he says.

I can't speak at first but manage a croaky: 'I will.'

'Do you want money, or something?' I say, digging into my bag, before realising Pete is watching with barely concealed disgust.

'It's not all about money,' he replies.

'I just... I want to help.'

'Do what you want.'

Pete strides past me towards the comfort of his community – and I'm riddled with humiliation for what my husband has done. For what I've done, too. Did I push Gabe into this? Has he been doing this for months? Years? And I somehow never noticed...

It doesn't take long to walk home and, when I arrive, Gabe's car is on the drive and he is back from work. He has shorter hours on Fridays, or so he says. I'm not sure what to believe any longer. I head upstairs, to where he's in his work suit, shoes off, feet up, playing on the PlayStation. I barely think about it as I cross the room, ignore his protestations for me walking in front of the screen, and pull the plug from the wall. The screen goes black.

'You're leaving,' I say.

He stares at me in disbelief. 'What? Leaving where? Why?'

'You know why. Now get out.'

Gabe doesn't move. The game controller remains in his hand.

'If you don't go,' I say, 'I'll call the police and tell them what you've been up to after dark.'

He is emotionless and blank. I expect pushback – anger, annoyance or denial. There's none of that. He puts down the controller on the side table, stands, and calmly leaves the room. He heads into our bedroom and then there's the sound of wardrobes being opened. I watch from the doorway as he coolly folds and slots his clothes into one of the suitcases we keep under the bed. He is methodical and deliberate, laying all his trousers into one area, his tops into another, and then his shoes, socks and underwear. When he's done, he zips it closed and lifts it off the bed onto the floor.

When he turns, there's a deadness behind his eyes and I

wonder how I've spent all this time with him. How I let him be around my daughter.

'Are you sure you want to do this?' he asks. There's nothing sinister there, nothing threatening. It's like he's asking if I want a cup of tea.

'I'm sure,' I say as I move out of the way of the door.

He carries the case past me and heads to the stairs. When he gets to the bottom, he stops and retrieves his keys from the rack in the kitchen. Finally, when he's at the front door, he opens it and drops the suitcase on the path outside.

'You won't need those keys,' I say.

'I live here, too.'

'No you don't.'

'You'll see me again,' he says, pocketing the keys. With that, he closes the door to signal the end of our marriage.

FIFTY-ONE

HEIDI

It's the excitable, hyper-organised Alison who is on the street this time. No sign of that cowed woman, struggling to deal with her mother-in-law. She's marching up and down with a clipboard, ensuring everyone is doing what they're supposed to be.

Freddie is up a ladder on one side of the street, tying the bunting to a lamppost in what I'm sure is some sort of health and safety violation. Diagonally across the road, Dylan is up a separate ladder, trying to affix the bunting to the next pole. There's a woman holding his ladder who I don't recognise. She's pretty and keeps pretending to shake the base and giggling. Even from across the road, I can tell there's affection there.

'Higher!' the woman calls.

Dylan moves the bunting up and then his daughter shouts 'lower!' He moves it up and down, while grinning down at the pair of them.

'You're not helping, Beth,' Dylan calls.

'Lower!' Orla calls again.

'Definitely higher,' Beth adds.

He looks across to me: 'Up or down,' he says.

'I think your lot have it well in hand.'

'Higher,' Beth calls.

Dylan calls for Alison and she scuttles across to sort things out. In the meantime, Freddie has attached his end to the lamppost and is on the way down the ladder.

We've only got the rest of the street to go.

Huntington Grove is a hive of action. Tables are stacked high on the lawn outside Alison's place, ready for tomorrow. Despite Alison being at the centre of everything, there is no sign of Kenneth or Chen, and it's as if her presumed husband and actual mother-in-law have disappeared. I keep looking to their windows to see if either of them is watching, though the blinds are closed. It's all a bit odd.

From the other side of the road, Willow and Isabella are working together, tying bows to the lower halves of the lampposts. There's no sign of Gabe. When they turn, I give a little wave and they both return the gesture. I wonder if Isabella has told her mother about this morning and the clinic. I suppose, in some ways, there's nothing to tell. She wasn't pregnant.

It's only as I turn to watch the full range of help along the street that I realise how few people I've spoken to over the past week. I don't particularly know any of my new neighbours. Perhaps this Beth has been living with Dylan the whole time and I've not noticed?

Freddie carries his ladder to the next lamppost as Alison passes by and thanks him for helping. I'm holding onto the bunting that's strung with red, white and blue flags, ready to pass it up to my husband.

'This is really impressive,' I tell Alison.

'Thank you.'

She half turns away but not quickly enough for me to miss the bruise that's cupping her eye. She's tried to conceal it but the mark is too dark to mask completely.

'What happened to your eye?' I ask.

'Nothing.'

'Did—?'

'No.'

I don't get a chance to ask anything else because she disappears to the other side of the road and starts to talk to Dylan.

I pass the bunting up to Freddie, who attaches it around the lamppost and then drops the rest to the floor, ready for Dylan to continue the stringing on the other side.

My husband clambers down, sits on the kerb next to the ladder, and has a drink of water. Maybe it's that which triggers the thought of how the liquid could put out a fire? My husband has been hiding this from me the entire time we've known each other. I watch him and wonder if it matters. It was before we knew one another, not the person he is now.

It doesn't stop me wondering, though.

Did he accidentally kill his friend and then run away? Even if it was an accident, it's still a terrible thing to do.

I turn and notice Willow by herself. She's standing with her arms crossed but it feels as if there's something different about her. I'm not sure if I believe in auras and the like but there's a sullen sadness clinging to her.

I cross the road and stand at her side. She's watching Freddie and, though the fire and Andy happened *after* they left school, I wonder if she somehow knows what I now do about my husband. It would explain the way they've been around one another – and why Freddie is so keen to move.

'How are you?' I ask.

'I've been worse,' she says. 'You?'

'I've been worse.'

Though I can't explain why, it feels like there's a connection between us. I'm lying and so is she but I suppose that's what people in marriages do. We convince ourselves that lies are true because it's the only way life can work.

Neither of us speaks for a while and then the woman who was with Dylan comes across. Willow suddenly uncrosses her arms and stands more loosely. She smiles but it's forced, not really there.

'This is Beth,' Willow tells me, introducing us formally.

We say hi to one another and then Beth turns to Willow: 'How did you know?' she asks.

Willow laughs. 'Just a guess – but it looks like you and Dylan are getting on well enough.'

That gets a smile as I wonder how they're all connected.

I excuse myself and cross the road back towards the house. Isabella is at the end of the street, holding her phone horizontally and filming what's going on. It's only as I watch her that I realise something I didn't ask Zoe at the hotel earlier.

Hi Zoe. It's Heidi. Sorry for bothering you. Was wondering if you have any photos from back in the day?

I'm not expecting a reply considering Zoe has what sounded very much like a bridezilla to deal with, but a text comes back within a minute.

Might do. Scanned a bunch a few years back. Will look later

'Oi!'

I look up and Freddie is on his way up again. I head towards him and steady the ladder.

'Everything all right?' he asks.

'Same as ever,' I tell my husband.

THE FUTURE

Police statement: Kelsey Evesham.

Officer: I realise you've been over this a couple of times but, now we're recording, do you mind if I ask your name, and that of your business.

Kelsey: I'm Kelsey and I own Poplar Place Parties.

Officer: I gather you provided some supplies for the Huntington Grove street party?

Kelsey: It was mainly tablecloths and place settings, that sort of thing.

Officer: Who ordered the supplies?

Kelsey: Alison – but I can't remember her last name. We met at a town gala thing a couple of years back and stayed in contact. She's very persuasive.

Officer: What do you mean by that?

[*Sound of laughing*]

Kelsey: Well, I ended up giving her all the supplies for free, so there's that...

[*Sound of laughing*]

Officer: I think I understand. I gather the street party was on the Saturday – so when were the items picked up?

Kelsey: The day before.

Officer: And who picked them up?

Kelsey: One of Alison's neighbour's. He had a big truck because she couldn't fit everything in her car.

[*Image shown of Dylan Wilson*]

Officer: Was this the man?

Kelsey: Yeah, Dylan. He was kinda cute and I looked him up after he'd gone.

Officer: What did you find?

Kelsey: Well, he's got a bit of history, hasn't he? His wife was killed a few years back. I remembered the story but didn't know it was him. I can't believe he went through all that, and now this happened.

Officer: Going back to that Friday, did anyone other than Mr Wilson pick up the supplies from you?

Kelsey: Just him.

Officer: What did he say he was going to do with them?

[*Inaudible*]

Kelsey: I don't think he said. I assumed he was taking them to Huntington Grove for the party.

Officer: How did he seem on the day?

Kelsey: Tired, I guess. I think there was more than he expected.

Officer: More supplies?

Kelsey: Right. I think I carried one bag but he had the rest. It was really heavy.

Officer: Did he say anything to you on the day that you remember?

Kelsey: Like what?

Officer: Did you talk about anything that stuck out?

Kelsey: I don't think so. We probably mentioned the party and maybe Alison. I was trying to find out if he was single but couldn't think of a way to ask, without actually asking.

Officer: So you found him charming?

Kelsey: I suppose.

Officer: Do you remember anything else about Mr Wilson from that day? Anything out of the ordinary?

Kelsey: No, he was really nice. After everything happened the next day, I couldn't believe it. I saw it on Facebook at first, then I texted Alison – but she wasn't replying. I wondered if…

Officer: What did you wonder?

Kelsey: Well, there was a time on Saturday when nobody really knew what happened. Someone put on Facebook that a bomb had gone off. Other people were saying there was a gunman on the loose, and I thought it was like one of those American things when there's someone with a rifle. I suppose I wondered if Alison had been shot, then I remembered Dylan from the day before. I'd been thinking about him after looking him up. I think he has a daughter, too, and I was hoping they were both OK. Did anything happen to her?

Officer: I can't say too much about what happened, Ms Evesham. It's still an ongoing investigation. That's why we appreciate your time.

Kelsey: But is she OK? Imagine if she wasn't? He already lost his wife and then—

Officer: Is there anything else you want to add?

Kelsey: I mean… I don't think so.

Officer: Thank you. Interview terminated at 16:03 hours.

FIFTY-TWO

SATURDAY

DYLAN

Orla is clinking her knife and fork on the table in the way I used to do when I was her age. Eggs are sizzling in the pan while the baked beans boil. When the toast pops, I turn off the flames and start layering everything together. The fried eggs go on separate slices of bread and then beans are poured over the top. It's an Orla special that my daughter is only allowed once a week *if* she gets enough stars.

I put down the meal in front of the girl it is named after – and she immediately pops both yolks and coos as the yellow oozes into the orange.

'I invented this,' she says proudly.

'You did,' I assure her.

'Is Beth coming round today?'

She forks the first mouthful of beans into her mouth, immediately dripping the juice into her lap. I've been trying to teach her to eat somewhat more tidily for years but nothing seems to work. Every mealtime ends up like someone's blown up a Sainsbury's.

'Concentrate on your food,' I tell her, knowing it'll make no difference.

'But is she coming over?'

'Maybe for the street party later.'

Orla takes a breath and I need the moment to marvel at how things have changed so much in the past day. From the darkest of shadows to this.

'What do you do at a street party?'

'Eat your food.'

'You eat your food at a street party?'

'Well, yes – but I mean eat your food now.'

Orla has another mouthful of beans and, this time, manages to swallow the lot without spilling it on herself.

'I've never been to a street party before,' I tell her. 'I think they used to have them regularly years ago. That's what your grandma reckoned, anyway. They used to do them for the Queen's birthday. I guess it's the King now.'

'What about *my* birthday?'

'I don't think you get a street party.'

She considers this by chewing on the end of the fork. 'That's not fair.'

'I know. Wait 'til you find out the King gets two birthdays.'

Her eyes widen. '*Two* birthdays?'

'One-two.'

'Does he get Christmas, too?'

'He does.'

'What does he do with all the presents?'

'I don't know.'

Orla ponders this, has a mouthful of toast and then says: 'Can I have two birthdays?'

'I don't think so.'

'Why does he get two?'

'One is for the day he was actually born; the other is for any king or queen to celebrate with the nation.'

Orla sups more baked bean juice and then shakes her head. 'I think everyone should have two birthdays.'

'I think it's probably better if everyone gets one.'

'No.'

With that issue sorted, Orla focuses back on her food. The sun is blazing through the window at the back, casting a haze of light across the kitchen. I only now realise that I didn't answer Orla's initial question.

'I think it's going to be like a giant picnic today,' I say. 'Everyone brings something and then it all gets shared out.'

'I like picnics.'

'I know.'

The smirk has returned: 'Does Beth like picnics…?'

The doorbell sounds, which at least gives some respite from having to go through the Beth questions once more. There were plenty last night. I tell Orla to eat up and that I'll be right back.

My stomach sinks as I pull open the door. There are two uniformed police officers, neither of whom I recognise. There's an older man and a younger woman, like something from a buddy movie. They're both grim-faced and I know this is where it ends. It felt like my life had changed last night. Beth said it best when she said I was getting my one and only pass. It wasn't only with her, it felt like that for my life in general. I'd made a terrible mistake but would now move on.

I was forgetting Jimmy, of course. Why *wouldn't* he tell the police what I did? I don't blame him.

If it's not that, then it's Alfie's parents who have finally gone to the police after Gabe's attack.

'Are you Dylan Wilson?' the male officer asks.

'Yes.'

'Can we come in?'

FIFTY-THREE

HEIDI

Freddie is on the sofa, eating some toast while half-watching the television. He looks up as I enter and, for a moment, it feels like he's going to bring up moving once more.

'Seems like a nice day,' he says.

I cross to the window and look out to the road. It has been barricaded at either end, with the fluttering Union Flag bunting zigzagging the street. There is something reassuring about the pair of girls sitting in the middle of the road tossing a Frisbee to one another.

'Alison asked me to help with the tables later,' Freddie says.

'Did she explain what happened with walking out from your office?'

'I didn't want to ask. She was acting like it hadn't happened.'

I turn and almost say the name 'Andy Westley'. It's on the end of my tongue. I want to know why Freddie has the other man's birth certificate, why he has the yearbook and other items from Willow. I would... I nearly do... but it feels as if I'm missing something. It's hard to describe. I know but I don't know.

Freddie joins me at the window and rests a hand across my waist. I wonder if he's watching the girls, like I am, or if he's more focused on Willow's house.

'I've got work to do this morning,' he says. 'It'll only be a half-hour. Promise.'

He heads to his study and closes the door. There is a bit of rustling and then quiet. I leave him to it, put on some shoes, and head outside. In the time it has taken me to get ready, a police car has pulled up outside Dylan's house. I stop for a moment, wondering what's going on, then head along the street to Alison's place. The tables are still stacked on the front lawn, ready for the party, but the blinds are pulled and there is no sign of anyone being home.

I reach the door and almost knock, except there's faint shouting from beyond. It's nowhere near as loud as when we first moved but still an unmistakable sound of two or more people going at it.

Instead of knocking, I head to the side. This time, there is no need to go over the gate because it's unlocked. I approach the side door.

The sight is not entirely a surprise. Alison is in the kitchen with the man I assume to be her husband. They are jabbing fingers at one another. Kenneth shouts something I don't catch and then, in a flash, Alison lunges and slaps him hard across the face. His head rocks sideways as the snap echoes like a gunshot.

It's almost as if everything stops as they both turn to see me at the same time. Kenneth touches his face but Alison stands unrepentantly. We all stand unmovingly for a few seconds and then Kenneth strides past his wife, out of view.

Alison is calm as she unlocks the back door. 'Can I help?' she asks politely.

'I, um... was wondering if I can help with something...?'

It looks like her black eye has faded this morning, though it's hard to tell for sure because she's not trying to conceal it.

'We can't do much before the tables go up,' she says. 'Freddie's helping with that in about an hour – but there'll be jobs afterwards.'

She glances inside, but there's nobody behind.

Her voice is lower now: 'That wasn't what it looked like.'

'What did it look like?'

Alison checks she's alone once more: 'I'm fine,' she says. 'Kenneth's fine. Everything is all right. We'll catch up in a bit, OK?'

'Sure.'

'And, Heidi...'

'What?'

'Use the front door in future.'

FIFTY-FOUR

WILLOW

Mum pushes her way through the front door before I've barely opened it.

'I need the toilet,' she says.

'Isabella's in the bathroom.'

'What?'

'She's having a shower.'

Mum stands indignantly on the front mat, blocking Dad from getting past her. It was barely days before they'd temporarily separated but now they're here together.

'Why have they blocked the road?' Mum asks.

'Because it's a street party, Mum. We can hardly put tables along the middle if someone's going to plough through it in an Audi.'

'I had to walk.'

Dad interrupts her by edging into the house and closing the door. 'We parked around the corner,' he says.

'It was further away than that.'

'It's literally around the corner,' he insists, pointing as if to prove the point. 'There's a corner up there, and we're around it.'

'I still had to walk – and now I need the toilet.'

'You went before we left!'

Mum and Dad glare at one another, then Mum heads upstairs to knock on the door and annoy Isabella. While she's doing that, I lead Dad through to the kitchen.

'Where's Gabe?' he asks.

'Not here at the moment. Do you want some breakfast?'

The idea of food is more than enough to wash over the absence of my husband and Dad tucks himself in at the table and takes out his paper.

'What's on offer?' he asks.

'I was going to poach some eggs on toast.'

'Ooh, your mother won't like that.'

'Why not?'

'Something about a dicky tummy. She'll tell you.'

I guess the contents of Mum's intestines is a conversation to look forward to.

I set the kettle boiling anyway and wait until I hear the inevitable crashing from the stairs as Mum barrels her way down again. She bumbles into the kitchen and plops herself opposite Dad.

'It's poached eggs for breakfast,' he tells her.

'So?'

'You don't like poached eggs.'

'Since when?'

'Since ever. I've never known you eat a poached egg without getting wind.'

'I've never got wind after eating an egg. Never.'

'Don't you remember Torquay. It—'

'OK,' I interrupt. 'Can we stop talking about wind and Torquay and whatever else is going on here. I'm making poached eggs on brown bread toast. Do you want that, or not?'

'Yes,' Dad says.

'Yes,' Mum says.

'Good.'

I pop four slices of bread into the toaster, then pour some hot water into a pan and set it boiling.

'Do you have white bread?' Mum asks.

'I do prefer white,' Dad adds.

'I've only got brown.'

'Guess that will have to do,' Mum says. 'You can get that half and half stuff at Tesco. Looks like white but it's supposed to be like brown. Amazing what they can do nowadays.'

Before I know it, Dad's off about how he's tried something 'new', called sourdough. Mum then insists on arguing over whether or not he's ever had a rye bread. I eye the kitchen knives and my wrists, and it doesn't seem like such a bad idea. I've got a whole afternoon of this. It would be bad enough if I hadn't kicked my husband out of the house less than a day ago.

When I tell my parents that, it really is going to go off.

Without thinking too much, I put the eggs into the poaching holders, dip them in the saucepan, and cover it with the lid.

I've not heard anything from Gabe since he walked out the door. I left the latch on last night in case his 'You'll see me again' was far more immediate than I thought. It felt threatening at the time but now feels more like something practical. We *will* see each other again. It's not as if he's simply walked off into the sunset and that's the end. He works in the area and most of his things are here. We'll have a mortgage to separate and a divorce to thrash out.

As I lay in bed last night, the self-preservation started to kick in as I wondered what will happen now. Will we have to sell? It's not like I can afford a mortgage by myself. Perhaps I should have departed with Isabella, and left Gabe with the house?

I think of homeless Pete and the marks across his face,

wondering how many others Gabe has paid to beat up over the years. Was he always violent and I somehow never noticed? He never raised his hands to me, nor, as far as I know, Isabella. That's hardly the point, though, even if picturing my daughter at the mercy of this man has set a fire raging.

Because a violent man is a violent man.

I woke up at three wondering if I should call the police, if only to get some justice for Pete and the people like him.

But, despite that fire, I didn't, of course. Would it make things worse for me? For Isabella?

I'm too much of a coward to find out.

The toast pops and I put two slices onto two plates, then scoop the eggs from the pan. When they're on the bread, I grind some pepper on top and pass both plates to my parents.

'This looks nice,' Mum says, although she somehow has a way of making it sound like, 'This looks like you scooped it off the floor'. I'm not sure how she does it.

Dad flips the egg off his toast and picks the bread up with his fingers.

'Don't eat with your hands,' Mum says.

'Why not?'

She starts to reply and then seemingly realises she doesn't have an answer. I leave them to it as I hear more footsteps on the stairs.

I head into the hall and cut off Isabella before she gets near the kitchen.

'She kicked me out of the bathroom,' Isabella says.

'I know. Sorry. I swear she wees out more than ever goes in.'

Isabella wraps her arms around me and we cling onto one another, out of sight of the kitchen door. If it was my choice, we'd stay like that for the rest of the day. Isabella is not much of a huggy person, especially with me. After everything from the past week – and probably the past seventeen years – I've craved this moment.

She releases me first, patting me on the shoulder until I let her go. 'Have you told them about Gabe?'

'Not yet.'

'It's just a little tiff, though... like me and Jarvis?'

'I think it's a bit more serious than that, love.'

Isabella strokes my arm sympathetically and it is as if our roles have switched. I'm the child and she's the adult.

'Do you think you're going to, y'know...' She checks over my shoulder and then whispers the word: '*Divorce?*'

'I've not thought that far ahead.'

That's a lie, because I definitely have. I've been googling solicitors.

'What happened?' Isabella asks. 'Did you argue, or...?'

'We'll talk later,' I say. 'Not while your grandparents are here. They'll never leave if they think there's a problem with me and Gabe.'

Isabella smiles gently, possibly patronisingly.

'Do you want breakfast?' I ask.

She is silent for a moment, as my parents' voices drift from the kitchen.

'I've never liked bagels,' Dad says.

'You used to always have a bagel in the morning,' Mum replies.

'When?'

'Always! You had one last week.'

'No, I didn't.'

Isabella catches my eye and the hint of a smile creeps onto her lips. 'I think I'm going over the road,' she says. 'Alison's collected all these foil blankets because one of the girls who lives at the other end of the street is autistic and shiny stuff helps calm her. I said I could help the other girl make something with the foil. Then I was going to help Alison set the tables.'

My heart melts. 'That's very kind of you,' I say.

It gets a small shrug as Isabella steps towards the door.

I catch my daughter's shoulder, not wanting the moment to end. 'I'm proud of you for all this,' I say. 'The bunting is amazing. I was looking out the window last night and it's perfect.'

There is a creeping whisper of a smile. 'I didn't make *all* of it.'

'You did enough.'

The grin widens, acknowledging the point. Craig was correct all along about the way I should have treated our daughter.

'I'll see you later,' she says.

FIFTY-FIVE

DYLAN

'My daughter's in the kitchen,' I tell the officers. 'Orla. I don't mind you coming in but do I need to get someone to sit with her? She's only seven.'

I imagine her being left by herself as I'm dragged off to the cells. I have no idea what happens to children whose only parent gets arrested. Are they taken into care? After everything that's happened to Orla in her life, I can't believe I've let her down so badly. Why did I storm into Jimmy's house like that? What was I thinking?

'I don't think you need anyone,' the male officer says. 'But we will need some privacy...'

'Oh...'

I'm not sure what to say. I was expecting handcuffs and a riot van. Instead, there is a single car at the end of the drive.

I step aside and show the officers into the living room. While they settle on the sofa, I tell Orla I need to talk to some important people and that she has to go upstairs. She takes it well enough. I think she knows when I'm being serious and the time for messing around is over.

When I return to the living room, the male officer introduces himself as Constable Hodges – call me George – while the woman is Constable Harding, but I'm fine to call her Janine. It's very informal for either an attempted murder of Alfie's father, or a definitive home invasion of Jimmy.

'You should probably sit,' George says.

I do, perching on the edge of the seat that Gabe always took.

'This is going to be something of a shock,' he adds.

'OK...'

'Two nights ago, a man who is already in custody on different charges confessed to killing your wife.'

I stare at him, then turn to the other officer, waiting for either of them to say this is some kind of wind-up. Janine is as serious as her partner.

'I don't understand,' I say.

'We're still checking the claim,' George says. 'We're not taking this as a definite fact – but we have confirmed that, although he comes from another area of the country, this man was in High Kingsley at the time of your wife's death.'

'Who is he?'

George ignores my question: 'He also knows a couple of facts about the case that were never released publicly. We wanted you to know this before anyone else. We're not saying it definitely will – but this information might leak into the media over the weekend.'

I turn between the two officers, unable to speak, barely able to breathe.

'You... know who killed her?' My voice is croaky, like a life-long smoker's who thinks giving up is for losers.

'We believe so,' George replies. 'Like I said, we're checking the particular facts.'

I suppose this is how cases are supposed to be. The police do their jobs and find the criminal. Knocks on doors like this come all the time. Victims aren't supposed to stalk courtrooms in an attempt unlock the puzzle.

It's madness and it always was.

'Who is it?' I ask.

'We can't say yet – but, honestly, even if we did, you wouldn't know the name. The individual isn't local and has no particular notoriety.'

'I'd still like to know.'

'You will one day – I promise – but there is no point in giving you that information now. This person is in custody. He's not going anywhere and your family is safe.' He waits a moment and then adds: 'Do you have any questions?'

So many swim through my mind that I barely know where to begin.

'Did he say why?' I ask.

Both officers glance to one another and there's something unsaid, at least in the moment.

This time, it is Janine who answers: 'We need to confirm his claims. It wouldn't be beneficial for anyone if we got too far ahead of ourselves.'

'But...?'

I've sensed it, anticipated it, and then it comes – from Officer George.

'...But there was something. He told us that he was in town, sleeping rough, when a man offered him money.'

'Money for what?'

'The man said he'd pay fifty quid if he could beat him up.'

I stare blankly at one officer, then the other, not sure what he means.

'I don't understand.'

'We're still asking questions but this man says he turned

down fifty pounds to be beaten up. Then the person who offered him the money slapped him around anyway. He says he was kicked in the head a few times. That the assailant stamped on him.'

I stare at the officer but, really, I'm picturing Gabe a few nights back, trampling on the head of Alfie's father barely a couple of metres away. I shiver at the memory but the officer misinterprets it.

'I know it's hard to hear,' he says. 'This man is claiming that, after he was beaten up, he was so furious that he took it out on the first person he saw.'

My mouth is dry, my wife's name almost stuck. How can this be true?

'Ciara,' I say, and it's a croak.

It gets a nod.

'This... man got beaten up and killed my wife as revenge...?'

There's another nod but then: 'That's what he says. We're not sure why he'd lie but we're still asking questions.'

'Who beat him up?'

The two officers exchange a silent glance. 'I don't think we have any way of knowing that,' Janine answers. 'Even if it's true, I don't know how we'd be able to find out three years on. It could be anyone. He's not been able to give a description because he says he doesn't remember.'

I don't know what to say. Somehow, I know it's true. The same thing led me to Jimmy's door, in that moment where I nearly destroyed more than one life. It's what had me grabbing for Alfie, the bully, then had his father showing up here before Gabe did what he did.

Violence creates more violence.

'We will pass on anything new that comes out,' George adds. 'You won't be left out of the loop. If it turns out this man is some sort of fantasist, we'll let you know that, too.'

I need a moment to think. Is this the end? It's been so long.

'Does it happen often?' I ask.

'What?'

'Do people pretend they've committed crimes they haven't?'

They glance to one another and then George answers: 'It does happen,' he says. 'But only usually with big cases. Some people want the infamy of confessing to something like that. I'm not saying your wife was unimportant but, on a national scale, it wasn't massive news. If someone was to claim they'd committed the crime it would be... unusual. I don't see what anyone would have to gain from admitting this.'

The officers sit a short while, probably waiting to see if I have anything else to ask, then they stand together.

'That's all we have,' George says. 'If there's anything more, we'll get back to you.'

He passes me a card and says to call if I have any questions.

I lead them to the door and they say they'll be in touch, before both heading towards their patrol car.

As soon as they're out of sight, the rest of the questions I should have asked swarm. Does this mean there won't be a trial? If this man's already in prison, will I ever get a chance to look him in the face?

How will I tell Orla?

I've spent these years dreaming of vengeance, of closure, and now... there's this. It was vengeance that killed my wife. I came so close to continuing the cycle.

Do I feel sorry for the person? I want to be furious, but the killer did the thing I so nearly did.

I was almost him.

Jimmy could have been Ciara.

The officers are at the car when I call them back. I hurry from the house, along the drive until I'm at their side. Both eye me with pity.

'The jacket,' I say.

'What jacket?' George asks.

'The foil jacket...'

I can tell from the joint looks that neither of them has any idea what I'm on about. Why should they? Tom told the police what he apparently saw and they dismissed it almost straight away. He was a drunk... *is* a drunk. The police knew that but, for some reason, I clung to his testimony as if it was gospel. I've been visiting him over and over, asking for reassurance over something that was never true in the first place. It was all I had and it was wrong.

'Sorry,' I say. 'I was thinking of something else...'

They turn slowly to one another and each say they will be in contact, before getting into the car. I watch as they drive off slowly along the street. George hops out to manoeuvre the barrier and then, after Janine drives around it, he puts it back in place. In a blink, they are out of sight.

At the other end of the street, the new bloke from across the road – Freddie – is lugging tables into place as his wife carries the other end. In the shade outside Alison's house, a young girl is sitting on the ground, wrapped in a foil blanket, playing with foil triangles. I stare for a second, confused because I have spent so long searching for the foil jacket Tom told me about. After everything with Jimmy, it now feels like such a waste of my time. A waste of my life. It was literally the ramblings of a drunk.

I'm watching the girl play when there's a flicker of movement from the other side. Alison is on her way across the street, next to Willow's daughter, Isabella.

Alison turns to look in the direction the police car headed. 'Everything all right?' she asks.

I look for any sense of the black eye I saw last night but she must have hidden it with make-up.

'Yes,' I reply.

She waits a moment, probably expecting more, then says: 'We were hoping to unpack the tablecloths...'

'Everything's in the back,' I say. 'The bags are heavy but you can climb in and unpack while you go if you want. I've got to check on Orla but I'll be back later if you need help.'

Alison looks to Isabella. 'Is that all right?' she asks.

'Sure.'

FIFTY-SIX

HEIDI

Freddie has worked up quite the sweat as he lugs the tables around with one of the other neighbours whose name I don't know. I was helping for a while but 'getting in the way', so left him to it. I don't think it helped that he dropped a table on his toe, then somehow blamed me, even though I was three metres away.

Isabella has been clambering up onto the back of Dylan's truck, unpacking the various place mats and tablecloths, then carrying them over to the tables that Freddie has been arranging into two long rows. I was half watching as she started but then she disappeared for about fifteen minutes. I felt guilty for not helping and it's only when she re-emerges from her house that I catch her.

'Do you need a hand?' I ask.

Isabella seems conflicted. She glances back to her house, then turns towards the tables. 'You can help me lay if you want,' she says. 'I was going to do some filming but, um...' she tails off and looks to the house once more.

'Are you all right?' I ask.

'Yeah, it's just... Granddad and Grandma are here. It's a bit, um...'

She doesn't need to finish the sentence. The poor girl looks traumatised.

I take the lead and head back to Dylan's truck, where we work on unpacking the bundles of cloths and place mats. We carry them over to the first row of tables. I set to work on spreading the main tablecloth, while Isabella lays the place mats.

'How's your mum?' I ask.

Isabella looks up, surprised: 'Oh... she told you...?'

'Told me what?'

She blinks and shakes her head. 'Uh... I shouldn't have said that.'

'I saw her last night and she seemed a bit distracted.'

Isabella flattens a crease. 'Don't tell her I told you but she kicked Gabe out yesterday.'

I blink at her, surprised. It was barely the other day we were all having dinner together. Not that Willow and Gabe seemed particularly happy to be around each other. 'Really?' I say. 'Why?'

'I don't know. She didn't say. You'd have to ask her – she might tell you.'

'Do they do this sort of thing often? Break up and make up?'

We head back to the truck together. 'Not really. They don't argue much. Not like me and Mum. This feels different.'

'How?'

'Like it's final.'

'Wow.'

When Freddie and I were there for dinner, there was definitely awkwardness and I found it hard to know why they were together. But then I think of what I now know of Freddie and suppose it's not that different. Seven days can be a long time. I wonder whether Freddie was something to do with their break-up. We all felt the tension when Willow got out her yearbook. The one that's now hidden in our house, that I fear my husband stole.

'How do you feel about that?' I ask, remembering where I am.

We stop at the back of the truck and Isabella turns to me. 'Nobody usually asks me that,' she says.

'I'm asking.'

She takes a moment to think: 'I don't know how I feel. I've never had a problem with Gabe, but it's not like he's my dad. I have my own dad.'

There is a moment of reflection and then she clambers up onto the truck bed. Instead of emptying another of the bags, she turns and sits, legs dangling off the back.

'If you found something you knew was wrong, something that would get another person in trouble, what would you do?'

I try to read her face but there's only confusion there.

'How do you mean?' I ask. 'Did you find something?'

'I mean in theory,' she replies, although it doesn't sound like a hypothetical. 'Would you tell the person, or would you go to the police?'

I don't know how to respond. Whatever Isabella is trying to say feels important and yet it's so general that I'm not sure there *is* a right answer.

'I don't think I know what you're asking,' I say. 'If someone was in danger, I'd probably go to the police.'

Isabella rocks her legs gently, like a swing caught in a breeze. She nods with some degree of understanding but that doesn't mean I've been any help. It's hard to know what she's talking about.

'Is this something to do with Gabe?' I ask.

Isabella has been gazing into the distance but blinks back to focus on me. 'Gabe? No...'

Before I can ask anything else, Alison is upon us. 'Thank you so much, ladies!' she beams.

Isabella jumps back to action by pulling another roll of tablecloths from the bags. She passes them to me and then the three of us head to the tables. As Isabella and I continue to lay them, Alison walks up and down with an iron, attempting to smooth the creases. It's plugged into an extension cord that is connected to a series of other extension cords, trailing all the way to her house. One of the other neighbours is behind her, placing plastic flowers and mini Union flags along the centre of the table.

I hang back a little, waiting for Alison to get to my section of table. 'How's Kenneth?' I ask.

'He's fine.'

'Is he coming out today?'

'Maybe later.'

'What about his mum?'

'Maybe later.'

Alison's black eye has almost faded, though it's still impossible to figure out quite what's going on with them. I'd say they were a dysfunctional family but, looking around, I think there are plenty of us who are guilty of that.

As I move back to help Isabella, my phone buzzes with a text from Zoe. I'd almost forgotten that I'd asked the party planner for a picture after visiting yesterday.

So young! Only pic I have of us 3 together. Andy in his grotty red vest, me, Fred

I press to open the photo and it fills the screen. The image is grainy and probably taken on one of the disposable cameras we all used to carry on holidays back in the day.

Zoe doesn't look that different from when she was a teenager. She's sickeningly stunning and must have some seriously good genes. She's in the centre, arms draped around the shoulders of two rake-thin young men. They're all in shorts and vests, showing off tanned arms and legs. Even from the captured moment in time, their grins and sparkling eyes show off the thrill of living day to day. I can see their youth and adventure; their joy of being alive. There's a part of me that craves what they had, that abdication of responsibility from the mundanity of work-rest-repeat.

There's one other thing, though.

I stop, stare, mouth open. It's barely believable, except maybe it is. All these years Freddie and I have been together and now... this.

I close the photo, then open it again – except it's the same as it was the first time.

Because, as incredible as the photo seems, all of a sudden, everything that has happened this week makes complete sense.

FIFTY-SEVEN

4:42 P.M.

DYLAN

'This is my friend, Lauren,' Orla says, putting on her best grown-up voice. She's been doing it for a couple of years but it's only recently that I realised my daughter was making a conscious attempt to sound more like an adult. It's endearing and yet another sign that she is actually growing up.

We are at the long table that almost runs the length of Huntington Grove. At first, they had laid them out into one continuous line – but then people realised it would take a five-minute walk to get to the opposite side of the street. Either that, or a bit of clambering over or under tables. From that, there was a bit of rearranging to put walkthroughs at regular intervals.

Beth is at my side and stretches a hand across the table to shake Lauren's, who is sitting opposite her, next to Orla.

'That's Beth,' Orla announces. 'She's Daddy's *girl*friend.'

The two girls explode into uncontained giggles, as if they've just heard the greatest joke ever told.

'Am I that funny-looking?' Beth asks.

Orla tries to answer but she's so busy laughing that there are only tears coming out.

Beth turns to me: 'Does this happen regularly?'

'At least once an hour when they're together.'

'I think I'll leave you to it for a minute. Be right back.'

Beth levers herself out of the chair just as Lauren gasps the word 'girlfriend', which sets the two girls off again.

Beth shrugs a part-bemused, part-amused look in my direction and heads along the tables until she reaches Willow. She taps her friend on the shoulder and crouches to have a conversation. There's no sign of Gabe and I wonder if he told Willow what happened in my house with Alfie's father. There's also a part of me that wonders whether she already knows? Perhaps the fury I saw is something she sees all too regularly? I wonder if I should have paid better attention.

Willow and Beth turn in unison to give me a joint wave – and it's only then that I realise I'm staring. I switch attention to Lauren and Orla, who are just about getting themselves together. Or they are until Orla whispers 'girlfriend', which sets Lauren off into tears of hysterics.

I lean forward in an attempt to be heard over the engulfing joy. 'I think the two of you need to calm down...'

Ciara was always the disciplinarian in our relationship. I still find it hard to be the serious one and the words never sound right in my voice. If I say 'calm down', it comes out as some sort of code for 'laugh a bit harder'. The girls certainly do that and I'm left scratching my head until Beth returns.

'Are you two still laughing?' she says.

Somehow, even though she's barely said anything, it's like a switch has been flicked. My daughter and her friend settle back into their chairs as if the past five minutes never happened.

'How did you manage that?' I ask.

'You've never been a little girl,' Beth replies. 'You wouldn't know.'

'But you didn't say much.'

'Subliminal messaging. You don't have enough X chromosomes.'

We're interrupted by a loud whine of someone pressing the button on a loudhailer. Everyone winces and then Alison's voice booms. She's standing behind her husband, Kenneth, who has his fingers in his ears.

Alison thanks everyone for coming, although it's not easy to make out everything she's saying because of the creaking feedback that's coming from the speakers. She says something about High Kingsley and then the people sitting closest to me all stand together. I'm not sure what's going on but everyone else is standing, so I copy. This is how every tale of authoritarianism seems to begin – people going along with things because everyone else is. The table in front of us is lined with sandwiches and slices of cake, however. I can't believe anything too imperialist has ever happened in the presence of Victoria sponge.

Next thing I know, the national anthem is blaring from the speakers. I immediately realise I'm wrong about the imperialism and cake thing – because almost everyone starts to join in until it feels like we are all determinedly imploring God to save our monarch. All except Beth. She isn't singing – or even pretending – and gives a cheerful shrug when I turn to look at her.

I mouth the word 'traitor' at her and she grins before leaning close to talk into my ear and replying with: 'We're both off to the Tower.'

'Why me?'

'Talking during the anthem.'

Orla and Lauren are oblivious. I'm not sure where they learned the words but, either way, they are perfectly happy about the whole God and monarch situation.

When the singing is over, we give three cheers for a reason I don't hear and then it's onto the reason we're all here.

Orla reaches for a gingerbread man but I tell her it's sandwiches first. She puts *her* gingerbread man on *her* plate to stop anyone else from getting in first, then turns her attention to the platter of sandwiches. Lauren is making short work of the cheese and ham ones, while Beth is searching for something without meat.

My daughter takes a couple of ham sandwiches from the platter and opens them up on her plate. 'Can I have Marmite?' she asks.

Beth turns between us: 'You let her have Marmite *with* ham? Are you some sort of monster?'

'It's how she's always had them.'

'Marmite? With ham? You are a terrible parent and, if I'm honest, an even worse human being. I'm going to have to get onto social services about this.'

I smile at her. Usually, I'd tell Orla to find something she does want but it's been a long week and I figure that, on this occasion, I'll let her be fussy.

'I'll find the jar,' I say, pushing myself up from the table.

Beth touches my arm as I go and grins up. There is a fraction of a second in which our eyes meet and I know, somehow, that things are going to be all right. The past three years have felt like swimming upstream. Now, I have crested the top.

I head along the drive and let myself back into the house. I shut the door behind but have only been inside a moment when I sense something isn't right. It's hard to say what or why but something prickles the back of the neck...

'Hello...?'

From behind, there is the gentle, joyous hubbub of the street party but my voice echoes around the house without reply.

I edge into the living room, poking my head around the

frame to see an empty space. After that, I move back through the hall into the kitchen. There is nobody there either, only a sink of dishes from Orla's over-enthusiastic baking.

I open the cupboard next to the fridge and take out the jar of Marmite, which is when there's a scuffling of movement from behind. When I turn, Alfie's father is standing in the doorway to the hall. There is a scabbed crack across one of his eyes, which is still rimmed by a mottled yellowy-purple. The other is covered by a bandage.

'What—?' I start, but don't get through a sentence.

He nods past me, towards the back garden. 'Nice little jump over the back fence. Where's your mate?'

'Gabe?'

'That his name, is it? Where is he?'

'I don't know.'

His movement is slow and deliberate as he reaches into his back pocket. I've never seen one before, not away from television, but, when he shows me what he's holding, I know what it is.

'I guess it's just you and me,' he says – as he points the stun gun at my chest.

FIFTY-EIGHT
4:49 P.M.

WILLOW

It's rather awkward singing along to the national anthem while facing people who are relative strangers. Freddie and Heidi are looking at spots close to their feet as the music plays. I only notice because of a quick glance up – and then I return to doing the same.

Mum and Dad are on one side, Isabella the other. Three generations of us all. My parents are belting out the anthem as if they've snagged the solo at the Royal Albert Hall. Dad even has a hand on his heart.

When the singing and three cheers are over, everyone sits, ready to eat, although Isabella remains on her feet. She crouches to talk into my ear: 'I'm going to head inside to film some stuff from up higher,' she says.

'OK. See you soon.'

I watch my daughter move into the house and, even though I'm here without my husband, even though I haven't heard from him since he left, there is a strange sense of a cloud having lifted.

Or partly.

It's true of me but, as I look across to the table to Freddie, I wonder if I should tell Heidi what I have figured out. It took that question about the that kid up on the school roof for me to know for sure. Perhaps I should ask Freddie himself?

He glances up, catches my eye for the merest moment, then holds it for an uncomfortable couple of seconds before turning away.

Is it *really* my place to get involved?

'This is lovely,' Heidi says in the way people do when small talk isn't coming.

I feel sorry for her, but perhaps I shouldn't? Maybe she knows and doesn't mind? Maybe it doesn't matter?

'It's great that everyone chipped in,' I say, knowing that I had very little to do with the spread.

Heidi and Freddie reach for a sandwich together and there's a strange moment as they touch and reel from each other. It's far more telling than the forced smiles that follow.

Mum picks up a sandwich and opens it up, showing me the slimy pinkish contents. 'What's all this?' she asks.

'I think it's tuna.'

'Oh. I don't like fish.'

She folds the sandwich back together and returns it to the main plate.

'You can't put it back,' I say.

'Why not? It'd be a waste otherwise.'

'Because you've already picked it up.'

'But I don't like fish.'

'So, don't pick up a sandwich with fish in it!'

She pulls a face and grabs what turns out to be a cheese sandwich instead. After a small bite, she foists it onto my father's plate. 'Don't like Cheddar,' she says. 'Never have.'

Dad picks it up and looks at it: 'You used to always go for Cheddar,' he says.

'Since when?'

'And tuna.'

'Name one time when I've ever eaten tuna. Go on. Just one.'

'Bournemouth in 1984. That chippy by the beach.'

When I glance across to Heidi, there is a knowing smirk on her face. She leans in a little. 'Have you met Alison's husband?' she asks.

'Kenneth? Once or twice. He doesn't seem to be around much.'

Heidi glances sideways to the next table, where Alison and Kenneth are sitting next to one another. It feels like Heidi wants to ask something but then has a bite of sandwich instead.

We continue eating politely as my parents bicker with one another. I'm nibbling the corners of a horrible cucumber sandwich but can sense Freddie watching. When I peer up, he doesn't turn away. Not this time. Our eyes lock and it's almost as if there's a psychic connection between us. Without a word, I realise he is ahead of me. He knows what I know – and I wasn't as clever as I thought I was when I blocked his car yesterday.

I push back my chair quickly and it catches on a small pothole in the tarmac, almost sending me over backwards. I just about keep my balance and stumble to my feet, using the table for support.

'You all right?' Heidi asks.

'Just need to pop inside for a minute.'

I ignore Mum's protests and hurry up the drive, into the house, waiting as I listen to Isabella moving from room to room upstairs. The living-room door is closed and, from nowhere, I suddenly feel flushed. Sweat pools around my ears, of all places, and I move into the kitchen, where I run cold water over a towel. It's as I turn off the tap that I hear the front door going. I assume it's Isabella leaving – but it's not.

When I turn, Freddie is advancing along the hall towards

the kitchen. It feels like the walls are closing in but he must notice my panic because he holds his arms wide.

'I'm not here for trouble,' he says, voice quivering. He stops a step or two into the kitchen, glances both ways and then: 'I know you made up the story about the school roof. About Alistair, whatever his name was, being up there. You used it to see if I'd go along...'

It's blunter than I suspected but at least the truth is out.

It was Gabe who triggered the thought. He was talking about me when he said 'people can't hide who they are' – but he was wrong. People *can* hide the truth about themselves. They do it every day when they go to work and pretend it's what they want from life. I've done it. I still do.

People can hide in plain sight and pretend to be someone they are not – but what they *can't* do is fake memories.

Which is what led me to Freddie...

'You never went to our school,' I say. 'You're not Freddie Potter. It's why you've been so keen to avoid me.'

The nod is slow but accepting. We both know it's true.

'Who are you?' I ask.

'It's a really long story...'

Neither of us gets a chance to say anything more because the door that connects the living room to the kitchen thunders open and there, standing in the doorway, is Gabe.

Nothing happens for a moment. I look at Gabe, who looks at Freddie, who looks at me.

'How long have you been here?' I ask eventually.

'It's my house, too, isn't it?' Gabe replies.

His words slur into one another. I've spent most of the day at the front of the house. He has his own key and could have let himself in at any point. He could have been in the living room for hours. Isabella would've gone straight upstairs, and I came into the kitchen.

Gabe turns between Freddie and me, looking us up and

down. 'This explains a lot, dunnit? This is why you want me out.'

'It's not like that,' I say.

'What *is* it like?'

Freddie only gets out the word 'Look—' before Gabe lunges sideways and crunches a vicious punch into his jaw. It's almost in slow motion as Freddie slumps sideways. His eyes are glazed, lids fluttering, and he doesn't use his hands to cushion the drop. When he hits the ground, there is a splintering *thwack* as his head collides with one of the dining chairs.

Gabe stands over Freddie's prone body, then kicks the other man's legs out of his way. He dusts off his hands like a saloon owner in a Western. He turns to me and cracks his knuckles.

'I guess this has been a long time coming...'

FIFTY-NINE

4:55 P.M.

DYLAN

I try to back away from Alfie's father and the stun gun but there's nowhere to go. The handle of the fridge digs into my back as I glance across to the knife rack on the far side of the kitchen.

'You don't even know my name, do you?' the man growls.

'No.'

'Kev,' he says. 'Your mate fractured my eye socket. I could've gone blind.'

'That wasn't me.'

'You didn't stop him stamping on my head, though, did yer?'

He tears away the bandage that was covering his eye and we stare at each other. The eye that was covered has no white surrounding the iris, only red.

'You were in my house uninvited,' I say.

He ignores that: 'You think it's all right to go around threatening kids?'

'Your son was *bullying* my daughter.'

Kev nods: 'Aye, well some things are for boys and some things are for girls. She shouldn't have been there.'

'My daughter can do whatever she wants.'

'That so?'

'Yes.'

'I guess she can grow up to be a doctor then.'

I don't get a chance to reply because, the next second, without warning, it feels as if the world is on fire. A thunderous earthquake has struck. There are green stars, pink stars, then black.

It's only after the trembling stops that I realise that isn't what happened at all. My thoughts are sluggish but there are prongs in my neck, attached to the stun gun via some sort of wire. The house wasn't moving: *I* was.

I'm on the floor with no memory of getting there.

As I try to push myself up, the vibrations come again, forcing my very bones through my skin.

There's a thought buried deep, reminding me of what's hidden under the cabinet in the living room. If I can only get there...

Except it isn't there at all.

I had it in my bag at Jimmy's house. JBG's. The initials burn as a third round of pain bursts into me.

There's no breath in my lungs, no thoughts, no...

I don't know what's happening.

The groaning is mine. I know that much. I can't breathe and it's dark. My eyes are closed but I've somehow not realised. It feels as if I need every muscle to try to force them open. My eyelids flutter, the lashes batting back and forth across my vision, until I can finally see.

A man is there... Alfie's dad... Kev... and I remember that my gun is in the bag I took to Jimmy's. I stretch, momentarily believing the bag to be at my feet, though there is only air. It's a murky, clumsy memory. A half-thought that might or might not be true. When I was parked at the railway station, after leaving Jimmy's, I put the bag in the back of my truck, next to all the table settings that Alison wanted. When I got home, Beth was waiting for me – and I... don't know what happened to the pistol.

It's not in the house any longer.

A face appears in front of mine and we're eye to eye. I can see the deep red of Kev's eye where there should be white. Then he leans back and cracks a punch into my stomach. The wind is gone once more, as I crease into a ball and gasp for breath.

'Didn't see that coming, didya?' he says. 'How'd ya like that?'

I manage to wrench the spikes from my neck and memories swirl as I remember he had a stun gun. I've been shocked. The hard kitchen floor is cool on my palms as I crawl towards the door.

Kev taps me on the back of the head and I twist to look at him. 'You're not going anywhere,' he says.

WILLOW

As Gabe steps towards me, I press back until there is nowhere left to go. The sink is behind and Gabe's in front. Freddie is on the floor, not moving.

'You did this,' Gabe says. 'You pushed me to it.'

'Pushed you to what?'

'Everything! Nothing was good enough for you. You couldn't just get a job, you had to become a student. What about me? I had to work longer and harder to keep us here.'

'We talked about me going to uni.'

'*You* talked,' he says. 'You'd already made your mind up. It always has to be about you.'

Gabe leans over me and the acrid smell of alcohol singes his breath. He hasn't shaven since he left and the prickles of his beard spike my chin as he presses so close that our noses touch. I push him away but he only moves back a little.

'What did I get from it all?' he asks.

'What did you want?'

'The only pleasure I had was the odd beer next door.'

'I never stopped you doing that – or anything else. It's not like I forced you to stay home.'

'But you never did anything to help, did you?'

'I'm trying to educate myself, to have a career.'

'You're almost forty,' he scoffs. 'There *is* no career for you. You wrecked your life and now you want to wreck mine.'

It takes a moment to realise what he means.

'Isabella never wrecked my life,' I reply but I'm stunned at the suggestion. My voice wavers. My daughter has never been that to me.

'That's not what it sounds like when you're screaming at one another.'

'She *never* wrecked my life,' I repeat.

Gabe takes half a step back, which gives me a microsecond to glance towards Freddie, who still hasn't shifted.

'Do you even love me?'

Gabe was slurring before but this is different. His words are haunting, riddled with betrayal. He knows the answer and I suspect he always did. I want to say yes but we both know it would be a lie. Both Craig and Gabe have said that I make everything about me but it's not true, not completely.

Everything is about Isabella and always has been.

I don't think it was necessarily a conscious thought at the time but Gabe has provided the stability for Isabella to get through her exams and become an adult. It's what I always wanted for her. Without Gabe to mediate, if it had only been my daughter and I, we'd have argued and argued until she stormed off to live with her dad.

It was unconscious, certainly at first, but I've used Gabe and we both know it.

'Maybe once,' I whisper.

Maybe once I loved him – but perhaps it was the thought *of* him. Of anyone stable.

It's not stable now.

'At least you're honest,' my husband says.

'Why do you do it?' I ask.

'Do what?'

'Pay people to beat them up?'

He chews his lip for a second and I wonder if he's been thinking on this since I kicked him out. Whether there's been any introspection. 'Don't you ever get angry?' he asks. 'Don't you ever feel that need to just...'

My husband doesn't finish the sentence but I watch his fist ball, his eyes narrow. I see it then, the thing I never spotted before. He assaulted that man – probably many others – and enjoyed it. The alternative was to do it to me.

To Isabella.

Should I be grateful it was somebody else and not me? Because I'm not. Gabe is a monster and I somehow never saw it. I'm disgusted I brought him into my daughter's life and wonder if he ever went further. If the people he hurt ever did something terrible to try to forget.

This type of violence never has a happy ending.

And now, in my kitchen, with my daughter upstairs, there's a tear in my husband's eye as he raises his fist. I cower, trying to crease back beyond the sink – but there is no space and no escape.

Then there's a bang.

SIXTY-ONE

5:00 P.M.

DYLAN

Then there's a bang.

It's distant but somehow close. I reel, expecting a blow, though when I look up again, Kev is hazy, not quite in focus. He has moved towards the back door.

'Was that a gun?' he asks himself. He bobs forward and back, between me and the exit – and then there's a second bang, louder than the first.

Or maybe there isn't?

My ears are ringing and it feels as if I've gone to bed after a long night of drinking. The world is spinning and I'm not sure which way is up, which is down.

What becomes clear is that Kev has gone.

The back door is open and, as I use the dining chair to pull myself up, I watch a dark shape disappearing over the back fence. The room is starting to swirl back into focus, though my neck burns. When I touch the spot close to my collarbone, I come away with a smudge of blood on my fingers.

Orla.

My thoughts are suddenly clear and I dash to the front door
– or think I do. I bounce off both sides of the hall before finally
getting there. When I open it, Beth is by the truck, Orla on one
side, Lauren on the other. Her mouth is open in shock.

'Are you OK?' I pant.

Beth steps towards me and opens my right eye with her
fingers. 'Are *you* OK?' she asks. 'You're swaying.'

'What was the noise?'

'I don't know. It was next door.'

I turn towards Willow's house, or try to, but almost spin
myself off my feet.

'It sounded like a car backfiring,' Beth adds. 'Either
that, or...'

I know what it sounded like. I know what it *was*.

A glance towards the back of my truck tells me too much.
The bags of linens have been emptied – but there was another
bag there, too.

'Get the girls inside,' I say. 'Go upstairs and barricade the
door.'

Beth doesn't question this. She pushes the girls into the
house and I hear them clattering up the stairs. As that's happening, I watch as the tables full of people turn to one another,
asking what's going on.

Only Heidi from over the road seems to have some idea.
She darts through one of the gaps between the tables and rushes
into Willow's house. I try to call after her but the words won't
come. The world is still spinning and, by the time I get to
Willow's door, a loud scream echoes from inside.

SIXTY-TWO
5:00 P.M.

WILLOW

My ears feel like they've burst. After the bang, all I can hear is someone ringing a bell next to my ear. Plaster splinters from the ceiling, caking my head with flakes of white.

Gabe was moving towards me but he's frozen, caught in Medusa's glare, about to turn to stone. Everything has stopped and then, as if someone snaps their fingers, my husband crashes to the side, landing on the floor next to Freddie.

There, in the doorway, is Isabella. She is inexplicably clutching a gun but her hands are trembling and the weapon drops to the floor. There is a second bang but I only know this because I feel it, rather than hear it.

My daughter's eyes are wide with terrified shock as she turns to me and mouths a single word.

'Mum.'

THE FUTURE

Police statement: Kevin Jamieson.

Officer: For the benefit of the tape, as well as myself, those present are Kevin Jamieson and his solicitor, Ms Moseley. It is 08:33 hours. Mr Jamieson, can I ask the name of your son?

Kevin: Alf… Alfie.

Officer: And am I correct in thinking that Alfie attended a football camp in recent weeks?

Kevin: Yeah.

Officer: Does the name 'Orla Wilson' mean anything to you?

[Inaudible]

Officer: Was that a no?

Kevin: I don't know her.

Officer: What about her father?

Kevin: Don't know him.

[*Image shown of Dylan Wilson*]

Officer: Do you know this man?

Kevin: I said no.

Officer: You have to actually look at the photo, before you tell us no.

Kevin: I don't know him.

Officer: Do you know anything about your son bullying this man's daughter?

Kevin: No.

Officer: Are you sure?

Solicitor: Just to remind you, we are talking about minors, all of whom are under the age of criminal responsibility. There's no reason to think Mr Jamieson has any knowledge of what his son might or might not have done, nor Ms Wilson for that matter.

Officer: Noted. Was there ever any interaction between you and *Mr* Wilson, in which he asked about your son bullying his daughter?

Kevin: No.

Officer: Are you aware of any incident involving Mr Wilson and your son, in which Mr Wilson asked about the bullying?

Kevin: No.

Officer: Are you aware of Mr Wilson possibly threatening your son?

Kevin: No.

[*Inaudible*]

Officer: OK, moving on. Do you know where Huntington Grove is?

Kevin: No.

Officer: Have you ever visited Huntington Grove?

Kevin: No.

Officer: What would you say if I told you your car numberplate was picked up by an ANPR camera very close to that area on two occasions in the days prior to Saturday – then again *on* the Saturday?

[*Inaudible*]

Solicitor: Mr Jamieson has already told you he doesn't know the area. You can't expect someone to know the name of every street in a town. You didn't state how close this camera is to the *actual* address in question, so I don't see how you can expect him to answer properly. I should add that Mr Jamieson is not under arrest and is here under his own volition. He is trying as best he can to cooperate.

Officer: Thank you for that. We do, um, appreciate his, um, cooperation. Mr Jamieson, the white of your eye is red and it looks very painful. Can I ask how that happened?

Kevin: Tripped.

Officer: What did you trip on?

Kevin: Carpet.

Officer: Did this happen at your home?

Kevin: Yeah.

Officer: Is that what you told the nurse in the hospital?

[*Inaudible*]

Solicitor: Again, Mr Jamieson is not under arrest. He has answered your question about his eye, even though there's no indication of why you're asking. His medical history is allowed to be private, unless you're accusing him of something.

Officer: I suppose I'm after a bit of clarity about your whereabouts on the Saturday.

Kevin: Why?

Officer: Because a serious incident happened at Huntington Grove – and, according to our ANPR camera, you were speeding away very quickly afterwards. This happened within days of what might have been a disagreement between you and Mr Wilson.

Solicitor: I hate to keep banging the same drum here – but my client has told you there was no disagreement. He says he has no knowl-

edge of Mr Wilson, or his daughter. If you have anything to say otherwise, you're free to present evidence. Other than that, the fact Mr
Jamieson might have been in the general area of what happened at
Huntington Grove is no proof of anything. Lots of people were there at
the time. Lots of people were driving at the time. Are you interviewing
everyone in a car from a mile radius?

Officer: You know we're not.

Solicitor: So I don't understand why we're here. Mr Jamieson has
answered your questions in good faith and, unless you have any
reason to say otherwise, I think we're going to leave.

Officer: Interview terminated at 08:41 hours.

SIXTY-THREE
SUNDAY

HEIDI

The sun is starting to come up as I reverse the car onto the driveway. The barricades have gone from either end of the road, though the bunting still zigzags across the lampposts above. The tables are once again stacked on Alison's lawn, while, over the road, the front of Willow's house is ringed by blue and white police tape.

A different kind of bunting, I suppose.

A police car is parked on the road outside, a single officer in the driver's seat.

As I put the handbrake on and turn off the engine, the officer turns sideways to look at us.

I turn to Freddie in the passenger seat. He's in a sling and there are stitches across the bottom of his hairline close to his ear: 'How long do you think he's been there?' I ask.

'No idea. Poor fella must've got the short straw.'

I unlock the house and wait for Freddie to move through to the kitchen before locking up behind us. Everything feels different. Everything *is* different.

I follow my husband into the kitchen and set the kettle boiling as we sit on opposite sides of the table. Freddie is looking at the floor and it's hard not to feel the eeriness. The kitchen in Willow's place is the exact size and shape of ours. The table is in the same spot.

'You're going to have one hell of a bruise,' I say.

Freddie half-winces, half-smiles, as he rests his arm on the table and fiddles with the sling using his free hand.

'Wait here,' I say – and he doesn't question me as I slip through the house, into his study. I retrieve the lockbox from its hiding place, plus Willow's yearbook and the rest of it. Back in the kitchen, it all goes on the table.

I think we needed a night's sleep before this.

'How?' Freddie asks. An eyebrow is twitching and, if he wasn't on so many painkillers, I figure his reaction would be much stronger.

The kettle plips off and I ignore his question as I fill two mugs with hot water and instant coffee granules. I'm not in the mood to make it properly.

After putting a mug in front of Freddie and placing the other on my side of the table, I push Willow's yearbook towards him. 'I'll tell you how I knew about all this stuff if you tell me how you got this...'

He's silent – but I suspect he knows what's coming.

I slide the stolen class photo across the table – and then, while Freddie is looking at that, I find the picture Zoe sent and offer him my phone.

'Do you want to tell me?' I ask.

He looks between the yearbook, the class photo, and the image Zoe had of her, Andrew and Freddie in Central America. I watch his eyes widen and his mouth open. He goldfishes a non-response and then manages a panicked: 'I can explain.'

'Go on then. Because, in the yearbook, Freddie has a small

scar on his nose. It's in the class photo, too.' I look up to my husband: 'Except *you* don't have one.'

He gulps and it's indisputably true. Two photos of a young Freddie, both with a clear scar the man in front of me doesn't have.

I point to Zoe's photo, then add: 'In *this* picture, Freddie has small ear lobes and brown eyes – but yours are green and your lobes are massive.'

I point to the image of Andrew Westley, standing and smiling next to Zoe.

'Like him,' I add.

Freddie presses back in his chair and turns from the pictures. I wonder if he knew this was coming. 'Where did you get that photo?' he asks, defeated.

'Does it matter?'

It takes a while for him to speak, and then: 'It can only be Zoe. I've looked her up now and again. It seems like she's been doing well. I always felt sorry for dumping her and running.'

'Tell me,' I say, 'Or you might as well leave.'

He glances up and catches my eyes. It's only for a moment but that's all it needs for me to realise quite what a horror show the past week or so must have been for him. I can only imagine the panic when he realised we'd moved in opposite one of the few people who could blow apart his life.

I shouldn't... but I feel sorry for him.

'My name is Andrew Westley,' he says, with a sigh. 'Andy. Or it was a long time ago.'

'How long have you been Freddie?'

'About eighteen years. We were travelling together.'

'Who?'

'Me and Freddie... the real Freddie.'

He sips the coffee and stares at the photo on my phone.

'I had my twentieth birthday when we were together. We were in Guatemala and Freddie, um...'

Freddie, *my* Freddie, winces at the name that isn't his. He takes a breath and continues.

'*Freddie* used to do this thing with a lighter. He'd snap it open and closed. I'd tell him all the time to stop but it was like some sort of stress relief. We'd gone to bed in this back room one night but I woke up coughing. It was hot and smoggy and I couldn't figure out what was happening. I thought it was a dream, then I realised there was a fire. I was sleeping near the door but Freddie was on the other side of the room. I shouted for him but the moment I opened my mouth, all the smoke went in. I couldn't stop coughing. He wasn't moving anyway. He was either unconscious, or...'

He turns my phone around and pushes it back towards me. I pick it up and stare into the face of the real Freddie. There are similarities between him and Andy – but the picture was taken almost two decades ago. Either of them could have changed enough to be the other. I wonder whether Willow figured it out.

'What then?' I ask.

'I grabbed both bags from the bottom of my bed and got out. The smoke was pouring from the building by then. There was some bloke on the street who tried to go in and grab Freddie but no one could get past the fire. It spread so quickly. It felt like two minutes later and the whole thing was black. There was no fire brigade, or anything. I don't know if someone called, or...'

'You had the real Freddie's bag...?'

'I didn't realise it was his at first but I had mine *and* his. He had all the money. I couldn't afford to do anything without him. I definitely couldn't have got a plane home. He kept saying he'd pay for the flight when the time came. The hostel was illegal and I didn't want to be there when the police arrived. I headed to this park just outside the city. I was going through the bags, which is when I realised I had Freddie's passport, too. There was this moment that I can't really describe where it felt like I knew what to do.'

I know already but ask anyway: 'What *did* you do?'

Freddie has another mouthful of coffee, then downs the rest. He stares into the empty reaches at the bottom, as if expecting more to appear, so I slide him my almost full mug.

'We looked similar enough,' he says. 'Not the same but tanned guys with dark hair. Freddie's life was so much more fun than mine... or it seemed like that. We'd both lost our parents but he had this massive inheritance. He was using that to get himself around the world.'

'You took his money?'

'It's not like he was going to use it.' Freddie bites his lip and sighs: 'I didn't mean that.'

He's quiet for a moment and I give him the benefit of the doubt. I don't think he *did* mean it in the way it came out, even if he's correct. A dead man wasn't going to use a bank account.

'Freddie could do something with his life,' my Freddie says. 'It's not like he had millions, but enough to give himself a decent start. I had none of that. If I'd gone home, I'd have no money. No anything. We were friends but I was still stuck with him because he was paying for everything. I couldn't suggest some-where to go because he made the choices.'

'You used his passport...?'

There's a long gap and then a solemn: 'Right.'

Freddie – *my* Freddie – looks up and his eyes are watery. 'I've never been more scared than when the guy at the airport checked the passport.'

'He let you through...?'

'Barely made a comment. Nobody did – not even when I got back to Britain and had to go through passport control again. I'd memorised his date of birth and place of birth but didn't need it. I couldn't go back to Marsh Vale because his friends would know I wasn't the real Freddie – and it's not like there was anything for me where I come from.'

'Where *do* you come from?'

He ponders for a moment, probably wondering whether he should say. Then it's as if he decides it doesn't matter.

'This little village near Swindon. Nowhere, really. I ended up going to Manchester, to get myself started. It was a city and there were things to do. I used Freddie's passport to get a replacement using my photo – and then everything else came with it. Before I knew it, I had a driving licence, National Insurance number, bank accounts, everything – all in his name. We were both orphans, so who cared?'

It's a lot to take in and yet, at its core, it isn't entirely abhorrent. It's not as bad as when I wondered if he'd killed his friend, accidentally or not, and did a runner.

I point to the lockbox: 'Have you had that the whole time we've been together?'

Another pause and then a gentle nod: 'The certificate used to be under the carpet in our bedroom – but I got panicked about some sort of water leak. It's the only piece of Andy that's left.'

He says the name as if it isn't his and I need to remind myself that *he's* Andy. This Andy is *my* Freddie. We both stare at the box for a moment and there's unquestionably something sad about the only remnant of a person being able to fit into something so small.

'Did you steal Willow's yearbook?' I ask.

He glances away. 'The window was open...'

'So you took it?'

'I was worried that if she spent too long looking at photos of Freddie, she'd figure it out. I saw the scar right away.'

'You don't drink,' I say, 'because Andy was a bad drunk.'

Freddie fiddles with his sling, then reaches behind his neck to undo the Velcro. His injured arm rests limply on the table.

'Zoe...?' he asks.

'I'm asking you.'

'Andy was a *terrible* drunk,' he says – and it sounds like he's talking about a different person. I suppose, in some ways, he is. 'So, I don't drink. I haven't since I got back to Britain. I guess I was always saying I'd never drink again and, eventually, that's one promise kept.'

I suppose that's one thing he has going for him. I wonder whether his lack of enthusiasm for travelling is due to a worry about his passport being checked too closely, or because he has some sort of phobia after what happened when he was in South America. I almost ask – but it doesn't feel like the time.

'How did you ever get used to answering to someone else's name?' I try instead.

'I used to think about it all the time. First thing in the morning, last thing at night, every minute in between. Then, gradually, I'd realise that I'd gone ten minutes and not thought of Andy. Then it was twenty minutes. Thirty. In the end, it was maybe once a day.' He pauses and then adds: 'Then I met you and it didn't matter.'

I swipe away the photo and pocket my phone.

'My name's not Potter,' I say.

'It is. I'm Freddie; he's me. I became him. I wanted to tell you, but...'

'But what?'

Freddie can't answer. Andy can't answer. We sit silently for a moment and I'm not sure where it leaves us. Everything's changed and yet, I suppose, nothing has. Freddie is the same person I married, even if that isn't his name. We've been together all these years. Despite the last week or so, we've been happy. Much of the confusion and suspicion from the past week can now be explained but that doesn't mean I've quite got my head around it yet.

'I'm going out,' I say, pushing myself up from the table.

There's a panic to his voice. 'Are you coming back?'

I head for the door, then pause in the frame. 'I'm coming back,' I tell him – because I know I will. Except I need time.

Outside, and an orange crescent of sunlight curves over the top of Willow's house, arcing across the police car in which the unfortunate officer is still waiting. He glances sideways to me and nods a slim acknowledgement, which I return with a head inclination of my own.

It's a strange sense that, after everything. Huntington Grove *now* feels like home. That dread I felt when I first carried boxes from my car a little over a week ago has been replaced by a sense of belonging.

As I glance across to the house and police tape, I think of Willow's daughter, poor Isabella, and wonder what will come next for her.

There isn't a lot of battery left on my phone but I try calling Willow, wanting to leave a message of support. I could text, of course, but sometimes a person needs to hear another voice. I figure she'll need that as much as anyone in the coming weeks.

It's a little after seven in the morning and, considering everything that happened yesterday, I really don't expect her to answer. Which is why it's a surprise when a woman's voice replies almost instantly.

'Heidi...?'

'I didn't think you'd...'

'Heidi?'

Willow is shouting and I have to turn down the volume a couple of notches until we both say 'How are you?' at the same time. There's a joint silence and then I ask where she is.

'My ears are ringing,' Willow says, still talking loudly. 'I can't hear properly. Hang on.' There is a muffled shuffle and then Willow adds: 'Can you hear me?'

'I asked where you are.'

'I'm at the police station. Where are you?'

'Home. How is Isabella?'

Willow says she needs to go somewhere more private and I

start to pace along the pavement as I wait until her voice returns. She's speaking much quieter this time.

'I think it's going to be all right,' Willow says, although there's a quiver to her voice.

'Really?'

'You can't just shoot someone – but the police seem to accept there were extenuating circumstances. It seems like they're more worried about where the gun came from.'

'Where *did* it come from?'

'Isabella says it was in one of the bags containing all the tablecloths.'

I miss a pace and almost trip over my own feet before catching myself: 'What do you mean?'

'That's what she told me, and that's what she's telling the police. She was going to hand the gun into the police but then Gabe showed up and...'

I stop and sit on the kerb, rubbing my temple as I realise this is what Isabella was asking about yesterday. I can't remember exactly what she said but it was something about finding a thing she knew was wrong. She was asking me what to do if it would get another person in trouble. If only I'd pressed further, she might have told me about the gun.

But, then, if she'd done that, she might not have been there to stop Gabe.

I almost tell Willow about the conversation, except some secrets are meant to be kept. What good would it do?

'Are you still there?' Willow asks.

'Yes. How's Gabe?'

'He's not dead – but with my statement and Freddie's, he's not going anywhere soon.' There's a pause and then she adds: 'I need to ask you something about Freddie...'

I don't reply, not at first, but there's a synergy between us, even though we're on the phone. 'Did you know?' I ask.

There's a pause but then clarity to her voice: 'Not at first. Did *you* know?'

'I do now.'

We sit on either end of a phone call, neither speaking. We don't need to. It's hard to describe the silence but it feels like some sort of sisterhood. An understanding. We each figured out the same thing separately.

'What are you going to do?' Willow asks.

There's a creak from behind and I spin to see Kenneth wheeling a bin along his driveway. He stops and starts to pick up small bits of litter from the lawn. When he sees me, he pauses, stares, and then turns and heads back into the back garden.

'Heidi?'

'I don't know,' I tell Willow. 'I don't know what I'm going to do.'

Willow has to go and I tell her that I'll be around if she needs me. She hangs up and I know it's true. We won't be moving house – and Willow and I will become the friend we each need. That phone call confirmed it. I need her in my life and, maybe, she needs me.

Except it's not only about me and her.

I should leave it, I know, but I can't. There are so many secrets in my life, on this street, that I have to ask.

I head to Alison's house and ring the bell at the front, as she asked. I wait, listening to voices beyond. At first, there's no sign anyone will answer – but then the door opens and Alison is there. The first Alison I met, with the tight bun and free facelift. She stares at me curiously, then towards the police car on the other side of the road.

'That was a shock, wasn't it?' she says.

I presume she means the gunshot of the day before. It was a street party that definitely won't be forgotten.

'Can we go for a walk?' I ask.

'I have to—'

'Can we go now?'

SIXTY-FOUR

DYLAN

I twist to look through the window towards Willow's house, where the police car sits outside. A bored-looking officer is in the driver's seat, who seems like he's tapping something into his phone. Diagonally across the street, Heidi is sitting on the kerb talking into her phone. It's hard not to wonder what each of them are saying.

Is it about me?

About the gun?

My gun.

A good five minutes pass before I finally stop watching the police car. The officer hasn't moved but it seems likely someone will come for me sooner or later. It was my gun that did the shooting, after all. My *illegal* weapon.

I caused this.

I wonder if Isabella knows it was mine? She must have taken it from the back of my truck, so will have some idea. Is that what she'll tell the police? Is it better for me to confess now, when they might not know, or to give it time and see what happens? I could say I'd never seen it before but who knows if that lie would hold? There were lots of bags in the back of the truck and everything had been left overnight and through the morning. So much time for anyone to have interfered with it. Nobody can prove otherwise.

Deny, deny, deny.

I was always so careful to wipe away any possible finger-prints. That gun could be anyone's. I bought it with cash from a guy at the back of a pub, knowing that money was going to end up injected into his arms. If he's still alive, he'll never remember me. If he somehow does, who'd believe him over a devoted father?

Deny, deny, deny.

Beyond all reasonable doubt and all that. They would have to prove it was mine, I don't have to prove it isn't.

That's what I tell myself anyway.

There's a snap from the back of the room and I spin quickly, expecting Kev to be holding the stun gun. My vision is still hazy but there is nobody there. I should tell the police what Alfie's father did, of course, but perhaps I deserved it for all those visits to Tom over the years? For all those times in which I made him repeat over and over what he thought he saw. Then there's what I did to Jimmy. To JBG. He'd be within his rights to tell the police how I barged into his kitchen.

There is a definite creak from the stairs this time and I turn to see Beth walking into the living room. She's bare-footed, wearing the biggest T-shirt I own, which hangs a little above her knees. We say nothing at first as she crosses the room and snakes an arm along my waist.

'Sleep well?' she asks.

'No. You?'

'Like a baby on Calpol.'

She presses herself into me tight. 'Orla's still out,' she says.

'She sleeps like her mum.'

I realise what I've said too late – but Beth is unconcerned.

'Is it like this every week?' she asks mischievously, nodding towards the street beyond.

I snort without meaning to. I don't deserve her and perhaps I don't deserve this life. Who knows how many more times I'll be able to enjoy these moments?

It might be a lifetime in which I get away with everything, or the police officer outside could open his door and put an end to it all. Either is as likely as the other.

'I reckon every street has its secrets,' I say.

SIXTY-FIVE

HEIDI

Alison looks to me from her doorstep and the sense of her dominance from the other day has shifted. Her brow somehow creases and then she nods.

We can go for a walk – and we can go now.

Without bothering to tell anyone inside that she's leaving, Alison closes her front door and steps into the warmth.

We start in the same direction from days before, though this time we're at my pace.

'Why did you walk out on the job Freddie got you?' I ask.

She probably knew it was coming and offers a 'Hmmm...' and then: 'I have a complicated relationship.'

'I gathered.'

'Kenneth's mother watched me getting into the car with Freddie and didn't like what she saw. She's old-fashioned like that. Women with men and the like. She got him to fly back, saying I was having an affair.'

I'm not sure why I ask but it comes out anyway: 'Are you?'

It gets a snort. 'I don't want to sleep with your husband, if that's what you're asking, Heidi. Either way, Kenneth came home, so I quit. He doesn't want me to have a job.'

Part of me wants to ask 'why' but we don't know each other well enough. It's hard to miss the parallels anyway. We both *want* to work but, for different reasons, because of our husbands, neither of us are. Is this the sacrifice we make for love?

We're on the towpath again, following the canal. It's early but still busier on a Sunday than the other day. There are kids riding bikes, adults strolling hand in hand, some teenagers eating breakfast ice cream from the van that's parked half on the pavement near the high street.

'Does Kenneth stop you doing other things?' I ask.

Alison doesn't answer at first.

'He doesn't *stop* me doing anything. You saw that the other day.'

I definitely saw her slapping him and the *crack* still rings when I think of it. She hit him so hard. I let that sit for a moment, replaying those images. I don't know him and I barely know her.

'So why give up the job?' I ask.

'Because I respect my husband's wishes.'

She sounds firm but cowed, and it's impossible to reconcile this enigma of a woman. She respects her husband to the detriment of her own career. And yet...

'Where did you get the black eye?' I ask.

Alison lets out a long sigh, then nods towards the ice cream van, where there's no queue. 'Want one?' she asks.

I tell her no, even though I probably do.

She buys herself a 99, then we continue walking. There's a strange calm as she eats. We've been talking amiably about domestic violence, one day after the shooting on our street.

'Kenneth's mother is someone else I respect,' Alison says – and I figure that's as much an answer as I'm going to get about her eye. Except it feels as if this will be my only opportunity to ask what I want.

'Do you hit Kenneth because she hits you?' It's perhaps the bluntest question I've ever asked but, after what happened yesterday, plus the morning with my husband, perhaps it's the day for it.

Alison doesn't reply for a while. She nibbles the top of the chocolate flake and then we stop to sit on a bench that overlooks a park, near the edge of the town centre. I let her eat in quiet and she doesn't speak until there's only a final piece of ice cream cone remaining.

'Do you have secrets in your marriage?' she asks.

I shiver because it's so direct, as if she's been looking into my life this past week.

'Doesn't everyone?' I reply.

'What if I was to tell you that Kenneth enjoys the thing you saw? That he begs for it sometimes? That his mother beat him so much when he was younger that he craves something even he doesn't understand?'

I shiver, wishing she hadn't spoken, almost telling her it's too much information. Except I was the one who asked. Her house is such a strange hierarchy of what she calls respect.

But who am I to judge?

I'm not sure what to say, so go with nothing. Alison twiddles the final bit of ice cream cone between her fingers.

'Did you get everything you wanted?' she asks, and it's almost cryptic.

At first I assume she's talking about my invasion into her life, whether her answers have been enough for me to not ask again. But then I wonder if she's talking about the past week. Whether Huntington Grove is a place I will call home.

'I think so,' I tell her.

'Good,' she replies, with a finality that I know means we'll never speak of this again. 'Welcome to the neighbourhood.'

THE FUTURE

Police statement: Peter Martin.

Officer: Thank you for attending, Mr Martin. For the sake of the recording, could you confirm your full name?

Peter: Peter Brian Martin.

Officer: Thanks for that. I wouldn't normally bring this up but I think it might be important. Could you confirm what you told me outside about your living situation?

Peter: I sometimes sleep in the High Kingsley shelter if there's room. It's at the back of the church.

Officer: Where do you sleep if there isn't room?

[*Inaudible*]

Officer: I'm sorry, I didn't catch that. Can you repeat?

Peter: In the park, usually. Near the war memorial.

Officer: OK, I've noted that. What I'd like to ask you about is what happened two weeks ago. I believe it was a Thursday night, probably early Friday morning…?

Peter: I already told you.

Officer: I realise – but it's important to get this for the recording.

[*Inaudible*]

Peter: There was a man who came by. He said he'd give someone eighty quid if they let him beat them up.

Officer: This was at the war memorial?

Peter: Right.

Officer: What sort of time was it?

Peter: You already said.

Officer: I know but I need you to confirm.

Peter: It was late, or early. Maybe two in the morning? Something like that.

Officer: And when he said he'd give someone eighty quid if they let him beat them up, is that how he phrased it?

Peter: He said something like, 'If you let me give you a bit of a kicking'.

Officer: Did anyone accept the offer?

Peter: You know I did.

Officer: Right – but for the tape.

Peter: I told him I'd do it.

Officer: Did he pay you?

Peter: Yeah, we went off to this alley and he did what he said.

Officer: What happened in the alley?

Peter: He kicked me about.

Officer: What then?

Peter: This woman showed up. They knew each other. She told him to stop.

Officer: And he did?

Peter: Yeah.

Officer: Then what?

Peter: He sort of ran off.

Officer: Did you know the woman?

Peter: Not then. I saw her again the next day, at the church. She was asking about the man, saying he was her husband. I think she was trying to say she was sorry.

Officer: Have you seen her since?

[*Inaudible*]

Officer: I'm sorry, I didn't catch that again.

Peter: I said she was on the news. My mate sent me the link. Her husband was the one who got shot by his daughter, something like that. There was a picture and it was her.

[*Image shown of Willow Ellis*]

Officer: Is this the woman?

Peter: Yes.

Officer: And do you recognise this man?

[*Image shown of Gabriel Ellis*]

Peter: Yes.

Officer: Who is he?

Peter: He's the one who got shot by his daughter.

Officer: Is there anything else you can tell me about him?

[*Inaudible*]

Officer: Can you repeat that?

Peter: He's the one who paid me.

[*Sound of shuffling*]

Officer: To be clear, for the recording, you're saying that Gabriel Ellis paid to beat you up – but that he was interrupted by his wife?

Peter: Yes.

Officer: Thank you, Mr Martin. I realise this is hard for you.

[*Inaudible*]

Officer: I need to ask you a little more about Mr Ellis. On the night he paid you, was that the first time you'd seen him?

[*Inaudible*]

Officer: Was that a no?

Peter: I'd seen him before.

Officer: When had you seen him?

Peter: He came by a few times.

Officer: Came by where?

Peter: To the park. The memorial.

Officer: The place where you sleep sometimes?

Peter: Right.

Officer: Why did he come by?

Peter: He brought money.

Officer: Can you spell out a little clearer what you mean by that?

Peter: He'd have money and ask if any of us wanted it?

Officer: Are you saying he had offered money to beat people up in the past?

Peter: Yes.

Officer: How often?

Peter: I don't know. I wasn't always there. I slept in the shelter most nights.

Officer: But how many times had you seen Mr Ellis near the memorial at night?

Peter: Maybe ten?

Officer: Is that ten nights in a row?

Peter: No. He'd come by two or three times close together, then not for a few months or so.

[*Inaudible*]

Officer: How long ago was it that you first saw Mr Ellis offering to pay people to beat them up?

Peter: Maybe a year or so? But I'm not the only one. Some of the others says he was coming by three or four years back. Maybe longer. You'd have to ask but they might not say.

Officer: Did someone always take him up on the offer?

[*Inaudible*]

Officer: Was that a no?

Peter: I don't know. I wasn't always there. Sometimes I saw people say no – but I think we all thought…

[*Inaudible*]

Officer: I need you to repeat that last bit.

Peter: … I think we all thought he was going to do it anyway.

Officer: Do you mean you thought he'd beat up someone anyway?

Peter: Right.

Officer: So you figured you might as well take the money?

Peter: Right.

[*Inaudible*]

Officer: I didn't catch that.

Peter: I said I'm glad he was shot. He deserved it. It's good it happened before he killed someone. It's a shame he's not dead.

Officer: I don't think—

Peter: Someone's going to get hurt one day. *Really* hurt. You're so angry, you know? You don't even want the money but it's hard to say no. Then, after he's done it to you, you're just so… *angry* that you let it happen. You want to do something about it but what is there to do? You can't fight back. It's hard to let go.

Officer: I understand, Mr Martin. I think that's all we need. Thanks for your help and your time.

Peter: Will it do any good, though? What does it matter now?

Officer: I promise you, Mr Martin, this has done so much more than you could imagine. I know it might not seem like it now – but one day soon, you'll know what you've done.

Peter: I don't think I understand.

Officer: I realise that. I'll talk more to you after. Interview terminated at 11:09.

AUTHOR'S NOTE

Home Is Where the Lies Live took seven years to write.

In that period, I moved four times, got two dogs, found out my dad had died while I was at an airport, had a severe concussion, lived through a pandemic, went through three UK General Elections and six Prime Ministers, won two literary awards, got hit by a car, ran a marathon (3hrs 26, thanks for asking), cycled up some big mountains, hiked up some bigger ones, finally saw Liverpool win the league, wrote a bunch of stupid radio quizzes for Ed Gamble and Matthew Crosby, discovered I *really* like sushi. A whole bunch of other stuff as well. Dr Pepper is so nice! Who knew?

I also wrote plenty of other books in that time, across genres, about all sorts of different subjects. They would be published and I'd move onto the next thing. I'm always thinking ahead.

But, somehow, this was always at the back of my mind.

I've started and abandoned a few books and don't mind leaving ideas behind if they aren't coming together.

The first draft of this didn't quite work, though I couldn't figure out why. There was so much I liked in it. I left it two years, re-read it, had a tinker, but it still wasn't there. Then another three years. Then two more.

I couldn't leave it alone because there was something about these three central characters that lingered.

It took seven years but I think I got it. I can see the changes in me as a person from that first draft to how it ended up. Maybe that's why the trio kept niggling away? There are different parts of me in each of them?

I need to thank my editor, Ellen, who read this for me seven years after it was first written. There was no contract in place and everything was on trust between us. But she read the whole thing and gave me some really useful notes. She didn't tell me how to fix the book but she did finally help me see what was wrong with it. And then, suddenly, I knew how to knit everyone's stories together.

I'm so proud of this book and it would not be out in the wild were it not for her.

Thanks for reading.

Kerry

PUBLISHING TEAM

Turning a manuscript into a book requires the efforts of many people. The publishing team at Bookouture would like to acknowledge everyone who contributed to this publication.

Audio
Alba Proko
Sinead O'Connor
Melissa Tran

Commercial
Lauren Morrissette
Hannah Richmond
Imogen Allport

Data and analysis
Mark Alder
Mohamed Bussuri

Editorial
Ellen Gleeson
Nadia Michael

Copyeditor
Jade Craddock

Made in United States
Orlando, FL
22 December 2024

56382725R00253